W9-BGJ-563

Her Last Letter

Her Last Letter

Nancy C. Johnson

Penwyck Publishing
Wolverine Lake, Michigan

Penwyck Publishing

This is a work of fiction. Names, characters, places, and incidents are the products of the author's imagination or are used fictitiously. Any similarity to actual events, locales, or persons, living or dead, is entirely coincidental.

Penwyck Publishing L.L.C.

Cover art by Angie Designs
www.angiedesigns.com

Visit the author's website at www.nancy-cjohnson.com

Library of Congress Control Number: 2006940230

ISBN-13: 978-0-9791909-0-2
ISBN-10: 0-9791909-0-8

Printed in the United Stated of America

First printing: May 2007

10 9 8 7 6 5 4 3 2 1

This book is dedicated to my wonderful family and friends. Thank you for helping to make *Her Last Letter* a reality.

Penwyck
Publishing

Acknowledgments

Publishing a book is a long, arduous process, and requires the efforts of many. I'm grateful to all those who helped me or wished me well. While I can't mention everyone due to the limitations of space, you know who you are.

I would like to thank first and foremost, my daughter, who has read everything I've ever written, and patiently advised me on all without complaint. She is the absolute best!

My thanks also go to Chief George of the Village of Wolverine Lake Police Department, who advised on matters involving police work and beyond. I'd like to thank also my friend Sharon Garant, LMSW, for reading my manuscript and bringing authenticity to my fictitious therapist. Thanks must also go to Mr. Nick Valenti - Faculty, Chair Fine and Performing Arts, Photography and Digital Imaging at Oakland Community College, for his detailed help with darkroom procedures. I thank also Mr. Dennis Greaney of Dennis Greaney Photography for my lovely website portrait, and for his additional darkroom expertise.

Numerous friends and family graciously volunteered to read and critique my manuscript(s). Thank you so much Angie, Anita, Ginger, Joan, Judie, Julie, Rachel, Sharon, and Theresa!

I would also like to thank Ms. Joyce E. for her professional editing skills on the first draft of the manuscript....

Chapter 1

The letter was in my sister's handwriting. My dead sister's handwriting. Kelly's writing, large looping script mixed nonsensically with block capitals. My sister's handwriting. I'd know it anywhere.

It was a single sheet of yellowed paper, violently creased. Kelly had folded it over, again and again, then taped it inside her dresser. Hidden it. Only time and age had caused it to come loose.

I sank to the edge of the bed, gently smoothed the paper on my lap. Slowly, through tears, her words returned to focus.

I'm so scared. He knows! And God if my sister knew I've been screwing her boyfriend she'd kill me anyway. Why in hell did I get into this whole situation? I've got to tell someone or I could end up dead ... like the last one. The look in his eyes when he told me about her was totally unreal. I don't think he was making it up, but he could have been, just to scare me. Maybe the best thing is to leave. Hope he calms down and forgets about it. Not likely, if he found the box. I've looked for it everywhere, and someone was in the house messing with things. God, what now? I'll think of something. I have to.

Later...I hear someone downstairs.

I had to read it several times before my mind would let me grasp the full meaning of her words ... "screwing her boyfriend ... dead like the last one." When exactly did Kelly write this? Was it true or was this only another plot to one of her fictitious stories? How many times in the years before her death had she stopped me in the middle of something and begged me to listen? "*Oh, tell me it's good. Please, Gwyn. No don't. Tell me the truth. I'll never get any better if you don't tell me the truth.*" And I had given her, as always, the encouragement she needed, budding writer that she was, my much-loved youngest sister.

But my gut was telling me this was no story. My gut was knotting, constricting, squeezing my heart already banging against my rib cage.

Was it possible Kelly had been screwing Trevor—now my husband? Or was it Wolfgang—now married to my sister Linda? How could Kelly do anything so unspeakable, so horrible to either of us?

Kelly knew how very much in love we were, that these were the men we hoped to marry. It was unthinkable to believe she could have betrayed us, or that one of our husbands had allowed an affair to happen. Or were they the catalyst? Heartbreaking and sickening as that possibility was rapidly becoming, it didn't even begin to address the most terrifying question. Could one of them be a coldblooded killer? Did one of them murder Kelly?

I sat there for many minutes fixated on the angled pattern of the morning sun slowly retreating across the floor. Finally, I brought my head up and gazed around the room, a room I'd only recently redecorated with Kelly's bedroom furniture. Janet, my therapist, would likely worry about the reasoning that led me to this decision—if she knew. She'd question the wisdom of bringing my sister's things here to the house, wonder if it meant I was regressing.

For the past two years since Kelly's death, I'd been seeing Janet off and on—the emphasis on off. I'd escaped her sessions using a variety of excuses, some real, some manufactured. The whole therapeutic process could be extremely painful, and I didn't like the idea of using professional help at all. If the majority of the population could go it alone when tragedy struck, then I should be able to also. Hiring Janet had been Linda's idea, not mine. She'd said I needed help, whether I wanted it or not.

Eventually, though, I began to rely on Janet's considerable strength as well as her friendship. And fortunately for me, my financial resources allowed me to continue my therapy indefinitely.

Then, two months ago, just as I'd started looking forward to the sessions, Janet announced it was time to stop. She'd monitor my progress with well-spaced phone calls only. I'd argued against such a drastic change, thinking I couldn't handle it, but Janet wouldn't budge. Surprisingly, I'd done much better than I'd thought, weathering her absence almost without a hitch. I'd worried that the sleepless nights with their draining anxiety would return, along with the depressing lows and spates of crying. Instead, I felt okay, my memory even began to improve. I lost only hours, not whole days. And sometimes, for the space of a moment, I'd forget that Kelly was gone.

I put the letter back in the drawer under one of her scarves and made my way down the curving mahogany staircase to the first floor. As I reached the bottom step, the phone rang, startling me. I wasn't sure if I should answer it, wasn't sure if the cacophony in my head would communicate itself through my voice, but I desperately needed to talk to someone. And I was fairly certain that the someone on the line would be Caroline, my best friend.

I plucked the phone off the kitchen wall.

"Hey, Gwyn. What took you so long to answer?"

"Oh hi, Care. I don't know. I was ... working. You know."

"In the studio?"

"Right, I was matting a painting, concentrating too hard I guess."

"I guess."

For a moment, I couldn't speak, my lips frozen, refusing to function. Finally, she spoke again. "Are you okay? You don't sound right."

"Sure. Why? How do I sound?"

"Like someone tied your vocal cords in a knot."

I laughed, but it came out like a strangled shriek. "No-o-o, I'm fine. Really."

"I don't think so. What's going on?"

"Nothing. I told you."

"Well, I was on my way over there anyway. That's why I called. That okay with you?"

"Sure."

"Did you eat lunch yet?"

"No."

"Then I'll pick up something. Sandwiches okay?"

"No, don't buy anything. I just went shopping. I'll make us sandwiches, and my soup."

"I don't want you to go to any trouble. It was my idea."

"Don't worry about it. I don't mind at all. Really."

"Okay. I'll be there in a few."

My hand trembled as I hung up the phone. I crossed my arms tightly to my chest, but even so, my shoulders began to shake. I sank down into a kitchen chair, then pushed my face into my hands and howled like a baby for several minutes. Finally, I cleared my throat and stepped to the sink. Splashing my face with cold water, I looked up and caught a glimpse of my splotchy reflection in the glass cabinet front.

Grabbing my purse, I pulled out cosmetics to try and repair the damage. Maybe I'd lie, tell Caroline I was getting the flu. I doubted she'd believe me, but maybe. Now that the fall cold snap had taken hold, a few people I knew had come down with the flu bug.

I put on a pot of coffee, hazelnut, Caroline's favorite, then idled next to the kitchen's bay window, watching dry leaves lift and skitter down the brick path toward my dying garden. Beyond the garden, the Rocky Mountains stood snowcapped, the towering peaks reassuringly familiar, reminders of winters spent skiing, of summers spent hiking through sun-dappled pines.

By the time Caroline arrived I'd thawed my homemade chicken soup and arranged a platter of turkey, ham, cheese, and bread. I was removing a vase of daisies from a spot near the window to place on the table when she blew in through the front door. Slim and athletic in worn jeans and hiking boots, her long auburn hair swept back in a ponytail, Care fixed me with that straight-arrow stare of hers. I tried to smile, opened my mouth to say hi, but she grabbed me and hugged me before I could manage a word.

"Okay, what is it? What's wrong?"

"Nothing," I said, squeezing a sizable lump back down my throat.

"Don't tell *me* nothing. You've been crying. Your face is deformed it's so puffy."

"I know. I think I'm getting sick. Maybe the flu. I started sneezing like crazy a few minutes ago."

"Oh." She withdrew, looking me up and down. "The flu, huh. Well, okay, whatever you say. I suppose you'll tell me the truth when you're ready."

I blew my nose. "It's true. But I'm still glad you're here, even though you shouldn't be. Come on. Let's eat. Everything's ready." I waved my hand toward the table.

"Wow, something sure smells good," she said. "Oh, you made my hazelnut coffee. You're an angel. Thanks."

She stepped to the counter and quickly poured herself a mug, then pointed toward mine.

"No, I'm good."

"Too bad you're not feeling well. I was going to ask you to go hiking with me today. I've got the whole day off."

I watched as Caroline began to ladle soup into bowls and slap sandwiches together. "I should do that," I said.

"No, sit, you're sick."

"I am," I said.

Caroline knew how much I loved the outdoors, how much I normally would have wanted to join her on a hike. It was an obvious ploy to try and pump the truth out of me.

"The hiking would have been fun," I said. "You should go anyway. It's beautiful out."

"I suppose." She shrugged. "Not so much fun—alone. You want cheese on this?"

"Sure. So how are things going with that guy, Phil?" I asked in an attempt to change the subject.

Caroline's lips pinched into a frown. "They're not. He's history. He hasn't called me in two weeks. And I'm glad. Asshole. He's dating another woman. Would you believe he brought her to the bar? I had to wait on them. If I didn't want to keep my job, I would have thrown the stupid drinks in his face."

"Oh."

"I made sure to water down their gin and tonics, barely put any alcohol in. I thought of doing some other things too, but ..." She smiled wickedly.

"Maybe next time."

"Actually, he did call—right after that happened. His way of saying

I may not be his true love anymore, but that doesn't mean we can't have sex. What a jerk."

"He wasn't your type anyway."

"No, although he did have his good points. At least I didn't need to use the electric blanket when he stayed over. Oh, but Gwyn ..." She started to laugh, then to really laugh, bent over at the waist, holding her stomach, unable to talk. I began to laugh too.

"What? What?" I pleaded.

"Oh God. When he'd stay over ... I don't know. You know me, I like ... Mexican food and ... he couldn't digest the beans, I guess. And he'd ... fart, under the covers, these sneaky silent ones ... or there'd be this long high squeak, like, you know, he was trying to hold it back, but no way. And then ... I swear the blankets would rise. I had to open the windows before we'd go to sleep or I'd die." She stopped to take a breath, still laughing, then gradually began to wind down. "God, I wish I could tell his new girl that, but maybe she already knows." Caroline grinned at me, then sighed. "I might have accepted it though, if he'd been decent. You know me. I don't expect perfection."

"But you deserve it," I said, knowing that though she was laughing, the man had hurt her more than she would ever admit.

She placed the soup bowls and plates on the table. "Looks good, Gwyn."

She ate with gusto while I had trouble forcing down a few bites of sandwich and a little soup. After we'd finished, Care put the remainder of the food back in the frig and we sat and sipped our coffee.

"I have dessert," I said. "Cookies, I think, and ice cream. You want some?"

"Nah, I'm full, thanks." She plopped her elbows on the table. "So, what else is going on? We haven't seen each other in a while. My fault, working *way* too much. Any new gossip? How's your sister and that burly, burly man she married? What's his name? Woof? Wolf man?"

"Wolfgang."

"Oh, right. How are those two doing? The guy cracks me up. Mr. Macho. He's got more muscle than any man I've ever seen up close."

"I don't know. I haven't talked to Linda lately. If I don't call her,

I don't hear from her."

"Why's that?"

"I don't know. Moody."

"Like you?"

"I suppose, though I am getting better."

She stared at me, her green eyes trying to bore through to my soul. I valiantly kept guard at the entrance.

"Well, I hope so," she said, slapping her thighs, then rising from the chair. "Okay, I seriously doubt you're telling me the truth about this so-called flu, but if so, maybe I'd better cruise out of here and let you get some rest. I wish you were coming along, but I think I'll take that hike after all. Need to stretch my legs and breathe in some good old mountain air. But call me later—if you want to talk. Whatever it is, we'll figure it out. Okay?"

"Okay."

I did feel sick after Caroline left, but now it was more mental than physical. I crawled into bed and tried hard to sleep, hoping to hide from myself for a while. I dreaded the moment I would eventually have to face Trevor. There wasn't a chance I'd ask him about any of this, not until I'd figured out what to do. Though I believed he had nothing to do with Kelly's death, and felt certain in my heart that he was, in fact, the man I knew him to be, still, I had to at least consider the possibility that my husband, the man I loved more than any man I'd ever known—had slept with my sister, and then murdered her....

The side door slammed downstairs, and I woke groggily. It seemed like only minutes later, but I'd slept for several hours. It was five o'clock, early for Trevor to be home. I could usually expect him around six or six-thirty, though many nights he arrived much later, depending on his workload.

"Hey, Gwyn," he called out.

"Up here."

I threaded my fingers through my hair, then turned toward the mirror. The puffiness around my eyes had receded, but sleep lines had formed along my cheek.

I rose and walked to the top of the stairs, watched as Trevor took them two at a time.

"Ah, you were sleeping, weren't you?" he said, a wry smile turning up his mouth.

"Yeah, you caught me."

"I had one hell of a good day. I might get the listing on a big group of condos, a new development outside of Denver, called Whispering Pines or something. You remember Robert Morris?"

"No, who?"

"You know, we met him at that party your sister gave. The sharp dresser. Oh, you met him. Anyway, I got a call from him today, and he's interested in possibly listing with us, and of course, I'm the guy he wants to do the selling."

I watched his eyes, animated as he described his project, and then his hands, moving deftly through the air, fingers pointing out architectural wonders only he could see. Those same fingers could at any given moment touch my arm or face and bring shivers of lust when even barely applied. He was six feet one to my five seven, his body trim and lightly muscled. He had thick dark hair and facial features faintly European, strong Roman nose, firm jaw. He possessed the capacity to summon at will a supremely confident charm that mesmerized women and drew the respect of men. And I'd seen his hazel eyes, sometimes a moody brown or a startling blue-green depending on the light, stop a conversation mid-sentence. But it wasn't the color, or the shape, or the thick flirty lashes that made his eyes so sexy, it was the way he looked at you—as if he could see no one else. He could have had any woman in the world, I believed, and yet he'd picked me. Countless times, I'd asked myself why.

"I think we should go out and celebrate," he said, loosening his tie. "And then, I think we should get some use out of that fireplace downstairs." He reached out and drew me to his chest, enveloping me in the lingering scent of his cologne, one I'd bought him last Christmas, something French and expensive. "We'll take our clothes off, sip some wine, and make love for at least three hours. How does that sound?"

"I love how that sounds," I said, nuzzling my nose into the warmth of his neck, temporarily filing the events of the day into some impenetrable place to be, for now at least ... forgotten.

That night I dreamt of my sister, who in the dream was still alive and only ten years old. We were playing hopscotch in the driveway, and I was letting Kelly win because I loved to hear her shrieks of happy laughter each time her stone hit the mark and mine overshot it. I was, after all, six years older and could win every game if I chose to. Linda had wandered over and immediately Kelly crossed her arms and stopped playing, her lower lip protruding. I assumed they'd fought about something and I asked Kelly, then Linda, what it was about, but neither would talk. As I watched, a thundercloud passed over the sky and when I looked back, Linda was holding a magic wand and waved it over Kelly, turning her into an emerald-eyed lizard. Then Linda, her expression one of pure evil, raised her foot to stomp on Kelly and I tried to shout, *No! Stop!*, but my mouth wouldn't move. I couldn't form the words.

I watched in horror, screaming and screaming on the inside—as Linda's foot came down.

I woke late the next morning. I hadn't gotten much sleep, and felt as if my brain were cloaked in a dismal leaden fog. I turned over in bed to look for Trevor, but only a concave impression of his body remained amid the rumpled sheets. He'd already left for work.

Though I'd managed to sidetrack thoughts of Kelly's letter yesterday while Trevor and I made love, now all the unanswered questions returned to haunt me.

My plan this morning, before my life had been turned upside down, was to complete a graphic design project I'd promised as a favor to my old boss. Now it would have to wait—at least until this afternoon. I took a fast shower and headed out the door.

I'd been over to the old house just two days before to tag the bedroom furniture that needed to be moved. My usual habit was to stop by the house every few weeks, then drive by every few days to make sure the lights went on at night and trash had not blown into the yard. Though the neighbors kept an eye on things to some extent, it wasn't their first priority. Linda kept after me to sell our old homestead, or at least to rent it, but I wasn't ready to let go. It was the last place Kelly had lived, the house where we all grew up, a repository of memories both good and bad. But that wasn't why I was going there today.

The two-story frame house was a mile out of Glenwood Springs and had been there for over fifty years. It sat on a small lot, a tiny square, with one towering pine dominating the front yard. For the last two years since Kelly's death the house had remained undisturbed, the furniture the way Kelly had arranged it, the kitchen utensils still in the drawers. The only thing that had changed since we were children was Kelly's room upstairs, a room that had once belonged to all three of us girls. In those days, two sets of bunk beds took up most of the room and fights had been frequent—the lack of privacy a constant source of irritation.

I parked my red Jeep Wrangler in the drive and walked up the stone path. Traces of snow still clung to the edges of the porch, but would probably melt by this afternoon, the temperature predicted to rise to forty, a mild and sunny end of October day. I unlocked the front door and stepped inside, assailed again by the stuffy lack of ventilation. Carefully, I surveyed the living room. Everything appeared to be in its place, still, something bothered me. Then I trained my eyes on the ashtray next to Dad's chair. Had it moved? Hadn't it been facing in the other direction the last time I was here? Well, maybe Linda had stopped by. She didn't often, but maybe she had.

I wasn't sure exactly where to start. The boxes with Kelly's journals had joined many other boxes when Linda and I had gone through Kelly's things. We had quietly sorted, sadly organized for over a month. And we'd fought. Linda wanted to throw out or give away almost everything, but I insisted we keep the majority. In the end, very little moved out of the house.

I began my search in the little room, the one my father had used for his business when he wasn't at the store. I opened the closet and stared in. Boxes sat upon boxes stacked three high. I pulled one off the top and began.

By two o'clock I'd found the box I'd been looking for, down in the cellar, but it had been opened and for the most part emptied. Only the very old journals sat at the bottom of the box. The rest were missing. I was too tired to look any further, so I gathered the box in my arms and took it out to the car. There was one other place they might be.

I dialed Linda on the cell phone from the Jeep. Unfortunately, Wolfgang picked up.

"Hi, Wolfgang, is Linda there?"

"Well hello, Gwyn, nice to hear your voice. How have you been?"

"Fine." I waited.

"Well," he said after a pause, "you must be in a rush, no time to talk I guess. Linda's outside in the hot tub right now, soaking in the bubbles, where I was heading. Would you like to join us?"

"Not today."

"I'm sure Linda has some extra suits, though I don't think I'll use one. That wouldn't bother you would it?"

"Wolfgang, I have to go."

"We could just hang out."

"Right. Very funny. Please tell Linda to call me later."

"Sure. I'll certainly do that."

He loved to tease me like this, hoping to amuse me I supposed, though he never did. I'd tried for Linda's sake to like him. Unfortunately, he always managed to turn me off. He was a good-looking man, classic Nordic blond, fair skinned, well built, clearly Linda's type, but he was way too into himself. I could see it bothered him enormously that I'd never warmed up to him. I don't know why. Maybe he needed women to like him for some reason. Still, it was hard to believe he could murder anyone. A flirt, yes, but a murderer? Of course, I'd met a lot of odd characters in my lifetime. How many had I ever thought capable of murder?

Kelly had known only three men that Linda and I would consider serious boyfriends: Wolfgang, Trevor, and before that, Josh, my friend since childhood. But there was no way I could believe Josh could commit such a horrible crime. He was just too good. And what possible reason would he have to harm Kelly?

Craig Foster, my sister's boyfriend, was the only one police were looking for in connection with her murder. He was the one who ran right after her death. He'd been the only real suspect. But now that I'd found Kelly's letter, it occurred to me that Craig may have had some other reason for running. And the one that was taking shape in my mind was that he'd been framed....

I worked in my studio for the rest of the afternoon. Along with the project for my old boss, I had a private art exhibition coming up soon in Denver and hoped to complete several new paintings. It was something I wanted to do, something I enjoyed doing. Though my training was in graphic design, I loved to paint, and I wasn't half bad.

Of course, I didn't need to work anymore to earn a living. That changed the day our father passed away and left the three of us girls accumulated assets worth over eighteen million dollars. Then Kelly died, and her share was divided between Linda and me. As if I wanted it. I'd have burned every dollar if it meant I could have my sister back.

I remember the shock I felt, and the looks on Linda's and Kelly's faces as we sat in the lawyer's office listening to our father's will. Certainly we'd suspected there would be something. Dad was always working, never home, at the sporting goods store or off somewhere. *But eighteen million.*

Our father had come from money, though he'd rarely spoke of his family or of their wealth, except on the few occasions when he'd been drinking. Huddled together on the floor behind the couch, my sisters and I would quietly listen in as he rambled on about the past. We learned that Dad had run away at nineteen to become a mountain man. He didn't want to work like his two brothers for his father, a successful Midwest beer distributor. Our father didn't like the changes he'd seen take place in his brothers, their bickering, their greed. He'd spent several years on the road, then met our mother in Cheyenne, Wyoming, my mother's birthplace. They'd moved on to Denver, Colorado, where my father opened his first sporting goods store. He was a natural, a good businessman. Making money ran in his veins whether he liked it or not. Wily and tightfisted, Samuel Everett let no man get the better of him. You did not ask him for money. You earned your money, you saved it, or you went without it. And that, of course, applied to his children. But harsh as it felt at the time, he'd praised us for our accomplishments, and encouraged us, loving us in his way. And each one of us had loved him back.

I lifted my paintbrush, stopping to eye the piece in front of me, a scene depicting climbers ascending an icefall, bright sunlight glinting off their crampons and pickaxes. Restless, I stood and walked to the easel in the far corner of the room and turned it toward me. It was Kelly's portrait, half-finished. She'd posed for this one even though I'd insisted I could use the camera. But Kelly had liked the idea of sitting for me, and she'd done a good job, hands folded quietly in her lap, meditating almost. Unfortunately, I hadn't been able to finish the painting, not for two years.

When Linda didn't return my call by five, I called her again. She answered this time, obviously intoxicated.

"Gwyn," she said too loudly. "Hi, how *are* you?"

"I'm okay. You still in the hot tub? You sound like you've been drinking."

"Not *that* much. I feel pretty good though."

"I need to ask you something. Is Wolfgang there?"

"Yes," she said. "Why, is it a secret?"

I heard water splash and worried she'd dropped the phone into the tub. "Linda, you there?"

"Ye-e-e-s."

"What happened?"

"Nothing. I told Wolfgang to cover his ears because we wanted to have a private conversation."

"*Linda.*"

"What?"

"Forget it. We'll talk later. I've got to go."

"No, come over. I haven't seen you in ages. I miss you."

"Yes, and I miss you too, but I can't right now. I have a couple things I have to do."

"But you'll stop by soon?"

"Yes, as soon as I can."

I hung up the phone and reached into the box I'd brought from the old house. I opened one of the journals and began to read. I could tell by the large cursive writing that Kelly hadn't been very old when she'd penned this one.

Nicole sat next to Jennifer today. I think she likes Jennifer better than she likes me, but she said she didn't. She told me I was her best friend at recess yesterday. I gave her a dirty look when she tried to talk to me when the bell rang. I wonder if they were talking about me? I hate the clothes Mom made me wear today and those old crummy shoes. Maybe if I lose them Mom will get me a new pair, but probably she'll make me wear those icky loafers instead. I'm not going to talk to Nicole the rest of the day. I don't like Jennifer. I don't know why Nicole likes her. Oh well.

I finished the notebook and opened another, picturing my sister at that age, her hair short and boyish, always in need of combing. Her chestnut hair had been silky though, and as Kelly grew older, her hair was one of her most attractive features. When she wore it long or piled it up on her head, there was no doubt she was the best looking of us three girls.

I flipped through the pages, reading a paragraph here, another there. Nothing in these journals was going to help me very much. All appeared to have been written when Kelly was still in elementary school.

But there had been several boxes of notebooks tucked away in Kelly's closet. The pages Linda and I briefly scanned during the cleanup after Kelly's death appeared semi-recent, bits and pieces of half-finished stories and ideas for more. Neither of us had read very much of it though, not even a tenth of what was there. It was too depressing, and felt too personal.

When I stopped by Linda's house the next day, her three-car garage was open. Fortunately, Wolfgang's commercial van with the company logo on the side was nowhere to be seen. Linda's Audi was there though, and their Subaru. I stared for a moment at the giant gingerbread house before exiting my Jeep. The idea to build this garishly overdone home could only have been Wolfgang's. My best guess was that he'd been trying to recreate Victorian architecture, but it was an insult to the form, a crazy blend of styles I could only guess at. Though the house embraced the lacy ornamented detail of Victorian architecture, plus the towers and turrets often seen, two large Greek columns flanked the front door of the partly white, partly beige stucco exterior. Traces of Colonial, Gothic, even Modern were present. Wolfgang was a builder, not a designer. That was certain.

I walked through the garage and knocked loudly, then yelled out, "Linda, it's me." After a while, I heard footsteps approaching.

"Gwyn?" Linda asked before opening the door.

"Yes, it's me."

"Wow," she said, pulling the door wide. "I almost didn't answer. Look at me."

I stared, amused, at my sister's purple head, the hair dye a slippery mess above her ears. "Guess my timing isn't the greatest."

"Doesn't matter. I'm still glad you're here." She tightened the towel she wore around her neck. "It's almost time to rinse it out. I gave myself an emergency fix. You can tell me if I look awful or not."

Linda parked me in the kitchen with a fresh cup of coffee and some strudel she'd warmed in the microwave. "I'll only be a minute," she called back as she trotted down the hall and out of sight.

I nodded and busied myself with the strudel.

She was back a few minutes later, the towel now wrapped around her head. "It's so good to *see* you," she said, her voice rising high like a child's as she seated herself across the table from me. "We're terrible. We're all we've got and we don't get together enough. So what was it you wanted to talk about yesterday? I wish you would have come over. We would've had fun. Wolfgang certainly wasn't much company."

"I had stuff to do. But I'm here now."

"We could have talked. What difference did it make that Wolfgang was there?"

"I just wasn't comfortable with him listening in."

Linda laughed. "He's not interested in our conversations, believe me. He was in and out of the hot tub the whole time anyway. I don't know why you let him bother you."

"Can we drop it, please?"

She frowned, stopping her coffee cup in midair. "Sure, we can drop it. What's with you?"

"Nothing."

She gazed at me, then resumed drinking her coffee.

"I'm sorry," I said. "I have a headache."

She nodded, but wouldn't look at me.

I bit into the strudel. "This really tastes good. Where'd you get it?"

"In town. Wolfgang picked it up on his way home yesterday." She chewed her lower lip, still avoiding eye contact.

"So how's the redecorating project coming along?" I asked.

"It's coming."

"No, really, Linda. Tell me. I'm sorry, okay. I didn't mean to hurt your feelings."

She sighed loudly. "Like I said, it's coming. But the whole thing's a real pain in the ass. Just try to do anything your way when your husband's a builder."

"Why? What happened?"

"Nothing huge. He just doesn't care about any of it. I show him color swatches and everything, but I know he's not paying attention. Then the paint comes out wrong and he just laughs and tells me his guys will redo it. I don't want them to redo it. I want it done right the first time. It's totally frustrating."

I nodded.

"I wanted the new bathroom painted a light airy blue-green," she said, "like you're in a meadow or something. Instead I get this murky swamp color. I almost cried. And don't say it. I know I could have hired a decorator for this, but I only wanted a few simple changes. Unfortunately, it's never that easy."

"Is it fixed now? Do you want to show me?"

"No, everything's a mess up there, tarps and paint cans everywhere. I'd rather show you when it's done. But enough about my stuff. How are things with you? How's Trevor?"

"Good. I'm doing a new exhibition in a few weeks, and Trevor's hot on some condo thing, a big project."

"A new exhibition? Did you tell me about this one?"

"No, I don't think so. It will be my biggest show to date. I'll be the only artist there. I guess they plan to feature one new artist each month. I'll be the first. I'm mentioned in their advertising too. Hopefully, this means I'll sell something."

"Of course you'll sell something. Artists don't get written up in the paper for no reason at all."

"It was a local paper."

"So what? You're incredibly talented. I wish I had even a little of your gift. So where's the exhibit going to be?"

"Denver, a new mall, Vista Meadows, real upscale so I've heard. I'll go down there a day early and check it out. Do you want to go with me?"

"How long will you be there?"

"A couple days. It's over the weekend."

Linda pursed her lips. "No, I'd better not. I need to be here to supervise things." She rolled her wrist between her fingers, then winced in pain.

"What?"

"Oh, I was trying to lift a chair by myself and hurt my wrist. I'm an idiot."

"Did you sprain it?"

"No, I don't think so, maybe a little. It's nothing." She rose from her chair and walked to the coffeepot. "I'm just glad it wasn't my tennis arm. Then I would be pissed."

"How's that going?"

"The league? Pretty good, we're moving up in the rankings. My backhand's improving. Wolfgang thinks so anyway. It's just hard to get over to the club and practice with all these workmen running in and out needing my approval, but I do. I have to work out just to preserve my sanity." She gave me a look, refilling my cup. "Is ... everything else okay?"

The *everything else* she was referring to was my depression and subsequent need for therapy.

"I stopped seeing Janet two months ago. Her idea. I'm doing lots better. I still have my moments, but they aren't as bad."

She stared at me for an instant, then smiled. "Good, I'm really glad to hear that." She took another sip of coffee, then reached her free hand up and touched the towel on her head. "Are you in a hurry? Can you wait a couple minutes for me to blow dry my hair and see how this all came out? I won't be long."

"Sure, as long as I can have this last piece of strudel."

"Please—enjoy. At least it won't end up on your hips like it would on mine. God help me if I ever stop working out. Wolfgang would leave me." She disappeared back down the hall.

I brought the strudel to my mouth and took a bite. If anything, Linda was getting too thin. She'd never been overweight really, but she did have a softer, more feminine look before Wolfgang came along. Now, her collarbones protruded and her face was much thinner. Despite the changes, she was still a beautiful woman, but she definitely didn't need to lose any more weight. It wouldn't do any good to mention this though. Linda would turn herself inside out if she thought it would please Wolfgang. Her love for him bordered on obsession. I would have to approach the subject of Kelly's letter very carefully or Linda would throw open the gates of hell and let the demon's fly.

"Ta—Da," she said with a flourish of her arms, a smile lighting up her face. "Do you like?"

I couldn't see a big difference, same blonde chin-length curls, but I hadn't seen her for over a month. "Oh, it's very pretty, very nice. I like the color."

"Yes, thank God. I was worried. I couldn't get an appointment with Audrey until tomorrow and I just had to do something about my roots. It's like they grew an inch in a day." Linda sat down, began tapping her nails on the table, then frowned. "I know this might sound a little weird, bringing this up now, but I was wondering, when exactly were you planning to get pregnant? I know you said you weren't going to try right away, but how long were you planning to wait? Have you and Trevor talked about it at all?"

"Sure, we've talked about it, though not in a while. Did something happen? Why are you asking?"

"Nothing happened. I've just been thinking about it lately. And well, you are thirty-four and I'm thirty-two and it just seems like we should be thinking seriously about it if we really want children. I mean, what if we wait too long and can't have them?"

"Are you pregnant?"

"No," she said, throwing her head back with a laugh. "No, of course not." But her smile faded and she began tapping her nails again. "The truth is, I'm not sure I want children. My life is so full. I just don't know."

"Well, it's not like you've got to decide tomorrow. But I don't understand. You've always said that you did. I've put off thinking about it because, well, we've only been married a year and the way I've been since—"

"You don't have to explain."

"Does Wolfgang want children?"

"Oh, I'm sure he does. Not right away, but in the future. A boy probably, you know, someone to carry on the Lehman name. Lehman and Son's Construction. Has a nice ring to it, don't you think?" She frowned, crinkling her brow. "Sorry I brought this up. It just popped into my head. Brain damage from the hair dye probably." She glanced at the kitchen clock.

I took the hint. "I guess I should get going."

"No hurry," she said, but rose from her chair and took our cups and plates and stacked them in the sink.

"I need to ask you something before I go," I said, "though I probably already know the answer."

"What?"

"Have you been over to the house recently?"

"No, why?"

"I was over there taking a look around and thought things were out of place since I was there last. The ashtray next to Dad's chair was turned around, facing in the wrong direction. There's no way it could have gotten that way on its own. And I was down in the cellar and noticed that the boxes with Kelly's journals seem to be missing too. The one box I did find was almost empty, and I don't think any of them were like that before. Any chance you moved them?"

"No, I haven't been over there. I certainly wouldn't go down in that creepy old cellar anyway. Maybe someone broke in."

"No, I don't think so. I just thought—"

"We need to sell the house, Gwyn. You have to stop living so much in the past for God's sake ... reading her journals, wandering around over there. It's not good for you and you know it. I doubt that you tell your therapist even half of what you do. I know you'd rather not hear this, but it's true. We're asking for trouble leaving the house empty like that. And it's dangerous, you hanging out there all the time. Who knows when that Craig creep might come back?"

"I can't get rid of the house, Linda. I can't. Maybe someday. But don't make me decide now. I just can't do it."

"I don't know why I even bring it up. Well, actually, you brought it up." She shook her head. "Stop going over to the house. It worries me. Or stop telling me about it."

"Okay."

"I didn't mean that. Just don't go over there. At least not alone."

Chapter 2

"Guess who I saw?"

It was Caroline on the phone, her voice mischievous and playful.

"I don't know. Who?" I asked.

"I said you had to guess."

"Okay. The Great Pumpkin."

"No-o-o."

"Witch Hazel."

"Oh, come on, Gwyn, you're not even trying. You'll never guess."

"Well, if I'll never guess, why should I try? Okay, give me a second. I see. I see ... a celebrity. Brad Pitt."

"Not exactly, but just as cute. I saw Josh."

"You saw Josh? Where?"

"In Aspen. I was over there yesterday hanging out with this guy I know. I guess there's an art fair going on, and Josh is in town checking it out."

"I know the fair you mean. I thought about going down there myself if I didn't have so much work to finish. Did you talk to him?"

"Yeah, for a while. I ran into him on the street. He asked about you," Caroline said slyly. "Said he might give you a call."

"But he can't. Our phone's unlisted. But you probably gave him the number."

"Well, he asked for it. It's not like he hasn't known you for most of your life. He would have got it anyway. Besides, I know you would have wanted me to give it to him."

"It's okay, Caroline. I'm not mad. You're right. I'm glad you gave it to him. So what did he say? Is he in the area for long? Is he coming to Glenwood?"

"He said he was, though I had the impression he was only going to be around for a few days, then fly back to Los Angeles. But he'll be cruising the art fair all this coming weekend. Probably hopes you'll turn up."

"No, he's an art lover and a collector, as you very well know. That's probably the reason he's in Aspen."

"Well, I still think he's there to see you, and you won't change my mind. So what are you up to?"

"Work, work, and more work. I've been diddling with this one piece for most of the day and it's just not coming together. Thank God I work in acrylics and not oils. I've erased half of it twice."

"Come over to the bar and keep me company. The place is dead and I'm lonely. I'll mix you up the best strawberry daiquiri you've ever had in you life and we can commiserate together. Please—ple-a-s-e."

"Okay, I'm not getting anything done here anyway."

Caroline worked at the Wild River Grill in Glenwood Springs. She was the only female bartender employed at the saloon-style restaurant, and was, in my biased opinion, the best. The job had started out as temporary work to pay the rent, since Caroline had for years professed interest in interior design and sporadically took classes at the local college. But now it appeared she planned to make it her lifelong career. She didn't like to sit for long. She enjoyed being on the move, and being part of the action when the nighttime crowds roared in. She also liked to talk, and customers at the Wild River were more than happy to indulge her.

I walked in and took a seat at the bar, and thought again of Caroline's recent conversation with Josh in Aspen. How was he doing now? What did he look like? Had he forgiven me in the two years since I'd last seen him? He hadn't called or attempted to contact me in all that time. When he left, I thought I understood why. Now I wasn't so sure. Was it possible that his abrupt departure from Glenwood wasn't just about me? Could it have had anything to do with Kelly? Try as I might, I couldn't believe it.

Caroline greeted me with a smile, sliding a humongous strawberry daiquiri down the bar to me. "I put a real strawberry in there, so don't drink it down too fast."

I took a sip. "Ooo, yummy. Berry delicious."

"I put in an order of buffalo wings for us too, my treat, in case you're hungry. I am."

"Thanks. I'm glad you called. I was going stir-crazy staring at that stupid canvas. Sometimes I wonder why I even bother. It's not like I need to do it, not for the money anyway."

"No, but you love your work. I've seen the look in your eyes when you're painting. It's like you're hypnotized."

"Yeah, maybe, but it's a love-hate relationship on days like this. Believe me, it was way easier to stay motivated when I was doing graphics for Crowley and Hoch."

"Uh huh," said Caroline, "needing a paycheck will do that for you."

I turned and looked around. I was the only customer seated at the bar, and other than some wait staff periodically moving between the tables with napkins and silverware, the restaurant was empty.

"It should pick up in another hour," said Caroline. "Maybe you could give Trevor a call and stay for dinner."

"No, he'll be home late and definitely won't want to go out. He'll want something quick. Besides, tonight's Halloween."

"Oh, right. Forgot. You mean he's going to miss the trick or treaters?"

"He won't mind. Actually, I'd rather turn off the porch light and sit in the Jacuzzi. Maybe I'll just leave a bowl of candy on the steps."

"And the first greedy little goblin will dump the whole thing in his bag."

"True."

Caroline leaned on the bar, her eyes level with mine. "Josh still looks good, better than ever. He got rid of the beard. Makes him look more professional."

"Yeah?" I knew that Caroline had always been attracted to Josh. When he and I broke up after I began dating Trevor, I thought

Caroline would finally do something about it. But she didn't, and then Josh moved to Los Angeles. He still had family living in Glenwood though, so there was always the chance that someday he'd move back. Maybe Caroline hoped so too. At the time he left, I was certain it was because of me, that he wanted to put as much distance between the two of us as possible. I'd never meant to hurt him. I still cared deeply for him. We'd been friends since childhood. He was my first real love, the man I'd lost my virginity to, the man I'd at one time dreamt of marrying. But then I met Trevor and was forced to make a choice. It hurt to let Josh go, but I loved Trevor more.

"You know," I said. "I always thought you and Josh might eventually get together."

"Hah." Caroline covered her mouth to keep from laughing too loud. "Not a chance. That boy has always, and only, had the hots for you. Sure, I can't say I didn't like him, but I'm not silly enough to waste my time." She leaned in closer. "Besides, you're my best friend, and though you won't admit it to me, you still care for him."

"Of course I care for him, but only as a friend."

"Right. The truth of it is, that relationship never got a chance to resolve itself, Trevor moved in so fast."

Her remark left me off balance. "Is that how it looked to you, that he moved in too fast?"

"About as fast as a jackrabbit homing in on a prize carrot."

I drained the last of my daiquiri.

Caroline quickly replaced it.

"No, don't give me another one."

"Don't worry. I won't let you leave until I know you're okay. Besides, the hot wings are up."

We munched on the wings and blue cheese dip, me trying to act as though Caroline's words hadn't upset me. *Love is blind. Yes, it is.* I'd never fully realized—or was it, wanted to realize—how quickly I'd become involved with Trevor. My perfect and perfectly wonderful husband. He'd shown me the house we were living in now, taking the place of another Realtor out sick. That's how we'd met. An accidental meeting, it seemed, but how accidental was it really? Everyone in town knew about eccentric Sam Everett and the truckload of money he'd left his girls. It's not like we'd tried to let it get out, but in a small town like Glenwood, riches of that magnitude didn't go unnoticed.

People talked.

And what about Kelly? Yes, Trevor and Kelly had been friends. They'd joked around a bit here and there, the usual stuff that goes on between a sister and her sister's boyfriend, nothing suspicious. Kelly seemed to like Trevor just fine, and Trevor liked her okay too. But that's all it was. Right? Or was I only kidding myself?

I reached for my drink and missed, instead brushing it with my hand. The glass teetered, then fell, rolling back and forth in a slow arc. The pinkish contents oozed out like a miniature lava flow.

"Sorry," I said.

"Don't worry about it." Caroline quickly wiped up the bar and removed the evidence.

I lowered my voice, aware that more people were sitting at the bar now. "Do you like Trevor?"

Caroline's eyes widened.

"Do I like Trevor? Sure, I like Trevor."

"Yeah, he's great. You know, I wonder if maybe he only married me for the money. I mean, he did know about my money. And I'm not bad looking and all, but he could have had anyone."

"Gwyn, now wait just a ..." She eyed a customer, his arm outstretched, beckoning. "Back in a sec," she said, aiming a finger at me.

I watched as she moved down the bar and mixed two drinks in rapid succession. Then, almost as an afterthought, she tossed a capped beer bottle twirling high behind her back and with barely a look up, caught it, uncapped it, and slid it down the bar where it stopped dead in the man's hand.

The man laughed as his beer overflowed in sudsy foam.

Caroline sidled back to me. "He's willing to lose some brew just to watch me do tricks." She shrugged, then placed a tall frosted glass in front of me. "It's water," she said. "You want a lime to dress it up?"

"No."

"Now you listen to me, and you believe me when I say this. You are special, really special. He's a lucky guy and he knows it. As for the money, sure, maybe he did feel like he'd won the lottery. Couldn't hurt, right? But that's not why he married you. The guy loves you. Anyone can see that. I don't know where you come up with this stuff."

I smiled, truly relieved. "Thanks, Care."

"Don't mention it."

When I returned home I quickly carved a pumpkin, a happy though toothless one, for my little guests. Ghosts and witches appeared in noisy groups, along with rock stars and dragons and winged fairies. Trevor walked in the front door a little after eight o'clock, just as one of the last groups of children scampered down the front steps. He smiled at me and shook his head. "Looks like I missed everything."

"We might get a few more. You look tired."

"I am. I don't think that couple even knew it was Halloween, and I doubt if they cared. They don't have children. But the papers are signed and it's pretty much a done deal. I was hoping to get home a little earlier though."

"I understand."

Trevor picked a Hershey bar from the candy bowl, stripped off the wrapper and took a bite.

I chose a Tootsie Pop. "There's an art show I probably should see this weekend."

"Where?"

"In Aspen."

"Oh," he said, "you know, that's a great idea. I need some new skis, and you could use some too. The mountain will be opening in a couple of weeks and this way we'll be ready. Do you just want to spend the day?"

"Sure—if we leave early."

"Well, we'll leave by eight and get there around nine. How's that?"

"That would work."

"We'll stay and have dinner. I'll make a reservation tomorrow. Anywhere special?"

"No. You decide."

"Feeling tired tonight?" he asked, draping his arm around my shoulders.

"Yeah, I sort of am."

"You sure?"

"I'm sorry, honey. I'm absolutely beat. I worked hard all day and nothing came together. Frustrating." I didn't mention my visit with

Caroline, for no particular reason. I just didn't feel like sharing it with him.

"Okay," he said, "then tomorrow for sure."

Chapter 3

I stood in my darkroom facing a row of polyethylene amber bottles, the soft glow of the safelight illuminating the tray in front of me. Carefully, I agitated the latest eight-by-ten in the solution, watching the image develop before my eyes, like a ghost coming out of hiding. This black and white photograph was from my most recent shoot. I'd trekked high above the canyon and taken several mountain scenery shots. Now I hoped they would turn out as good as when I'd aimed the camera. As I watched, the photo became clearer, the mountain stream seeming to gurgle as it swirled around sunlit rocks, while stately fir trees created the necessary shadows needed to camouflage the sleepy bear I planned to insert there, taking a long cool drink.

As I hung the photo to dry, the phone rang out in the studio. I listened as the answering machine clicked on, but didn't recognize the caller, a woman. Hungry and curious, I finished up and left the darkroom, then pressed the message button.

"Hope I have the right number. The writing in this old address book is a little smudged. I'm calling for Gwyn Sanders who has the house on Stockard road next to mine. I noticed last night that some kids were over there, the lights were off; that's why I'm calling. They threw some toilet paper into the trees and bushes, and were throwing something at the house. I hope they didn't do any damage. I would have shooed them off, but they were the bigger kids that come later on Halloween so I didn't want to go there. I was just about to call the police when they took off. Someone shined their headlights on them and I think it scared them so I—"

The answering machine cut her off at that point. I quickly flipped through my own address book and found the number for Louise Carmichael.

She picked up on the first ring.

"Mrs. Carmichael," I said, "I just got your message. It's Gwyn Sanders."

"Oh, I'm so glad. I wasn't certain I dialed it right and I guess you're not listed."

"No. I'm coming over there in a little while, so if you see a red Jeep in the drive you'll know it's me. Does the house look okay in the daylight, or did you look?"

"Oh, I looked. Tissue in the trees, but no broken windows, not that I can see from here anyway. I should have called the cops, but I didn't notice anything right away, and being it was Halloween ... well, I ... but I should have called."

"You said the lights weren't on?"

"No, not all night. It's the first time I've noticed it, though it could have been like that the night before. I went to bed early and slept through for a change, so I wouldn't have noticed anything. Before that everything's been fine, though I'm not checking all the time. I usually watch TV in the evenings."

"Well, I'll see what's up with the lights and make sure they go on tonight."

"I doubt if those kids will be back, but if they are I'll definitely call the cops on them this time. Have you thought about renting the place at all? There must be lots of young couples that would like to live in a house as nice as that. But maybe that can be its own problem too. It's none of my business anyway."

"My sister and I will probably make some arrangements one of these days. I'm sorry about all this."

"Oh, it doesn't hurt me. Kids are kids. They probably didn't mean any harm anyway."

I fixed myself a tuna sandwich and a Thermos of coffee, then left for the old house. I should have guessed that something might happen last night. The house, empty for so long, made an easy target for neighborhood children. And on Halloween night, with all the lights out—what kid could resist? If I'd been completely sober when I left the bar, I might have thought to swing by, though I wouldn't have noticed if the lights were off then. It was still daylight.

I waved as I climbed out of my Jeep, knowing Louise Carmichael was probably watching, though I couldn't tell from where I stood. Sunlight reflected off her windowpanes into my eyes. Toilet paper streamers fluttered like tiny white flags from the trees, and on closer inspection I saw what appeared to be human excrement on one of the windows.

Everything inside the house looked okay though, so I walked directly to the timer on the floor in the living room. It was unplugged. I knelt and plugged it in, then pulled it out again. Though not a snug fit, it couldn't have come out on its own. I checked the windows and doors on the first floor and all were secure. I walked back from the kitchen to the living room and glanced at the mantel over the fireplace, then stopped. Something looked wrong. Then I noticed one of the framed pictures face down on the wood floor. I knew immediately whose picture it held. I walked over and picked it up. The glass was shattered, but jagged pieces still lay tightly in the corners of the frame. Kelly's smiling face stared out. All of the rest of the family photos had shifted slightly from their dusty arrangement.

I sank down in my father's oversized chair and held the frame with both hands, gripping it as I wished I could grip my sister, the tension and frustration I'd suffered over the past few days suddenly boiling up and over the top. "Tell me what happened, Kelly. And don't you *lie* to me. Do you understand? I need to know what you did." I shook the frame for emphasis, staring into her unblinking eyes, willing her to talk back. When, of course, she didn't, I dropped the frame into my lap and laid my head back, exhausted.

A full hour had passed by the time I realized I'd fallen asleep. I sat up, cursing myself softly, then stopped halfway out of the chair. Something skittered across the kitchen floor past the open archway, then instantly backtracked across the linoleum. The intruder revealed....

I crept to the front door and opened it wide, peeked into the kitchen, then stepped slowly to the broom closet and took out the broom. But the squirrel, tail twitching, seemed wise to my plan and streaked across my shoes into the living room, then frantically tried to jump past the fireplace grate and up the chimney.

I moved closer, reached out with the broom, tried to poke at it gently. My hope was to change its course of direction while gingerly staying out of its way. Those claws could do more than climb curtains and break pictures.

It scurried back and forth, each time missing the open doorway and trying the chimney. Finally, I opened the back door off the kitchen, and like lightening ... it bolted.

I closed both doors, then crossed my arms over my stomach and laughed. After a few minutes, I walked out to the garage and found a tall ladder for the trees, then filled a pail with soapy water for the window cleaning.

"So now I have to find someone to put screening over the chimney so no more squirrels find their way into the house." I turned toward Trevor, who was in the driver's seat of the Cadillac, cruising down Highway 82.

"You're right, with the weather turning colder, they'll all be looking for a warm place to stay."

I chuckled. "The little guy yanked out the plug to the timer with all that running back and forth trying to find a way out. I'm sure that's what happened. But it might have starved to death if it didn't. I probably wouldn't have gone back over there for a while." This wasn't exactly true, of course. I don't think Trevor realized how often I actually did visit the house.

I glanced at the clock on the dashboard and saw it was a quarter to nine. In another fifteen minutes we would be in Aspen.

"How do you want to work this?" he asked. "Do you want to go with me and look for the skis first, or should I come with you to the art thing?"

I knew by the way he said "art thing" that he wasn't interested in joining me, and I'd counted on that reaction.

"No, you don't have to go to the art fair. You'll be bored after a while, and I know you're anxious to look for the skis. Let's meet somewhere if you want, for lunch, see what we've accomplished."

"Okay, leave your cell phone on and I'll get in touch."

I nodded.

Trevor dropped me off a block from the fair, situated between Galena and Mill Street in the open air Aspen Mall. Because of the crowds, he'd park the car farther out, then walk back in.

I was in a better mood as soon as I joined the people filling the streets. Obviously, the event was going well, and I looked forward to losing myself for a while admiring the work of local artists and those more renowned. I loved Aspen. Though it had changed over the years and become a playground and haven for the super rich, it had still retained its charm. The Elk Mountains, the majestic backdrop for it all, inspired awe and also a sense of serenity. Standing in this valley town, surrounded by mountains on all sides, you felt protected and yet aware of how small and fragile you actually were, how insignificant your existence in the overall scheme of things. These wise old mountains passively watched as centuries slipped by, looked on as we humans triumphed and failed, loved and hated. They didn't take sides and they didn't judge. And with any luck, they'd still be around when the sun sputtered and blinked out forever.

As I stood on the sidewalk, the sun slid from behind a bank of clouds and poured over the street. Colorful tents dotted the mall, protection in the event of bad weather, though a majority of the artists had ignored the risks and displayed their work out in the open.

I'd dressed casually in a lightweight ski jacket, jeans, and comfortable hiking boots, knowing I would be on my feet for most of the day. If I found artwork that particularly interested me, I planned to buy it and take it with me, or have it delivered later. I could have displayed my own paintings here, but with the show coming up next weekend, it would have been too much.

I decided to walk the length of the fair and determine its scope before concentrating on any one artist. And though I tried to convince myself that I wasn't looking for anyone in particular, I did study the faces of everyone who passed me on the street, knowing Josh would look a little different now without the beard.

I traveled down Mill to Cooper, back to Mill and over to Hyman, then back to Mill. I saw several places I would have liked to stop, some sculpture I admired, some beautiful pottery, some oils and watercolors bordering on unbelievable, but rushed by them all.

Finally, I came to a halt, pedestrians passing by me on both sides. Chances are I wouldn't find Josh like this anyway, running back and forth like a mouse caught in a maze, so I might as well stop and focus on the art. Josh would probably call anyway. After all, he'd asked Caroline for my number.

I walked through a tent displaying the portraits of Jean LaRoche, luxuriant oils already catching the attention of the larger art world, and the artist was only twenty-two. This young man was definitely going somewhere. The price of his work would probably shoot up in the near future, and I wanted to own at least one. Jean LaRoche himself was not present at the art fair, and that added to the mystique, but he could afford to be elusive.

I stood before a LaRoche I'd seen in a flyer that had been sent with the information I'd received advertising the art fair. No prices appeared on the painting itself. The portrait was of a small boy, dark-skinned, no more than two years old, and naked. His hands pulled at some weed in the dry earth, and I could tell somehow that he was hungry, though his body didn't appear to be starved. It was completely lifelike. I could almost feel his struggle, and it touched me. I decided to buy it.

"I'm sorry to disappoint you," said the pierced-eared young man in charge, "but we already have a buyer. I was just about to place a sold sign on it."

My shoulders slumped. I'd already imagined myself hanging the painting in my studio, proud to finally own such an extraordinary LaRoche.

"Well, what are the odds?"

I swiftly turned around, recognizing the voice in an instant. "Josh," I exclaimed, wanting to hug him, but knowing I no longer had the right.

He was dressed in a sport coat, his shirt open at the collar, looking handsome and cultured and younger than I remembered, though he was a few months older than I was. His blond hair seemed lighter, bleached, I supposed, by all that California sun, and his face was clean-shaven as Caroline had mentioned. I studied the square jaw line and chin that had matured since I'd known him as a child, and the playful brown eyes that smiled back at me now.

"I should have known you'd want it too," he said, nodding toward the painting I'd just tried to purchase.

I shook my head. "I did, but at least I know it sold to someone who will treasure it as much as I would have. Caroline told me she saw you here. How are you, Josh?"

"Not bad." He rubbed his chin, his smile sincere.

"You shaved your beard."

"I did. A mistake or an improvement?"

"Not a mistake, but the beard was good too."

"It made me look older, and I'm old enough now that I can afford to look younger, if that makes any sense."

I laughed. "It does."

He began to stroll down the aisle, and I followed alongside him. It felt so natural to be there, as if it hadn't been two years since I'd seen him last. "So, how's your business?"

"Good, considering the economy. Actually, I have more work than I need, pays to specialize I guess. But what I really need is a vacation, so that's why I'm here. I decided to come down and visit some of my old friends, see the relatives."

"How are they? How's your mother?"

"Better ... now. Mom had a stroke a few months ago, and we were very worried, but she's doing okay. She'll make a full recovery. Fortunately, my sister recognized the symptoms, got her over to the hospital right away. They were able to give her a clot-busting drug before any major damage was done."

"Thank God."

"Yes."

He stopped to point at another LaRoche, a pregnant young woman staking a tomato plant in an urban garden. "I like this one too," he said, "probably less expensive than the other one, though I could be wrong. What do you think?"

"It's wonderful. They all are."

He nodded at me and we walked on.

We left the tent and for the next two hours slowly meandered through the mall. It was enough just to be near him again, talking, laughing. I carefully avoided any subject too personal, and so did he.

Instead, we simply enjoyed each other's company, comparing notes on the artists' talents.

Finally, he looked at his watch and then at me. "I'm hungry," he said. "Can I buy you lunch?"

I couldn't refuse. I just couldn't. If I did, I knew he would take it as his cue to leave, and I didn't want him to. I didn't want this happy feeling to end. Josh had forgiven me. Josh didn't hate me anymore. Josh still cared about me. I didn't deserve it, but he did. I could tell by the way he placed his hand lightly under my elbow as we walked along, by the way he wouldn't leave my side when I stopped briefly to unzip my jacket. And I could feel him watching me when I turned to examine a piece of pottery, or trace my fingers along the edge of a frame. How entirely ridiculous to think he could have ever been with my sister. From the time Josh and I were small, I'd known that I occupied a very special place in his heart. He could never betray me. Josh could never hurt anyone.

He decided on a café a good two blocks from the mall. We still had to wait in line, but the time zipped by. Once we were given a seat and had ordered, I excused myself and found the restroom, then hurriedly checked the messages on my phone. I'd discreetly turned down the volume so that it wouldn't ring, knowing I'd make my excuses later. And, of course, Trevor had called—twice—and the familiar trust in his voice made me feel even more guilty. I dialed his cell phone from inside the bathroom stall.

"So why didn't you call back?" he asked, his annoyance coming through loud and clear.

"I'm sorry. I didn't hear it ring. I guess the volume was down or something. I just checked."

"Well, I need a break so why don't we meet over at the Chalet, unless you have a better idea."

"Now?"

"Yes, now. It is lunch time."

"I can't. I'm hoping to negotiate a price on a painting and it would be a bad idea to leave now."

"Then how long?"

"Maybe a half-hour."

"A half-hour? I don't think I feel like waiting around for a half-hour. But—okay. I'll wait. Try to hurry. I'll be in the bar."

I was anything but composed as I took a seat across from Josh, but he didn't seem to notice. "So," I said brightly, "tell me about all this work you've got. It's going that good, is it?"

"California has its advantages. Still a lot of building starts going on. Plus having a specialty like I do makes it easier."

Josh was a registered architect, a designer, but he'd gradually moved into a related field where he could put his artistic interests and talent to work. He, along with his staff, created digital renderings of proposed developments for architects and builders; the architects used them to sell to builders, the builders used them to sway the planning commissions and other decision makers whose approval they sought. In these big money deals, Josh's beautiful renderings were well worth the stiff fees he charged.

"So does that mean you're not planning to come back to Glenwood?" I asked.

"Financially, I might as well cut my own throat. But sooner or later I'll get tired of the pace and want to slow down. Then I might be back. In the meantime, I'll visit." He gave me a quick smile.

I had literally gobbled down my Turkey Rueben, knowing my half-hour was almost up.

"You're hungry, aren't you?" he asked.

I nodded, my mouth full of food.

He waited until I'd swallowed, then began again. "It's good to see you, Gwyn. Unfortunately, I thought I was completely over you, but I see that's not exactly true. I'll go out on a limb and ask you something, and you can cut me off or leave me dangling. Are you happy with your marriage?"

I hesitated, stunned by the question. "It's fine," I said. "It's fine."

"But are you happy?"

"If I'm not totally happy, it's not because of Trevor. I'm still not over losing my sister. I've been seeing a therapist, though I stopped going about two months ago. I may go back. I haven't found a way to handle it yet on my own."

"Did they ever—find the guy?"

"No."

"That might help, when they catch him. At least you might find some kind of closure then."

I shook my head. "They don't even really know it was him."

"They don't?"

I'd said too much, and regretted it. "How can they know? They questioned him once and then he took off."

Josh blinked, staring at me. "They'll find him. Eventually they'll find him and then you'll know."

I didn't want to argue the validity of that premise, since Josh didn't have all the facts. But at least he wasn't talking about my marriage anymore. "I'm sorry, but I really do have to run, Josh. I want you to call me though." I gave him my cell phone number and he took it and didn't ask why. "It was great seeing you. You will promise to call, won't you?"

"Don't worry. You'll be hearing from me."

He rose as I stood up from the table to leave, but didn't try to follow me out.

It had been forty-five minutes since I'd talked to Trevor on the phone. I race-walked through town, then ran, getting a few dirty looks as I narrowly missed fellow pedestrians. I burst through the door of the busy restaurant and quickly scanned the bar. But Trevor wasn't there.

I asked the hostess if he'd left a message, and the girl, her eyes glassy with disinterest at first, suddenly showed life. "He's still here. We put him upstairs." She turned to locate a menu, but I didn't wait and hurried toward the stairs.

I saw his back first. He was leaning over the woman's table, nodding his head and gesturing with his hand. The woman was younger, very attractive, loose brown curls cascading down her back. She smiled up at him, her skirt riding high, tan legs crossed, flipping the toe of a high-heeled pump. It left no question about her feelings. She liked the attention.

I chose to ignore him, noticing instead his jacket draped over the back of a nearby chair. I took the seat opposite his, still facing him. After several minutes, he turned and looked back toward the table. Again, he turned toward the woman, but he was standing straighter and I guessed he was about to leave. He reached into his back pocket and presented the woman with a card, then walked over.

He took a seat and looked at me, but I couldn't tell what he was thinking.

"I ordered an appetizer," he said, "but I already ate it. Did everything get settled? Did you get the painting for the price you wanted?"

"No, it didn't work out after all. They wanted too much, and I just couldn't see it. But I'm looking at some others."

He waited, as if I might have more to say on the subject. "Oh, well."

"I'm sorry I'm late."

"Couldn't be helped."

He was obviously upset, but I decided not to comment on it. "Did you find some skis?" I asked.

"Yes, as a matter-of-fact, I did. And I found some for you too. I've got them on hold for you to look at, if you're done with your—browsing."

"What are they?"

"Actually, I found two pair you might like, but the graphics are a little bolder on one. You can see them after we eat."

The waiter appeared and we ordered. I complained of a nervous stomach and chose a small salad and decaf coffee. Trevor chose a steak sandwich, soup, and dessert.

"So, who were you talking to over there?" I asked finally.

"Maybe a potential client. She might be looking to buy a place in Aspen. Might be bullshit too."

"I'm sorry I was late."

"It's over. Forget it."

He smiled more on the ride back to Glenwood. We had visited the ski shop, purchased the skis, along with two ski sweaters and a one piece ski outfit for Trevor that he seemed interested in. He joined me at the art fair and I took him through it. I ended up making a few minor purchases, but decided to wait on the LaRoche, though I knew that would probably be a mistake. At six, I changed into the good skirt and leather boots I'd left in the car and we walked to The Chart House and had dinner. I didn't see Josh again, and was thankful I wouldn't have to explain anything to Trevor.

"So, it was a good day?" he asked as we pulled into the driveway, the garage door rolling upwards as the Cadillac neared.

"Yes, I enjoyed it. Did you?"

"Yeah, can't wait to go there again and ski. We'll need snow first."

He closed the driver's door and walked with me to the side entrance. "I saw Joshua Newbury today," he said.

"You did?"

"Yeah, this morning after I dropped you off. I don't think he saw me though. Did you run into him?"

"Yes, I did see him, but we barely talked. I guess he's visiting his family."

Trevor yawned and covered his mouth. "I almost didn't recognize the guy. The beard's gone. It never looked good on him anyway."

I shrugged noncommittally, then started for the stairs and bed. Trevor moved in behind me, pulling me backwards into his arms. "You're not tired tonight, are you?"

"No, not really."

"Good."

But as we walked up the stairs, I had the uneasy feeling that Trevor could see right through me.

Chapter 4

"Thanks for getting me in on such short notice, Janet," I said. "I really appreciate it."

"No problem at all. I've been meaning to call and say hello anyway. It's good to see you, Gwyn."

I hung up my coat and took a seat in one of the comfortable chairs that faced each other, my usual spot near the window.

"You've made a few changes," I said. I noted a new lamp on a corner table, some chocolate-brown throw rugs on the wood floor, and updated pictures of her teenaged children, Ben and Sarah, atop her desk.

"Yes. Small improvements. Thanks for noticing."

Janet herself had not changed, a wisp of a woman, wide-eyed with a warm engaging smile. She barely looked thirty, though I knew for a fact she would be celebrating her forty-second birthday in December. I found her easy to talk to, extremely likeable, and worldly savvy in a way that couldn't be taught. Though I'd never asked, I'd sometimes wondered what life experiences might have drawn her to this particular profession.

She took a seat opposite me, crossing her ankles, mirroring my own. "We haven't seen each other in a while, not for a few months.

What brings you here today?"

"Well, I needed to talk to someone I trusted, someone who would keep my secrets," I said with a short laugh.

"Oh. Secrets. Well, this is serious."

"Actually, it's not so much secrets. It's more—things I can't talk to anyone else about right now." I took a deep breath, folding my hands one into the other. "I've been having some issues concerning Trevor. I haven't been treating him all that well lately, but every time I think I should be more ... truthful with him, I back off. He tried to make love to me the other night and I just couldn't connect, and that's not usually a problem for me at all."

"So, what is it you're not being truthful about?"

"Well, I ran into Josh, my old boyfriend, in Aspen this past weekend. He's in town, just visiting. It was an accidental meeting. We bumped into each other at an art fair, but I felt guilty about it and didn't say anything to Trevor. The problem is, I enjoyed seeing Josh—a little too much, I think—and might want to see him again."

"And why does that worry you? What do you think will happen if you see him again?"

"I don't know. Actually, I don't think anything will happen. I just want to see him again. It's almost like I need to. I hated the way we broke up. Our relationship ended so quickly. After all the time we'd been together, Josh just took off and left the state, disappeared from my life completely. My fault, of course." I glanced up, but Janet's expression hadn't changed. "I don't want to lead him on, but if I start to see him again, of course, I will be. It's totally selfish. I'll be hurting Josh, and I could end up hurting Trevor too, severely damage what we have. It's crazy."

"So, knowing this, why do you think you're still willing to take the chance?"

"I think I need closure with Josh. I need to try and explain to him why I left. He was more than a boyfriend to me, he was a friend. I miss him ... a lot. As for Trevor, I don't want to talk to him about this because he's the reason I left Josh. And I still have a lot of mixed emotions about that. As much as I blame myself, I blame Trevor more. Recently, I've been questioning his reasons for marrying me."

Janet reached for her glass, took a sip of water. "Go on."

"I really didn't get to know Trevor all that well before I became involved with him. I was seeing Josh, in love with him—not wildly anymore, we'd been seeing each other for so long—but it was love. Then Trevor came along and I wanted him so badly I couldn't think of anything, but him. I literally forgot about Josh—just threw him away—for a man I barely knew. Now, looking back, I'm wondering if the money had more to do with Trevor's decision to marry me than I thought. He likes having money. He enjoys spending it and he does, though not ... excessively. Oh ... what am I saying? He's not bad about it. I encourage him to spend on himself. I spend money on him. I want to. I mean, what is it for if not to make the people you love happy? The thing is, with Josh I always knew I was loved for me. I didn't have a dime when Josh loved me. I barely had two cents in my savings account."

"So, seeing Josh has made you question your relationship with Trevor?"

"Yes."

"Has anything else happened that would make you feel this way? Besides, Josh, I mean."

"No ... well, maybe some little things. Trevor has been working a lot lately. That bothers me. I don't get to see him as much."

"Have you talked to him about it?"

"No."

"What's stopping you?"

"I don't think it would do any good."

"Hmm. I'm sensing some anger here." Janet stared at me, waiting for me to respond. Finally, after what felt like an interminable silence, I did.

"If I'm angry, I'd have to say that I'm mostly angry at myself. I'm stupidly naive when it comes to the people I care about. I blindly accept whatever they put in front of me, when instead I should take a step back and see what's really going on."

"Are you still talking about Trevor here?"

"Trevor, sure."

"Not Kelly?"

"Well, yes, Kelly too. I was certainly stupid with her. If I hadn't been so stupidly naive, maybe she'd still be alive." I had to stop talking for a moment, reign in all the old feelings that engulfed me whenever I spoke her name. "I didn't know her either. I really didn't. When you love someone that much, you can't see them. I couldn't anyway. And maybe I didn't want to see who she really was, because then I'd be forced to admit she wasn't everything I wanted her to be. Still ... why couldn't she trust me? If she had a drug problem, why couldn't she tell me about it? I could have helped her. I wouldn't have stopped loving her. Didn't she know that? I never would have stopped loving her."

"But maybe she wasn't willing to let you. Unfortunately, we'll never know why she was reluctant to seek help."

"I wish so much that I could talk to her. I do, sometimes, when I'm alone. I want so much to know what happened ... why it happened. How could anyone do that to her? Only a monster could have slaughtered her like that. He ran her down—like she was nothing—like she was dirt. I swear if I could, I'd kill him. I'd kill him and never regret it for a single moment." My stomach rolled and I felt the searing hatred rise in my throat, bubbling up its caustic acid.

"Linda told me Kelly was on drugs, said it was obvious, but I didn't believe her. I even took Kelly aside one day and stood her in front of me and asked her point blank, 'Are you taking drugs? I don't want to think so, but if you are I need to know. So please, tell me the truth.' Do you know what she said? Right to my face she said, 'I'm not doing drugs, Gwyn. I wouldn't do that. God, I can't believe you're asking me this.' I told her I had to ask because I was worried about her, that she didn't seem ... right. She got a little angry, then told me I shouldn't worry about her, that I worried about everything, that I've always worried too much and maybe I was the one with the problem. Then she took that back and apologized, told me again that, no, she didn't do drugs. Well, maybe a little weed, when she was in school, but that was stupid and she knew it, so she'd quit. She had me convinced that Linda was absolutely wrong. It was a real relief at the time. But then, of course, they found cocaine in her system, and other drugs I can't even pronounce were stashed in her medicine chest disguised as cold medicine or cough drops or whatever. God, it hurt. It hurt so much to think she would lie to me like that."

Janet sat quiet, then finally spoke.

"You can't blame yourself, Gwyn. We'll never know exactly why Kelly felt she had to lie. But you do have to stop thinking you could have changed her."

Numbly, I brushed away tears with the back of my hand.

"I know how very much you loved Kelly, and I believe she knew that too. Maybe she felt you were the only one left who still believed in her, who saw something in her that was truly special. Maybe she wasn't willing to let that go. Though I've never spoken to her, I think from what you've told me that she must have loved you too, very much. After all, you looked after her after your mother died."

"Well, my father was there too."

"Yes, but from what you've told me, he wasn't around too much."

"No." I took a deep breath, finally shaking myself of the bizarre feeling that had taken hold of me a while ago. "You are right, of course. Kelly couldn't have handled the thought of losing me too, losing my love. She'd lost Mom, then Dad. And Linda, well ... Kelly and Linda weren't exactly best friends. I suppose Kelly couldn't take the chance that maybe she'd mess things up with me too.... It's so strange. I've had dreams since she died where I died too, where I lost my footing and fell into this cold dark bottomless crevasse, and for one horrible instant, I feel my insides shrivel, because I know this is it. No one can save me. I can't even scream I'm so terrified. Maybe that's how it was for her that night. I don't know. I'm not sure I want to know, because if it's as bad as it must have been, how can I ...?" I stopped abruptly, sat very still. Finally, I looked up at her. "I have said all this before, haven't I?"

"Gwyn, you are not at fault. You are not the one to blame."

"No?"

"No."

"You're right. He is."

"I'm going to give you a referral to that psychiatrist friend of mine, just for some medication, something to help you relax, nothing heavy duty. I want you to—"

"No, I don't want to take anything. I'm okay."

"Of course. But you can always call me if you change your mind. I do think we should see each other again. Maybe next week, if that's all right."

"Sure."

"Talk to Rachel on your way out. Tell her I said to fit you in."

"All right."

I stood and my knees buckled slightly. I hoped Janet hadn't noticed, but she glanced down, then back up into my eyes. "You're certain you're okay?"

"Yes, I'm fine."

I bypassed Rachel. I just wanted out of there. I'd call and make the appointment later on ... or maybe not.

I was consumed with thoughts of Kelly on the drive home.

Initially, police surmised she'd been a random victim of a drunk driver who'd swerved out onto the gravel shoulder, hit her, then panicked and fled. But no one could supply the answer to one important question. What was Kelly doing walking alone on a deserted road so late at night?

The morning after she died, reeling from the news, I drove over to the old house. When I opened the garage door, I found Kelly's pickup parked inside. She'd almost never bothered to pull her truck in, so I'd inspected further. Her right front headlight was smashed and the fender creased. Dried blood stained both the glass and metal.

Her killer had taken the time to drive her truck back to the house, pull it into the garage, and close the door. Everyone had assumed it was Craig Foster. He didn't have an alibi, and he did have a record, drug offenses and other assorted crimes. He must have known they wouldn't look any further. After he ran, the police had focused entirely on him.

As soon as I got home, I walked into the studio and checked my answering machine, which flashed ominously with seven messages. I started to play them back, but cut them off after the first one, from Linda.

I nervously dialed her number.

"Linda, I just got home. Are you all right? Why aren't you at the hospital?"

"I think I'm okay now, well sort of, and I tried to call Wolfgang, but he hasn't called back."

"Call an ambulance—right now—or I will."

"No, Gwyn, don't. Please, you come and take me there. I'm only a little dizzy now. I don't want an ambulance in the driveway flashing its lights. I don't want to explain to the neighbors, okay? I swear. I'm not that bad."

"I'll be there in five minutes. Don't hang up."

I drove with reckless speed, hoping Linda was telling the truth, that she wasn't hurt badly. But how can you fall down a flight of stairs and judge that for yourself? And who the hell cared what the neighbors thought?

I rushed through the front door calling her name. She was laid out on the couch, eyes shut, and for a second I wasn't sure if she was conscious. Then she turned her head and tried to smile.

"God, Linda, don't scare me like this." I knelt beside her. "You look awful. Is anything broken? How's your head?"

"I don't know. I tried to get up and I felt nauseous, a little dizzy."

"Let me call an ambulance. This is ridiculous."

"No, don't. I'll be fine. Just give me a minute."

Slowly, Linda tried to rise, easing her legs off the couch and gradually coming to a sitting position. "Whew—okay. One second, then we'll try it."

"Linda, this is really stupid. What if you faint and I drop you? It's a long way to the Jeep."

"No, we're going to do this."

I helped her up, supporting her under the arms as she attempted to come to her feet. Holding her tightly across the back and shoulders, I felt her legs shake from the effort to take her own weight.

"Are you sure you're okay? You're not going to pass out?"

"No. I'm okay."

We carefully made our way out the front door and down the concrete walk to the driveway. Still holding Linda tightly, I struggled to open the car door. Finally, I managed to unlatch it and push it open with my knee. I stopped to take a breath, knowing this was one of the dumbest things I'd ever let Linda talk me into. "Okay, can you get in the car?"

"Wait," she said, and I could almost see the nausea roll over her deathly white face.

"God, Linda. What are we doing?"

She lifted one foot onto the floor of the Jeep, then reached up for the seat. Lifting and pushing, I shoved her inside, then fastened her seat belt.

I scrambled to the driver's side, jammed the Jeep into reverse and backed onto the road. Linda groaned, then coughed, her head listing toward the window. I watched from the corner of my eye, experiencing a wave of panic so strong I felt close to passing out myself.

I barely remember the drive to the hospital, but the look on my face must have been something because two orderlies rushed out to help me get Linda into the emergency room.

The doctor, a silver-haired gentleman with a dimple in his chin, seemed to take it all in stride. I watched as he went about his preliminary examination of Linda.

"She wouldn't let me call an ambulance," I added quietly as the doctor held her chin up and shined a small beamed instrument into her eye.

"And do you always do what your sister says?" he asked, never taking his eyes off his patient, who appeared too sick to say a word.

I stood there, shamefaced and silent, knowing he'd assessed the situation exactly.

"We'll need to keep her overnight for observation," he said. "She has a concussion. That's the most serious issue, and some contusions, scrapes. We'll check her out thoroughly for any internal problems. Do you know how this happened?"

"She fell down the basement stairs. I don't know the details. She called me and—"

"I tripped," Linda breathed softly.

"That's okay," said the doctor. "Don't talk if it's difficult for you." He turned to me. "We'll get her into a room as soon as we finish here and receive the results of the tests. You can take a seat outside now and we'll call you when she's settled in." He smiled briefly.

"Thank you, doctor."

I continued dialing Wolfgang until he finally returned my call on the cell.

"Your wife's in the hospital," I stated darkly.

"She's where?"

"You heard me."

"Is she okay? What happened?"

"No, she's not okay. She has a concussion, bruises, maybe other serious stuff. They're still checking her out. She fell down the stairs and she's been trying to reach you ever since."

"Oh, man. Oh, I'm so sorry, Gwyn. Really. I'll be right over there."

"Why didn't you call her?"

"Oh—work. I don't know. You're right. I should have."

"Yes, you sure should have. If not for me she might have lain there waiting for who knows how long."

"Listen, Gwyn. It's not what you think. She calls me every minute of every freakin' day with something. If I called her back every time she called me I'd never get any work done."

"Well, that's still no excuse. Look what happened."

"I know. You're absolutely right. I'll be right over."

Fifteen minutes later he stepped through the sliding glass doors. I watched as he approached the desk and spoke with the nurse in charge. He acknowledged me with a raised hand as the woman before him pulled out forms and a clipboard with a pen attached. He walked over and took a seat beside me.

"I guess they're putting her in a room pretty soon," he said.

"Yes." I looked him over. He wasn't in his work clothes, but a pair of tan slacks and a brown leather jacket. I had to assume he'd taken the time to change at the house before coming over.

He studied the forms on his lap, flipping the pen between two fingers. "I need a coffee. You want one?"

"I guess. Sure."

He stood and looked down at me, and I could see the impression of his muscular thighs bulging beneath his slacks.

"How do you like it?"

"What?"

"Your coffee. How do you like it?"

"Oh, cream and sugar. But don't bother. I can get it."

"Don't worry about it. How much sugar?"

"Just a little, a spoon."

He stepped over to the coffee machine.

He made me uncomfortable. I didn't like being alone with him, especially being this near to him. Could this be the man who'd killed my sister? I'd never bothered to try and figure the guy out, or to look behind the obvious flirtatiousness to see what might be lurking there.

Wolfgang held the Styrofoam cup toward me. "It's hot. Be careful."

"Thanks," I said.

"You're welcome."

He sat down and scooted his chair closer to mine, then balanced the clipboard on his knee. With a half smile, he leaned in toward me. "Tell me why in this age of instant information we still have to fill out these idiotic things."

"I don't know. Guess they need updated information."

"Yeah, guess so." He bent forward and began filling in the blanks.

After a minute, I glanced over his shoulder. "So, what is it they need to know so badly?"

He turned to face me. "Boy, you must be bored."

"No. Just asking."

"You sure are a funny gal. Now don't take this wrong, because *I'm* just asking. But I get the feeling you don't like me very much."

"What?"

"Hey, it's okay. I can see you're a very private person. You don't warm up to people that easy. I'm a little that way myself. Not everybody can take my sense of humor. And ... maybe there's something about me that kinda turns you off. I don't expect everybody to like me. It's not a problem."

"I don't dislike you, Wolfgang. I don't. I just don't know you very well. I'm sorry if you got that impression."

"Okay, that's fair."

"But I do worry about Linda. You didn't call her back when she needed you. That upset me very much. And she absolutely refused to let me call her an ambulance."

"She did?"

"Yes."

"Why?"

"I don't know."

"Well, she should have. What, you think I'd care? If she's hurt, for sure I want her to call *somebody*."

I studied his body language. He appeared sincere, but there was something glib and rehearsed about his answers, as if he'd already anticipated the questions. "Will you excuse me for a minute?" I said. "I need to call Trevor and tell him what's going on."

"Sure thing."

I walked a short way down the corridor, then dialed my cell. Trevor didn't answer, so I left a message explaining everything and telling him to drop by the hospital on his way home, or if that wasn't possible, I'd see him later. I stopped to use the restroom, and when I returned to the front desk, Wolfgang was gone.

The nurse motioned me over. "Mrs. Lehman is in a room now if you'd like to make a short visit."

"Yes, I would."

She gave me the room number and directions.

Linda and Wolfgang were talking softly as I entered the private room. Wolfgang was seated close to the head of the bed, his hand gently stroking Linda's hair. Though still sickly looking, Linda seemed happier.

"Hi, pumpkin," I said. "I stopped to use the restroom or I would have been here sooner. Of course, they only announce anything when you're not available. How are you feeling?" I pulled up a chair on the opposite side of the bed from Wolfgang.

"Better now. Tired though."

Wolfgang looked over to me. "We have to keep it short. The doc just stuck his head in and doesn't want her getting too tired. I told him you were on your way."

"What did he say? Is she okay? Did they find anything internal?"

"No, she's fine. Concussion and bruises, some scrapes. They'll probably let her out tomorrow. She's tough." He patted her arm.

Linda smiled weakly at Wolfgang, then turned to me. "It was so stupid. I was moving some boxes and I tripped. I dropped the box, but missed the handrail. It happened so fast."

"You have to be more careful," I said.

"Oh, I know. I don't want to come here again. Gwyn, could you call the club, let them know I won't make my tennis lesson?"

"Of course."

She sighed. "I'll have to ask the doctor when I can play again, and Thanksgiving's coming up."

"Don't worry about all that," I said. "Just get well."

A few minutes later a nurse appeared in the doorway and shooed us out.

Wolfgang hurried alongside me down the hall. "She's out of it," he said. "But she'll be okay."

"Yeah."

It was already dark outside the double doors of the hospital. A raw icy wind had kicked up its heels, and I stopped to button my jacket before heading out. Wolfgang waited for me, then walked with me across the parking lot to our cars. I called Trevor again, but no answer, so I left another message, told him I was leaving the hospital and not to come by.

Trevor's Cadillac was parked in the driveway when I pulled in. I walked inside, noticing a fire in the fireplace as I hung up my coat. A clinking of plates and silverware came from the kitchen. "Trevor?"

"In here, my tired girl."

He smiled as I stepped into the kitchen.

"You're cooking?" I asked.

He finished placing silverware on the table, then came over and hugged me. "I felt bad about not making it over to the hospital. So I thought you might like dinner-a-la-Trevor as an apology."

"That's so sweet."

"How's your sister doing? Okay?"

"She's hurting, but she'll be okay. I didn't really expect you to make it to the hospital. I knew you'd come if you could." I squeezed him closer still. "What a day. How was yours?"

"All right, except for your news. I was in a meeting when I got your message. I wanted to call back, but I had to play happy, I-have-no-other-life, Realtor. You know how it is."

"Mm-hmm." I sniffed the air. "So what did Chef Trevor prepare for dinner tonight?"

"Well, I had big plans in the beginning, thought maybe I'd try something gourmet. I actually looked through a couple of your cookbooks for ideas. But that scared me off, so instead we're having broiled chicken with a really awesome barbecue sauce, plus a baked potato and a salad. I still have to make the salad. You got here sooner than I thought you would."

"I'll help you."

"No. No you won't. I'm looking for hefty paybacks in the form of sizzling female flesh. Whoa, hang on a minute. Need to add a log to that fire, I think. Don't want it to die down too quick."

I laughed as he hustled from the room.

When dinner was ready, he pulled out my chair and brought our plates to the table. He actually wasn't a bad cook. The chicken was done, not raw or overcooked, as was the potato. Of course, at that moment, it didn't matter to me one bit how it tasted. I wouldn't think of criticizing his efforts.

He lit a candle for the table and turned down the lights, and by the time we'd moved to the living room and the hypnotic warmth of the fire, I was ready to love Trevor again, the way I'd loved him in the past, before I'd discovered Kelly's letter.

Chapter 5

The drive to Denver was bleak. Rain turned quickly to sleet, a heavy slushy mess that my windshield wipers struggled hopelessly to remove. I strained to see the road, slowing to just under fifty, made more nervous as other less intimidated drivers flew by on Route 70 hurling splatters of the heavy stuff against the van.

I'd rented a large cargo van to carry all of my artwork and the panels I would display it on. The Jeep was just too small. Unfortunately, I didn't expect to be driving with an unfamiliar vehicle in such nasty weather. Still, it would take a lot more than bad driving conditions for me to cancel. I'd arranged this particular mall exhibition at Vista Meadows a year in advance, before the mall was even completed. An art agent I'd met at one of Linda's parties had mentioned that the new mall would be a good opportunity for newer artists, if they moved quickly.

I'd brought twenty pieces to display, a feat, considering all the setbacks in the past two weeks. Eight of the paintings were new. I also had a large stack of four-color brochures I'd designed which had turned out really spectacular, and a nice looking mauve plastic name tag with my name in gold.

It would be late afternoon by the time I arrived at my hotel, enough time to have dinner, then call and make sure all the arrangements I'd made earlier, and confirmed by phone, had not somehow been lost in the shuffle of changing mall personnel.

As much as I wanted to do this show, I didn't like the idea of leaving when things were so unsettled. They'd discharged Linda from the hospital on Thursday, yesterday, and I'd visited her at home and brought her favorite pastries and other treats, along with lots of sympathy. Each time I asked her about the accident, as subtly as I could considering her tendency to close up on me, I got the same response. She'd tripped on the stairs. She said again she hadn't been able to reach Wolfgang and she didn't want the neighbors asking a lot of nosy questions, so she'd called me. Simple as that.

I'd made a decision to show Linda the letter as soon as she recovered. I suspected Wolfgang was the one responsible for Kelly's murder, but I had no answer as to why. At the time Kelly died, Linda and Wolfgang had been married for a year and a half, certainly sufficient time for him to get to know Kelly fairly well. Maybe something had been going on. Was he afraid that Kelly would expose the affair and jeopardize his marriage to Linda? No, that didn't seem reasonable. Wolfgang had to know that Linda wouldn't leave him. Not for any reason. Not as crazy as she was about him.

Kelly had mentioned a box ... that he may have found the box. This box must certainly be the clue that tied everything together. Could Kelly have stumbled onto something, some secret Wolfgang didn't want revealed? Or possibly, Kelly, with her habit of writing everything down, had put what she'd learned into the box, and Wolfgang had found that. Or maybe not. Maybe it was something entirely different. What was so important about this box?

I worried about showing the letter to Linda. I worried that she wouldn't be able to keep her mouth shut, that she'd either intentionally or accidentally reveal the contents of it to Wolfgang. Then the both of us would be at risk.

The sky was the same dull gray and still sleeting when I pulled the van into the parking lot of the four-story Bingham hotel. I folded a newspaper to cover my head, then stepped outside the van and peered through the rear windows. None of my artwork appeared to have seriously shifted. I'd protected it well.

The van came equipped with an alarm system, so I wasn't too worried about theft. Plus, it seemed to be a good area of town, though I'd never been on this side of Denver before. Tonight, after the mall closed for business, I'd drive over and set up for tomorrow.

I checked into the hotel and took the elevator to the second floor. The place wasn't exactly new or exactly old. Its best quality as far as I was concerned was its proximity to the mall, just a few miles away.

The elevator doors opened and I stepped out onto plush green carpet framed by walls of pale mint. I found my room number, inserted the keycard into the slot, which signaled green and allowed me to enter.

The room was decent enough, continuing the green motif of the hall, patterned spread on the king-size bed, ginger jar lamps, telephone. I pitched my suitcase onto the bed, then sat down to use the phone. I called home first. Trevor wasn't there, so I left a message, said I'd arrived safely, the weather was crummy here too, that I was starving and thirsty—and lastly—that I loved him. I told him I'd call later in the evening. I left a similar message on his cell phone.

I ordered room service, turkey sandwich and tomato soup, then lay back on the bed and tried to relax.

The hotel was on the northeast edge of Denver, not so far from downtown that I couldn't sightsee if I had more time. It had been three years since I'd made a trip to Denver purely for pleasure. Kelly had been with me. We'd visited the Denver Art Museum, exploring the many wings of the huge free-form structure. Since then the museum had added an entire floor devoted to European paintings and textiles. I wanted to see them, but it would have to wait until another time. I tried to remember why Linda hadn't come along on that trip, some excuse, but she'd rarely joined me if Kelly was invited.

My snack arrived and after I finished it I checked my voicemail for messages. I had only one since I'd last looked, the time given, eleven a.m. I didn't recognize the number, though it seemed vaguely familiar. And then it clicked ... Josh.

"Hi, Gwyn. It's just me. I said I would call and here I am, calling. I'm over at my mom's again, a short trip only, but since I'm in town I thought of you and our lunch date in Aspen. I wouldn't mind seeing you again. I'm bored as hell here. I love the family, but I can only eat, sleep, and yak with them so much. Are you very busy? Could you drop whatever you're doing and meet me for a drink? I realize this could be awkward, but we are old friends, more than old friends. I got the feeling last time that there's more we need to talk about. I could anyway. So, give me a jingle."

He'd left his mother's number and his cell phone. I checked the time. It was now five-thirty. He sounded nervous and needy and I could have punched myself if I thought it would do any good. Look what I'd done.

I debated returning his call. Rude if I didn't, considering I'd given him my number though he hadn't asked for it. Of course, maybe he wouldn't answer and I could leave a short message, tell him I was out of town, thank him for the call, and leave it at that. Then let a week go by. He'd get the idea. He was no idiot.

I moved to the edge of the bed, thinking, contemplating the phone. I picked up the receiver and dialed. It rang once, twice, and just as I was about to believe it would all work out, he answered.

"Hello?"

"Hi, Josh. It's Gwyn."

"Oh—well great. I'm glad I picked up the phone. I'm in my car."

"I got your message, a little late. I just got it now."

"Oh, well I'm glad you called. I didn't think I'd be in town again so soon, but I am."

"Is anything wrong?"

"Wrong? Oh, you mean my mother? No, she's fine. They're all fine. No, my sister's getting married, and at first I didn't think I'd be able to make it, but I did. The wedding's tomorrow. You want to be my date?"

Before I could answer, he continued. "I'm kidding, of course. It's that whole church, morals thing. You know, married woman, single man. My family is *so* not with it. I don't give a damn, but they might."

He had me laughing now.

"Oh, Josh. So, which sister is it?"

"Amy."

"Well, give her my congratulations."

"I will. Say ... do you have a minute? For that drink, I mean."

"Would you believe I'm in Denver?"

"You are? No. Why?"

"A good reason. A big solo exhibition at a mall."

"I see." Then sounding happier, he said, "That's great. Are you done for the day?"

"No. No, it doesn't start until tomorrow. I set up tonight after the mall closes."

"Which mall?"

"I don't think you'd know it. Vista Meadows. New, kind of classy, I guess."

"No, I don't know it. But I'll be going to the airport on Sunday. I have some business in Denver. Maybe I can stop by."

"Well, I guess you could," I said, hesitating, "but I won't have much time to talk. I'll be busy trying to sell."

"Then maybe I'll buy something. I haven't seen anything you've done in a while. Are you expensive?"

"If I don't sell anything Saturday, the prices could get a lot lower by Sunday."

"You'll sell. Maybe I'll buy the whole bunch."

I smiled. "I don't think you have to do that. Maybe just do a lot of gushing about my work in front of the customers, pretend to be an art critic or something."

"I certainly will, but actually I can't guarantee to make it. I have a few things to take care of on Sunday, so don't count on me."

"If you're there great, if not, some other time."

"Yeah."

I couldn't think of anything else to say, and felt as if we might drift into dangerous territory if the conversation continued. "Well, it was nice talking to you, Josh. I probably should call the mall and do some last minute—"

"Gwyn?"

"What?"

He was silent, then cleared his throat. "Have a good time tomorrow. Enjoy yourself. You'll do fine."

After we hung up, I made a list of questions to ask the mall people, just to reaffirm what they'd told me before. I'd get over there by eight tonight, before the mall closed at nine, look at the layout, plan how to set everything up, then get started.

Unfortunately, by the time I drove over, the sleet, still heavy—and now made worse by the addition of wind—had glazed the roads and made them icy. The van didn't handle as well as the Jeep, a stick shift, enabling me to downshift quickly when needed, and I had my reservations about the quality of tread on the tires. The van slid at every corner even though I was barely moving.

To make matters worse, a line of traffic grew steadily longer behind me. A truck, its headlights flooding the interior of the van, loomed inches from my bumper.

I could see the mall lights up ahead on my right as I began to ascend a small hill. The rear end of the van swished right, then left. I clutched the steering wheel, willing my foot off the brake. The truck faded back.

I pulled into a well-lit area of the immense parking lot and stopped to take a breather. According to my instructions, I was to go to a loading dock marked B-7, where I could back the van inside, shielded from the weather. I'd impressed upon the mall people that I couldn't unload my paintings and panels unless they were well protected. They'd assured me everything would be fine.

But, of course, I couldn't find B-7. The way they'd spoken, I'd assumed it would be easy to locate. But there weren't any markings of any kind outside, or else the dark night and inclement weather had erased them. I parked the van as close to an entrance as possible and ran inside.

Despite the weather, the mall was busy. It was quite nice, better than anything near Glenwood, and new. It gleamed like a shiny new coin. I hurried past walls adorned with striated marble tile and under vaulted ceilings with antique gold accents. Lush greenery and brilliant flowers of red, yellow, and purple sprouted from giant pots around every turn. Store windows spewed forth their offerings, glittering jewels, Rolex watches, full-length sable coats. I spotted Saks Fifth Avenue and Neiman Marcus, smaller stores, Liz Claiborne, Gerard Heath, and Le' Spa.

My instincts told me to head to the center of the mall. Maybe I'd find some kind of information desk.

I did find a circular booth, and calmly explained my dilemma to a kind-faced, smartly dressed woman in a rose colored suit. She quickly spoke to someone on the phone, pulled out a folded map, marked off

B-7 in red ink, along with the area I described as the location for my art show. I thanked her profusely and headed off.

By the time I crept back to my hotel that night, I was exhausted. I'd found B-7, but again had to get out of my van and get drenched because a huge delivery truck was blocking the entire entrance. I found the driver and convinced him to move his empty truck—he had stopped to have a coffee and donut and was reluctant to leave the donut box—but the delay cost me another half-hour of setup time.

Fortunately, it was all done now. It took me countless trips to carry it all inside and a lot of thinking and planning to put it all together, but it looked great. They'd given me a good location, a carpeted island surrounded by aisles going in several directions, central to foot traffic. I had potted plants for background, pots of flowers I could use or remove. And they'd remembered to provide a decent looking desk for me to sit behind when I wasn't on my feet roaming or talking to potential customers.

Though it was almost eleven p.m. and Trevor might already be asleep, I decided to call. The phone rang four times and then the answering machine clicked on. But as I began to speak, the machine beeped once, and I knew Trevor had picked up the receiver. His sleepy voice mumbled something resembling hello.

"Hi, honey," I said, "sorry I woke you."

"So'kay."

"I'll call again in the morning. You go back to sleep." He grunted something unintelligible and I couldn't be sure if he was agreeing with me or not. "Trevor?"

The phone disconnected.

I sighed and hung up, then pulled back the blankets on the tightly made bed. Without another thought, I crawled between the cold sheets and turned off the light.

The mall opened at nine and I arrived by eight-thirty. I wore a charcoal gray skirt and low shoes, a lighter gray jacket and mauve blouse that matched my name tag, along with a pair of pearl earrings. Not too dressy, but not too casual.

I inspected my small domain. Desk with Visa machine—a must— and several small stacks of my brochures, a business card tucked into each. I also had a large floor bin of prints I'd made of my original paintings, three copies of each one. I could, of course, take orders for more. The prints were priced to sell for much less than the original artwork and would likely be the smaller percentage of my profits.

I walked between my panels, painstakingly put together last night and hung lovingly with the canvases I had labored over the past few months. They were some of my best work. My painting of climbers ascending an icefall looked almost real. You could almost feel them sweat as they swung their axes in the warm sunshine. And my painting of a mammoth bear balancing on the rocks, extending its neck into a cold mountain stream for a drink, was breathtaking. I'd also recently completed one of hikers on the trail up to Hanging Lake, stopping to wait for their young son, and to take in the beauty surrounding them.

I had arranged and rearranged it all in as attractive a fashion as I could imagine, allowing for traffic flow and room to stand back and admire. It looked spectacular.

There was a deli close by, and before the mall became too busy I planned to buy my lunch and put it in the small cooler below my desk. That was the only problem. I couldn't leave for any length of time. It would be a long, long day.

A little past nine a.m., a stray pedestrian, a twenty-or-so male dressed nicely in slacks and a golf shirt, sidled into my area. I tried not to pounce on him, instead stood near my desk ready to answer his questions should he ask any. He walked through it all, then gave me a quick smile and rummaged through the bin.

"Nice," he said when he was done. "I might be back later."

I nodded and watched him walk on.

I experienced a few more of those, then at ten o'clock things got busier. I casually walked among the panels. Potential customers strolled in and out, wives with husbands, wives without husbands, single women, single men and, of course, children.

An older gentleman, his face deeply lined, but his gait rapid and sure, came up to me and signaled me to follow him to one of the paintings. "I love this," he said. He was referring to my painting of a lone young man in a kayak moving through a turbulent river, the youth's paddle dipping forcefully into the churning water. "My grandson would love this. Can I buy it?"

"Oh, yes."

"What river is that?"

"The Colorado."

The gentleman smiled. "Really? He kayaks there. It almost looks like him. Did you paint this?"

I nodded, remembering taking the shot last summer, but painting it within the last month.

He turned to gaze at it again. "Oh, he will absolutely love this. It's his birthday tomorrow and I didn't have any idea what to get him, but this is perfect. Do you take Visa?"

He didn't question the price, which I'd displayed on a small card beside the painting, though it was one of my most expensive. I wrapped the painting in brown paper for him and he strolled off, an apparently happy man.

I sold two prints and one smaller original before lunch, and was feeling very good about it all. I sneaked a few bites of my turkey sandwich when I had a chance, and sipped iced tea through a straw in a paper cup.

My mouth did drop open when I overheard a young woman wearing stilts for shoes bray to her boyfriend. "*Well, yeah, but it's not worth that!*"

I backed off immediately, not hurt exactly, just surprised by the girl's loud mouth rudeness.

I rearranged my paintings to cover the empty holes made by the morning's sales, then sat for a while. I'd tried to call Trevor an hour ago, but got his voicemail, so left another message. Suddenly, I missed him, and wondered why he didn't answer his phone, though he was probably working hard too. Realtors, at least the successful ones, couldn't work strictly from nine to five. He hadn't mentioned his condo venture in a while, though he had talked nonstop about it at first. Had something gone wrong with that?

By nine o'clock Saturday night, my feet were sore and my temperament dark. The show had gone well, but I couldn't enjoy my success. I just wanted to be home. I had a bad feeling I couldn't shake. I didn't believe Linda's story about the fall down the stairs. She was lying. But it was more than that. Something was telling me I was missing something important. And I hadn't talked to Trevor at all. Why didn't he call?

It was past eleven before I returned to the hotel. I debated calling

Trevor again, though I knew he'd be asleep. I dialed the house anyway. No answer. Then his cell phone—the recording again. Calmly, I left another message, then climbed into bed, tossing and turning until I finally fell asleep.

Sunday was more of the same, decent sales, nice conversations with some very nice people, and it improved my mood. I started to attribute some of the bad feelings on the previous night to exhaustion, both physical and mental.

By three o'clock in the afternoon I decided that Josh wasn't coming. He hadn't said what time he might come by, and now I wished I'd asked, because I was torn between hoping he'd show at one moment and hoping he wouldn't the next. But I wasn't worried about my motives anymore. We were old close friends, and to my great relief, I didn't want us to be anything more.

I finally connected with Trevor late that afternoon.

"God, it's good to hear your voice, Gwyn. I've really missed you. I'm sorry I didn't get a chance to call until now. You forgive me?"

"No, but I guess you had your reasons," I answered cautiously.

"Gwyn, now don't be mad. I honestly couldn't help it. Every time I stopped to pick up the phone I got interrupted. And I figured you were busy anyway. You were, weren't you?"

"Yes. I made quite a few sales. But I stayed up late, and I didn't see any messages on my phone. Not one."

"You were up late? I swear I would have called you if I thought you were up. I've had some incredibly late nights. Sales are popping all over the place with the condo project. There might be a Whispering Pines two if sales are any indication. In fact, I might be making a trip to Denver myself in the near future to train new associates. But I know. You're not interested in that. I should have called."

"Yes."

"I love you. You still love me ... right? Just a little?"

"Maybe."

"Gwyn?"

"Okay ... a little."

"That's better. We'll work at improving on that when you get home."

I had to cut Trevor off at that point because a teenaged boy was standing in front of me anxious to purchase a print. I gave a smile to my new customer, apologized to Trevor, then hung up.

When I arrived home late Sunday night, the lights were still burning, but Trevor didn't rush out to greet me as I'd hoped he would. I quietly shut the side door entrance and glanced up the stairs, then toward the kitchen, but Trevor definitely wasn't around. Home though. His car was in the garage. I walked upstairs and heard his muffled snores as I stepped into the bedroom. I thought about waking him, but instead listened to him breathe for a while, then walked back downstairs.

As I entered the kitchen, I caught the unmistakably sweet scent of roses. Two dozen or more red ones, my favorite, swelled out of an antique-style vase on the table. A note poked out from between the petals.

I'm sorry if I'm not awake to greet you. If you walk in and I don't run out and carry you to bed in my arms it will only be that the spirit was willing, but my body was shot... I love you with all my heat, (heart). Trevor

I laughed softly and leaned down and breathed in the rich perfume of the roses. He hadn't given me roses in a long time, not two dozen anyway. Maybe I was being too hard on him. All of the questions, all of the worry, had created so many doubts.

I undressed in the upstairs hall bathroom so as not to disturb him, then tiptoed into the bedroom once more. I laid my clothes neatly beside the bed, then eased in beside him. I laid my head back on the pillow, then blinked, turning my nose into the soft folds to again test what I'd sensed when I put my head down. It was perfume—not a leftover impression made by the roses—but the undeniable scent of another woman there on my pillow. My heart picked up speed, thudding wildly as my mind searched for an explanation to replace the unthinkable one that was rapidly filling my head.

I turned to look at him, wanting to take my foot and shove his body right out of the bed. So, he was too busy to call me all weekend. Too tired to talk when I called. Then as a cheesy afterthought, he'd bought flowers to assuage his guilt. How very predictable and ordinary of him.

I slowly climbed out of bed and crept back down to the kitchen. I cried for a while, then sat staring at the flowers, wondering what would be my next move.

Chapter 6

I pretended to be asleep when Trevor tried to wake me and make love the next morning. Not surprisingly, he didn't try all that hard. He patted me patronizingly on the shoulder, then headed to the master bath and turned on the shower. I watched him through the slits of my eyes. It had been all I could do not to reach up and slap him.

He picked his keys off the dresser, then leaned over the bed and kissed me on the cheek. "I'll call," he whispered, "you get some rest."

When I heard the side door slam downstairs I leapt from the bed and ran down to the foyer. I stood there, cold and naked, my arms clasped tightly to my chest as he backed out of the garage. Last night, after I'd gone back upstairs, I'd been tempted to find my flannel nightgown and put it on, but Trevor would have noticed, and I didn't want him to notice a thing.

Padding across the foyer tile to the kitchen, I spotted a note he'd left behind on the table.

You must have been a tired puppy too. I missed you this morning. I might be late again tonight. Sorry, honey. Please forgive me. Don't save me dinner, and call "immediately" when you get up. Love you, Trevor

I crumpled the note into a tiny ball and pitched it into the garbage. Shaking, but not so much from the cold, I stomped back up to the bedroom and threw on some clothes. I spent two hours brooding into my coffee cup, then dialed Linda.

She answered on the second ring.

"Well, hi, Gwyn. I was just making some blueberry muffins and thinking of calling you too. Want to come over and have some with me?"

"Sure."

"I think I'll be able to play tennis sooner than the doctor said. I've been slowly moving my arm and it's starting to feel almost normal."

"I think the doctor was talking about your head, not your arm, when he said that."

"Why? I don't play tennis with my head."

"You know what I meant."

"Hey, what's with you? I'm trying to be funny. You could at least try to laugh."

"Sorry, rough weekend."

"Oh. That's right. The art show. I didn't even think to ask. How was it?"

"Okay."

"Just okay? You did sell some of your paintings, right?"

"Yes. Actually I made more sales than I expected."

"Well, that's great. So what's the problem?"

"Nothing. I'm just exhausted. It was a lot of work."

"I'm sorry I couldn't go with you—to help you out."

"That's not why I invited you. I could have hired someone to help me. I didn't want to."

"So tell me about it. You were so excited."

I didn't feel like talking about it, but Linda would think it odd if I didn't. I had been excited about it ... before.

"Well, all right. It turned out to be a nice mall, a lot of foot traffic. I did have some trouble setting up. It started to rain, then sleet. I couldn't find my area, but when I did, saw that I'd gotten a good one—sort of an island with shoppers passing on both sides. By the end, I'd sold at least half of what I brought and took several orders for prints and maybe an original. But the woman needs to give me a deposit for materials, and I'm not sure she won't back out. She was kind of flighty."

"Well, that doesn't sound bad."

"I guess."

"Come on over. I'll cheer you up. We'll have a nice visit."

"Actually, there is something I need to talk to you about."

"What?"

"Not over the phone. And, please, promise me you won't come unglued. I just couldn't handle it today."

"Well, what is it for pity sakes? You can't drop something like that on me and expect me not to react."

"Just promise me you'll stay calm."

"Why, what is it? Are you and Trevor getting a divorce?"

"No," I said, wondering if this would eventually prove true.

"I think you should tell me *something*, so I can at least prepare myself."

"Okay, I'll tell you this much and no more. It's about Kelly. Something I found."

For a moment, she didn't speak. "I'm not sure I want to hear what it is."

"Yes, I'm certain you're right, but I have to tell you anyway."

Linda had left the front door unlocked and I walked on in. I found her seated in the kitchen, elbows on the table, a blueberry muffin in one hand, her mouth working on half of it. She swallowed, giving me a sullen look. "Have a muffin. There's coffee too."

"Thanks."

I poured a cup and took a muffin, then sat down next to her. She quickly shifted her chair back, as if I'd moved too close to personal boundaries.

"So, what did you find?" she asked.

"I found a letter—in a dresser drawer. Kelly wrote it. I'm assuming she wrote it not long before she died. I have it here. I'll read it."

"I can read. Let me have it."

"No, I'd rather read it myself, because I don't want you ripping it up or anything stupid."

Linda stiffened, then glared at me. "That wasn't necessary, was it?"

"We'll have to see."

"Huh," she said. "Must be bad. Go ahead. Read it."

I unfolded it and began. " 'I'm so scared, and God if my sister knew I've been screwing her boyfriend she'd kill me anyway.' " I looked up to gage her reaction, but her face was blank. I continued reading until I'd finished the letter.

Linda pushed her tongue into the inside of her cheek, then looked off to one side. "Well, that was a waste of time. It's not true. Sounds like one of her stories. I'm surprised you believed it."

"You've got to be kidding. She says she's scared she'll end up dead, and she is *dead*, and you think she was writing a story?"

"Yes, that's exactly what I think."

I shook my head.

"Case closed," she said, standing. "So, are you and Trevor coming over for Thanksgiving?"

"Damn it, Linda. We have to talk about this."

"No, we don't," she yelled back at me. "You want to talk about it. I don't."

"Someone killed her, and it obviously wasn't Craig."

"No, Kelly wrote it knowing we'd eventually find it, just to drive us crazy. She was a lunatic, a drug addict, and you just don't want to see the truth."

"No, I think you've got that backwards. Linda, we could be in a lot of danger—our own husbands."

"Well, at *least* you included Trevor in the equation."

"We don't know who it is, but we sure as hell should try to find out."

Linda stood there, her back against the counter, one foot tapping furiously. "It's not Wolfgang."

"Right, it's not Wolfgang. Hard to believe you'd say that," I said sarcastically.

"Let me see the letter."

I held it back from her. "You can't rip it."

"Oh, give it here. I won't rip the damn thing."

I slowly handed it over, watching as she perused the letter.

"What is this box?" she asked.

"No idea. Probably something she found that would incriminate ... whoever."

She handed the letter back. "Has Trevor ever done *anything* that could even remotely make you believe he's a murderer?"

Though I hated his guts at the moment, I had to agree it didn't seem possible. "No, not really."

"Not really? What do you mean, not really?"

"Nothing. I'm just ... mad at him right now."

"What about?"

"Don't change the subject. It's nothing."

"So, what are we going to do? Turn them over to the cops based on this letter, something really dumb like that?"

"Of course not."

She looked toward the ceiling. "Did you consider that it might be Josh? She did say—boyfriend—and she knew him too."

"I thought of that."

"Thought and dismissed it, sounds like."

"It's just so ridiculous. Josh and Kelly having an affair. Josh running her down. Come on."

"Not any more ridiculous than the other two choices. Maybe it was an accident."

I laughed at the absurdity of it. "An accident?"

"Well, not an accident, maybe.... Oh, I don't know."

I checked behind me and down the hall. "Where's Wolfgang?"

"At work."

"Oh."

"Relax, Gwyn, he's not hiding in a closet plotting to do away with us."

I stared hard at her. "And that's another thing. You *cannot* tell Wolfgang about this. I know you don't think it's him, and I honestly don't think it's Trevor, but the fact is neither of us knows anything. We have to be smart. Someone killed our sister and it's not much of a stretch to believe they'd kill us too if they thought we knew something. We have to be the same, act the same, protect ourselves. I think we should hire a private investigator."

"For Trevor and Wolfgang, or for Josh too?"

"Just our husbands."

"I think for Josh too."

"Linda, we've known Josh all of our lives. We played with him, went to school with him. Come on. We know hardly anything about our husbands, just what they've told us. We inherited a lot of money, and though I'd like to believe that Trevor would love me with or without it, I have to admit I rushed into this marriage. So did you. I've met Trevor's relatives once, at the wedding. You and Wolfgang eloped. Both men are from out of state. There could be a ton of stuff we don't know."

"Okay, then we'll start with Trevor and Wolfgang. We can always look into Josh later if nothing comes up with them. And I happen to know someone who can help us, someone reliable that one of my girlfriends used. Spied on her philandering husband. I'll call her and get the guy's number, make up some story she'll believe."

"Okay, let's do that."

I'd called Trevor earlier in the morning as he'd requested, continuing to act as if everything were normal, like I hadn't noticed he'd slept with another woman in our bed.

"Well, there you are," he'd answered happily. "I was wondering if you were ever going to roll out of bed."

"It was an exhausting weekend. Sorry I was asleep when you left this morning."

"My fault. I should have stayed awake for you last night. I should have glued my eyelids open, drank massive amounts of caffeine, whatever it took."

"It's okay. We'll see each other tonight."

"Ahh ... it's going to be pretty late. Morris is coming in, bringing another backer. I have to be there. There's no way I can get out of it. Dinner and drinks, the whole nine yards. I doubt if I'll be home before eleven."

"Where are you meeting him?"

"Probably at the office, but could be he'll want to go straight to dinner and talk there. I can't say."

"Which restaurant?"

"No idea, no *fricking* idea. God, how many times can I say I'm sorry? I want to make love to you in the worst way. I feel like I haven't touched you in a month. I get hard just thinking of—"

I could hear only muffled voices now, Trevor with his hand over the receiver.

"Gotta go, Gwyn. I'll call you soon, baby. Soon as I can."

"Sure."

Like so often in the past, he'd given me clipped answers concerning where he'd be. Most of the time all I knew was that he was "working late" or "out with clients" or that I "wouldn't be interested in all the nitpicky details." He was right. I hadn't been. I'd trusted him. Why shouldn't I? Didn't he tell me he loved me all the time? Make love to me in a way that left no doubt? Wasn't he home just often enough to allay any fears?

The private investigator was a good idea, and I was relieved that Linda had gone along with my plan so readily. Maybe I'd be able to find out who Trevor was fooling around with, then confront him, and be done with him. One big boot out the door....

But as the day droned on and I sat lonely and incredibly empty in my studio, I realized I would miss Trevor horribly if it did all have to end, and I wondered if possibly something I'd done had driven him to betray me. I knew that was stupid, of course. Yes, he could have used some slight, some offense I'd committed, as an excuse to justify an affair, but that's all it would be, an excuse. The affair would have been the primary goal.

But he wasn't a murderer. He couldn't be. Could he? I'd have sworn on everything I'd ever believed in that he wasn't capable of anything so monstrous.

Of course, until I'd come home last night and found another woman's perfume on my pillow, I'd have sworn he'd never cheat on me either.

Chapter 7

Thanksgiving was the twenty-third of November, four days since my trip to Denver, three days since the confrontation with Linda.

We were joining Linda and Wolfgang for dinner, and like the year before, they required only that we dress for the occasion and bring a big appetite. Still, Trevor and I brought wine, two bottles, a merlot and a chardonnay. The gathering would include only the four of us.

It had snowed earlier in the morning, so as I approached the walkway leading to their front door, Trevor was quick to take my arm, though I didn't slow down to wait for him.

"Whoa, what's the rush?" he asked. "Remember, I've got breakable wine bottles here."

"Oh, sorry. I'm just cold. In a hurry to get inside."

"I can see that."

A huge wreath adorned their front door, and tiny multicolored Christmas lights twinkled around the entrance. Off to the right, in an elaborate manger scene set amidst a stand of evergreens, angels and wise men knelt and paid homage to baby Jesus.

I pressed the doorbell and it chimed softly.

Wolfgang swung open the door, greeting us. "Welcome, good to see you, Gwyn, Trevor. Come in. Come in. It's cold out there."

I nodded and stamped my feet on their bright Christmas mat.

Trevor helped me remove my coat, and I made small talk with Wolfgang for as long as holiday protocol required, then continued on inside, following the tantalizing aroma of roast turkey drifting in from the kitchen. Linda stood at the counter, tasting and arranging appetizing treats.

"Hi, Gwyn," she said when she spotted me. "Taste this." She held a stuffed mushroom up to my mouth. I opened obligingly and let her poke it inside.

"How is it?"

I chewed on the hot mushroom, then nodded rapidly.

"Good," she said, smiling. "I thought so."

Linda wouldn't be cooking today, only supervising. She always hired someone to help out on special occasions. It wasn't that she disliked cooking, but on the holidays she wanted to join the group and make merry.

Trevor entered from behind us with the wine bottles. "Happy Thanksgiving, Linda." He kissed her on the cheek. "What would you like me to do with these?"

"Oh, how nice of you both. Thank you so much. Here, let me take them. I've already got two bottles open."

He handed over the wine, then stood gazing at the food.

"Can you do me a favor?" she asked. "Can you take these out to the living room?" She handed him a silver tray of mushrooms and one of canapés. "I have my hands full right now."

"Sure, no problem."

She watched him leave, then lowered her voice. "Yes, shoo fly, shoo, and don't come back. Why is it men always want to stick around the kitchen and get in the way? At least Wolfgang knows better than to come in here when I'm cooking."

I glanced at the hired chef, a lanky older man Linda had used on other occasions. He didn't look up from his stirring and seemed happy to be left alone.

"How are you feeling?" I asked.

"Fine." She rotated her shoulder for me. "I still feel it a little, but less and less all the time."

I looked back toward the door leading to the living room. "And did you talk to her?"

"Who?"

"You know."

"Gwyn, not in the kitchen." She motioned toward the cook, then whispered, "Big ears." She took me by the arm. "Come on, I want to show you the new bathroom."

She led me down the hall past the living room and on upstairs, then she stopped and turned to me. "I called my girlfriend, Sheila, and everything is set. I talked to the investigator just last night and we decided to do a background check on them, then go from there."

"That's all?"

"Well, if there's a red light somewhere in their past it will probably show up there."

"But I thought maybe he would follow them and see what they're up to."

Linda studied me. "I don't understand. What would we gain by doing that? I don't think they're going around committing murders right and left. We would have read something in the papers by now."

I rolled my eyes. "It just seems like we should try to find out as much as possible, as soon as possible. You know, bug their phones. I don't know."

"We'll do the background check—for now. It's what he suggested."

"Did you tell him why we were asking?"

"Hell no. Why, did you think I would?"

"I didn't think about it until just now. What *did* you tell him?"

"Just that I wanted to check out their past. I didn't tell him more than that and he didn't ask."

I nodded. "Did he say how long it would take?"

"No, but he'll leave a message on my cell phone when he's got something."

We walked toward the remodeled bathroom even though I'd seen it the last time I came to visit.

"You saw this already, didn't you?" she said.

"Yes." I peered inside at the new shower, white embossed wallpaper, and green and white striped towels. A painting I'd done for Linda of a marina lined with sailboats adorned the wall.

"We should get back," she said.

The men were standing near the front window by the Christmas tree as we approached. Wolfgang held a glass of red wine. Trevor was reaching for another stuffed mushroom.

"So when do we eat?" Wolfgang asked with a smile at Linda.

"When it's ready," she answered, coming close to him and whispering something up toward his ear. He bent down to listen, then laughed.

"Hey, no secrets," said Trevor, wagging a finger. "Very impolite."

"She's making lewd suggestions."

"I was not." Linda bopped him on the arm.

"Yes, you were." He drew Linda into his waist and held her there. I looked across to Trevor, my arms folded tightly to my chest.

"Gwyn," said Wolfgang, "don't look so stiff. Relax."

I ignored him and nodded toward the Christmas tree, delicately ornamented in silver and gold. "Your tree is so pretty. I don't even have ours up yet."

"I didn't do it this year," Linda said, "what with the accident. Wolfgang wouldn't let me."

"I don't know why she bothers," he said, "too much work if you ask me."

"I like decorating the tree," she said. "It puts me in the mood for Christmas."

"Seems silly," said Wolfgang. "We're not even going to be here."

"You're not?" I said. "Where are you going to be?"

"Hawaii," said Linda. "Isn't it great? It's Wolfgang's idea, a surprise Christmas present for me. He sprung it on me this morning."

"How long?" I asked.

"Two weeks," she said, "over Christmas and New Year's. We'll have the remodeling done by then and we'll both need a break."

"And," said Wolfgang, "it will give her an excuse to buy a whole new wardrobe for her new enormous walk-in closet."

"And for you to parade around in front of all the young chickees on the beach."

Wolfgang raised his eyebrows. "Hadn't thought of that." He flexed an arm. "I'll have to add a few extra reps to the workout."

We turned our heads at the jingle of a small bell. The dining room table was now set with an elaborate array of food.

Linda leaned in toward me. "The bell is his idea, Renard, the cook. But I guess it's better than yelling–*hey, come and get it.*" She shrugged.

On the table were platters of turkey, sliced ham, and roast beef, along with bowls of bean salads and tossed salads, asparagus and squash, twice baked potatoes and au gratin. And Linda was pleased to inform us that she had four different desserts out in the kitchen, so we'd better save some room.

Wolfgang pulled out a chair for Linda, and Trevor did the same for me. We toasted to the holiday season and almost forgot to say grace until I spoke up.

"Oh, yes," said Linda. "Wolfgang, would you do it, please?"

"Me?"

"Yes, you."

"Okay." He bowed his head. "Thanks, God, for the really great food. And ... and all the other stuff. Amen."

Linda turned to stare at him.

"What?" he said.

"It's okay. Next time I won't ask. Let's try that again." We bowed our heads once more. "Thank you, dear Lord, for the bounty we are about to receive, and our many blessings. We pray for those less fortunate, that they too might enjoy this day, and we humbly ask that you feed the hearts and souls of those who need your guidance, and lead them to the path of righteousness in your name's sake...."

Finally, she finished the prayer and smiled.

After dinner and a round of desserts, we sat at the table drinking coffee. Wolfgang leaned forward on his elbows and addressed Trevor. "So, what are you and Gwyn doing over Christmas?"

"I don't know. Skiing, maybe. I'd like to do a little of that."

"Downhill?"

"Yeah, what else?"

"Sometime I'm going to take you out in the backcountry with me, ski the deep powder. You don't know what you're missing."

"Sounds like too much work. What do I want to walk uphill for when I can take a chairlift?"

"You don't have to walk uphill. I like to do it that way, but you don't have to."

"What do you mean?"

"Snowmobile. You take three guys, one drives and carries another guy uphill. You take turns."

"You've done that?"

"Sure, but I'd rather climb. You can ski a lot of powder if you use a snowmobile, and I know where the powder just hangs around for days waiting for tracks."

"I don't know. I'm a decent skier. But I'm not sure I'd enjoy it that much."

"Oh, you should go," said Linda. "You'd love it. I've gone out with him ... not on a snowmobile. I like to use my telemark skis and skins. Gwyn does it."

"Yes," I said, "but Trevor just learned to ski a few years ago. He hasn't had a chance to ski much powder—"

"Now wait a minute," Trevor said. "I could handle it, no problem. I'm just not sure it's something I want to try. But hey, I might go out there with you, at least once I do a little downhill skiing and get the legs in shape."

Wolfgang smiled widely. "Then we'll do it."

The conversation turned to talk of the good old days. Linda spoke of how the family used to go sledding when we were kids and the fun we'd have. "Gwyn would scare me half to death. She'd get me on that sled and we'd fly down so fast that when I finally tumbled off I flipped over at least three times. She'd never let me go in front and steer."

"You didn't want to go in front and steer," I said.

"Well, you were the oldest. And the daredevil. Gwyn's quite the athlete."

"I'm okay."

"You're a lot better than okay," she said.

"Yes, she is," said Trevor. "She's a much better skier than I am. No contest."

"Well, then," said Wolfgang, "maybe you should join us too." He motioned at me with his coffee cup. "In the backcountry."

Linda laughed. "Wolfgang, she goes out in the backcountry all the time in the winter, and she hikes in the summer. She hikes all over the place taking her pictures. She hikes, she skis, and she can handle a snowmobile better than most guys. You don't know Gwyn."

"Oh," he said. "Well, I guess I don't."

"Shows how much you listen when I talk."

"So, sounds like the whole family was into sports," Wolfgang said.

"Not exactly," said Linda. "Dad liked to snowshoe sometimes, when he wasn't working, and that wasn't much. Mom, she mainly stayed in the house. She liked to cook and do her embroidery. She could do sports, but she wasn't that interested, I guess."

"She liked to cross-country ski sometimes," I said. "She'd take me out."

"Yes, but I think only because she knew you liked it," said Linda, "and you didn't go far."

Linda put her hands on the table and pushed herself up. "More coffee anyone? Renard's gone home, so we're on our own. How about more dessert?"

Trevor patted his stomach. "No can do."

I watched Linda leave the room, then turned toward Wolfgang. "So, where is your family now?"

"What's left of them are in Washington, Washington state, that is. My parents are gone, died a long time ago."

"What happened to them?"

"They were killed ... in an accident."

"An accident?" I asked.

"They were buried in an avalanche in British Columbia. Bodies didn't turn up until spring."

"My God," said Trevor, sitting up straighter.

Wolfgang shrugged. "I was three years old. I barely remember them."

"So who raised you?" I asked as Linda reentered with the coffeepot and a tray of desserts.

"An uncle," he said. "I hear from him from time to time. Still lives in Washington, same house, same everything."

Linda began pouring coffee, squinting her eyes and frowning at me. "Enough of this depressing conversation," she said. "It's snowing outside." She dipped her head toward the dining room window.

"Well, Aspen is open," said Trevor. "I checked. And Vail too, not as much snow though. Did I tell you Gwyn and I bought new skis?"

"What kind?" asked Wolfgang.

Linda motioned for me to follow her back to the kitchen, then glanced around the corner once we'd reached it. "What were you doing out there? Don't ask Wolfgang a bunch of questions about his past."

"Why not?"

"Because when you do it, it sounds like you're grilling him for information. And don't think he doesn't notice."

"I was just asking."

"Well, don't. We'll know what we need to know soon enough. Here, take this." She handed me clean forks and napkins, then pushed me toward the dining room.

"Now wait just a minute," I said. "Why didn't you tell me you were going to Hawaii? You could have told me upstairs."

"There wasn't time. And I only found out this morning."

"And you knew I wouldn't like it. And you're right, I don't."

"Well, I like it."

"What are you thinking, Linda? It's an incredibly bad idea. What if something happens? You'll be so far away."

"What difference does that make? Something could happen here too. Oh, don't worry about it. I'll be fine. Come on, we can't stay in here. It will look suspicious. And, please, don't ask any more questions."

Later on, Linda tried to convince the guys to watch a special remake of *A Christmas Carol*, but Wolfgang just laughed and turned on the football game. Linda and I made popcorn. I tried to enjoy the game, but couldn't concentrate on any of it, including the halftime show, my usual favorite. Trevor kept glancing over at me and it made me uncomfortable. I tried to smile and pretend to be enjoying myself, but I had the feeling I wasn't very convincing.

By the time we drove home, it was dark out, and snowing harder. We sat in silence watching the snowflakes whip across the road in the glare of the headlights. Suddenly, Trevor reached across for my hand. I almost pulled it back, but managed to stop myself.

"What's the matter, Gwyn?" He squeezed my fingers gently.

"Nothing. I'm just tired."

"Of me?"

I swung my head to face him. "No. No. Why would you say that?"

"Oh, I don't know. Maybe because you never look at me. Maybe because you're stiff as a board when I touch you. I catch you looking at me like you hate me. Things like that."

"No. I told you. I'm just tired."

"So, it's not me? Because if it is, I'd really like to know. I can't take this much longer."

I looked away.

"Gwyn, if it really isn't me that's upsetting you, maybe you should see that woman again, that therapist. Maybe you really should."

"I have started seeing her again."

"Is this about your sister? Is that what it is, the holidays, and you're thinking about her?"

"I guess so."

His shoulders slumped and I could almost see the tension drain from his body. "You should have told me. You can't keep these things from me. We're a couple. We need to share what's bothering each other. We can't allow problems to grow, not if our marriage is going to work."

I wasn't sure how to respond to that, and I still didn't trust him, so I didn't say anything.

"I want our marriage to work," he said. "I want you to tell me when things I do bother you, even things that have nothing to do with me. Can you do that?"

"Yes, I can do that."

"Good. I feel better."

As we continued toward home, I thought back to the night Kelly died. Trevor told the police he'd been working alone in his office that evening, that he'd returned home around nine. Actually, it had been a lot later, more like eleven. I'd fallen asleep, and when I woke up, Trevor was just hanging up his coat. I'd never asked him why he lied. But I knew he hadn't forgotten the time.

The following day I drove to the cemetery. I didn't ask Linda if she wanted to join me, probably she wouldn't anyway, because then she might have to talk about Kelly. And that, it seemed, was something Linda never wanted to do.

A wreath lay on each of the family graves, delivered yesterday and on each major holiday, an arrangement Linda and I had made in case one or both of us were out of town. But I'd brought my own flowers today, a mix of tinted orchids and carnations, and placed a spray on all three graves. The markers had been recently cleared, though a dusting of snow had already begun to obstruct the names. I bent down and wiped the snow away with a gloved hand, starting with my mother.

She'd died one winter morning while Linda and I were visiting friends in the neighborhood. Only Kelly was at home. It appeared Mom had lain down for a nap, something she rarely did, and never woke up. Kelly, nine years old at the time, found her and phoned us. "I can't wake Mom up," she'd cried. "I shook her and shook her."

They determined that our mother had died of an aneurysm, a blood vessel popped in her brain. No reason given ... these things just happen.

I knelt near her marker and read the inscription.

Ruth Ann Everett. Beloved wife and mother. Receive her into heaven, oh Lord ...

My mother's friends and relatives had called her Ruthie. In the pictures I'd seen of her as a child, she'd appeared quite happy, always smiling, though I didn't remember too much of that. To me, she'd seemed subdued and resigned. I could only guess that she'd been lonely, not for us kids, but for my father who was almost never around. When he was, he holed up in his little room, doing his books or talking on the phone ... in the house, but not really at home.

My father, Samuel Titus Everett, lay in the grave beside my mother. And it occurred to me, that at least in death, my father was forced to stay near my mother, like it or not. But he had been a good man, a stable provider, and he'd stop what he was doing to listen to his children, though we couldn't hang out for long before he'd tell us to scoot. He'd amassed a fortune virtually behind our backs, though my mother must have known. We owned the sporting goods store in town, Titus Sports Authority, and there was a catalogue that came out each month, and frequent mention of "the plant," though none of us girls had ever been there. We did help out often in the store on vacations and holidays to earn our spending money, but we had no idea of the wealth he'd accumulated until he died.

It was obvious he wanted it that way. Our home was modest. We lived modestly. I could only wonder why he'd chosen to live so simply, though in the will, he'd given a clue. "And to my girls I bequeath all my earthly belongings, and urge them to remember that money makes no guarantee of happiness, but instead can usher in a world of woe. Choose wisely your path, and those you keep close to you now. Forgive me the burden I have placed on you."

He'd sold off the store after the first heart attack, and soon after liquidated the rest, leaving everything in order, as was his way. He died of a second, massive attack, no doubt due to a lifetime of stress, or perhaps, I liked to think, he'd missed our mother more than he'd ever cared to show.

Kelly's grave was next to my father's. I stared at it the longest. My dearest baby sister. How would I live my life without her? I couldn't go a day without thinking about her, without wishing she were still here.

She was born Kelly Alan Everett. The middle name belonged to our paternal grandfather, since Kelly was the hoped-for boy that never materialized. She was a wild little child, tearing through the house, bouncing off the walls, always smiling, especially at me. I carried her around like a favorite doll when she would let me, helped give her baths, played hide and seek, and read her stories. I thought of myself as Kelly's second mother. She was our baby, and we spoiled her accordingly. I, especially, hated to tell her no.

I looked up from her grave. A frigid wind had picked up, blowing snow around my ankles. I watched as a plastic bag took flight across the cemetery, skipping over and over. I reached down one last time to adjust the flowers, then pulling my coat close, headed back to the Jeep.

Chapter 8

A week and a half later on a Saturday, Trevor left for Denver to "motivate the troops," as he'd put it. He would be away for the weekend, possibly longer depending on how everything worked out. He'd left in a good mood, mainly because I'd fooled him, convinced him he was not the reason for my recent coldness.

Every few days I talked to Linda with the excuse of asking about her health, which I was, of course, concerned about, but more concerned to hear what was happening with the background check.

"Nothing yet," Linda would say. "Give it time, Gwyn."

I thought about hiring my own investigator, but didn't know of a good one, and if I hired a private detective, I wanted them to be very good. Other than looking through the phone book, I didn't know of a way to find a reputable one. For now, I'd try it Linda's way.

She assured me that "Mr. I Spy"—not his real name, but Linda's attempt to be covert about the situation—was a thorough and well-respected investigator. I was glad to hear that, but more concerned that the guy be fast.

I was certain Trevor was meeting the woman, whoever she was, in Denver—or somewhere—and the thought made my insides churn. After we'd kissed good-bye this morning, I'd curled up, fetal position, on the couch and stared at nothing for hours. It wasn't good. I could feel myself wanting to return to the mindless vegetative state I'd experienced following Kelly's death.

Finally, I willed myself off the couch and managed to get myself moving. I would visit the old house ... have a word with Kelly.

A layer of new snow covered the front porch, but instead of the smooth unblemished coating I'd expected to see, the snow was marked with footsteps. It didn't alarm me. I'd seen this sort of thing before. Solicitors who didn't know the house was empty probably had come by. I studied the pattern of footsteps, but didn't see anything out of the ordinary. Only the front walk and porch were marked. The snow surrounding the rest of the house appeared intact.

I inserted the key in the lock, and stepped inside.

It wasn't warm, but it wasn't freezing either. The thermostat was set at sixty degrees to protect the plumbing, which I'd left in working order for the times I stopped by. I didn't see any signs of squirrels or other visitors; the screening over the chimney had taken care of that, and the timer was still plugged in.

I walked farther inside and glanced at the mantel over the fireplace. I'd replaced the broken glass in Kelly's frame, and now her picture was back where it belonged, at the edge of the mantel with the rest of the family photographs.

I strolled to the kitchen and turned on the cold water tap. The pipes chugged with stale air for a moment, then released a burst of water. I let the faucet run for a while—not that I needed water for anything—but it seemed like a good idea. I turned on the hot water tap, and after a minute or so, it flowed with the beginnings of warm water. "There you go, Kelly," I said, "just in case you want to take a bath."

I knew it might sound crazy to be talking out loud in an empty house to my dead sister, but as long as I knew I wasn't crazy and no one could hear me, who cared?

I opened the back door off the kitchen and looked out to the detached one car garage. I thought about going out there, but decided maybe not, or else maybe I'd check it out when I was done roaming the house.

I stepped into my dad's little room and stood looking at his desk, then walked over to the swivel chair and sat down. The rolling wheels beneath it creaked and slid backwards slightly, then stopped. I rolled myself up to the desk and looked at the room from my father's perspective.

Screwing my face into the frown I'd often seen him wear, I mimicked his low growl. "Quiet down, you girls. I'm trying to work. You're making *way* too much noise and I've got a *lot* of work to do.

"Right, Dad," I answered back at him, "your work should have included your family, don't you think?"

I stood up from the desk and walked to the window that looked out over the backyard. No more swing set. That had rusted and collapsed years ago. I remembered digging holes with kitchen spoons back there in the yard. Kelly and I were going to dig a hole to China, save on airfare.

I left my dad's room and walked to the stairs leading to the second floor bedrooms.

In a way, it was good that Linda didn't come by the house too much, because she'd be upset to see the small change I'd recently made. It wasn't a big thing, so there really was no reason for her to care, but I knew she would. I turned right at the top of the stairs and entered our old bedroom, the one Kelly had converted to her own after Dad passed away.

I liked the change. It looked right. Two bunk beds sat on opposite sides of the small room, almost exactly like the ones that used to be there. It wasn't as if I'd gone looking for them, but the room was empty, and the secondhand store didn't want much for the beds, and if a family did end up renting or buying the house, the kids would have a place to sleep.

I hung on the doorframe for a while, then inspected our parents' bedroom, and finally, the small bath. I pulled aside the shower curtain and looked into the tub, and was disgusted to see dead bugs upended there. I unrolled a length of toilet paper to scoop them up, deposited them into the wastebasket, then removed the plastic liner from the basket and replaced it with a new one.

Washing my hands with soap, I looked at my reflection in the mirror over the sink and thought that I looked tired. Trevor wouldn't be home tonight. The house would be empty. I'd get to eat dinner alone, or I could go over to the Wild River and see Caroline, have dinner there. But I didn't feel like talking to Caroline just now, and she would be busy anyway on a Saturday night.

I walked back downstairs and after one last look around the house, including a peek in the basement, headed out the front door. I glanced over to the garage, but didn't feel like going out there anymore. All I'd need would be to find a dead mouse or something else equally disgusting to cap off my day.

What I really needed was to do something fun, something I wouldn't do if Trevor were home.

It was three o'clock in the afternoon, still early, and I had an idea. First I'd go home and pack a small bag with a change of clothes and my bathing suit, and then I'd go over to the hot springs pool and soak in the thermal waters. If that didn't make me feel better, nothing would. And the water had the power to heal, I was sure of that, maybe not psychological wounds, but certainly it could help.

I was smiling as I drove toward home, and pleased to see sunshine finally break through the clouds after the gray skies of this morning.

I could do all kinds of things this weekend. I could go cross-country skiing with Caroline, or alone, or go snowshoeing up in the mountains. I could take more pictures, or just commune with nature, hike down on the lower levels. I had all kinds of choices.

But I liked the hot springs idea.

I packed my bag, then fixed myself a tuna sandwich and tomato soup, eating it at the kitchen table. I wondered what Trevor was doing now, and if the woman he was seeing was someone he worked with. How convenient for him. I'd met some of his associates at the office parties, when I was invited, when I'd bothered to go. Maybe that was a mistake, not going. I was glad Trevor was happy in his work. He liked being the boss, running his own office. Unfortunately, though I enjoyed Trevor's enthusiasm, real estate and sales were not my favorite subjects. I always listened whenever he talked about it, never let on how I felt, maybe even fooled him to a degree. Wasn't that all anyone could expect of me? I couldn't be someone I wasn't, feel something I didn't. And Trevor would sometimes shut down completely when I talked about art, and I forgave him.

Marriage certainly wasn't easy, even under the best of circumstances.

I lifted a spoonful of soup to my mouth and slurped it, something else I wouldn't do if Trevor were around. No, marriage wasn't easy, and if you threw in a dash of murder and a sprinkle of infidelity, just watch the odds for success go down.

So who was Trevor screwing? And had he been screwing Kelly too, right under my nose? It made me sick to even think about it.

After my lunch, I drove into town. I decided to make a stop at the Hotel Colorado, a favorite of mine, before heading to the hot springs pool nearby. I hadn't visited the historic hotel in a while, nor had I been to the mineral pool since last winter.

The lobby of the over one-hundred-year-old hotel was truly vast, and reputed to be one of the most attractive in the western United States, having been modeled after Italy's Castle Villa de Medici. The lobby had been renovated, now done in beige, and boasted myriad chandeliers, fireplaces, fountains, oil paintings, and potted palm trees. As I strolled about, stopping to gaze out into the hotel's courtyard with its beautiful Florentine fountain, I wondered what sort of people once roamed the rooms of the venerable Hotel Colorado, what secrets it held, whose hearts had been broken here.

I changed into my bathing suit in the athletic club and walked out to the vaporous hot springs pool, huge in its length—two blocks long—the largest in the world.

Dipping slowly into the water, I gazed around at others enjoying themselves, a pair of giggling teenagers, a woman with flowing gray-flecked hair, a potbellied man in a fishing cap, all soaking in the comfortably heated mineral waters. If I wanted to, I could also take advantage of some of the hotter smaller pools, or go over to the Yampah Vapor Caves, enjoy a steam, get a massage, listen to soft music. So much to do, so much I took for granted, living here in Glenwood. But I wouldn't want to live anywhere else.

I gazed at the surrounding mountains rising above the steam and felt at peace for the first time that day. I'd stay in this cocoon of warmth until my fingers shriveled and my cares seeped away. Maybe I'd call Caroline, or maybe not. It would be okay to be alone now, have dinner by myself, go over to the Italian Underground and have some pasta and perhaps too much wine. And later, maybe Trevor would call; maybe guilt would set in, and he would remember he was married....

I did enjoy dinner, a big plate of lasagna, and did drink a little too much wine, and afterwards sipped my coffee dreamily and pretended to be a reclusive movie star hiding from the public.

It was dark on the drive back to the house, and snowing again, fat flakes that slid carelessly down the windshield, swept away by the constant flip-flop of the wipers. I was still slightly buzzed from the wine, but not so much that I worried about getting stopped by the police. Why would they stop me? For going too slow?

I watched as an SUV approached from behind and stayed there. I wasn't used to that. Usually cars passed me on this open road, most of them uncomfortable going the speed limit or below. But it stayed, continuing to follow me. After a while, I slowed even more, encouraging the driver to pass. Finally, I turned on my signal, pretending to make a right turn, then actually made it, though I wasn't going in that direction. But the car turned, continuing to follow me, and that's when I started to worry. I made several more turns at random, and still the SUV stayed behind me. Then, at the very last second, risking sliding out, I veered right into someone's driveway, ready to rush out and go pounding on doors if the vehicle dared slow down. But it didn't, and I sat there, breathing hard, until a porch light came on and I rolled down my window and shouted to the stranger in the doorway, "Sorry, thought I had a flat tire."

I backed out and drove the rest of the way home, pulled into the garage and waited for the door to roll completely down before unlocking the Jeep and getting out.

Once inside the house, I locked all the doors, even doors I usually didn't worry about, and closed all the blinds, then turned on all the outside lights. I carried my cell phone with me and peeked out the windows now and then.

Suddenly the cell phone rang in my hand and I dropped it, then picked it off the floor and answered.

"Hello?" I asked, fearing who might be on the other end.

"I scared you, didn't I?"

I didn't know the voice, or did I?

"Who is this?"

"Gwyn, it's Josh. It's only Josh."

"Oh." I exhaled, my heart pounding out of control. "I didn't recognize your voice. I'm sorry."

"I was following you, not on purpose. I was on the road going home and I saw your Jeep, thought it was you anyway, knew it was you after a while. I didn't mean to scare you. I did scare you, didn't I?"

"Nothing I won't live through."

"God, I'm sorry. It was just such a coincidence. I was thinking of you, thinking of calling you, and there you were."

"Where are you now?"

"I'm parked outside your house. I knew better than to go in the driveway. Why, are you alone?"

I thought for a second. "Actually, I am. Come on in."

It occurred to me as I ended the call that he wasn't supposed to know where I lived.

I unlocked the front door and watched as he drove up the driveway through the falling snow. He was in a green Ford Explorer, though I hadn't been able to tell that when he was tailing me. The snow had been too thick to see very well.

He had on jeans and a ski jacket, and snowflakes in his hair. He smiled up at me as he climbed the two steps to the brick porch.

"You're sure I'm not intruding?" he asked.

"Absolutely not."

He gazed around the entrance. "Wow, some place. What a spectacular house, Gwyn."

I smiled. "A little better than the one I grew up in."

"Well, true, but cozy is good too."

I was glad I hadn't yet had a chance to get really comfortable with Trevor away. Everything was still neat and clean. "Would you like a cup of coffee? Then I can give you the nickel tour if you want."

"Sounds good."

He brushed himself off and I led him into the kitchen. I walked him past the white marble counter tops and antique oak cabinets that went on and on. He nodded his appreciation, then smiled as I pointed out the large brick pass-through fireplace that opened out into the dining room.

"Great kitchen, Gwyn. I like it. Roomy, but tasteful. It looks like you, something you'd like. Is this house custom built?"

"No, but it's fairly new." I began making coffee, then reached into a kitchen cabinet for an unopened bag of chocolate chip cookies, poured them onto a plate. I handed it to Josh. He sat down at the table, legs outstretched, and watched while I worked at the counter.

"So where's Trevor?"

"He had to leave ... for a little while."

"Oh."

"So you're back in town," I said. "I didn't think I'd see you here again so soon."

"And I didn't think I'd be here either, but it's only for the weekend, though I'll probably be coming out more often now. I ... worry about my mother, alone like she is. She's worried too. The stroke's on her mind, though she tries to pretend otherwise. And what else do I have to do?" He paused as I brought the coffeepot to the table and filled our cups. "I'm joking, of course. I'm swamped with work, and I shouldn't be here. But sometimes you have to remember what's really important."

"Yes, I agree with that."

I sat across from him and we stared at each other. "So," I asked, "how was your sister's wedding?"

"Oh, it was fun. Amy looked really happy, got lots of gifts. It cost a fortune though. I helped my mom with that. How's she supposed to do it all, living on my dad's retirement money and not much else? Amy sure doesn't have any money."

"Is your mom still working ... at the clinic?"

"No, she's too tired for that. Maybe if she feels better she can go back part-time. She misses it."

"That's too bad. I always looked forward to seeing her there. She was the one receptionist who would greet you with a smile even if you were grumpy and miserable with the flu. Such a sweet lady."

"She liked you too."

I nodded.

"She hasn't been the same since my father passed away," he said. "Getting old really sucks, I guess, and it's even worse if you don't have anyone." He looked up at me then and smiled. "I can't believe I went so long without seeing you. Stupid of me. No reason we can't still be friends."

"No, there isn't."

"Aren't you just a teensy bit worried about what Trevor is going to say when he walks in and sees me here?"

"I would be, but he's not coming back for a couple of days."

"Oh. Good. I'm glad. I'll admit it. I'm glad." He reached over for a cookie.

"How did you know where I lived, Josh?"

He sat up a little straighter. "Oh. Well, I didn't follow you here, if that's what you're thinking. It came up in a conversation with Caroline. I was over at the bar one night and we got to talking. And you know how she likes to talk."

"Yes."

"And I was curious, drove past just to see."

"You could have called me. I would have told you."

"I know, but ... it doesn't make any difference, does it? What possible difference could it make how I found out where you lived? It's not like it's a secret, is it?"

"No, just ... I wondered, that's all."

He stared at me, and I saw something in the set of his mouth I couldn't quite identify. Embarrassment? Anger? He brought his coffee cup to his mouth and took a sip.

"So," he said, "how have things been with you? Oh, I know what I wanted to ask. How did your art show turn out? I'm sorry I never got over there."

"It went well. I sold, let me see, about half of the originals, and most of the prints, and got orders for others I ran out of. I was actually surprised with the results."

"I knew it. Hey, you know what? While I'm here, why don't you take me through your studio?"

For a second, my thoughts jumbled. It was the way he'd said, *your studio*, like he was familiar with the layout of the house. I'd never mentioned that I had a studio—though maybe he'd just assumed I would—in a house this size. Or Caroline—of course, that was it—Caroline had mentioned it to him. "Yes, I'd love to show it to you."

"Great, I'd love to see it."

I began a guided tour of the house. We decided to make my studio the last stop, since Josh might want to spend more time there.

I walked him through the main floor, the entrance with its two-story ceiling, marble floor tile, and walls adorned with paintings—none of which were my own. Then we moved on to the living room with its natural stone fireplace and large windows that overlooked the mountains in daylight, but now sparkled with cascading snow made visible by the incandescent spotlights outside. We stopped and looked out for a while, and I thought how romantic this scene would be if Josh and I were still in love.

He reached over and touched my arm. "Look how beautiful that is. Something, isn't it?"

We continued on.

"When we're done with this floor," I said, "I'll have to show you the basement. I've got this huge cedar sauna down there, and a whirlpool tub, and a shower, and this big exercise room. It was all here when I bought the house. It's so perfect."

He nodded and smiled at me.

Finally, we walked downstairs to the basement. "It doesn't feel like a basement at all," I said, "with the door walls looking out at the mountains here too."

Josh stepped into the sauna and gazed around. "You've got a really nice place, Gwyn," he said, stepping out again.

I was reluctant to take him upstairs, not because I didn't trust him, but because showing him the bed Trevor and I slept together in night after night, seemed not very nice.

"Well," I said, "you're probably getting bored. Maybe we should move on to the studio."

He pointed upstairs. "You missed a floor."

"Oh. Well, it's just bedrooms and baths."

He raised his eyebrows. "I want the whole tour. I paid my nickel."

I laughed. "Okay."

We started up the stairs.

I paused before the first of the four bedrooms. "This is the guest room, though it's never been used for that." I thought of it as the blue room, the spread on the queen-size bed and the rest of the furnishings all in matching shades of blue.

"Nice," he said.

We walked to the next door.

"And this is just an extra room. Trevor uses it sometimes for a study, though he also has the real study downstairs." I didn't add that this and one of the other upstairs rooms would eventually belong to our future children. Of course, that all rested on me still being married. I gazed into the room with its television, nubby-textured couch concealing a pullout bed, and oak bookcases.

"I like this too," he said.

"And this is just another room," I said, about to brush by.

"Wait, I want to see it." He opened the door and flipped on the light, then looked at me.

I knew he had noticed how the room did not go with the rest of the house. The bedroom furniture was cheaply made and morbidly dark. Kelly had purchased it at a thrift shop and painted it black, probably during some drug-induced euphoria. It was truly ugly.

"Well, I'm not sure I like this," he said, "but if you do." He turned to me again.

"It's Kelly's old stuff. I'm going to get rid of it."

"How did it get here?"

I turned out the light. "I brought it here—a long time ago."

I spent a few moments showing him the hall bath, then moved on to the master bedroom. It was the largest room of all, the king-size bed lost in the spaciousness of it. We stepped into the walk-in closet, Trevor's things on one side, mine on the other, my side looking empty in comparison to Trevor's.

"He's got a lot of suits," Josh said, so close behind me now that I could feel his warm breath move past my cheek.

I ushered him into the master bath with its gold rimmed and marble tiled Jacuzzi tub, big enough for two people to stretch out comfortably. He pulled open the glass shower door. "Nice. I really like the gold fixtures."

We left the bath and I walked quickly across the bedroom, hurrying past the bed again. I stopped only after I'd reached the hall. "Well, all that's left is my studio," I said, and practically raced for the stairs—afraid to look at him and read something in his face—afraid he might pull me close and try to kiss me—afraid that in my weakened state I might not stop him.

I detoured to the kitchen first and poured more coffee, waiting for my heart to slow down, thinking that I had to get him out the door soon. There was something in the air drifting around us, a soft sensual smoke winding through and circling, curling ... coaxing.

"There you are," he said.

"I got more coffee. You want some?"

He nodded slowly.

I handed him the cup, black, the way he liked it.

"I'm making you nervous, aren't I?" he said, and took the cup from my hand.

"No." But I almost spilled the coffee at the brief touch of his fingers on mine.

"Do you mind staying here all alone tonight?"

"Of course not."

"You're not afraid?"

"No, and stop it," I said, knowing he was teasing, and annoyed that he knew exactly what I was feeling. I moved quickly past him before the smoke could draw us any closer. "You have to go."

"But I haven't seen your studio."

"I know, but I think you should go. This wouldn't look right if someone were to come by."

"Who's going to come by?" He looked at his watch. "Oh, well it is eleven o'clock. I suppose you're right." I could see a smile beginning to crinkle his eyes. "But I'll go, Gwyn. I'll see the studio another time."

"And I promise I'll show it to you," I said, already able to feel the tension easing away, the smoke dissipating.

I let him finish his coffee, then showed him to the door. I waved goodbye as he backed his Explorer down the drive and swung out onto the road, kept waving until his car drew completely out of sight. I felt sad, oddly let down. Though I didn't want him to, I truly didn't, it surprised me that he hadn't so much as tried to kiss me on the cheek.

Later, as I stood looking out the kitchen's bay window at the heavily falling snow, the phone rang. I knew it was Trevor. It was eleven-thirty, very late for him to be calling, and for a second I thought about not answering, then reached for the phone a moment before the answering machine clicked on.

"Hello?" I said, drawing the word out, trying to sound as if I'd been asleep.

"Hi, honey. I woke you, didn't I?" It *was* Trevor, his tone of voice appropriately apologetic.

"Yes, I kinda dozed off."

"Sorry I called so late. I lay down for a minute after dinner and woke up two and a half-hours later. I'm glad you answered."

"I almost didn't."

"It looks like I'm not going to be home until late tomorrow night, unfortunately, but I'll call if that changes. But everything is going great here. I might even need to hire a few more sales people to take the pressure off the rest of the staff. I did a few interviews this afternoon."

"That's good."

"You do sound tired. Did you have a nice dinner? What did you do?"

"Oh, I went over to the house for a while, then drove into town and used the pool, and later I had dinner at the Italian Underground."

"Well, that sounds like fun. Did you go by yourself?"

"Yes. I thought about visiting Caroline at work, but she's too busy on Saturday, but I still could have gone over there. I think I just wanted to be alone."

"Well, that's okay. You know, you can call me if you want to. I'm not always busy."

"Sure, but I know you probably are."

"I miss you, Gwyn. I wish I could come home sooner. I really do. If there's any chance of it, I will."

"I know."

"I'll try to call tomorrow, a little earlier. Okay?"

"Okay."

"Did you remember to lock all the doors?"

"Yes."

"Make sure, and check the windows too."

"I will."

"And get some sleep. Sorry I woke you, but I wanted to call even if it was only to leave a message."

"I'm glad you did. I would have worried otherwise."

"I'll talk to you tomorrow. Okay?"

"Okay," I said, and hung up the phone.

I had trouble sleeping. Though I'd locked every door and checked every window, the slightest sound awoke me, a gust of wind, the furnace rumbling on, a creak from who knows where. I tossed and turned and hugged my pillow.

I had a brief nightmare, and in it Trevor had indeed come home early, and zombielike, floated up the stairs, a razor-edged knife held high above his head. His face, large in the doorway, smiled at me as it bobbed into the room. I was, of course, helpless to protect myself, frozen to the bed, terror flowing out from my body in cold waves.

My eyes snapped open and I inhaled sharply, then lay so completely still I was aware of my lungs expanding and contracting. I reached over and felt for the bedside lamp, fully expecting to see Trevor looking down at me from the end of the mattress. But like magic, he'd seeped through the floor.

After my eyes adjusted to the light, I put on my robe and walked to the bathroom. Something had awakened me, though it might only have been remnants of the dream.

Of course, if someone actually *were* in the house, I would be unable to protect myself. Where was the gun I was supposed to remove from the nightstand when my assailant waltzed through the door? Where was the growling barking attack dog? Where was the elaborate alarm system tied to the police, and the SWAT team, guns hoisted to fire, ready to surround the house?

I walked downstairs, flipping light switches at every opportunity, goose bumps on my arms and the back of my neck. I hummed a tune, comforted by the sound of my own voice. No one was in the house. I'd had too much coffee before bed, that's all. I should have brewed the decaf, but I knew Josh didn't like it. Well, at least maybe he wasn't sleeping well either.

I opened the refrigerator, poured a glass of milk and drank it down. I wasn't going back to sleep for a while, so I'd use this time to do what I'd thought of doing earlier this evening when I'd led Josh into Trevor's study. I'd look for clues....

It wasn't my nature to spy. It was bad enough to hire someone to look into Trevor's background, but even worse to rifle through his things when his back was turned. I respected Trevor's privacy, or I had ... but ignorance, though blissful, could also be dangerous, I'd decided.

His study was off the hall on the main floor, the last room on the left. I passed the staircase and turned on another light.

His door was open as it usually was. I entered and looked over at the desk and file cabinets, all neat and orderly, not a stray pen or paperclip in view. His computer sat atop his desk, but it would be useless to go into the computer. I didn't know the security code, and knowing Trevor, he wouldn't have written it down anywhere.

Should I use gloves? Well no, of course not. No one was going to be looking in here for fingerprints, and certainly they'd expect to find mine, considering it was my house. And it was my house, in my name only. I'd never changed it. There was never a reason to. It would all go to Trevor anyway if I died. I'd named him in the will, along with my sister, should anything happen to Trevor.

I cautiously opened the top right-hand drawer to his desk. Pens and pencils lay side by side, along with a small tube of white glue, a box of paperclips, a paper hole punch, a small stapler, and a roll of stamps.

In the drawer below I found a stack of business envelopes. I laughed softly under my breath. My, lots of incriminating stuff so far. I tried not to disturb the envelopes as I checked far back in the drawer for possible notes from Trevor's lover, or a romantic card Trevor had been too enchanted with to throw away.

The first drawer on the left-hand side of the desk had bank statements held together with rubber bands. These would be his business statements, or maybe some personal account I wasn't aware of. I kept the household bank statements in my studio, since again, everything was in my name except for a small account that Trevor had access to, containing less than fifty thousand dollars. I'd thought about changing it all to include his name, but as long as Trevor had enough cash when he wanted something or could use a credit card, he didn't seem to care.

And, as I had thought before, money was only one possible motive to murder Kelly, and probably not the right one.

His file cabinets were filled with copies of real estate transactions, probably spare copies matching the ones at his office, and, of course, he kept everything on disk.

I returned to the bank statements and studied them, but didn't see anything to raise an eyebrow there.

I perused his desk, then picked up his large maroon address book and began going through the names, starting on page one. Here, Trevor wasn't so neat. His handwriting was practically illegible, but oddly he could read it. I stared at the names, listed alphabetically. I was able to decipher an Aberton, Aiken, Allen, and Ashton, all with male first names, clients or former clients, or at least no one I knew. I stopped at the first female name listed, Alicia Averhill. There was a phone number, a local one, but no address, and nothing to set it apart from the hundreds of other names in the book. I looked carefully at each page, searching for any special notation, something unusual to raise my suspicions, but couldn't find a thing.

What about phone records? Not for the phone in the house, I saw that statement every month. But where did Trevor keep the records for his cell phone? Surely, if he were having an affair, he would be calling his girlfriend frequently on that phone, and the calls might be longer. I realized, with a lurch of my stomach, that those statements didn't come to the house, and were probably billed to his office. Trevor considered it a business phone, so, of course, he would have the bills sent there. And, of course, that worked out perfectly since I would never be able to look at them.

It was the same with his Visa. He had two cards, one card he used strictly for business—or at least that's what he told me. The other card—in both our names—we used for everything else. Those statements came to the house. But the business Visa statement, like the cell phone statement, likely went to Trevor's office.

I peeked into Trevor's wastebasket, but I knew before I looked that it would be empty. Trevor was very neat and orderly, not one to do anything sloppily.

Still, after I'd finished in his study, I thought it might be a good idea to check the pockets of his coats in the foyer closet, and his suit pockets upstairs. But after another half-hour, the only items I turned up besides the usual folded tissue and small change, were two ticket stubs, maybe from a movie, or a concert, or even a raffle. And though the stubs might mean nothing, might even be from some event I'd attended with Trevor myself, I sat on the bed and studied them, my thoughts fixated on Trevor and his mysterious secret lover....

Lascivious pictures of the two of them rolled like an x-rated film through my head. Trevor, standing naked facing her, one hand threading his fingers through her thick lustrous hair, the other hand pressing firmly against her smooth round ass—lifting her, sliding himself into her wetness. She'd groan from the force and fullness of him, and they'd move together in hot sexual rhythm, his mouth pressing against hers, their tongues probing. His muscular body would pump ceaselessly, slowly at first, then faster and faster, incensed by her cries of lusty pleasure. Finally, they'd fall to the bed and wind their bodies into the sheets, continue the tortuous build-up of tension and heat, his touch on her shoulders, his kiss on her breasts, lips teasing, traveling down the soft flesh to her belly, then slowly, slowly, going lower, finding the soft throbbing nest....

Somehow, I eventually managed to get back to sleep. I woke groggily the next morning, opening my eyes to see sun shining through the blinds. Rising to my knees on the bed, I peeked out the window at the sparkling beauty of the newly fallen snow, thick on the evergreens.

The sight of it instantly lifted my spirits, and I knew what I was going to do. Today was not a day to be spent worrying and wondering. Today was a day to spend outside, enjoying nature's gift. Today I would go cross-country skiing. Better yet, I'd call Caroline and we could enjoy it together. I grabbed the phone.

"Rise and shine, my dear," I chirped. "Up, up, and away."

"Huh? What time is it?" she asked, her voice heavy with sleep.

"After ten. Why, did you have a late night?"

"Sort of. What makes you so cheery this morning?"

"Look outside. There's got to be two feet of new snow."

"Oh. Really?"

"Let's go cross-country skiing. I need to get out. Can you do it?"

Caroline yawned loudly. "I suppose. I don't have to be in today until late. But please, can you let me sleep for a couple more hours first?"

"No, I don't want to wait. Are you *that* tired?"

"Yeah, but you don't want the truth. Okay, I'll drink a couple pots of coffee—as soon as I can get my eyes open. Call me back in a half-hour."

"All right. Don't fall back to sleep."

I scampered around the bedroom, yanking drawers open and throwing underwear and ski tights, socks and hats, on the bed. I wasn't going to let Caroline wiggle out of this. If necessary, I'd go over to her apartment and physically drag her out of bed. We'd drive up to the cross-country ski center located at the base of Sunlight Mountain Resort, ski the groomed trails like we often did in winter, and it would leave us both feeling young and alive and full of energy. Then I'd buy Caroline lunch in town, to thank her for climbing out of bed and making her best friend happy.

I showered and dressed, then sat down to a bowl of oatmeal and an English muffin topped with strawberry preserves. I found my skis, poles, and boots in the storage locker in the basement, then carried them out to the garage and put them in the Jeep. I located my fanny pack and washed two plastic bottles to carry water in, one of them for Caroline, since she'd be sleepy and might forget.

Exactly a half-hour later, I called back.

She answered on the second ring. "Okay, I'm up. Tell me what I've forgotten." She proceeded to name off all her equipment and clothes.

"Do you have goggles or sunglasses?" I asked.

"Nope, forgot that."

"Sunscreen?"

"Not going to bother. I want to tan."

"Bad idea, you know you'll burn."

"I don't care, and I don't have any sunscreen."

"You can use mine."

"Whatever."

"What about gloves?"

"Forgot those too. Wow, you are good."

"And bring your fanny pack, or else I'll give you one of mine. I already washed two bottles and filled one for each of us."

Caroline chuckled. "Thanks, Gwyn. Bring the extra pack. I don't have a clue where I put mine. Are you ready to go? I still have to get something to eat."

"Well, looks like I'll have to clear the snow in front of the garage or I'll never get out. My snowplow guy didn't show up yet. Probably swamped."

"Meet here in a half-hour then?"

"Sure." I smiled and hung up the phone.

As we pulled up to the cross-country ski center, Caroline was still cradling her coffee cup and in no hurry to move from the warm Jeep. I jumped out and started unloading our equipment. The snow grooming machine had already been by this morning, the path for the trail well marked. I could see three skiers farther on ahead, sliding gracefully along. Anxious to begin, I stepped into my skis to do a quick warm up. Using traditional classic skis, the type I preferred, I skied over to the trail, slipped my skis into the pre-made slots grooved into the snow, and took off. I swung one arm forward with my long pole, briefly touching the snow with the sharp tip, while the other arm dropped back. My legs slid forward in sequence too, and it was like accelerated walking, though much more athletic the way I liked to do it—fast and free—charging on the uphills, descending fast on the downhills. But this portion of the trail was mostly flat, so I skied up a few yards, then back, continuing to watch for Caroline to make her move from the Jeep.

"Hurry up, woman," I called out happily as Caroline finally emerged and stepped into her skis. I slid over to her.

"Do we really have to do this?" she asked, but was already moving toward the trail.

"You'll be awake in a few minutes, and I'm going to treat you to a great lunch when we're all done."

"You are?"

"Anywhere you want."

"Good. I'm always starving after this, and you owe me big time. I'm seeing spots I'm so tired." Caroline swayed, pretending to be on the verge of fainting. "I think I only slept five hours, and that was off and on."

"How come?"

"Overtired. I was up late. The place was packed last night, new country western band. But I made some serious money in tips."

I never let Caroline pay for anything when we were together, considering the discrepancies in our incomes, though sometimes she insisted. I'd also made a point to include her in the living trust I'd arranged through an attorney, leaving her a considerable amount of money, though I hadn't told her about it. She wouldn't want to hear it, would laugh it off, say I'd outlive her anyway. Caroline didn't seem to care about any of that. As long as she could live in the mountains and do as she pleased, she was happy. I did wonder sometimes if she ever felt lonely.

We moved side by side into the deeper reaches of the forest, the sun shining high above the mountains, the trail before us glittering with snow.

"This was a good idea," Caroline said as we skied a little faster up a gradual hill. "I'm awake now."

"Told you."

"So when's Trevor coming home?"

"I guess tonight, but probably late. I don't know and I don't care."

Caroline glanced sideways at me. "That didn't sound good."

I didn't say anything, debating whether to tell her the whole truth.

"Trouble in paradise?" she asked.

"Oh, I don't know." I slid to a stop and unzipped my fanny pack, pulling out the water bottle. Caroline stopped too.

I took a long drink, then made my decision. "I think Trevor is having an affair."

She didn't react right away, then shook her head. "What?"

"I think he's screwing someone."

"No. What makes you think so?"

"The weekend I was away, for that art show in Denver, I think he had her over to the house."

"How do you know?"

"I came home and he was asleep and he'd left like two dozen roses for me in the kitchen, and this romantic note, but he hadn't had time to call me all weekend, and then I climbed into bed and I smelled her."

"Huh?"

"Her perfume was on my pillow."

"Her perfume was on your pillow. You're sure?"

"Positive."

"Did you recognize it?"

"No."

"Have you ever smelled it on anyone, anyone you know?"

"No. I don't think I've ever smelled it before. It was sort of sweet, but light. Expensive, I think. I'd know it if I smelled it again."

"But that's all it was? Perfume?"

"Yes. Why? Don't you think that's enough?"

"Well, I guess so. But it's not a lot to go on. Is there any other way it could have gotten there on your pillow?"

"I don't see how."

I was beginning to think she didn't believe me. Maybe she thought

I'd imagined all of it, considering my history. I'd gone off the deep end in a big way after Kelly died. Caroline hadn't forgotten.

I could feel a rush of emotion filling my chest, and I didn't want her to see me cry. I picked up my poles and pushed off, charging down the trail—fast.

"Hey, hold on," she called out. "Come on, Gwyn, slow down."

I kept on going, but eventually braked, sliding to a stop.

She finally caught up. "Listen, I know you're ... upset with me. But you have to admit, it's not a whole lot of evidence."

"No? Then why would perfume be on my pillow? I didn't put it there. And I didn't imagine it either."

"I don't know why, but let's talk about it, okay?"

We resumed skiing at a steady walk speed.

"Okay, you smelled perfume on your pillow. You're absolutely sure, right?"

"Yes."

"I mean—maybe Trevor washed the sheets with a new detergent or something. It's possible, isn't it?"

"Not a chance."

"I want to believe you, Gwyn. But sometimes ... sometimes you let things get blown all out of proportion. You know? You do ... do that sometimes."

"I'm not doing that. I used to do that. I don't do it now."

"Did you confront him?"

"No. I don't want him to know that I know."

"So what are you going to do?"

"Nothing. At least right now. He'll give himself away sooner or later. Then I'll decide."

She nodded slowly.

We didn't talk for a while, just kept skiing, then I remembered something. "Did you tell Josh where I lived?"

"Ah, I don't know. Let me think. I guess I could have."

"He said you did, but ..." I was going to say that I'd gotten a funny feeling about the way he knew about my house and the studio, but figured Caroline would think I was overreacting again.

"But what?"

"I wondered, that's all. I wondered why he didn't call and ask me."

"When did you talk to him?"

"A while ago. He called."

She stared at me. "Well, he did come over to the Wild River one night, just hanging out. In fact, it was the weekend you were in Denver. I probably did tell him about your house. Did he come over?"

"He wanted to, but no. Trevor wouldn't want him there."

"No, I wouldn't think so."

I dropped back and moved out of my track and into hers, as skiers were approaching up ahead on the left. A long easy downhill was coming up, and as soon as the skiers passed by, I came around in front of Caroline and crouched down, ready to try for more speed. It was fairly straight, so I didn't worry about the tall evergreens on either side of the trail.

I coasted effortlessly down, the wind buffeting my face, hoping to put some distance between the two of us. When I stopped and stepped off the trail and looked back, Caroline was a small speck in the distance. I waited for her to catch up.

"Whew," she said, finally stopping beside me on the trail. "You were flying."

"I felt like it."

"You're not still mad at me, are you?"

"No."

"Please don't be. I only worry about you, that's all."

"Well, don't worry about me. I'm fine. I promise I'm not going to do anything stupid. And I won't turn into some kind of nutcase again. You don't have to worry about that."

"I know."

"I'm really okay. But he is having an affair. And it would be nice if my best friend believed me for once."

"Oh, Gwyn," she said, reaching for my arm. "I do believe you. I just don't want it to be true, that's all."

"Yeah," I said, "neither do I."

We finished around two o'clock, having skied approximately ten kilometers.

"I wish you had the whole day off," I said as we drove the remaining miles back into town.

"So do I. I'm going to be dead on my feet tonight. Happy, but dead."

Caroline decided on Mexican food for lunch, so we stopped by one of our favorites, the Fiesta Guadalajara, just across the street from the Hotel Colorado. We walked in and took a seat by the window.

I ordered a margarita and Caroline ordered a cola. She rarely drank, having been exposed to the heavy drinking of her father, a retired railroad engineer. Unfortunately, a coherent thought was a rarity for him now, but when it came, Care said it was as if the sun had broken through the clouds. She visited him often, along with her mother, still in good health and Caroline's father's main source of care.

"To us," said Caroline, and we clinked our glasses together.

"Yes, to us, and to a long winter with lots more skiing."

We ate chips and salsa and guacamole dip, then ordered a bean burrito and fajitas as our main entrees. I was pleasantly high by the time I finished my second margarita.

"If you see Trevor in town," I said, "keep on eye on who he's with and let me know."

"I doubt if I'll see him, but I will."

"Maybe you'll hear something at the bar. People gossip."

She took a sip of her cola. "Have you been working on anything since you got back from Denver?"

"Working on anything?"

"You know, your paintings."

"Oh, sure, of course," I said, though I had actually done very little.

"Got your Christmas tree up?"

"Do you have yours up?" I shot back at her.

"Yeah, the little fake one."

"I put the tree up yesterday," I said, though it was a lie. I hadn't done a thing, not even my Christmas cards. "I bought a spruce, a really nice one, and spent all of yesterday morning decorating it. Any more questions?"

"No."

I hailed the waiter and ordered another margarita, ignoring Caroline's sad pensive expression.

"The holidays are hard on everyone," she said, "very stressful."

"Well, you don't know everything."

"What does that mean?"

I shrugged.

She continued to stare at me and it really bugged me.

"I'm doing fine, Caroline. Don't worry about me, okay? Whatever happens with this, I'll be fine."

The waiter set the third margarita before me and I drank half of it down in two gulps. I waited for her to lecture me about it. But she didn't.

I did let Caroline drive my Jeep home, and when I asked her if we could stop by the old house since we were in the area, she didn't object.

The driveway was cleared of snow, but only because I'd made an arrangement for it to be plowed after each heavy downfall.

"How often do you come by here?" she asked as we stepped out.

"Whenever I feel like it, maybe once a week."

"Wouldn't it be easier to just sell it?"

I didn't answer. Instead, I unlocked the front door.

Even in my inebriated state, I knew immediately that something was wrong. I stopped in the doorway, blocking our entrance.

"What is it?" she asked.

"Things have moved."

I walked slowly inside.

My father's chair was farther forward, as if he had pushed it closer to the television set, and the throw rug was askew.

"What?" she asked.

I sniffed the air. "Do you smell that?"

"No, what?"

"I'm not sure. I've never smelled it in here before." I turned slowly in a circle. "Someone's been here."

I walked into the kitchen and turned on the water. It flowed smoothly, telling me that someone had used it recently, since yesterday, when I'd visited. "Someone's been in the house."

"Does anyone come over here besides you? What about the neighbors?"

"No. Linda is the only other person with a key. And I don't think it was her. She doesn't like coming over here."

We checked the first floor, but could find no signs of a forced entry.

"These locks look old," said Caroline. "I doubt if they'd give much of a problem to someone who knew what they were doing."

I didn't mention that the locks were the same ones that had always been here. I'd changed nothing after Kelly died, even though Linda had thought we should.

We inspected the second floor, and I thought I could discern the impression of a body on my parents' bed, even though the bedspread was still neat.

"You might have a tenant you don't know about," Caroline said.

"I think you're right."

We walked back down the stairs and into the kitchen. The refrigerator was empty, but still, it smelled as if something, some type of food, might have recently been inside.

"Why do you keep the refrigerator on?" she asked.

"It's either that or leave it open, and sometimes I keep a cold drink in there when I come over and clean stuff."

"I think you should call the cops and have them take a look around. Keep an eye on the house. And you should definitely change these locks."

Well, duh, I thought, feeling tired and increasingly annoyed at each of Caroline's many suggestions. Hoping to taunt her, I said loudly, "Maybe we should check the basement, see if we can catch them."

"No, I think we should leave—pronto."

"No, I'll check it. I'll be right back."

She grabbed the back of my coat. "Don't you *dare.*"

At that precise moment, glass shattered in the basement.

"My God," she shrieked, pulling my arm. "*Come on!*"

Caroline sat at the wheel of the Jeep, now parked a block away, talking on her cell phone to the police. "Yes, it looks like we have a break-in." She gave the address, which I had written down and held up for her to see. "We heard glass break in the basement as soon as we said aloud we were going down there."

She ended the call, then turned to me. "It probably would have been better if you'd talked to them yourself."

"No, they'd know I've been drinking and might not believe me."

Caroline drove the Jeep to the head of the street and we waited for the police car to roll by. When it did, we followed it back to the house.

Lights whirling atop the squad car, two male cops emerged, slamming doors. We pulled beside them into the drive. One of the guys came over to the window of the Jeep and looked in.

"Thanks for getting here so quick," said Caroline. "She owns the house." She pointed at me.

"Best if you stay in your car while we make a search of the premises. Do you have a key?"

I handed it over and watched as the blue-eyed cop, fresh-faced and exceedingly cute, walked to the front door. "He was looking at you, Care."

"No, he wasn't." But I saw the corners of her mouth twitch into a faint smile.

The other cop, an older guy, had already gone around to the back of the house. For ten minutes, the two men searched, first the house, then the garage and surrounding yard. Finally, after several short trips to our window and more questions, not all related to the break-in, the cute one leaned up against the Jeep. "No one in there now," he said. "We found a glass jar, broken, down in the basement. We'll take what's left of that back and check it for prints. How long has this house been vacant?"

"About two years," I said.

"Ever notice signs of anyone before?"

"No."

"Who else is allowed in the house?"

"My sister, but she doesn't come by, really. And my husband, but he never comes over here, well almost never, and my sister's husband. He might have a key too."

"I'd strongly suggest that you change the locks, get dead bolts, a better system. If the house has been empty this long, you might have a vagrant who thinks he's found a rent-free place to stay. It doesn't look as if the house has been disturbed too much. I'd also check to make sure one of your relatives wasn't over here and didn't tell you. You might want to think about renting the place or selling it too. Save yourself some grief. We will make a point to come by and check on things." He smiled at Caroline, who had managed to flirt with him and find out his full name, Nathan Tobias. "And I wouldn't advise coming here alone. Call us. We'll swing by and give things a look first."

He touched his cap, then both men got into their car and sped away.

"I've seen him before," Caroline said as she drove toward her apartment. "I think he comes by the Laundromat I go to every once in a while, but not in a uniform." She tapped her fingers to her lips. "God, the last time I was over there I looked like hell. I won't anymore." She turned to me. "You have to promise me you won't go in that house alone anymore. Okay?"

"I promise."

"And if you do have to go over there, for anything, make sure you call me first. Got that?"

I was sober now, and quietly hating myself for being angry at my best friend, who was certainly a better friend to me than I'd been to her recently.

Chapter 9

The drive was plowed by the time I returned home. I drove immediately to the Christmas tree lot and purchased a tall spruce, dark green and full, then paid extra to have it delivered and set up within the hour. Usually Trevor helped me buy the tree, and he'd offered to before he'd left this weekend, but I figured I might as well get used to doing things alone. After all, I might be forced to fairly soon.

I was in the middle of dragging boxes of Christmas decorations from the basement when the phone rang. I dropped the box on the floor and grabbed the receiver.

"So where have you been all day?" my sister inquired.

"Oh, hi Linda. Caroline and I went cross-country skiing this morning, then lunch."

"Good for you."

"So what's up?"

"Oh nothing—except I got a message from Mr. I Spy earlier today."

"You did?"

"Yes, and he thinks he'll have something for us early this week."

"Did he give any details at all?" I asked, my heart picking up speed.

"No, but I'm sure there'll be lots of those."

I noticed an odd lilt to Linda's voice, a happiness that shouldn't be there, and wondered if she already knew something about the report. "So, he'll call when it's ready?"

"That's the plan."

I knew I should mention the possible break-in at the house, but I hesitated to do it since I knew how Linda would react—badly—but I couldn't have her going over there unaware of the danger.

"Caroline and I stopped over to the house today."

"Yes, and ...?"

"We probably should put new locks on the doors, make the house more secure."

"What happened?"

"Nothing exactly, but someone may have been in the house. Actually, I don't think so, but Caroline thought we should have the police check the place out."

"You had the cops over there? Come on, Gwyn, give me the whole story and quit tiptoeing around the truth."

"I am telling the truth, but before we both start jumping to conclusions, I think we need to be certain there isn't a simpler explanation. We need to be sure no one else has been in the house. Have you?"

She didn't answer for a moment. "No, not recently."

"But you have. When?"

"I don't know, a few weeks ago, maybe not that long."

"Why would you go over there?"

"I was trying to help you out. I was looking for those stupid boxes, the ones with Kelly's journals. The problem is I think I may have thrown them out, before, by accident."

"You what? You threw them out? How could you do that? You knew how important they were to me."

"I found them in a damp spot in the basement. They were moldy, Gwyn. It was sickening. It was like it was her, all yuck and moldering in her grave. I think I may have tossed them when I was cleaning up. I didn't mean to. I changed my mind about it, but I threw out a lot of stuff that day and they may have gotten mixed in."

"But I *wanted* them," I cried, feeling sick, my insides doubling over on themselves.

"I know, and I'm sorry. I really am. I guess I shouldn't have told—"

I slammed the phone down, tears spilling onto my face. Thanks. Thanks a whole bunch, Linda. Thanks for always wrecking *everything*. You *meant* to do it. I know you did. You *hated* Kelly.

The phone rang and I let it ring until the answering machine began to click on, then picked up the receiver and slammed it down again. *"Don't call me!"* I shrieked at her. *"Don't ever call me again! You're rotten, rotten, rotten!"*

I realized much later that the house was dark except for the one security light burning in the living room. I slowly rose from the kitchen chair and flipped on the overhead light. The clock on the stove read nine p.m. The phone was ringing again, but I ignored it, as I had for hours.

I walked into the living room and stared at the unlit Christmas tree, so dark and depressingly dead. I stood looking past it for many minutes, my arms wrapped tightly to my chest, my fingers vice grips in my flesh. I'd cried again for Kelly, given the night over once more to my terrible grief, begged that the one I loved most be returned to me.

It would do me no good. I could plead all I wanted. I could curse, and scream, and pound on the gates of Heaven itself. It would do me no good. The Lord had taken away. He'd giveth and he'd taketh away. My baby wasn't coming back. I'd never be with her again—not here.

I had only one remaining fragment of family left. Linda.

I stooped to plug in the Christmas tree and it glowed with light. I opened a box and picked out a shimmering ornament, hooked it to an empty branch. I watched as the bright ball swung delicately on the limb. Some of the ornaments were old and cheap, relics from my childhood. Always before, I'd placed them all on the tree, no matter how battered. Now, I left the worst ornaments in the box. I wanted my tree to be truly beautiful again.

Still, when it was done, the tree needed something more, and I promised myself to buy new ornaments tomorrow.

And I would call Linda too, and forgive her.

I remembered how it had been, though I'd sometimes ignored the increasing hostility between my sisters as we were growing up. Kelly had not liked Linda either, though Linda had tried hard to fit in, to be a part of the group. Kelly had wanted to shut her out, but I—when I was around—always put a stop to it. No doubt there were things only Linda knew, times she had suffered, but held them inside. She'd been the baby until Kelly was born. Surely, the close bond between Kelly and I had been very difficult to accept.

I heard Trevor come home at one a.m., and I debated going downstairs to greet him. I missed him, but it was like missing someone I used to know. I wanted to ask him about the woman, wanted to get it all out in the open, wanted him to admit it or deny it, but for better or worse, let him know I wasn't in the dark any longer.

I wouldn't do it, of course. Somehow, the deceit might all be related. If he could have an affair with this woman, then he might also have had an affair with Kelly. And if I let him know I was aware of his true character, he might begin to wonder what else I might know, what else I might have deduced.

He turned on the light in the hall. I pulled the blankets up around my chin and shut my eyes. I could hear him quietly drop his keys on the dresser, hear him pulling open a drawer. For just a minute, I wished I could be in his head. Was he remembering delicious details of the woman's body, her kiss as they parted, their plans to meet again very, very soon? Why did he say he loved me? Did he? Did he ever?

He silently rolled in beside me and I tensed as I waited for his hand to come up around my shoulder, for his warmth to close in on my back. I loved the way he loved me, even now, unsure of him as I was. But he didn't touch me, and that was even more painful.

Chapter 10

I called Linda early the next morning.

"I'm so sorry I didn't answer the phone last night. I know you kept trying to call."

"Oh Gwyn, I'm sorry too. I—"

"It's okay. I know you didn't mean to hurt me. It was an accident, and I understand why you might have wanted to throw the journals out."

"I didn't want to. I told you. Not after I thought about it. If I did, it wasn't on purpose. I wouldn't do that."

"But maybe you were right to do it. I have to stop obsessing so much about things I can't change, stop living in the past. It's taken a huge toll on me—on you—on all of us. I loved Kelly. I always will. But she's gone. And we're still here."

"I loved her too, Gwyn."

"I know."

"I never wanted anything bad to happen to her. I didn't—even when I was hating her."

"You don't have to explain."

"No, I need to say this. You know how awful it was between us. She knew exactly how to get to me. I'm not sure why it started, except maybe she knew I wanted to be closer to you. Ever since we were small, there was a kind of competition between us for your attention. Over the years, she and I did a lot of mean things to each other. After a while, I don't think either of us knew how to stop."

"I should have done something."

"I'm not sure it would have helped. Some things are so bad they can't be undone."

"Do you want to tell me? Any of it ...?"

"No."

"Wouldn't it help?"

"No. I don't want to speak ill of the dead. Kelly's not here to defend herself. And I don't want to make it real again."

"I should have done something."

"Well ... you didn't."

The barbed retort stabbed at my heart, but I knew I deserved it. "Linda, we've been drifting away from each other lately. I know a lot of it's my fault. I've been so preoccupied. But you don't call me like you used to. I feel like you're closed off somehow."

"I called you yesterday."

"I know, but it's so rare."

"I'm busy, Gwyn. Good grief, I've been up to my neck with this remodeling, and then you bring up all this stuff about Kelly's letter, and—"

"No, before that, for a long time now."

"I'll try to call you more often. Okay?"

"Okay."

"Besides, as soon as I get that report, I'll be calling you immediately."

I decided to drive over to Trevor's real estate office at lunchtime. He wasn't at his desk, so I did a quick survey of his quarters, then headed back into the main part of the office. The agency consisted of three rooms, a small reception area, a large open space with four desks for the sales associates, and Trevor's office.

On my way in, I'd walked past the reception area, which was devoid of a receptionist, then strode past the one lone agent, a beefy linebacker-type guy about twenty-five, shirtsleeves rolled up, elbows on his desk. He was inhaling a submarine sandwich, but stopped chewing as I passed.

"Can I help you?"

I'd waved and smiled and kept on going.

But now I returned to question the man. "Hi, I'm Gwyn Sanders, Trevor's wife. Do you happen to know where he might be?"

"Lunch, I think."

"Yes, I was supposed to meet him, but I forgot where he said."

"Really? Oh ... well you know, I'm not sure. Ask Molly. I think she's in her car out back. Molly keeps track of everybody around here." He pointed to the rear door. "She likes to eat her lunch out there."

"Thanks," I said. "I'll go check."

I saw three cars parked close together, but no Molly. Carefully, I stepped between the vehicles. Then, like a corpse arising from the dead, Molly popped into the passenger window of a tan Chevrolet. I stumbled back, landing on the adjacent car.

She rolled down her window. "Sorry, were you looking for me?"

The girl wore thick glasses and a piece of food—probably bread— was stuck to her upper lip. As if aware of it, she quickly wiped her mouth with a napkin.

Not Trevor's type, was my first thought.

"I didn't mean to scare you," she said. "I dropped my pickle on the floor."

"No problem. I'm looking for Trevor. I'm his wife, Gwyn." I held out my hand to her through the open window. "Sorry to bother you on your lunch break, but I'm supposed to meet him and I forgot where he said."

"Trudo's."

"Oh, that's right. Thanks. How long ago did he leave?"

"Half-hour ago, at least. Do you want me to call him?"

"No. I'll call. I should have before, but I don't want him to know I forgot where to meet. Silly." I shrugged.

Molly smiled and raised her eyebrows, the window slowly rolling back up.

"Thanks again," I said before it closed completely.

I rushed to my Jeep. Trevor would probably take a long lunch, and maybe, just maybe, I'd catch him with his amour of the moment.

Trudo's was packed.

I stood in line, trying to remain partially concealed as the hostess came by and asked, "How many?"

"Two," I said, for no particular reason.

I scoured the restaurant from my cramped position in line. I'd decided not to act surprised if Trevor were with a woman, instead I'd appear innocently ignorant. I hoped to spot him long before he spotted me, for it would give me time to study his body language. Although, how openly affectionate could he be in public? Surely, he'd want it to look like an ordinary business lunch.

Well, I knew him better than anybody else, except *her* possibly, and I was aware of Trevor's secret little ways of telling a woman she was special. Of course, the possibility existed that the woman he might be lunching with today was not a lover, might actually be a client, or an associate with no close ties to Trevor.

Either way, I had to try this. I couldn't sit still any longer.

As I was being seated in the bar area, the main dining room still a half-hour wait, I glimpsed Trevor on his way toward the back of the restaurant. No doubt visiting the restroom. I positioned myself so my back would be toward him when he exited the john, and so I was directly behind a man whose girth would certainly hide two people adequately.

While Trevor was occupied, I used the time to move out of the bar and peek into the main dining room. I concentrated on finding an empty chair and a beautiful woman. I saw a few of both. But one woman in particular caught my attention.

I ducked back into the bar area, thinking how different scenarios might play once I finally faced him. I didn't like this picture of myself as the jealous spying wife, but I was limited in my choices, since I couldn't ask him directly about the affair. And I had to know.

I waited five minutes, long enough for Trevor to return to his table, then I walked cautiously toward the dining room and glanced inside again. There was Trevor. There was the woman, and as I had correctly guessed, the woman was the same I had spotted earlier, the most gorgeous brunette in the room. I stepped quickly back to my table, slumped into my seat, and took several quick breaths. I realized now how clearly I had wanted to be wrong.

After several minutes, I gathered my courage and walked purposefully toward my husband. His back was toward me, and the woman didn't seem to recognize me as I approached.

I walked slightly past Trevor, then turned. "Hi, honey," I said, kissing him on the cheek. I carefully observed his expression, expecting ill-concealed horror, but instead was met with a wide delighted smile.

"Gwyn," he said, rising from his seat. "What a surprise."

I turned to the woman, hoping to at least catch her off guard, but could read nothing in her face, an inscrutable porcelain mask of full-lipped mouth and intelligent almond eyes.

Trevor pulled up a chair for me.

"I didn't realize you were busy," I said, smiling first at Trevor, then at the woman.

"Oh," he said, "let me introduce you two. Gwyn, this is Sylvia Breslin. Sylvia, my wife, Gwyn."

Sylvia offered her beautifully manicured hand. "Hello, I've heard so much about you." But her smile was only a slight one.

"I feel like I'm interrupting," I said.

"No," Sylvia assured me, "we're done talking business. We've been at it all morning. Lunch and small talk are very welcome right now."

Trevor waved a hand at the waiter, then looked at me. "Did you see my car parked out front? You were in town?"

"No, I stopped by your office hoping to catch you at your desk and invite you to lunch. Molly said you were here, so I took a chance."

My hands lay on my lap beneath the table, and I felt Trevor's fingers slide over mine, then withdraw.

We ordered drinks, then seafood, and I tried to remain quiet and listen to their conversation. I felt entirely foolish and ridiculous. Either Trevor and this woman were a lot sharper than I ever could have imagined, or it was a business lunch, one between a luscious woman and a gorgeous man, but still a business lunch.

I endured the rest of the meal, slowly becoming aware that this woman was "big bucks," the controlling financial force behind Trevor's condo project in Denver. She was in Glenwood to discuss another possible project, being extremely pleased and impressed with Trevor's handling of the first. I did notice that the woman's ring finger was empty, and that Sylvia Breslin was an extremely cool and polished cucumber.

Sylvia wanted to stop back at the real estate office, and I excused myself from joining them, claiming to have important errands to run.

Instead, I went home and reluctantly dialed the office of my therapist and scheduled another appointment.

Trevor was home by six o'clock, and I was happy to see him, incredibly relieved that Sylvia Breslin had turned out to be a false alarm. I'd made a special dinner for him too, prime rib, his favorite, and twice baked potatoes.

"What's the occasion?" he asked, sniffing the air. "Something sure smells good."

"I'm just glad to have you back. I missed you this weekend."

"Then I'll have to go away more often if I get this kind of reception." He put his coat away and walked into the living room where I'd started a fire, the flames curling peacefully around the logs. "The Christmas tree looks great," he said. "You did something different."

"I added some new ornaments. I left a lot of the old ones in the box."

"Nice." He strode over to the tree and reached for a gaily festooned replica of Santa on his sleigh. "Such a lot of detail. Where did you get these?"

"In town. It's the work of a local artist over in Redstone. I was totally intrigued and bought a whole bunch of them."

"And a fire in the fireplace." He smiled.

"And prime rib."

He came close and kissed me on the forehead, then on the mouth, lingering for a while. "You're totally amazing," he said. "And confusing. I swear I will never figure you out."

"Don't try."

"I take it you're feeling better?"

"What do you mean?"

"Well ... you were depressed. That's what you said. I was concerned, that's all."

I pulled back. "And you had to mention it."

"Now wait, don't beat me up if I say the wrong thing. I'm not good at this."

"Not good at what?"

"Gwyn, don't. I didn't mean anything bad."

"But somehow you managed to remind me again that I'm the one with a problem."

He held my shoulders. "Gwyn, don't. I didn't mean it that way. I didn't. Okay?"

I tried to let the anger slide away, not sure where it had come from. I closed my eyes along with my lips, determined not to spoil the romantic evening I'd envisioned. "I'm sorry," I said finally. "I guess I'm a little oversensitive. I'm tired of everyone seeing me as the recovering manic-depressive."

He hugged me. "I don't see you like that." Then kissed me. "Not at all. Will dinner burn if we leave it in the oven for a while?"

"No, I guess not."

He continued to hold me and the tension gradually eased away, my body relaxing, responding to his kisses. We made love on the floor, there before the fire, as I'd hoped we would, and I enjoyed myself more than I had in a very long time, and wondered if it were possible for a man to make a woman feel this loved, this special, and still be a cheat. At the moment, I didn't care to guess, but hoped that it wasn't possible, and that I was wrong about him.

Finally, we unwound ourselves from each other, and I moved to get up. But Trevor stopped me, placing his hand on my arm.

"I'm glad you came by today, that you found me in town."

"I probably shouldn't have interrupted you."

"Didn't hurt."

"She probably didn't like it."

"I doubt it, but it wouldn't matter."

I waited for him to continue. He rolled over and gazed down at me. "You were jealous, weren't you?"

"No," I said, suppressing a laugh.

"You were right to be. She is hot for me."

"You're kidding."

"Why? Is that so hard to believe?"

"No, but it's hard to believe you'd tell me about it. Especially now."

"I just didn't want you to get the wrong impression. If that's why you're mad. I'm not interested in her."

I looked away, then back into his eyes.

"But," he said, "I am interested in her business, and I have to pretend a little."

"Why?"

"Because women like Sylvia want to feel attractive and powerful. She likes to think she's irresistible, that if she truly wanted me, she could have me. But she knows I'm married."

"So why would that make any difference to her?"

"It might not.... I think you are jealous."

"Not at all."

"Liar."

I tried to get up, but his weight pinned me down.

"I have to take the potatoes out," I said, "or they'll burn."

"You don't have to worry about Sylvia. I told you. I'm not interested."

And the question just sort of dangled there at the tip of my tongue, ready to slip out. *But what if you were interested? What would you do then?*

I let the subject drop and served Trevor dinner in the dining room, poured his wine, and spoiled him with attention for the rest of the meal.

Later that night, I watched as he relaxed in his favorite chair and checked stock quotes in *The Wall Street Journal*, while I pretended to read a book. I thought again of the lie he'd told police about the night Kelly died, how he'd misrepresented the time he'd returned home by a full two hours, and never given me a good reason for it. I assumed he'd worried it would make him look bad, that he might come under suspicion if no one could corroborate his whereabouts. I'd understood, I thought, and said nothing. But *was* he alone, as he claimed, catching up on some work?

Back then, he was employed by Sun Realty. It wasn't until later, when we married, that Trevor was able to open his own office. I'd provided the up-front money. I'd wanted to do it. He was so enthusiastic, so eager, and so obviously ready for the move. He had a lot of contacts, and was sick and tired of working his butt off and making money that didn't end up in his pocket, but that of Sun Realty. And he had been right to do it. He'd made the business a success.

He looked up from his paper and noticed me staring at him. "Thinking about me?"

"Of course."

"I didn't wear you out?"

"You wore me out."

"Good—though if you're interested, I'm up for another round."

"As nice as that sounds, I'll pass. I'm tired."

"Me too." He folded his newspaper and set it aside.

I had to ask him, before he got up to leave. "Do you think they'll ever catch him?"

He frowned, then looked at the floor. "Sure, they'll catch him."

"Are you certain?"

"Yes. Eventually they will. You'll feel better when that happens, won't you?"

"Yes."

He rose from his chair and walked over. "You coming up?"

"In a little while."

"Don't stay up too late," he said, caressing my shoulder.

"I'm just going to read a little more."

"Fine."

I remembered one time coming into the kitchen. It was during the housewarming party I'd given a month after moving in, and seeing Trevor and Kelly alone talking quietly at the counter. I'd felt an odd kind of jolt, seeing them together, Kelly looking so absolutely gorgeous, showing just a little too much cleavage, her eyes overly made-up, heavy on the mascara, lids drooping alluringly, then lifting, gazing up at Trevor so intently. She was leaning in a bit too close, the way she did when she was attracted to a man, and it was apparent she was already on her way to being drunk, or maybe it was more than just the alcohol. Trevor had spotted me first, and stepped back.

It was only the one time, and I hadn't thought about it since. After all, Kelly was a born flirt, but I'd always believed she meant nothing by it. It was just her way. She'd never step over the line. She had flirted with Wolfgang too, and Josh, yes, lots of times, and he had good naturedly put up with it, but never gave me any reason to doubt his loyalty. Besides, Kelly had Craig, a guy she seemed pretty taken with. Why would she go after anyone else's boyfriend?

I had met Craig only a few times, usually when I stopped over to the house to visit Kelly. The two weren't living together. Craig had his own place. Kelly hadn't known him long, maybe four or five months, but he was often there when I came by. He seemed okay, friendly enough, but I hadn't tried to get to know him. Kelly might have a new guy by the next week, though she did seem to have a thing for Craig.

With his long blond ponytail, rock-star good looks, and "whatever-baby" attitude, he seemed to have a lock on what Kelly was all about.

I'd been certain he'd murdered my sister, and so it appeared had the police. He didn't have an alibi, and a young woman at a party store thought she'd spotted him earlier in the evening with Kelly, though the girl wouldn't swear to it. The police had questioned Craig later. Shortly after that, he'd left town in a big hurry, leaving most of his possessions behind. No one had seen him since. Possibly no one ever would.

But now that I'd found Kelly's letter, I wished I could talk to him and find out what he knew. Maybe there'd been a good reason why he'd left town in such a hurry. Maybe he knew who'd actually killed Kelly, and was afraid he would be next.

Chapter 11

"Gwyn, is Trevor home yet?"

It was Tuesday afternoon and Linda was on the phone, speaking slightly above a whisper.

"No."

"I've got it."

"The report?"

"You guessed it."

"What's it say?"

"I can't read it to you now. Wolfgang could walk in here at any second. I'm upstairs. I'm not even sure—he might be out of the bathroom already."

"He could also pick up the phone. Are you sure he's not listening in?"

"I'm on my cell. He can't listen in on that."

"Come over to the house," I said. "No, let's meet somewhere. I'd be too nervous looking at it here. Can't you tell me anything?"

"I'd rather you look at it yourself."

At that, my stomach flipped over. "Why, is it bad?"

"Don't start second-guessing. Where should we meet?"

"Not in a public place, someone might overhear us. What about in a parking lot? How about behind the library?"

"Okay, way in the back. For sure, no one *I know* will be there."

"What time?"

"As soon as you can."

"What about Wolfgang?"

"Oh, I'll tell him I'm going to the drugstore, that I need cotton balls or something. He's in the middle of his workout. He won't even care."

"Okay, I'm leaving now."

I could barely keep my mind on my driving. In the space of a few hours I would know more of Trevor's history than in the whole two and a half years I'd known him. He didn't talk much about his past, mostly about current things, the business, friends he'd made in the business, his hopes for the future, and things we could do in our free time, ski trips, vacations we could plan.

He also talked very little about his family, who lived in Sacramento, California. I had met his mother, Ester, a petite shy lady, at the wedding here in Glenwood more than a year ago. And he had a sister, Laurel, whom I didn't meet, who had apologized over the phone for not being able to attend. She was in the hospital for surgery, a torn ligament in her shoulder, as I remembered. His older brother, Joseph, was at the ceremony and was pleasant enough, but came alone. I'd talked to him at the reception and learned he'd never been married, though according to Trevor, his brother had a sometime girlfriend, but for whatever reason, didn't invite her along. Trevor's old childhood friend, Stan, a prominent lawyer with extensive land holdings in California and a lot of influential political friends, showed up for the wedding and stayed for part of the reception. Trevor had shown more animation and spent more time with him than with anyone else.

Trevor's father did not attend. Trevor had shrugged, said his dad didn't want to upset his mother. Though still legally married, his parents had separated years ago at his mother's request. Trevor didn't seem too upset about it, or surprised that his parents had not taken the final step and divorced. I wasn't sure if Trevor ever contacted his father. He never said so. At times when I mentioned his dad, Trevor changed the subject—jokingly, but still he changed it. He did phone his mother fairly often, but he hadn't seen her since the wedding, and he didn't have any future plans to visit as far as I knew. Not exactly a close-knit bunch.

Linda's Audi wasn't in the library parking lot when I arrived, so I cruised the last row, surprisingly full of cars, and realized that parking was becoming scarce the closer it got to Christmas. I found an empty space and pulled in. A few minutes later, Linda pulled up behind me. She waved her arm, beckoning, and I hopped out and got into her car.

"Do you believe this?" she said. "How many of these people are really in the library?"

"Drive around," I said, glancing around the car for the background check.

"In the backseat."

I reached over and grabbed the manila envelope. "Are they both in here?"

"No, just yours."

I frowned at her. "Where's yours?"

"At home, where I left it."

I noticed that though the envelope was glued closed and clasped, it wasn't anything Linda couldn't buy at an office supply store. But if I asked if she'd looked at the contents and transferred them to a new envelope, Linda would freak—and it wouldn't change a thing. "How come you didn't bring yours?"

"Because it's private, and certainly I'd tell you if there were anything that needed telling."

I held the envelope and silently counted to ten—very, very slowly. "I thought the idea was to share information."

"Yes, but only if it might lend some light on Kelly's death. I thought you might want to keep Trevor's matters private also. Are you going to open it?"

"Give me a minute."

"I agree. It's scary."

Linda located a narrow parking space and edged in.

I slowly released the clasp and pried the envelope open, then reached in for the papers. I held them at an angle so Linda wouldn't be able to see. I saw my husband's name, Trevor Taylor Sanders, first, then our home address, his business address, and Trevor's social security number. No aliases. I took that as a good sign.

It listed previous addresses, and I briefly perused those. Several were in California, but one was in Denver, and I calculated that it must have been shortly before I met Trevor, before he came to Glenwood. I thought he had told me he'd moved directly from Sacramento to Glenwood, or at least that's what I remembered.

It listed relatives: mother, father, brother, sister, aunts and uncles, many more than Trevor had ever mentioned, and their last known addresses and telephone numbers. It listed our current neighbors and their addresses and phones also.

I looked up, but Linda was staring absently out the window. "You can drive," I said. "I can't study all of this here."

"I know. It's a lot of stuff."

I brought the papers into my lap. "So there wasn't anything questionable in Wolfgang's background?"

"No, it was almost boring there was so little of interest."

"He was telling the truth about his parents dying in an avalanche?"

"Yes."

"I'm only asking, you know. It's not like you're volunteering anything here."

"It was just such a waste of time." She turned her face toward me. "Unless there's something in yours you haven't told me about."

"No, but I've barely read it." *But I bet you have.* I'd even be willing to bet that Linda had been studying it for several days, since she'd called on Sunday.

I turned back to the papers, flipped through the pages, skimming information, then stopped—and focused. The word, "incarceration," brought me to an immediate halt.

Ronald J. Sanders, alias Roger Sutter, alias Randolph Simms ... Pueblo Minimum Center, Pueblo, Colorado, currently serving a five-year sentence, convicted on racketeering charges, eligible for parole on ...

They were talking about Trevor's father, in prison, in Colorado. I thought quickly. No, I would not give Linda the satisfaction. I wouldn't admit to her that Trevor's father was a jailbird. Though Linda wouldn't say it, she certainly must have thought it—that the apple doesn't fall far from the tree—and perhaps Trevor, more rotten than his father, had taken it a step further.

"Do you want to stop somewhere?" Linda asked, "or do you want to go back?"

"We should go back. Isn't Wolfgang waiting for you?"

"He won't be worried, believe me." She drove around the block, heading toward the library. "If nothing shows up in the report, nothing incriminating or suspicious, what are we going to do?" she asked.

"I don't know."

"Do you think we should let the police know what's going on?"

"No. I haven't even read this thing yet. I need some time. And the only evidence we have so far is Kelly's letter, and that's no proof of anything."

"True.... Make sure Trevor doesn't see you've got that."

"Of course I won't."

"Call me if there's anything, anything at all in the report. We have to be super careful. I don't want us tripping over any land mines."

When I returned home I sought a good hiding place for the report. Later tonight, after Trevor went to bed, I'd read it in depth. I'd decided that my discovery didn't mean a thing, that if anything, having a father in prison had taught Trevor one thing and one thing only. *Don't end up there.* Look how diligently he went about his business, about his life. Of course he didn't want his father's mistakes to reflect on him. That's why he'd kept it a secret.

His family had kept it a secret from me also. I wondered if Trevor had coached them, or if they regularly forgot to mention Ronald Sander's imprisonment.

And I wondered why Trevor hadn't trusted me, his own wife, with this, then realized a moment later that the background check would have been totally unnecessary if I'd fully trusted him.

I hid the envelope in my darkroom. It was the one place Trevor rarely stepped foot in, and if I needed to, I could close the door and lock it and Trevor wouldn't question me about it. He'd assume I was developing pictures.

I placed the manila envelope in the midst of other envelopes containing actual prints. I didn't have time now to look at the documents further. It was already five o'clock and Trevor could walk in soon and would expect to find me in the kitchen making dinner. I also needed to get my thoughts together and calm myself, so I wouldn't inadvertently say something that would give me away.

I took two packages of frozen shrimp out of the freezer and poured them into a metal bowl to soak in water, then filled a saucepan with water to heat for the redskin potatoes. I washed fresh asparagus and put that aside. What else? I poured myself a glass of wine, a small one, to steady my nerves.

By the time Trevor arrived, the dining room table was set, candles were burning, and music, a piano concerto by Bach, filled the rooms. At the last minute, I turned on the gas jets for the pass-through fireplace.

Trevor was smiling as he walked into the foyer, and his arm was behind his back, hiding something.

"You must have been a good girl," he said, grinning mischievously. "'Cause Santa stopped by the office today and dropped off an early Christmas present for you."

"Santa did that?"

"Yes he did, and I'm wondering if the old elf's got a thing for you." He held out two small boxes exquisitely wrapped in gold foil and ribbon, tiny gold bells attached.

"Well, if he has a thing for me, wouldn't he have brought the presents here?"

"Subterfuge. Won't look suspicious this way."

"Should I open them now?"

He crossed his arms. "Sure, open them now, because I have another surprise for you after that."

I carefully unwrapped the smallest package. Inside was a lovely blue-velvet box. I flipped the lid to reveal astonishingly brilliant diamond-encrusted earrings. "Oh Trevor, they're absolutely beautiful, just gorgeous."

"Uh huh, now open the other one before you start with the big wet kisses."

I unwrapped it as slowly as the first. "You know, it's still three weeks until Christmas and I don't have anything to give you back."

"Not to worry. I've been known to barter in flesh."

Again, it was a blue-velvet box, but larger than the first. Inside was an equally astounding and brilliant gold and diamond tennis bracelet, at least fifty diamonds running down its center.

"Wow," I exclaimed. "Santa must really love me."

"Yeah, he really does."

I looked at him, wanting to believe him. His face, so incredibly sincere—how could he possibly be lying? Why go to all this trouble to convince me?

We kissed and I hugged him tightly, pressing my cheek against his warm chest. Why couldn't all of this mess just go away? Why didn't I just drop it? But no, I couldn't drop anything. Someone had viciously murdered my sister, and that someone deserved to be caught and punished, whatever the reason for the crime ... and certainly before they might feel compelled to kill again.

Finished with dinner, I sat near Trevor at the end of the dining room table. I played with a stalk of asparagus, steering it with my fork around my plate like a swimming eel. Though full, I continued to nibble, because we were having such a nice time together. I reached for Trevor's hand.

He took mine in his and squeezed it, then reached for his wineglass, sipping the last of his wine. "You tell me when you're ready for my next surprise."

"You're spoiling me, Trevor."

"I know."

"Okay, I'm ready. Go ahead."

"Well," he said, drawing it out. "I've made arrangements for us to spend the weekend in Aspen, a mini ski vacation."

"Really? You have the time? You can take a whole weekend off?"

"Yes and no ... just listen. First, we'll have luxurious accommodations, a private two-bedroom condo, adjacent to the slopes and a short walk into town. We'll be dining on steak and lobster and grilled calamari, chilled caviar. I know, you don't like caviar, but if you want it you can have it."

"Just the two of us?"

"In our condo, yes. For the weekend, no."

I sat waiting for the obvious catch.

"We'll be the guests of Sylvia Breslin and Robert Morris."

"Oh," I said, then realizing I should appear more excited, added, "well that's wonderful. We'll have a great time. They want me along?"

"Of course. You've met Bob. I know you don't remember him, but you might when you see him again. He remembers you."

"At Linda's party. I remember you said I did, but I don't remember him. Short guy?"

"Hardly. He's six-two. Dark hair, wavy. Skin a little craggy. About forty years old. Always has a good-looking woman at his side."

"Not married?"

"Divorced some years back."

"Where will they be staying?"

"In another condo, same complex."

"Together?"

"Yes, but there's nothing going on between them. They're business partners. Actually, partners isn't the right word. It's more like—what benefits one benefits the other. Associates, I guess."

"And they ski?"

"Yes, they ski. I don't know how well, enough that we can ski together. It will be fun."

I smiled. Sure, a weekend with the woman who was after my husband. Of course, what could be more fun? And if Trevor were lying, it might have progressed far beyond that. Sylvia might have already caught him.

I cleared the dining room table and Trevor helped me, following me into the kitchen. While I rinsed dishes and placed them in the dishwasher, Trevor perused the small stack of mail he'd tossed on the kitchen table earlier.

"Something from your sister and Wolfgang. Looks like an invitation."

He brought it over.

"Open it," I said, my hands wet.

"It is. Your sister's giving another party."

"When?"

"Two weeks from Friday. She calls it a 'Holiday Hiatus'."

"I had a feeling she'd try to put something together before they left on vacation. She probably didn't want to disappoint her friends."

"Kind of short notice."

"Yes, for Linda, but Wolfgang surprised her with that Hawaiian vacation. She probably thought she'd have more time."

"It would be nice for the two of us to take a trip, if I could arrange to get away. If I had the time. Things might slow down eventually. This weekend will be fun though. We can try out the new skis."

"Can't wait," I said, closing the dishwasher and setting the dial.

I hoped Trevor would go to bed early, but it was almost as if he could read my thoughts, and frustrated me by first staying up to watch a gross program about sharks and shark attacks, then wanting to make love. I kept thinking about the envelope in my darkroom, and how odd it would look when I crawled out of bed to go downstairs, when normally after sex I'd roll over and fall asleep.

I decided I'd have to wait until Trevor was asleep himself, then sneak downstairs. If he woke up later on, I could always say I was restless or something. He probably thought I was half crazy anyway, the way I'd been acting lately, and wouldn't see anything I did as too unusual.

At close to midnight, I eased out of the covers and put on my robe and slippers. I tiptoed carefully around the bed and into the hallway, then grasping the stairway banister, slowly descended the stairs. Eerily bright moonlight streamed through the windows. I'd almost made it down to the first floor when a stair creaked. I stopped, listened for sounds of movement coming from the bedroom. Nothing. I inhaled a deep breath, let it out slowly.

My darkroom was located below our bedroom, or more specifically, below the master bath. My studio was directly below the bedroom. If I made too much noise Trevor might hear me, or think we had a prowler. But Trevor didn't own a gun, so at least I didn't have to worry that he'd shoot me and call it an accident later.

I entered the studio, then closed the door and locked it. That in itself would look odd if Trevor did get up and search the house for me. I never locked my studio door, and rarely locked my darkroom since Trevor knew better than to open it if I was working in there. I changed my mind and unlocked the studio door, but kept it shut with the overhead light on.

I closed the door to the darkroom and turned the lock, switched on a small fluorescent lamp, then found the envelope. I sat on a stool, my elbow resting on the counter near the sink.

I drew out the contents of the envelope, dusted off the counter with my arm, then laid the papers down.

I returned to the part about Trevor's father, noticing that he would be eligible for parole in the next year. How did Trevor feel about his dad? Would he be glad if he made parole? I thought for a moment about my own father. What if he had been involved in something shady? Would I have loved him any less? Or would I have instead worried about him, tried to figure out the reasons behind his convoluted thinking, his lack of respect for the law, and his failure to foresee the probable consequences of his actions.

I couldn't ask Trevor about any of this, but I was glad I knew. Before, Trevor always seemed to me so assured and confident, so unscarred by life, and sometimes—not cool exactly—but too removed from the difficulties of ordinary people. Now, it appeared, that wasn't true.

His credit was good, but I'd known that before. That alone said a lot about his character, about his respect for others, about the value of his word, and, of course, the stability of his financial position.

He'd said he had attended college in Sacramento, and that was true, though I had assumed—was it something he'd said?—that he'd graduated. Now I could see that he hadn't. Why lie about that? Pride? To appear on the same educational level as his business associates, his friends? Actually, I could think of several extremely successful men who'd never attended college at all, my father for one, and who instead of hiding the fact, had bragged about it.

Well, whatever the reason, it wasn't a huge deal.

He didn't have a criminal record. He had been issued several tickets, many for speeding, when he was younger. He'd once owned a boat, a small speedboat it appeared.

I was happy to see he hadn't been married before. He wasn't divorced and lying about it, or a bigamist running off to Denver to visit his other wife.

I wondered. Did he ever visit his father in prison? Was it only accidental that he'd moved from California here to Glenwood, in the same state his father was imprisoned? In the time I'd known Trevor, he'd gone to Denver many times, but always, I thought, for business. Perhaps he'd driven a bit farther, to Pueblo.

I continued to read all the minutia of his life, his previous employment record, including his first job as a busboy, the genealogical records of his family, the who, the when, and where of their lives. Trevor probably didn't know a tenth of this, and if he had, most likely would have forgotten it by now.

But I didn't find anything that would make Trevor a likely murder suspect. In essence, I was no further along than before.

I lifted my head, thinking I'd detected a noise outside in the studio. Holding my breath, I watched the doorknob, waiting for it to turn. When it didn't, I eased from the stool and pressed my ear against the door. Finally, after several minutes had ticked by without event, I returned to the stool and slid the papers back into the envelope, placed it on the shelf, and unlocked the door.

The studio door remained shut, as I had left it. I flipped off the light to the darkroom, then the studio, and quietly entered the hallway. Turning my head to peer up the stairs, I tiptoed past them to the kitchen to pour myself a glass of milk—as good a reason to be up as any—in case Trevor was, indeed, awake.

I opened the refrigerator and drew out the milk carton. No, I decided, it didn't appear there was anything in the report that would cast a dark shadow on Trevor. I did wonder, however, why Linda had been so secretive about Wolfgang's report.

Chapter 12

I hired a locksmith to change all the locks in the old house. Just to make sure he didn't damage the old wood doors too badly, I'd watched him for a while as he did his work. But he was a fastidious worker, so after a while I'd roamed the house, particularly the basement.

The police had gotten back with me and found only my own fingerprints on the broken pieces of glass, the remains of a jelly jar I'd saved for whatever reason. Maybe I'd set it too close to the edge of a table, and movement generated from Caroline's and my footsteps on the floor above had finally sent it plunging to the floor. That was what I wanted to believe. In any case, I planned to keep a much closer eye on the house than before.

With Mr. Garvey, a muscular man of fifty or so, installing locks above me on the first floor, I didn't worry too much as I descended the stairs to the basement. I was certain no one was down here now, and was curious to see if I could do a better job than the police at finding signs of an intruder. After all, they didn't know how Linda and I had arranged things.

I stopped momentarily on the stairs to call back to Mr. Garvey. "I'll be in the basement if you need me." Not because I thought he might need me, but in case I needed him.

It was warmer in the basement than in the rest of the house, as the furnace resided there, its tangle of ancient pipes reaching up to the ceiling like arthritic arms. Two basement windows covered by dusty plaid curtains let pale light into the room, and the usual dampness and soggy odor had diminished since summer.

The basement had never been a favorite part of the house for me and my sisters while growing up. Strange sounds emanated from it, especially at night, after we'd gone to bed. Oddly, the noises had abruptly ceased after our father died, making me wonder if he'd been up to something.

I stopped to reach overhead and pull the string for the bulb installed in the ceiling. Instantly, everything was brighter. Still, it all gave me a case of the creeps. Nothing to worry about, I told myself. Only an idiot would still be down here.

There wasn't much to see. The walls were cement block and had never been painted. My dad's tool cabinet, tall and four feet wide, faced the stairs. On the shelves were various saws, hammers, and widgets of all descriptions.

On every table were boxes, most of it Kelly's stuff; other boxes contained my parents' things, mostly items of sentimental value. I checked the outside of some of the boxes for the mold Linda had said she'd found on the ones containing Kelly's journals, but they were dry. I didn't feel like checking the interior of the boxes, which could very well be covered with the stuff.

But nothing seemed at all suspicious, or out of place.

I turned around and studied the dark shadows behind the stairs. Yes, back there, it would be possible for someone to hide, ducking down if an unsuspecting soul began to descend the steps, and they would be close enough to hear the conversations of those on the first floor, maybe even all the way upstairs, on the second floor.

I stood very still, gazing into the shadows. I glanced up toward the main floor, heard Mr. Garvey shifting around, the thud of a tool placed on the floor.

"Was it you?" I asked quietly into the dark void. "Was it you, Kelly? Did you break the glass?"

The shadows remained still, but I felt something, a soft current of air, and I quivered with fright. "You can tell me," I said. "You can. It's okay."

I inched closer, still aware of Mr. Garvey's faint shuffling and scraping overhead. I'd almost reached the shadows when the booming sound of his boots on the top steps brought my head up and around.

"I'm almost done here," he called down, "but I'm going to take a break, have lunch in my truck. You can look over what I've done and see what you think. I'll be sanding and touching up the paint next."

I nodded up to him. "Okay." But stood still and listened as he pounded across the floor and closed the front door. I eased around the stairs and wiped a damp palm on my hip. "Don't be afraid," I said.

A cobweb caught on my face and I wiped it away. Stopping, surrounded by darkness, I turned and looked out into the basement, then ducked my head behind the stairs. I waited for a hand to touch my shoulder, for some sign, my heart thumping wildly. Goose flesh traveled electrified up my spine into the small of my neck.

I waited until I could stand it no longer, then reached farther into the darkness and touched something that made me squeal and run headlong up the stairs. It was slimy and cool, and later, when I'd calmed myself, I realized it wasn't anything other than mold—more moldy boxes.

Mr. Garvey's flashlight confirmed it.

It wasn't, as I'd thought in that instant, Kelly's hand reaching out to me, trying to warn me, telling me who and what to fear.

Chapter 13

Trevor and I arrived at our condo on Friday night overloaded with suitcases, boot bags, and skis. It was five o'clock, almost dark, but the silhouette of Aspen Mountain could still be discerned black against the night sky. Trevor held the key in his hand and smiled as he turned it in the lock.

"This is going to be a great weekend," he said, pushing the door open for me.

I stepped into a wide entrance with a coat closet running along its length. Trevor followed me in, dropping the suitcases and bags on the carpet, then went back outside for the skis. He leaned them, clattering, against the wall.

"Let's look around first," he said, walking forward. "Nice. Very nice." He looked back at me.

"Yes, I agree."

The entrance opened into a spacious living area with a kitchen at the far end. A log fire burned in the fireplace on my left and I could tell from the scent of cherry wood that it was real. "Are you sure we're in the right condo?" I motioned to the fire.

"Yes, she said they'd get it ready for us." He stepped to the counter that separated the living room from the kitchen. "See, chilled champagne." He pulled the bottle from the ice bucket. "And munchies. Cheese, crackers, fruit, salami. But let's not eat now. Let's save our appetite for dinner."

I continued toward the hall on my right to the first bedroom, which contained a king-size bed covered with a multi-colored patchwork quilt. Lamps on either side picked up the rust shades of the spread. Around the corner I found a spacious bath, complete with fluffy towels and a whirlpool tub and shower. A vase of yellow roses sat atop the counter. I finished my tour with a peek into the second bedroom, decorated in the same manner as the first, but this one with twin beds.

Trevor was slicing salami onto a plate when I returned. He shrugged. "Couldn't wait." He handed me a cracker topped with cheese and salami, along with a glass of bubbling champagne.

"Pretty nice, isn't it?" he asked, and I could tell he was looking for my approval since I'd hardly said a word since we'd parked the car.

"Oh, it certainly is. You should see our bedroom. I love the bedspread. And roses too."

"I guess we don't have to dress up too much tonight," he said. "I'm not sure what they have planned. We might be walking into town, or we might go over to their place first."

"When are we supposed to meet them?"

"Actually, I should call."

I carried my suitcase to the bedroom, but tried to listen to Trevor's conversation as I unpacked. I could hear him laughing, his voice rising and falling, his words a little too low to hear clearly, then he was off the phone.

"Six-thirty," he called in to me. "We're going to meet over at their condo."

Though I had showered earlier in the day, my hair looked limp, and I decided more hairspray would only make it worse. And in spite of my efforts not to feel that way, I knew I would be in a competition tonight. I decided to start from scratch and shower again, begin the canvas with fresh paint and clean soft brushes.

By the time I'd spritzed on perfume, I felt I was a match for anything Sylvia could throw at me. I had chosen a long suede skirt and leather boots—the ones with decent tread on the bottom—and a soft burgundy sweater.

"Should I wear my new jewelry?" I asked as I approached Trevor, relaxing on the couch in front of the fire.

He frowned. "I don't know. Maybe save it for tomorrow. I'm not sure where we're going tonight." He stared at my boots. "Are you going to be able to walk in those? There's a lot of snow out there."

"Yes, they're okay."

"You look nice," he added with a smile. "And don't worry. Bob and Sylvia are good people. They're not going to be talking about business with you there."

Sylvia's condo was similar to our own, only the general color scheme differed, this one in contrasting shades of blue and beige.

"Welcome," Bob said, standing aside as we walked through the doorway. "Gwyn, nice to see you again. You're looking as lovely as ever. Hey, Trevor."

I looked around for Sylvia, but she wasn't in the room.

"What can I get you two?" Bob glanced in my direction first.

"The champagne was good."

"We have more." He stepped to the counter and poured me a glass, then looked to Trevor.

"She's right. The champagne was good."

Bob poured another glass for Trevor and one for himself. He held his glass toward ours. "To a fantastic weekend of great skiing and absolutely no work."

"I hear you," said Trevor.

"She'll be out in a minute." Bob motioned toward the bedroom. "She needs to hear the *no work* part of our toast."

"I'm listening, Robert." Sylvia's voice floated in from the hallway. "Now don't go making me out to be some kind of workaholic." She entered, dressed in a red beaded jacket and slim black velour slacks that hugged her petite frame. Her lipstick, nail polish, and earrings matched the red of her jacket exactly. "Hi," she said, taking my hand demurely in her own. "I'm so happy you could join us this weekend. Is everything okay over there? I didn't get a chance to look, myself."

"Everything's great," I said, withdrawing my hand slowly.

"Yes, it is," said Trevor. "Perfect."

She turned to him and patted him affectionately on the cheek. "Mr. Charming, you are. There could be an elephant standing in the kitchen and you wouldn't complain."

"Yes, I would."

She poured herself a glass of red wine and leaned on the counter. "The snow is supposed to be excellent this weekend." She gazed at us. "Sit, sit. Everybody sit." She pushed the air with her hands, driving us toward the grouping of chairs and couch. "We have an entire hour before dinner."

"An hour?" Bob said.

"I pushed it back."

He stared at her.

"It's important, Robert. I have to take the call, here, without interruptions. You can go on ahead. You should go on ahead."

"No," said Trevor. "We're not even hungry. We never eat this early." He looked to me to agree.

"No, we never do. And we ate a lot of that cheese and salami before we came over."

"I'm so selfish," she said, "and you're all so nice to put up with me."

We all shook our heads in unison.

Sylvia collapsed into a chair and crossed her legs. "I love the scent of cherry wood. I always ask for the cherry wood."

I scratched at my ear, feeling as if I were a part of a dutifully respectful audience. I wondered if Sylvia ever bowed and left the stage.

Bob took several trail maps off the end table and shuffled through them. "Does anybody have a preference where they'd like to ski tomorrow? Here? Over at Snowmass? The Highlands?"

I waited for Sylvia to voice her views, but she sat quietly.

"Nobody?" said Bob. "In that case, I say we stay here. That way if I get tired and desire a brewski, I can leave everybody and quit early."

"I might be joining you," said Trevor. "I haven't skied at all this year."

The phone rang and Sylvia popped up and out of the room.

"It will be better when we get out of here," Bob said in an aside to Trevor. "The proverbial shit could hit the fan. She's worried."

"I know," Trevor said.

When Sylvia finally returned fifteen minutes later, her smile was wide with triumph. "Well, let's go. I'm hungry now."

We had reservations at The Silver Strike, a new restaurant in Aspen that Sylvia had heard good things about. Located on Cooper Avenue, it was a few short blocks from our condo complex.

We walked two by two through the frigid winter night, Bob and Sylvia leading the way. I threaded my arm through Trevor's, bringing him close, hoping to send a clear message to Sylvia that she would have a fight on her hands. I also prayed that Trevor was telling the truth, that he wasn't interested in Sylvia, or any other woman for that matter.

We checked our coats at the door. The restaurant was dimly lit, decorated western style, coarse wood beams crisscrossing the ceiling and walls. Thick linen tablecloths and napkins adorned the tables, along with what appeared to be authentic silver silverware. Candles flickered seductively.

The host led us to a reserved table in a secluded corner where we were attended to by several helpers, who offered goblets of ice water and a lavish assortment of bread, cream cheeses, and butter. Our waiter, Hugh, tall and sporting a thin goatee, greeted us soon after.

In his pronounced English accent, he quickly made several wine suggestions, but Sylvia smiled pleasantly and requested a French wine at the top of the wine list. Though no prices were given for any of the wine selections, my guess was that the best and costliest were listed first. Our waiter's delighted grin at the choice confirmed my thinking.

We were not to be insulted with actual dinner menus. Hugh rattled off four gourmet entrees offered that evening—a filet mignon with portabella mushrooms—a seafood medley with crab legs and lobster, flown in fresh this morning from the east coast—a roast leg of lamb accompanied with a "spectacular" mint jelly—and pheasant.

I ordered the steak, not my first choice, but I didn't want to wrestle with crab and lobster shells in front of strangers. Sylvia, as expected, ordered the seafood, and Bob and Trevor ordered the lamb and pheasant, respectively.

"I love Aspen," Sylvia said to the group. "I wish I'd discovered it sooner. And I'm learning to love skiing too, though I'm absolutely frustrated by my inability to get off the easier slopes."

"You've taken lessons, right?" asked Bob.

She waved a hand. "Dozens. I thought about hiring someone

tomorrow, to accompany us, lead us around the mountain—save my ass if I get in trouble." She nodded slightly at me. "Trevor tells me you ski very well."

"I've been skiing a long time."

"So, is that what I need, time on the slopes?"

"Sure ... and patience. It takes a little while to get the basics down."

"Well, that's one thing I don't have. Patience. Maybe you could help me a little tomorrow, and we can skip the instructor?"

"Ah ... an instructor is probably not such a bad idea. I don't think I can teach—"

"Nonsense. No instructor. Gwyn will show us how it's done."

She directed our waiter to bring us another bottle of wine, then with a delicate flip of her fingers, expertly cracked and removed another length of crabmeat from its shell.

I was up by seven the next morning. I could have slept a little longer, but Trevor wasn't being exactly quiet, singing in the shower, using his electric shaver with the bathroom door wide open, and clomping around the bedroom in ski boots.

I looked up from the covers and smirked at him, dressed only in men's briefs and the boots. "Should I ask what you're doing? Is it really going to be warm enough for that outfit?"

"I'm breaking the boots in a little, so my feet don't hurt later. You'd be wise to do the same thing."

"I'll take my chances." I sat up in bed. "What are we doing for breakfast?"

"I don't know. I don't want to take a long breakfast. And the lines could be bad. There's food in the frig. Eggs and English muffins and cereal."

I climbed out of bed. "Okay, then I'll make breakfast."

The sun was shining through the blinds promising a beautiful day for skiing. I opened the front door and looked up toward the steep intimidating face of Aspen Mountain—also known as Ajax—then shut the door against the incoming rush of freezing air. "It's cold out there," I called to Trevor. "Better dress warm, honey."

"I plan to." He stepped from the hall and held up two outfits he'd brought to ski in, a royal blue ski suit, and a maroon jacket and ski pants. "Which do you think?"

"Which one is the warmest?"

"How would I know? I've never worn either one."

"They're probably both good, just wear a thick sweater underneath, a wool one. Which one would you rather wear?"

"I think the jacket. It would be easier to take off when we go inside to eat, but I like the ski suit. You know, I think I'll wear the ski suit." He walked back out of the room.

So glad I could help, I thought, then headed to the kitchen and pulled a carton of eggs and muffins from the refrigerator.

The plan was to meet at the gondolas. We arrived before Bob and Sylvia, and at eight forty-five in the morning, there was already a long line.

"I can't wait to try these skis," Trevor said. "Where are those guys anyway?" He slid his skis back and forth in place on the snow. "The wax seems good. It's not sticking. How's yours?"

"Great, so far."

He pointed at my skis. "Those are the exact same skis a lot of the women World Cup skiers were using last year."

"I know. I'm sure I'll absolutely love them. Good choice."

"You'll have to slow down just so the rest of us can keep up with you."

"Trevor," I said, looking around to make sure Sylvia and Bob hadn't skied up without me noticing, "she's not really expecting me to try and teach her to ski, is she?"

"I have no idea. But don't worry about it. Give her a couple tips and leave it at that."

"I *know* how to ski. I *don't* know how to teach people. There's a big difference between skiing well and having the proper training to instruct someone."

"She probably just said it to make you feel good."

"I doubt that."

"What?"

"Nothing. Is she going to be able to ski here? There's a lot less beginner terrain on Ajax than there is over at Snowmass or Buttermilk."

"Maybe she was exaggerating. Maybe she's a better skier than she let on."

"She'd better be." Then I realized Trevor wasn't listening.

"Hey," he shouted. "It's about time. The lifts close at three-thirty."

"It's nine a.m.," Sylvia called back. "We're right on time."

She was wearing red again, a red ski suit that emphasized every curve, and so tight I wondered how she moved. She didn't intimidate me though. My own navy stretch pants and silvery-blue ski jacket looked just as good, better in fact.

Sylvia sidled up to me, but smiled at Trevor. "What a glorious day."

"Incredible," Trevor agreed.

Each of us reached down toward our ski bindings, unsnapped our boots from the skis, then brought our skis upright. We quickly moved into the line for the gondolas, the crowd so thick now that skiers' bodies pressed against one another, jostling for position. I glanced over my shoulder and saw that I'd already become separated from the group. I suspected Sylvia was responsible for that move. I stopped and waited for the three to catch up, letting the crush of skiers carrying skis and poles push past me.

"The joys of being first on the lift," said Trevor. "It will be better once we're on the mountain."

"I don't know. This isn't so bad," said Bob, "depending on where you're standing." He was positioned behind a tall Nordic-looking blonde. "Anywhere else I could get sued for this."

"Shut up, Robert," said Sylvia.

"What'd I say?"

Finally, it was our turn and the gondola swung in and slowed. Trevor, Bob, and I jumped inside. But Sylvia took so long at the door putting her skis into the slots outside the cab that no other skiers were able to hop on.

"I did that on purpose," she said, stepping in just before the door closed and the gondola picked up speed, "so we could ride with each other in private."

"I'll bet you did," said Bob.

"I did." She stared at us all.

For a while, I ignored their conversation and simply enjoyed the view from the gondola as it smoothly swept us high up the mountain.

Tiny skiers seemed to dance on the slopes below, the town of Aspen disappearing behind us as the cab ascended a rise and sailed past colossal pines toward the farthest reaches of Aspen Mountain.

Finally, the gondola slowed again at the top. We exited and retrieved our skis. The four of us stood there, surveying our trail maps.

"Looks like we can get over to Spar Gulch from here," said Bob, "and that's an easier run. But all the other runs are difficult, true blacks or blues."

"And that's what I'll be if we take them," Sylvia said.

Trevor leaned on his poles, taking in the panoramic view of the mountains. "It would be good to warm up on something easy. I'm for that."

"So am I," said Bob.

"Sure," I said.

Trevor skied off first, then Bob, then Sylvia. I took off last.

I watched as Trevor swung his skis back and forth smoothly over the snow in parallel consecutive arcs, having no difficulty. He was a good athlete, a confident skier who could handle any terrain, though he wasn't at ease on extremely steep slopes. Given that he'd skied only a few years, he'd picked up the sport quickly.

Bob, from what I could tell watching him make a few turns, appeared to be a good intermediate skier. His skis were parallel most of the time, but he skidded his turns instead of carving them. Other than the fact it was early in the season and his form was probably rusty, chances were good he could ski something more difficult, though I couldn't tell on this flat ballroom slope.

Sylvia tried to make parallel turns, but forced them, almost willing her skis to turn. I had no idea what would happen should she end up on something steeper. If she could resort to a good aggressive snowplow, and stopped often to slow her speed, she might be okay.

I liked the skis Trevor had picked out for me, fairly lightweight and not too stiff. They worked the soft snow smoothly, and the edges were sharp, should I hit a patch of ice. Though it didn't appear there would be any ice today, certainly not if the sun stayed out.

We stopped farther up and rejoined.

"Wow," said Bob. "The snow is great." He was breathing hard, and I suspected the altitude had winded him.

"Yes," said Sylvia. "How did I do, Gwyn?"

"Fine. How did you feel?"

"Great, but of course it isn't steep at all here."

"I'm not crazy about steep," said Trevor. "I like the intermediate runs, where I can cruise. And these new skis, I can't believe how great they turn. You'd love them, Bob."

"Yeah? Maybe I should try a pair. What are they? Volkls?"

We continued down, stopping and starting several times, all managing to stay on our feet. I didn't try to show off, though I could have. I could have easily picked up speed and left them all a half-mile back in no time. But then I might also never find them again. And I wasn't about to leave Sylvia alone with Trevor.

We wound our way down the mountain and stopped in the line to a four-place chairlift. Bob and Trevor studied the trail maps again.

"It looks as if we can pick up several different trails from here," said Bob, "including several black runs we need to avoid, unless you and Gwyn want to ski them." He looked up.

"Not particularly," said Trevor. He pointed to a spot on the map. "But here's a great one we might try, Ruthie's to Roch Run."

Bob and Trevor both looked to Sylvia.

"Maybe I'll try that after lunch," she said. "So far I'm having fun on the easier runs."

"True," said Bob. "And we haven't skied this one."

We took the chair up.

It appeared to me that Sylvia was going to make all the decisions unless someone stopped her. As we slid off the chair at the next stop, I sidled over and whispered to Trevor, "Why don't we do Ruthie's ourselves and meet them at the bottom? We're never going to ski anything good this way."

"I can't."

"Why not?"

But he didn't answer because Bob and Sylvia skied over to join us.

"You two go ahead and ski the difficult run," said Sylvia. "Bob and I can do this one and meet you at the bottom."

I looked to Trevor.

"No," he said. "Let's all ski together. It's more fun that way."

Sylvia seemed pleased with that response, but added, "Well, I tried."

I again followed them slowly down the slope, but I was steaming. Eventually, Sylvia crossed the tips of her skis and tumbled. Trevor rushed over to her and gently helped her up. Watching this made me so angry I thought about leaving and skiing to the chair alone, but I knew that was exactly what Sylvia would have liked.

Eventually, I cornered Trevor again. "Are we ever going to get to *ski* anything?"

"Look," he said. "I can't leave them. Obviously, you don't see that. We're their guests. Okay?" His tone softened. "But you go on and ski. I'll make some excuse, say your boots are hurting or something."

"No."

"Why not?"

"I just don't want to."

"Then don't complain."

We stopped for lunch at twelve-thirty, and though we could have stayed on the mountain, we—that is—Sylvia, decided to have lunch in town.

I didn't say a word as I brought my skis through the door of the condo and changed into my snow boots.

Trevor was quiet too. Then, as we walked back out the door, he turned to me. "Would you rather I'd left you at home for the weekend? It's not my fault we're not as free as we'd like to be. But we're here, aren't we? I'm not working."

I nodded.

"And we're skiing," he said. "And now we're going to have a great lunch. I'm having fun. Try to have fun with me. Please."

"I just don't like Sylvia."

"Why not?"

"I just don't."

He frowned, then shook his head. "It's because of what I said before, isn't it? About her being attracted to me. Gwyn, I work with her. I have to be nice, but I'm not interested in her. Don't go and get jealous on me. It's flattering, but it's silly."

"I am not jealous of her. She's bossy and self-centered, that's all."

"Okay, but she's basically *my boss* right now, and this deal is very important to me, so try to remember that the rest of the weekend."

Lunch took an hour and a half, and by the time we were back on the gondola, it was past two o'clock. Again, we took an easy run, the same we had started the day on.

Midway down the slope, Sylvia skied over and stopped near me. "I think I'm ready for that ski lesson now, Gwyn, if you don't mind. My legs feel warmed up enough to try something more difficult, though maybe not right away. What am I doing wrong?"

Trevor gave me a look, and I understood. *Do not say anything that could offend.*

"Well, it's not that you're doing anything wrong really."

Sylvia nodded eagerly.

"But on a slope like this, I like to let the terrain help me make the turn, let the ski do what it's shaped to do. Actually, if you press the ski on its edge into the snow even slightly, it will start to turn." I demonstrated. "Bend each knee into the slope to put the skis on their edge."

Sylvia tried it, but fell. She raised her gloved hands in the air and laughed. "I'm such a klutz," she said, "but don't help me. I can do this myself." She struggled to her feet.

Bob and Trevor watched all this with interest.

"The thing is," I said, "you have to change your approach on a steeper slope, otherwise you'll be going ninety miles an hour into a tree."

"I knew there was more to it," she said.

"Actually, you should practice making"—I hated to say it, since so many skiers considered it a beginner move—"snowplow turns, in tight arcs, very slowly. Because that's what you need to be able to do on a steeper slope if you get into trouble. Also, as a last resort, you can always stop and side-step down the slope until you reach a place you feel confident."

"Snowplow turns? I thought I was all done with those."

"They come in handy," I said, "and even good skiers resort to them if they get in a really tough spot."

"Well then, let's try a more difficult blue run," she said.

I didn't think she could handle it, and I didn't want to be the one responsible should she get hurt. "I really think you should practice the snowplow turns first. It's not as easy as—"

"Oh, everybody knows how to do those."

"Yes," I said slowly, patiently, "they do, for most situations. But you have to realize that a good percentage of the blue intermediate runs here on Ajax are steeper than on say, Buttermilk, or even Snowmass."

"Well, I have to try sometime, and I feel like trying now."

I was wondering if the wine she'd downed at lunch had something to do with her bravado now. I looked to Trevor to talk the woman out of it.

Bob skied up to her. "It's kind of late in the day. I'm getting a little tired. Aren't you?"

"No, I'm not that tired. I plan to celebrate in the bar after we're done. My first steep run on Aspen Mountain." She slid away from him, trying to arc her skis as I'd demonstrated, but fell flat again, losing both skis.

We took Spar Gulch to Grand Junction and made a left turn into Kleenex Corner, then headed toward a blue section called Magnifico. At the very least, it was one of the shorter blue sections on Ajax.

Though it looked easy to me, I knew it wouldn't to Sylvia. The slope dropped off sharply from the easy catwalk we'd been skiing.

Sylvia stared at it, looking back and forth as if trying to decide.

"You don't have to do this, Sylvia," Bob cautioned. "I think you should wait."

"Yes," said Trevor. "Let's continue on down the catwalk. You can save this for tomorrow."

"No," she said. "I want to do it. It's just snowplow turns, right? And I can do those."

Bob shook his head. "Sylvia, this is no time to try and prove something. You're not—"

She shot him a look. "That's not what I'm doing at all. Gwyn, show me again what I'm supposed to do."

I looked toward Trevor, but his face was unreadable.

"Okay," I said, "if we're going to do this, then we need to do it safely. What we'll do is have you traverse across the slope, slowly. First, you'll get into your snowplow position, then traverse across the hill, then plow to a stop. Sound good?"

"Yes, I can do that."

"This would be a good place to start." I pointed to a spot near me on the left side of the slope. "From here you'll ski across the hill at a slight angle. And remember, *never, ever*, point your skis downhill unless you're in your snowplow. In fact, you should keep the skis in a snowplow the entire time."

Sylvia slid into position. I skied to a spot down the slope twenty feet below her on the far right side, then waved for Trevor and Bob to join me. Together we formed a line across the hill. "You can ski toward us. If you do pick up speed, we'll stop you. Use a wide snowplow, Sylvia, really wide. Make sure you don't let the skis come together."

She adjusted her skis, pointing the tips together, her knees bent inward, inches from each other. The tails of the skis were spread apart so that the skis formed a V-shape.

"No—spread the tails wider than that," I said, "as far as you can."

"I'll split my pants," she said, but spread the skis.

"I know it's awkward, but that's the only position that will really slow you down on a steep slope, and it's important to be aggressive and maintain it. *Now one last thing.* If you do get out of control—and you shouldn't—*fall*, just lean over and *fall*. That will stop you."

"Okay." She took a deep breath and exhaled, then with a slight smile began plowing slowly forward. She managed to ski to us and stop. "I'm a little nervous," she said, then looked for sympathy from Trevor.

"You're doing fine," he said.

She continued in this fashion on down the slope. Once, she lost control and slid into us, but everyone laughed, not hurt.

About a quarter of the way down, Sylvia seemed to become a little more at ease with the steepness, and managed twice to traverse across the hill, turn and traverse in the other direction. She stopped and smiled. "I think I can make it the rest of the way down on my own. I don't need you standing there anymore."

I was about to object, but knew she wouldn't listen. Plus I was still angry. Fine, I thought, you're the boss.

"Sylvia, I don't think it's a good idea," Bob said.

"I didn't ask what you thought, Bob."

Trevor kept his mouth shut, but I caught a slight shake of his head.

My guess was that she was trying to impress Trevor, or maybe all of us, otherwise I couldn't see why she'd take the risk.

"You don't need to worry about me," she said, looking back as she started off. "I've got this down."

For a time, it looked as if Sylvia might be right, but I knew that even a second's lapse of concentration could be a serious mistake surrounded by trees as we were. In spite of my anger, I decided to remind her of my previous advice. "Remember, Sylvia, if something goes wrong, make yourself fall. Just lay yourself out on the snow."

She never even turned her head.

We followed her down, and I watched each time she eased into the fall line—the most direct route down the face and the most critical— and held my breath until she'd crossed it and again traversed the hill. We still had half the slope to cover and I could see her legs twitch from the effort her muscles were making to control her speed. Any minute now, I kept thinking.

I knew it would happen, and I saw exactly what started it all. She crossed her tips, only for a moment, but that was all it took. As she turned into the fall line, the skis jerked, locked up, and surprised by it, Sylvia came out of the snowplow and let the skis go parallel.

A split second later, she shot off down the mountain at warp speed.

"Fall," I cried out, taking off after her. "Fall, dammit."

I could hear her squeals of terror as she raced out of control. She was veering right, streaking toward the solid wall of pines. I tucked low, gaining incredible acceleration, realizing in a panic how deadly serious this had all become. If I didn't reach her soon, it would be too late even for me to turn away from the trees. We'd both die.

"*Come on*," I screamed at myself. "*Fasteeer.*" Wind roared in my ears. I could see the pines like grim death ahead, see Sylvia. *Still time, still time.* Careening downward, I raised my body slightly, ready to deliver the blow. I shot in beside her and threw my body forcefully into hers, knocked her off balance. She crashed instantly. I flipped too and went airborne, cartwheeling, spinning through the air, then hit, tumbling over and over, skis and arms and legs flying and spiraling down the slope.

Eventually, I slammed down on my chest—spun crazily to a stop. I couldn't breathe, the wind knocked completely out of me. I lifted my head, saw that all my limbs were still attached, and that I'd missed certain death by six, maybe seven feet. I couldn't see where Sylvia ended up.

Finally, I was able to suck in some air, then tried to move my arms and legs and felt no pain. Nothing appeared to be broken, though my neck hurt.

The men skied up. "God almighty," said Trevor.

I pushed myself to a sitting position and saw that Sylvia was a few yards down from me, not moving. "Sylvia, are you okay?"

She still didn't move, but a small shaking voice issued from the snow. "Yes, my lip is bleeding, but I think I'm okay."

"We need to get the Ski Patrol," said Trevor.

"No," Sylvia said weakly. "I'm okay. Just let me lay here for a minute. Nothing hurts. Just my lip."

Eventually, Trevor and Bob helped each of us up. Sylvia clutched at the two men, her body shaking.

Someone who'd watched it all from the chair must have called for the Ski Patrol, because they showed up with a sled. Though Sylvia protested, she let them tuck her safely inside and tow her down the mountain to the Ski Patrol shack where they checked her for injuries.

They put a small bandage on her bloody lip, and when she insisted again and again that she was okay, they let her leave, warning that it might be prudent to make a stop at the hospital—just to be sure.

I didn't mention my own neck, though I knew it would be really sore by tomorrow.

Despite everything that had happened, Sylvia insisted that we hit the bar, promising not to drink anything stronger than a Coke with a lime.

"I can hold the cold glass against my lip," she said, "bring down the swelling."

Trevor walked beside me as we entered the bar, already filled with skiers celebrating the day's good weather and skiing. "God, Gwyn," he said quietly. "You saved her life."

"Don't remind me."

He laughed. "You really *don't* like her, do you?"

I shrugged, then stopped to rub my neck, pushing my fingers into the soreness.

"Here, let me do that," he said, but removed his hand once we caught up to Sylvia and Bob.

There was no place to sit, except for one seat at the bar. Sylvia took that spot. I stood by while the men ordered drinks, then excused myself and shouldered through the crowd to the john. I combed my hair and washed my hands, wondering how I was going to make it through another day of Sylvia.

As I approached Bob and Sylvia—Trevor was farther off securing a table from a group that was leaving—I overheard Sylvia's harsh accusing words. "From now on I'll make sure I have a *real* instructor, someone who won't get me killed." I shrank back, hoping they wouldn't see how close I'd been. In any other situation, I would have given it right back at her, saying, *I didn't volunteer to teach you, Sylvia.* Or nastier, *Even a real instructor would give up on you—bitch.*

I bypassed the two and walked over to Trevor. He smiled and handed me the glass of wine I'd requested. Maybe when the weekend was over I'd let him know what an ungrateful ass Sylvia had turned out to be.

Bob and Sylvia joined us at the table. I was the only one seated, and as I looked back over my shoulder I saw Sylvia whisper something into Trevor's ear. He saw me watching, frowned and pulled his head away.

He sat down next to me, and Sylvia followed him, anchoring herself between Trevor and Bob at the small round table. She leaned forward and stole a glance at me, a tiny smile forming. "I'll take your advice next time, Gwyn, and hire an instructor. I shouldn't have placed all that responsibility on you."

Was it an insult or an apology? I wasn't sure. Maybe she did know I'd heard the callous remark. "It's okay. Everybody's fine and it was a great day."

She held her glass to her lip, then withdrew it. "Yes, and we have one more day to look forward to."

I didn't like it that Sylvia was sitting next to Trevor. Her hand, the one at Trevor's side, was hidden beneath the table, and I could only guess what she might try doing with it. I suddenly wanted to grab her by the hair and swing her—Tarzan style—up and into the rafters of the bar.

"You're planning to ski tomorrow?" Bob asked Sylvia.

"Of course. All I have is a small cut on my lip, though it does hurt a little to smile." At that, she grinned at Trevor.

I held my empty wineglass toward him. "Could you get me another, honey?"

"Sure. The merlot?"

"Yes."

"Anybody else ready?"

Bob shook his head, siting the two beers in front of him on the table. But Sylvia nodded yes.

As soon as Trevor stepped up to the bar, I scooted over, taking his seat, eliminating any further funny business under the table. I leaned in toward Sylvia and Bob. "It's really hard to hear in here," I said. "Have you two decided where you'd like to ski tomorrow?"

"Well, I always love Snowmass," said Bob, "though we'd have to rent a car or else take the shuttle bus."

"Yes, Snowmass," said Sylvia, turning her face from me and placing the glass to her lip again. "I hate Aspen Mountain."

That evening we again met at Sylvia's condo, and because she had enjoyed it so much the night before, we repeated dinner at The Silver Strike. After the meal and a quick stop at the Red Onion and The Little Nell, we strolled through town, the four of us walking arm-in-arm at Sylvia's insistence. Always, she managed to place Trevor on one side of her or the other.

Finally, I'd had enough.

"Let's go," I said, pulling Trevor aside as we stood before one of the storefronts, admiring ten gallon Stetson hats and impressive leather saddles. "I'm tired."

"It's not late," he said. "It's only ten."

"Please, Trevor." I gave him a look he couldn't fail to understand.

"Okay." He walked forward and put his hands on the shoulders of Bob and Sylvia. "I've got to call it a day, you two. You wore me out."

"Oh-h," Sylvia cooed at him. "It's so early. At least come back to the condo for a while."

"No, can't do it. I'm a sleepy boy."

I smiled at them both. "Well, thanks again."

"Okay," said Sylvia, "then we'll all go back."

I quickly wrapped my arm around Trevor's waist and urged him forward before Sylvia could pull the four of us together again.

Back at the condo, Trevor was quiet, and though I was boiling with anger, I readied myself for bed, determined not to argue with him, afraid I might let everything spill.

He eyed me from across the bedroom. "Anything you want to say to me? I can see the steam coming out of your ears, you know."

I shook my head. "No, I'm fine."

"No, I'm fine," he mimicked in a high whine. "I can tell you're not fine, Gwyn."

"Let's not get into it, okay?"

Naked, Trevor flopped onto the bed and reached over and shut off the lamp, leaving me in darkness.

Still undressing, I turned on the lamp at my side of the bed.

"Maybe you should sleep in the other room," he muttered, not looking at me.

I suddenly wanted to slug him and cry at the same time. I'd been hoping … needing, actually, for him to hold me. After all I'd been through today. "Sure, I can do that. I'd be glad to do that." I stomped around the foot of the bed and past him out the door.

I yanked down the blankets on the twin bed across the hall.

"Gwyn?" he called out.

I refused to answer.

"Gwyn, baby?"

"What?"

"Come to bed, okay?"

I crept to my doorway, stood there, snuffling back a tear.

"Please?" he said.

I hesitated, then raised my chin and walked over. He reached up and drew me down on top of him. "I'm sorry," he said, kissing my cheek. "I'm a dick. You forgive me?"

"No." And then … "yes."

He rolled me beneath him, tucked his hands into my bra and released my breasts, then eased the straps away and unlatched the bra. His breath was warm on my face, and I could catch traces of the cologne he'd worn earlier. I heaved a sigh, excited.

"Never go to bed mad," he said, his voice low, his kisses trailing alongside my hair, my ear.

"Should we turn out the light?" I asked, shutting my eyes, wrapping my arms around him.

"No, let's leave it on." His mouth moved in slow hypnotic circles down the side of my neck, while his hand deftly pulled at my panties. I wiggled out of them.

"I need you," he said, entering me, filling me completely. I thrilled to his touch, warmed to the sensual rhythm as I lifted my pelvis close, scooped him up, squeezed him. I rotated against him—stoking the fire, again and again.

He reached between my legs and touched me, and it was like an electric shock. He began to stroke softly, slowly, round and round ... taking me higher ... hotter, then moving faster, working me into a frenzy. I clenched with ecstasy as he brought me almost to the brink. "Do you want it?" he said. "Do you want it?"

"Yes ... yes."

"Then, take me," he groaned. "Take me. Fuck me."

For over an hour, he concentrated his attention on every available crevice of my body, bringing me to the edge, then back again, making my heart race, driving me crazy, as it seemed he was always, and easily able to do.

Afterwards, I lay spent, perspiring, my body limp—satisfied. I looked over to him. He lay on his back, hands behind his head, looking up at the ceiling. He turned and smiled at me. "I'm dead," he said. "You killed me."

"You killed me first," I said, grinning back at him, and was suddenly struck by the depth of my love for this man. I was in deep—way, way too deep.

The next morning, Trevor and I met Bob and Sylvia for breakfast at a quaint gourmet restaurant, one of my favorites, complete with lace curtains and delicately embossed silver coffee and teapots. I ordered coffee and a western omelet. Trevor ordered eggs Benedict, and Sylvia, thinking Trevor's choice a wonderful idea, ordered it too. Bob chose a tall stack of pancakes.

Though Sylvia wanted to rent a car equipped with a rooftop ski rack for the trip to Snowmass, Bob insisted it would waste time and wasn't necessary for the one day. Instead, we waited for the shuttle bus, which picked us up promptly at ten o'clock.

Sylvia had removed the bandage from her lip, and I could barely tell that she'd been injured at all. My neck was sore, but this morning's hot shower and a large dose of ibuprofen had helped to take my mind off it.

The bus was only half filled with skiers, so the four of us were able to find seats near each other. Trevor and I sat together. Sylvia and Bob sat directly behind us. Trevor was on the aisle and turned around frequently to talk to them. I wasn't interested in talking, but I did listen.

"I spoke with the ski school earlier," said Sylvia, "and my instructor will meet us out in front of the building."

"So," asked Bob, "are you going to be able to ski with us?"

"Of course," she said, "for the money I'll be paying him, he should be happy to accommodate me in any way I choose."

"How do you know it will be a *him*?" asked Trevor.

"Because I asked. His name is Andreas."

I heard Bob laugh softly, then some whispering, then a smack, as if Sylvia had slapped Bob on the lap.

"Stop it," she squeaked. "If you're going to tease me, you can move to the back of the bus."

He laughed again, then the conversation settled down to comments about the sunny weather and the rising price of lift tickets and its affect on skiing as a whole.

The four of us met at the ski school and collected Sylvia's instructor, a great looking guy, maybe thirty-five years old, tall and broad shouldered with a pronounced Austrian accent. His hair was a thick blond, and he wore silver Oakley sunglasses that perfectly matched his blue and silver ski suit.

As we made our introductions, Andreas removed his sunglasses and slid them atop his ski hat, revealing friendly and knowledgeable blue eyes. I decided as I looked him over that Andreas had summed up our party pretty quickly, and likely his only real concern would be how thick a wad of cash would be in his hands by the end of the day.

Sylvia gave him the game plan, and of course, he acquiesced to all she suggested.

"If one of the others wants a little help, could you do that?" she asked. "Of course, I'd compensate you."

"Certainly," he said, his smile as bright as the sun overhead.

He bypassed the long line to the chairlift and led our party to the front, our privilege for paying for the lesson. Sylvia had hired him for the entire day.

Bob and Trevor high-fived one another as the chair carried us up the mountain. Sylvia rode with her instructor. Bob, Trevor, and I rode up on the chair immediately behind them.

"All day it's going to be like this," Bob said. "What a great idea. Hire an instructor to cut the lines."

"I know," said Trevor. "Pay him and tell him to leave you the hell alone. Can you do that?"

"Why not?" said Bob. "He's getting paid. Instruct him not to instruct. Tell him you just want to ski. Why would he give a damn?"

"Yeah, why would he? Unless he's got some kind of ego problem."

Sylvia looked back from the chair and waved. Trevor and Bob waved back. I lifted my hand, sort of, then dropped it into my lap.

We took the chair halfway up the mountain in the direction of Sam's Knob, a peak Andreas told us would be our ultimate destination this morning. And morning was rapidly departing. My watch read eleven twenty-two.

Once we were again on the snow, Andreas took Sylvia aside, presumably to test the limits of her skiing ability. Trevor and Bob hovered nearby, while I waited not so patiently for instructions from my husband. Today I'd promised to do whatever he asked, no questions.

I watched as Andreas led Sylvia through some kind of drill, demonstrating bending his knee into a turn, exaggerating it, helping her repeat the move. Once, he glanced over at me, and I could only surmise that Sylvia had given him her version of the near disaster the day before. *And then she purposely led me down a run I had no business on. Tried to kill me, in fact.*

Andreas motioned to us, told us to go on ahead, to meet him and Sylvia at the bottom near the chair.

Finally, I could let loose. I swooped down the mountain, bypassed the beginner run and instead dropped into a blue run, Velvet Falls, waving for Trevor and Bob to follow. They did, and the three of us whooped and hollered on our way down, not stopping until we'd reached the bottom of the slope near the chair.

I was laughing, out of breath.

"Wow, you were great, Gwyn," said Bob. "I saw that little jump, but I was afraid to take it, but not you."

"I probably shouldn't have. I don't know how well these bindings are set. I could have released on the landing."

Trevor smiled at me too, then looked up the slope. "I think that's them over on the right."

Sylvia and Andreas slowly made their approach. Sylvia was all smiles. They stopped and she reached up, placed her hand on her ski instructor's shoulder. "According to Andreas, I'll be skiing like a pro by the end of the day."

He pointed skyward. "Ve'll be going all da vey to da top of Sam's Knob dis time."

Again, Sylvia and Andreas took the first chair and we followed behind. I was glad Sylvia had hired an instructor because it looked as if she wouldn't get an opportunity to sit near Trevor the entire afternoon.

From the top, ski runs spread out in several different directions down the face. Andreas led Sylvia off onto Max Park, another beginner run, and the three of us took Banzai Ridge, a blue run that paralleled Max Park until it turned into an easy green run, Lunch Line, and traversed the mountain. Again, we were to meet them at the bottom.

I led the way down the slope—finally having fun. I cruised at high speed, aware that Bob and Trevor were somewhere behind me. I stopped just past the Lunch Line cutoff and waited for the two men, but only Bob came into view and skied up beside me.

"What happened to Trevor?" I asked.

"Don't know. He was behind me. Maybe he stopped for something."

We waited for several minutes, then continued on down. I wasn't worried. This run wasn't difficult. Trevor could handle it easily. Maybe he was fiddling with something, or had taken a freak fall and was dusting himself off.

We waited at the bottom, and I was disgusted to see Trevor come into view skiing slowly down the mountain with Sylvia and Andreas.

Trevor and Andreas were having a conversation as they skied up, then Trevor slid over to me. "Thought I'd take advantage and get some pointers. He's good."

At first I didn't say anything—then, "Thanks for telling me. I didn't know what happened to you."

"I ran into them at the cutoff and Andreas yelled over for me."

"Oh, I see."

I didn't talk much to Trevor until lunch at the restaurant atop Sam's Knob. Though I was pissed again, it wouldn't do any good to express it, because I'd agreed earlier to be a good girl today and not cause trouble. Trevor would be the first to remind me of it.

After lunch, we headed to the Big Burn, the entire top of that peak covered with long wide-open cruising runs, mostly blue, intermediate, and easy. Sylvia would have room to maneuver without putting her thick skull in danger.

Even so, she appeared to be frightened, and wasn't waving back at us from the chair as she had the entire day. She sat close to the instructor, who probably also sensed her fear, and placed his arm behind her on the chair.

This time I waited for Trevor to begin skiing first, so he couldn't dart off and leave me. But he stayed with Bob, the two of them watching Sylvia's slow progress down the slope.

I was impressed with Andreas. Whatever he had done, whatever he had said to her was actually working. He had brought about a change in Sylvia's skiing. She was doing better, her turns exhibiting a fluidity of motion I wouldn't have thought possible in so short a time. Partway down the Big Burn, Andreas instructed her to follow him, repeating his turns, slowing her down.

Sylvia was jubilant by the time we stopped for a rest near the chair. "I love him," she said as Andreas skied over to cut the line. "I have his card. I'm never going to hire anyone else. I told him I'd pay him double, triple, what he normally gets for a lesson. I may ask him to move in with me for the winter."

We stayed on the Big Burn for the rest of the afternoon, Sylvia more eager to continue than anyone else.

Bob had tired and was anxious to call it a day.

"Oh, one more run," Sylvia pleaded with him. "Just one more."

"You go," he said. "I think the rest of us are done."

"Are you, Trevor?" she asked.

He shrugged.

She glanced at me. "I don't think so, Sylvia."

"Oh, all right. Andreas and I will ski one more time and meet you down here, unless you don't want to wait for me."

"We'll wait," said Bob.

The three of us found an empty picnic table facing the slopes, and Bob and Trevor ordered beers from the slope-side café and brought them outside into the sunshine.

"It's been a great weekend," said Bob. "I'm glad the two of you could make it. We'll have to do this again soon."

"You name the day," said Trevor.

Not in this lifetime, I thought, but said agreeably, "Yes, we had a great weekend, Bob. Thank you so much, for everything."

"I can't take the credit," he admitted. "It was totally Sylvia's idea, but she gets some great ideas, like bringing Trevor on board. That was one of her best."

And I remembered suddenly the conversations I'd had with Trevor when the project started, only Robert Morris was mentioned. Sylvia didn't exist as far as I knew.

I didn't risk a look at Trevor, better to play dumb about this too.

But I wondered, later, as I packed up to leave for home, just how long Trevor had actually known Sylvia Breslin.

Chapter 14

Feeling vulnerable, I crossed my arms as I walked into Janet's office the following Wednesday morning. Somehow, needing to see my therapist again felt like a personal failure. But it was all so confusing now. I didn't know whom to trust, what to believe, where to turn.

Janet stood in the corner of the room, closing a file drawer. She looked up at me and smiled. "Hi, Gwyn. Cold out there, isn't it?"

"Yes," I said, unfolding my arms. "And it's snowing pretty hard."

"Supposed to get five inches."

"Yes, I heard that too." I settled into my favorite chair facing the window and watched as snowflakes fell softly out in her courtyard.

She walked over and took a seat across from me.

"How are things with you, Gwyn?"

"Well, you know, just once I'd like to come in here and say, wonderful, never better. But, of course, I'd be lying."

Janet laughed softly. "Well, maybe that day isn't too far off. You do appear troubled, tense. Am I right?"

"If I were a coiled spring I'd be bouncing around the room."

"That bad."

"I suppose I should have made an appointment sooner than this. I haven't been following your advice. I've been keeping things, a lot of things from you. But I really hoped to handle this on my own. Unfortunately, I can't."

"Oh."

"I found a letter that my sister Kelly wrote. She must have written it shortly before she died. I'm certain she didn't want me or Linda to find it, because it was taped to the inside of her dresser. The only reason I did find it was because it came loose and got caught as I was trying to open the drawer. She wrote that she'd been screwing her 'sister's boyfriend' and was scared for her life. She also implied that this man may have killed a woman, a girlfriend possibly. That part wasn't clear. She also said there was a box, that he may have found 'the box.' I have the letter in my purse if you'd like to see it."

"Yes, I would."

I handed it to her.

Janet read it, then looked up at me. "How long have you had this?"

"Since around Halloween. And there's something else I'm very worried about, though I don't know if one has anything to do with the other. I think Trevor may be having an affair, possibly with a woman I met this past weekend. I'm not certain about the woman. It could be someone else. And I could be wrong altogether. I hope I am. But I came home after a weekend away and smelled another woman's perfume on my pillow. It definitely wasn't mine."

"This letter does seem authentic. If it is, then I definitely would be worried too. Who else have you told about this?"

"Linda, she's the only one."

"And what did she say?"

"Actually, she refused to believe it. She thought that Kelly made it up, that she wanted us to find it, in order to drive us crazy. Of course, Kelly did write a lot of fiction, short stories, poems, but nothing like this. And if she was making it up, why would she hide it?"

"Linda didn't suggest that you notify the police?"

"No, not at first. But I didn't want that either. Not until we could find out more. We've since hired a private investigator to do a background check on Trevor and Wolfgang."

"And?"

"And ... nothing. Nothing at all," I said, choosing to leave out the information about Trevor's father. It didn't seem sufficiently relevant at this point.

"Nothing on either man?"

"Well, I didn't see Linda's report. She wouldn't let me. But she swore there was nothing bad about Wolfgang. Unfortunately, I have a difficult time believing that." I shifted in my chair. "And there's a third person that Kelly could have been talking about, Josh, the guy I dated just before Trevor. I can't see how he could possibly be involved in any of this, but he *was* my boyfriend, and he *did* know Kelly very well."

"Gwyn, I think you should give this letter to the police and let them handle it."

"And not tell Trevor? But maybe I should tell him first."

"No. I don't think so. I mean—"

The look on her face scared me. "God, Janet, it's not Trevor. It's not. Trevor couldn't hurt a fly. And what if Linda is right? What if Kelly made it up? I love my husband. We're not on solid ground as it is. If he finds out I've kept all this from him, spied on him, and then the police pick him up...."

Janet stood. "That shouldn't be your main concern. And I don't think you should let anyone know you've confided in me either."

"Not even Linda?"

"No. I hesitate to say this, because it could be nothing, but you've told me that Linda and Kelly didn't get along. Did it ever occur to you that Linda found out about the affair?"

"Well, actually, it did, but I didn't.... She would have said something."

"She would have? You're certain of that?"

"You're not saying that Linda could in any way be responsible, are you?"

"I don't know. My only concern is you."

I turned and faced the window.

"I'm sorry if I've scared you, Gwyn. I can't be sure if your sister is hiding anything. But not showing you the report on Wolfgang, suggesting Kelly's letter has no significance, not insisting you both contact the police—"

"Linda did ask if we should go to the police. At the library, after she gave me the background check. I was the one who thought we should wait. I hadn't read Trevor's report yet."

"Well, then certainly that could change things, but the police still need to know what's going on."

I turned again to face her. "Everything I say in here is confidential, isn't it? It doesn't leave this office?"

"Of course."

"I'll think about what you've said, Janet. I'll give it some serious thought. Then I'll make my decision."

She slumped back in her chair.

"Don't worry. I'm not planning to get myself killed. But as far as I'm concerned, the police haven't done such a hot job of finding the man they believe murdered my sister, and I can't think of any reason I should trust them now."

I was so unnerved on the drive home that I didn't see the squirrel dart over the snowbank and under my wheels until it was too late. I screamed, waiting for the telltale thump, then swiftly checked the rearview mirror. The squirrel had made it to the other side of the road. I watched as it scampered up a tree.

Janet had to be wrong. Linda had nothing to do with any of this. She loved Kelly, would never have hurt her. How ridiculous to even suggest it. But ... would she cover for Wolfgang if she suspected that *he* was somehow involved? Loving him as obsessively as she did, would she choose to look the other way?

And the journals. Why did Linda throw out the journals? Was it really because they were moldy? Or was she afraid of what I might find in them?

Chapter 15

I stared at the phone in my studio. The number for the City of Glenwood Springs Police Department stared back at me on the speed dial. I picked up the receiver and listened to the dial tone, then carefully placed the receiver back down.

Instead, I dialed Linda.

She didn't answer, and I waited as the answering machine voiced the recorded message, then beeped. I left my own message. "Hi Linda, received your invitation to the party. Of course, Trevor and I will be there. Just wondering about the dress code. Formal as usual? Call me back."

I gazed across the studio at the easel turned to the wall, then rose and walked toward it. I studied the half-finished portrait of my youngest sister, then took a seat facing her. Maybe if Kelly and I stayed here together, some thought would come.

I picked up my palette and selected several tubes of paint, squeezed a dollop from each. I studied the photograph tacked to the wall and positioned the easel, then picked up a fine-tipped brush. Concentrating, I watched the brush move, as if guiding my hand, down the curve of my sister's cheek.

An hour later, Linda called.

"Got your message," she said, "though, of course, I assumed you'd be attending the party."

"Yes, but I thought it might be nice to call anyway."

"And the dress is semiformal, same as last year. We are planning to do something a little different after the party. It's not my idea, believe me, and you're not obligated to join in, though it might be fun. Then again, maybe it will be too cold."

"What?"

"Wolfgang wants to rent snowmobiles, go tearing around the property on the trails, have everybody bring warm clothes and change, build a bonfire. It's a radical idea."

"For sure. And we do this after the party's over?"

"Yeah."

"Well, that is different."

"Maybe we can just let the men go out on their own."

"They'll all be drunk."

"True, though I could have the bartender water down the drinks after the first couple. I just may do that. But you're right. It's probably not the best timing."

"I'll mention it to Trevor."

"So, how's everything? Looking forward to Christmas?"

Not especially, I wanted to say, but instead gave a stock answer. "Sure, but I have a lot of shopping left to do. I've barely started on Trevor's gift list."

"What does he want?"

"Oh, whatever I decide to give him, but nice, of course. I have a few things, a watch he mentioned, cuff links, a leather jacket he admired and tried on a few days ago. And he wants a sports car, maybe a Porsche, to drive around this summer. Though I can't exactly put that under the tree."

"No."

"Is Wolfgang there?"

"No, he's still at work."

"I've been thinking. Maybe we should inform the police about the letter."

"What now? Right now? Before Christmas, before I go on vacation, before my party? No, bad idea. Very bad idea."

"Then when?"

"I don't know, but not now. And I thought we were going to do a background check on Josh, first. Isn't that what we said?"

"We're not detectives, Linda. We're two scared wives afraid that someone's going to send our husbands to jail. We're not equipped for this. We can't think rationally."

"No, we're being sensible. I'm still not sure Kelly didn't make it up, or exaggerated it, or—"

"You know she didn't."

Linda was silent, and I could almost sense her shifting gears. "And how do you think showing the police the letter is really going to help us? What? Now they'll stop looking for Craig? Who, by the way, they haven't been able to locate so far.... So now they'll focus on our husbands, or maybe poor Josh, the guy you've already put through holy hell and doesn't deserve any more crap from you than he's already gotten. And if it does turn out that our husbands are innocent, or even guilty, but with no evidence to convict, how do you suppose they're going to feel about us? I don't see Wolfgang massaging my back with scented oils after putting him through all that."

"We can't just sit and wait, Linda."

"All right. Then we'll do it after I get back from Hawaii. Please, Gwyn, don't spoil my vacation. I deserve a break from all this. We both do. Come on, how much possible difference can a few weeks make?"

I hesitated, frustrated, growing angry. "All the difference in the world. Anything could happen. I don't like this at all. I'm scared."

"Please, Gwyn. I don't ask much from you. Do this for me. It's going to be okay. Really."

"I don't know."

"*Please*, Gwyn."

"*All right. We'll wait.* But I'm going to the police with or without you as soon as you're back."

"And I promise I'll go too."

Chapter 16

I was just finishing my breakfast when the doorbell chimed, followed by a loud knock. I stepped into the foyer and glanced toward the snowy drive, but didn't see a car. Putting my nose to the beveled glass beside the door, I glimpsed a square ribboned box a foot or more high on the porch.

I opened the door a crack and cautiously stuck my head outside. My first thought was that it might be Caroline playing a joke. She was supposed to stop over later, but maybe she'd changed her mind and arrived early. I reached down to pick up the package and as soon as I touched it, it emitted a howl. I jumped back, then heard the whimpering cries of a puppy.

"Oh, for pity sakes," I said, lifting the box and bringing it inside. As I tore away the wrappings, I noticed round air holes cut into the back of the package. Inside was a floppy-eared puppy, a tiny bejeweled collar around its neck, a child's pink blanket beneath it. The puppy, a cocker spaniel it appeared, eyed me quizzically, attempted to throw up, then stopped and panted. I bent down to read the gold tag at its neck. *My name is Annabelle.* I checked the box for a note, but didn't find anything, then stopped to pet the pup, who was feeling comfortable enough now to put its front paws on the edge of the box and gaze around.

My cell phone began to ring in the kitchen. I ran and picked it up off the table.

"Hello?"

"Hi, Gwyn. Did you like your present?" It was Josh, laughing softly.

"Joshua Newbury," I said in mock anger, "you wrapped her in a box. She was scared."

"Sorry, but it was only for a minute. And I was watching. I wrapped her up in the car and walked her to the door. My sister's dog had a litter and I thought of you, remembered thinking you needed someone to protect you while your husband's away. But you don't have to keep her."

Back in the entrance with the puppy, I lifted her into my arms. She swiped at me with a wet tongue. "I'm not sure how much protection she'd be."

"Well, maybe not a lot, but she can make a lot of noise."

"Yes, I've noticed that."

"Could I come in?"

"Sure—umm, Caroline might drop over soon."

"Oh. Then maybe I should wait."

"No, don't be silly. Come on in."

This time, Josh didn't park in the drive, but arrived at the door on foot.

"Where's your car?" I asked as I let him in.

"Down the road. I felt like walking."

The puppy began to wiggle in my arms at the sight of Josh and I handed it over to him. "I guess she's forgiven you for the whole box thing."

"I guess." He smiled at me, but he looked tired. His eyes seemed dull and his complexion pale. "Well, Merry Christmas, Gwyn, though like I said, you don't have to keep her."

I was wondering what I would tell Trevor. *Funny thing, Josh stopped over this morning and gave me a Christmas present, thought I might need a dog since you're away so much.*

He must have guessed what I was thinking, because he added, "I don't expect you to tell Trevor I gave you the puppy. Maybe you could say Caroline brought it over or something."

"Yes, she'd probably agree to that."

I took Annabelle from Josh. "She's so cute. I could build a little fenced area for her to play in, until she's trained." The pup looked up at me with heart-melting brown eyes. "Are you hungry, Annabelle?" I asked, hugging her to my chest and kissing her on the head.

"Well," he said, "I guess I'll go back out and bring in the puppy chow I left in the car. It appears you've made your decision." He glanced at his watch. "And then I should get going. Wish I could stay longer."

"Are you sure? I could show you the studio. You missed it the last time. And Caroline probably won't be here for at least a half-hour."

"Well, maybe I could stay a few minutes more."

As soon as we walked into the studio, Josh noticed my portrait of Kelly. "When did you start to work on it again? You've accomplished a lot," he said, walking over to it.

"Recently, since I saw you."

"It's beautiful. She would have liked this. It captures her perfectly, the subtle mystery in her eyes ..." He turned sharply to me, I suppose to see if he'd hurt me with his comment.

"Thanks," I said. "I think she would have liked it too."

He redirected his attention to my other works in progress, nature scenes and the like. "I can see why your work sells so well. Such fine detail, and your sense of color is inspired. Will you let me buy something? Please? I'd really like to."

"Sure, pick something out." I motioned to the finished paintings hanging on the walls. "And no, I won't let you buy anything."

"Gwyn."

"Consider it a Christmas present—from me."

"Then how about this one?" he said, moving across the room toward the far wall. I turned my head to see which one he meant. I'd forgotten about it, had painted it years ago.

"Yes, this is the one I want."

It was a small painting, a self-portrait—me—standing in my garden, arranging a vase of wild flowers, wearing a yellow sundress. I'd staged the shot, took it using a timer and tripod. I'd been trying out some new photographic equipment.

"Yes, this one," he said.

"That's so old. Look, there's even dust on the frame. You can pick a better one than this."

"No arguing. You said I could pick."

"Okay. It's yours." I lifted it from the wall and placed it in his hands.

He stared at the picture, then at me. "Well, I'm off. Tell Caroline I said hi. And good luck with the puppy. Hope it works out. If not, give me a call. Maybe give me a call anyway."

"I will. Thanks, Josh."

He placed his hand gently on my shoulder. "And thank you for my present. Have a great Christmas, Gwyn."

"You too."

I watched from the window as he trudged down the snowy driveway, then onto the road, the painting cupped in his hand.

By the time Caroline arrived, I'd carried Annabelle out to the drive twice to do her business, and the pup was quickly taking possession of the kitchen, sniffing every chair and table leg, puppy paws clicking as it ran in sudden bursts across the tile floor.

"What's this?" Caroline asked, standing in the foyer.

"This is Annabelle."

I tried to lift the pup from a spot near my feet, but she tore into the kitchen.

"When did this happen?"

"This morning, when you gave her to me."

"What?"

"Josh brought the pup by. His sister's dog had a litter. He thought I might like one. I'm hoping I can say you gave it to me so I don't have to explain to Trevor. Is that okay?"

"Sure, I guess. But are you sure you want to do that? Lies have a way of backfiring, you know."

"Don't try and sound like my shrink. Better to lie than to listen to Trevor not talk to me for hours."

"O–kay."

"You working today?"

"Nope. Nope. Nope. Today I am shopping. You can join me if you like, though one of the presents I was going to shop for is yours."

"No thanks. I don't feel like shopping, and I don't want to leave the pup alone right away."

We walked into the kitchen where I'd already brewed coffee and warmed a pound cake.

"You planning to go to Linda's party?" I asked, slicing a piece of cake and lifting it onto a plate for Caroline.

"I guess."

"Bringing anyone?"

"Okay, now I know why you wanted me over. Details."

"No, but I am curious."

"Nate and I have a date this weekend, and if it goes well, maybe I'll invite him to the party too."

"Sounds like you and Nate are doing a lot of laundry lately."

"Hah," Caroline said with a laugh. "I've got more clean clothes now than when my mom did my laundry."

"The couple that scrubs together.... Oh, I don't know. What rhymes? Rubs together?"

"We're not doing any rubbing yet. But I have to say I wouldn't mind. God, he's cute."

"What do you know about him?"

"Enough. He moved here four years ago, because they offered him a job. I guess he used to live in Crowley. He's not married. He let me know that right away. He doesn't have any kids either, and he's not moaning over some broken romance and boring me to death. He actually has some smarts."

"I like him already."

"Yeah, so do I. But I hate that giddy stuff, looking in the mirror every two seconds to see if I've left spinach in my teeth. I want to be past all that." Caroline brought a fork full of cake to her mouth, then glanced toward the floor. "Well, what's this? Annabelle wants to be one of the girls and eat too. She's chewing my shoelace."

"I hope Trevor is okay about the dog. Normally, I'd give him some notice. Actually, he might think it's a good idea, think it's better for me to have some company during the day."

"Yeah, he could. And she is a cutie." Caroline lifted the puppy into her lap, and it immediately brought its paws up and tried to leap onto the table. "No, no, Annabelle. Down you go. Bad Annabelle." She placed the puppy back on the floor. "She's a handful." Caroline's smile quickly dissolved into a frown. "Hey, what's that look you're giving me? What's wrong?"

"I've got something I need to show you. It's the real reason I asked you over here."

"What?"

"I should have told you before. But ... this is so bad, I wasn't sure I wanted to involve you. I'm still not sure."

"What is it? Is this about Sylvia?"

"No. Here." I handed her Kelly's letter.

She read it, then looked up at me.

"Where did you get this?"

"I found it taped inside Kelly's dresser—hidden. I've had it since Halloween. I think Kelly must have written it right before she died. No one knows about it except Linda, my shrink, and now you."

"God."

"We've hired a private investigator—well—Linda hired one. I didn't know of a good one."

"This is unbelievable. How did Linda react to it?"

"Not good. She's in denial. She wants to believe Kelly made it up. I think if it were up to her, she'd destroy the letter and pretend she never saw it. And I still haven't told her the rest. I haven't told her about Trevor, that he might be cheating on me. She'd blame him, say he's a cheat and a murderer. But he's not. If anyone's a murderer, it's Wolfgang. So far, all we've done is a background check. And Linda won't show me the report on Wolfgang. Says there's nothing in it. She's treating this whole thing like it's all going to blow over. They're even planning a trip to Hawaii over Christmas and New Year's. I can't talk Linda out of it."

"Whoa. That doesn't sound like a good idea. Do you think Wolfgang suspects anything?"

"I don't know. God, you'd think Linda would have better sense than to tell him. But she's so stupidly in love with the guy, who knows what she'll do? I've warned her. I think she has an idea of how dangerous the man could be—for both of us."

"And—I have to ask this. But what makes you so certain it's Wolfgang?"

I could feel my face warm at the question. "Why? You don't think it's Trevor, do you?"

She shook her head. "I'm totally—I have no idea. Was there anything that could implicate him in the background check?"

"No. Nothing. He's never been in jail. He's never done anything."

"Well, that seems promising."

"What I really need is to find another investigator, one who will dig deeper. And I don't want to tell Linda about it."

"Why not?"

"Because she doesn't want to face the truth about Wolfgang. She won't pursue this. I need to find out what he's up to—and fast. And I want to do some checking on Trevor, not because I think he's a murderer. I need to know if he's cheating on me."

"Gwyn, this is serious business. You have to go to the police. *Kelly is dead.* This guy's not fooling around. If he finds out—"

"That's exactly why I *can't* go to the police, not yet. What if they botch things and decide to interrogate the guys? Either man could retaliate, or at the very least skip town, like Craig did. The cops never found him. It's too big a risk. Right now, I have the advantage. I think I should keep it that way."

"Yeah, but I still think you should go to the police."

"And I plan to, as soon as I have something more to give them than this letter. That's why I'm going to hire my own investigator. Do you know anyone that's good?"

"I've never hired a private detective, but I guess I could ask Nate. He should know of a good one."

"And don't tell him it's for me."

"Geez, I hate to start out by lying to the guy. But I suppose I could say that somebody at the bar asked about one, and wants to keep it hush, hush. Yeah, I guess I could do that. I'll call him as soon as I get home. I'll get in touch as soon as I know something."

"Okay, great. Thanks, Care. I really, really appreciate this."

"You might want to think about hiring yourself a bodyguard too. I'd sure feel better if you did."

"I think Trevor might notice someone hanging around."

She shook her head. "You're scaring me, Gwyn. Big time."

"I shouldn't have told you."

"No, you definitely should have, and before this."

"I was worried for you. I guess I figured the less people that knew, the better."

"Gwyn—about Kelly's letter. You didn't say it, but you do realize she may have been talking about Josh too. Right?"

"You can't believe that any more than I do."

"No. But I had to mention it."

After Caroline left, I got a call from Trevor. He wouldn't be home until after eight, though he'd thought earlier he would be home in time for dinner. Some contracts needed signing. Details of the transactions required clarification, and whereas it was supposed to be done tomorrow morning, it turned out it would have to be settled tonight. He was apologetic—too much so. I didn't mention the puppy, since he sounded so harried already.

I couldn't sit still, so drove into town to the pet store to buy Annabelle some things she needed, a doggy bed, leash, and toys to chew. I brought her with me in the Jeep, first disconnecting the passenger-side airbag with my key, then snugged her into an old blanket on the front seat. She appeared to laugh at me and just as quickly unsnugged herself and disappeared into the recesses of the Jeep—leaving me to wonder about her safety. I did prepare for her rapid-fire running sprees at the pet store with a makeshift leash I'd fashioned from a rope I'd found out in the garage.

After the purchases, I drove by the old house. Dusk was slowly turning to dark. I pulled the Jeep to the opposite side of the street and turned off the engine, then watched for several minutes as the lights inside the house switched on. I just had a feeling I couldn't shake.

For a half-hour I trained my eyes on the front window, crouched low in my seat, Annabelle watching too, apparently sensing something afoot. Just as I was about to call off my vigil, a human shadow passed behind the curtains. I stiffened, hair rising at the back of my neck. I ducked lower as the silhouette stopped, stood for a moment, then backed away. Though the curtains were drawn, they were also thin. The intruder was possibly unaware of how easily he could be seen.

I dialed Caroline, who answered on the first ring.

"It's me," I whispered. "Care, someone's in the house."

"Which house?"

"My old one."

"Where are you?"

"I'm parked across the street."

"Don't you dare go near it. I'll call Nate."

"Should I leave?"

"Yes, leave."

"Maybe I should stay, just in case they take off. Maybe I'll see whoever it is."

"Leave and go park at the head of the street. Now let me hang up so I can call Nate."

"What if it's Linda?"

"Linda?"

"Maybe she's over there and didn't tell me, or maybe she sent Wolfgang over to check on the new locks."

"Do you see her car?"

"No, but maybe she parked in the garage."

"Well, call her and find out, but leave."

I stayed put, though now it was too dark to see should anyone exit by the back door. I dialed Linda's cell phone, but didn't get an answer, only the recorded message. Linda's home number was no better, again the machine. I pulled Annabelle into my lap, and the puppy, perhaps sensing my fear, settled down, watchful.

Another few minutes passed. Then out of the darkness a car pulled slowly in behind me, its headlights flooding the Jeep. I froze and fumbled for the key in the ignition—too late. A frightful visage with empty eye-sockets materialized at my window. It almost stopped my heart until I realized it was Caroline, her features grossly distorted by the bright light.

Annabelle jumped up, barking furiously.

"Shush," I said, pulling her back. I rolled the window down partway.

"You were supposed to meet us at the head of the street," Caroline said.

"I was just leaving."

Nate appeared behind her. He was wearing street clothes, but held a gun at his side. He took off across the road and disappeared behind the house. Another police car sped to a stop a moment later. Caroline and I watched as two more cops jumped out and ran to the porch.

"I didn't see anyone leave, but I couldn't see the back," I said.

"What are you doing here?"

"I was in town buying stuff for Annabelle. I just thought I'd drive by and take a look."

"Well, that was a good idea," she said sarcastically.

I studied Caroline's face. She looked normal now, but I was tempted to mention how awful she'd looked a few moments before. I decided against it. "Did you get a chance to ask Nate about the detective?"

"Yes, I did. He said he'd look into it. Gwyn, you can't keep doing stuff like this. I told you—you're scaring me. It's way, way too dangerous. Promise me you'll stop. Okay?"

"Okay."

"And let me in. It's freezing out here."

"Sorry, forgot."

Nate came out ten minutes later and put his face to the window. "No signs of anyone now, except for old footprints near the back door and in the drive. Those could be mine or one of the other guys. We've been coming by to check every so often. We're taking a closer look at those."

"Well, I saw someone. Thanks for getting here so fast, Nate."

"Sure. And don't worry. We'll catch him eventually. And there's a good chance he'll decide things are getting too hot around here and move on."

I turned to Caroline, then again to Nate. "That does it. I'm selling the house. I've had enough of this. I'll tell Trevor to put a sign up tomorrow."

The following day, Trevor, Nate, Caroline and I met at the house. Trevor wanted to take inventory before putting the house on the market, make note of some minor fix-ups that might improve its resale value. Care brought Nate along to check things out before we entered—just in case.

I'd also talked to Linda, who agreed immediately to the sale, and assured me that neither she nor Wolfgang had been by the house the previous evening.

I held Annabelle in my arms and followed Trevor as he listed items that needed repair. The puppy, making all the right political moves, had campaigned and won Trevor over, wiggling and running in circles on his arrival last night, acting as though Trevor were an old and valued constituent. Unfortunately, I suspected that Annabelle had mistaken Trevor for Josh, returning for a visit.

"It needs paint," I said, gazing at the kitchen walls and cabinets.

"This house needs a lot of things, carpeting, curtains, counter tops. But it's salvageable," he said.

Just then, Nate walked in, joining me and Trevor. "I have to go on another call. Caroline wants to stay. That okay?"

"Sure," I said. "Where is she?"

"Upstairs."

"I'll go find her."

Trevor grabbed his coat and began to follow Nate out the door.

"Where are you going?" I asked.

"Outside. I want to inspect the exterior of the house."

I found Caroline standing in Kelly's old bedroom, the one Linda, Kelly and I had shared as kids.

"Strange, isn't it?" I asked.

"What?"

"Being here."

"Yes, it is."

"I wish I didn't have to sell the house. I really don't want to. You'll probably think I'm crazy, but sometimes when I'm alone here, I swear I can feel her presence." I glanced sidelong at her. "Not like a ghostly presence, just her essence, I suppose. Somehow, it's still here. And a lot of memories are connected to this house, most of them good."

She nodded. "I don't think you're crazy. She is here. I can feel it too."

"Really?"

"Yes."

I sighed. "But I guess I should sell it. Linda wants to, and all this trouble.... And I don't like the idea of anyone else in here, some vagrant taking advantage. Kelly wouldn't like it either. I guess it's best. Get a new family in here. Bring some life back into the place. It might be nice to drive by and see kids playing in the yard again. You think so?"

"Yeah, I think so."

The front door slammed and Trevor shouted up the stairs. "Hey, you two, get down here. I want to show you something."

We ran down the stairs and followed Trevor outside to a spot next to the window of my father's little room.

"Maybe I should join the police force part-time," he said. "Watch this." Carefully, he eased his fingernail into the edge of one of the four glass panes just below the mid-point of the window. With a flick of his finger, the pane dropped into his hand. "There's no caulk around this pane. Someone used gum or something to stick it back in place. But as you can see, it's easy to dislodge."

"Nate probably couldn't see that last night," said Caroline.

"After that," Trevor said, "it's just a matter of reaching in and releasing the lock. Slide up the window and he's in. The lights were off in this room."

He pointed out the many windowpanes with loose and flaking caulk. "And the walk goes right by the window, so nobody's going to notice footsteps."

"The storm windows are out in the garage," I said. "It seemed like such a waste of time, putting them on, taking them off."

"That would have made it harder," said Trevor, "but not impossible. I think this guy was going to find a way in either way."

Chapter 17

"You're sure you want to talk about this here?" asked Caroline. She'd quit work early, and was seated near me at a table in the far corner of the bar at the Wild River Grill.

"Sure, why not?"

"Well, once I'm off my shift all I want to do is get the hell out of here. And someone could come over and interrupt us. I'm a magnet for all the drunks and deadbeats."

On this Wednesday night, the Wild River was packed, shouts and laughter arising from every table. A mechanical bull-riding contest was underway, the action of the evening.

"What did you tell Trevor?" she asked.

"He's working late. I told him you wanted to get together—girl stuff. He believed me. Why wouldn't he? And he can call my cell. Doubt if he will though."

"She said she'd be here by seven. She knows the place, though I guess she's only been in here once before."

"What's her name?"

"The name she gave me is Sue. Something tells me it's not her given name though. Nate says she's good at what she does."

"Any reason he picked a woman?"

"Don't know. Maybe he's worried I'll get interested if I hang around another guy too much."

"I thought you told him the detective was for one of your customers?"

"Yeah, but I'm not sure he believed me. Hey, I have no idea why he picked a woman. If you don't like her, I can—"

"No, it doesn't make any difference to me. Actually, it might be better. I'm just a little nervous about all this, that's all."

"I think it's cool that I get to meet her," said Caroline.

"Well, of course you should meet her. My story will be that she's a friend of yours, in case Trevor sees us together. That okay?"

"No prob'."

"You want to get something to eat?" I asked. "I'm not hungry, but you must be."

"I was just about to suggest that. Maybe some ribs and chicken. How's that sound?"

"As good as anything. Order a salad too. That might be all I can eat."

"Done."

Caroline stuck two fingers in her mouth and let go a shrill whistle. All heads in the immediate vicinity turned in her direction. She hooked her finger at a waitress. "Hey, Vicki. When you get a minute."

By seven, we'd finished the salad and ribs and were licking our fingers. As it turned out, I was hungrier than I thought. I kept watching the door, not sure what this detective would look like. Caroline had described the exact location of our table to her, along with an imprecise description of each of us.

"I wonder how old she is?" I said.

Caroline shrugged. "Let's guess, and then ask her."

"I'm not doing that. Don't do that."

"I was kidding. Boy, you are a bundle of nerves."

"You got that right."

A large group came through the door, but scattered and found tables. "Where is she?" I said. "It's five minutes after seven according to that clock."

Caroline shook her head. "That's bar time. That clock runs fast. Check your watch."

"Hi," said a voice just behind me. "Caroline?"

I looked up to see a straight-haired blonde of medium height, decked out in a cowboy hat, cowboy boots, jeans, and a beaded denim shirt. She wore a tan and sunglasses, though the sun had gone down a while ago. I guessed her to be in her early to mid-thirties.

"That would be me," said Caroline.

The woman thrust out her hand, ringless, but on her wrist she wore a beaded bracelet. "I'm Sue," she said with a mild southern accent. "Mind if I join y'all?"

"Please do," said Caroline, giving Sue's hand a shake.

I jumped up and pulled out a chair for her. "We were just talking about you."

"I know. I've been sitting over there for the last twenty minutes." She pointed to a table not far from us near the wall. "Got here a little early, and I was hungry so I grabbed a bite. Good barbecue here."

"Sure is," said Caroline.

She smiled. "So, my first question is, will I be working for you, Caroline? I'm assuming not, since you brought a friend. And your name would be?"

"Oh, I'm sorry. I'm Gwyn."

"Nice to meet you, Gwyn."

Caroline scooted her chair closer to the table and leaned in. "Nate didn't tell me a whole lot about you."

"No, probably not. I'm sort of a friend of a friend of his—once removed. I've never met Nate in person."

"Actually, I have a question for *you*," said Caroline. "Before we begin, I need to know if you'll have to tell Nate who your client is. Would that be necessary?"

"No. Can't think of any reason for that at the moment. Course, he might ask."

"But, you wouldn't—"

"It's none of his business."

"Good."

Caroline looked at me and dipped her head, prompting me to speak.

"I would be the client," I said.

"I assumed so," she said. "Do you want to talk here?"

"Well, I don't know."

"Not too private."

I looked from detective Sue back to Caroline, then back to Sue. "Caroline's my best friend. I'd trust her with my life, if that's what you mean."

"No, just kind of noisy in here." She idly glanced back toward the mechanical bull. I followed her gaze and watched as a yelping girl slid off its rear.

Caroline stood up. "I need to use the washroom for a minute. I'll be right back."

Sue smiled, then turned to me once Caroline walked away. "Not trying to be rude to your friend, but I can't just assume you're ready to talk money and contracts in front of your buddies."

"No, I guess not."

"What I have is a standard agreement. I'll give you a copy. Nothing fancy, no frills. I try to give folks a fair deal. I do require a retainer to get started, and of course, details on what you hope to accomplish. I don't think this is the best place to talk about that. If I got a handle on what y'all were saying earlier, then I suppose others might be able to also."

"You could hear us?"

"Yes and no. But for the most part, yes. I believe Caroline made some remark about asking my age, and you objected."

"You heard that?"

She smiled. "Sort of. I'm not telepathic. Though sometimes ... I wonder."

I looked around at the people sitting nearest to us. None seemed to be paying any attention. "We were joking. I mean, Caroline was joking ... about asking your age. She's not—"

She held up her hand. "Don't worry. I thought it was funny. I almost laughed out loud. And I'm not quick to take offense, or to make hasty judgments. I wouldn't last in this business if I did. I'd like to talk to you tonight for a few minutes, if that's possible, so we don't waste each other's time. But I can't talk in front of your friend. I'm sure she's all that you say she is, but it's not the way I do business."

"Okay. Where do you want to go?"

"How about my van. What windows it has are tinted, and nobody's going to hear us in there."

"I'll just tell Caroline we're leaving."

"Sure."

Her van was parked a block away on a side street with minimal traffic. The minivan looked fairly ordinary, white, and was due for a wash. I noticed the windows were tinted a dark black, except for the driver's and passenger's, which were a lighter black tint.

She unlocked the doors and let me in. The passenger compartment appeared like any other, and was clean and organized. The only personal items were a box of tissues and another pair of sunglasses on the floor. I looked toward the back of the van, but couldn't make out a thing. Light shielding curtains covered the windows. I did get the feeling that whatever equipment she carried back there wouldn't be found in your average family van.

She reached behind her seat and grabbed a black briefcase, then punched in a code that released the lock. She pulled out a single document printed on white paper.

"This is my contract. You can read it over if you like, but you don't have to sign anything now. Unless you're in a big rush. Like I said, it's fairly standard in the trade, and my rates are in line with other good P.I.s."

"I'm not worried about the money."

"Well, that's always good news. How soon did you want me to start?"

"As soon as possible. Is that a problem?"

"No, no problem."

I took a deep breath, then let it go. "Whatever I tell you ... I mean ... I guess what I'm trying to say is ... I need to know if I can count on you not to involve the police, if it turns out ..." I hesitated, thinking. "Are you a cop? Were you ever on the police force?"

"No, I'm not a cop, though I was interested—well no, I wasn't—to tell you the truth. I'd rather work on my own. But I know people, a lot of people, who are officers of the law, and they don't mind helping me out now and then, and that goes both ways." She stopped, waiting for me to respond.

"I don't want you to do anything illegal," I said, "or to do anything illegal myself. I guess what I'm trying to say is that if you do uncover something, could you at least tell me first before you go to the police with the information?"

She finally took off her sunglasses, and I could see that she looked quite young for her age. She wore no makeup, but wasn't unattractive, clear tanned skin coupled with light blue eyes and blonde lashes.

"I can't promise anything until you give me a clue as to what you expect me to do."

"Okay, that's fair. Sorry. Two things, essentially. I want to find the guy who murdered my sister, and I want to know if my husband is cheating on me."

She nodded her head. "I know about your sister. Awful thing. Sorry. I know they're still looking for the guy.... So, you want me to try and flush this creep out, and you want me to find out what your husband is up to, if anything."

"Yes, basically that's it," I said, then looked down at my hands.

"But not everything."

"No, that's about it."

"Gwyn, the more information you give me up front, the better I'll be able to help you. I can't guarantee anything if you leave stuff out. Believe me, I've heard it all. Nothing shocks me. But it's your dime. However you want to play it." She gave me a half smile. "Why don't you look over my contract, think about it, then get back to me. I will say this. I don't go out of my way to hurt people or to mess up their lives. You can trust me there. I'll do everything in my power to help you, within reason."

Afterwards, I walked back toward the Wild River where my Jeep was parked. I wasn't ready to be alone, or to go home to an empty house. I pulled out my cell phone and dialed Caroline.

"Hey," she said, "how did it go?"

"Good. We talked a little. I have her contract. I like her. I think I'll hire her."

"Great. So where are you now?"

"Walking back to my car."

"You going home? Do you want to stop by?"

"I kind of would like to stop by."

"Then come on over. I cleaned up the place, and no one's even seen it yet. I figured maybe you and that detective might want to meet here. Hate to waste a clean apartment on just myself. I'll make us coffee."

"Okay. I'll bring dessert."

"Super."

I could feel my spirits lift as soon as I stopped by the grocery and picked out chocolate ice cream and home-baked sugar cookies. As I mounted the stairs to Caroline's second story apartment, I caught a whiff of freshly brewing coffee. She'd left the door ajar, but I gave it a knock anyway.

"Come on in," she yelled out.

Her one bedroom apartment was spacious, the way apartments used to be built years ago, with full country kitchens and large bathrooms. The building itself housed ten units, and was over forty years old.

Caroline sat watching television, knees curled beneath her on the L-shaped couch. She picked up the television remote and clicked off the set as I walked over.

"What'd you bring?" she asked, rising.

"Ice cream and cookies. Your place looks great," I said.

"Yeah, took me two days. I would have hired a Jiffy maid, but I would have been embarrassed to let her see it. You use those guys, don't you?"

"Once in a while. Trevor doesn't like strangers in the house. I need to be there."

"He thinks they'll steal something?"

"No, I think he's worried they'll break something, or scratch something."

We settled onto the couch with our ice cream and cookies. Later, after second helpings and extra cups of coffee, I drew out the contract and pushed it toward Caroline.

"What's this?" she asked.

"My contract."

"Ooo, I want to see." She snatched the paper from my hand and began to peruse it.

"I didn't tell her everything," I said. "She knew right away I was hiding something. I suppose I'll have to fill her in eventually."

"Why didn't you? What are you afraid of?"

"Everything. God, Care, what if it is Trevor? What if he had something to do with Kelly's death? It sounds so bizarre to even say it, but what if he did? Maybe I don't know him at all."

"Good reason to find out then, right?"

"Yes. I'll call her. I'll tell her everything I know."

"Investigative Agreement," she said.

"What?"

"That's what this contract is called. Yep, and it says right here, 'you agree to provide accurate information as a basis for this investigation ...' And here's a big one, all capital letters, bold print ... says they don't have to promise or guarantee the outcome of the case. Well, that sucks."

"I know. I read it. And she implied as much."

"But Nate did say she was good. And I don't think he'd vouch for her unless she was. I wonder what she'll do? You'll have to tell me everything. Unless—you don't want to."

"I'll let you in on it."

"She didn't trust me, did she?" Caroline handed the contract back to me.

"No, it wasn't like that. She doesn't know you."

A pen lay on Caroline's coffee table. I reached for it, then signed my name on the dotted line. "Can I use your phone? Guess I might as well get this thing started."

Chapter 18

"Okay, sounds like you want the deluxe package with all the trimmings." Sue held a clipboard and took notes as I walked her through the house. She was wearing jeans and a baggy sweatshirt, and outside the sign on her van read *Cybernetics*, computer installation and repair. She'd dropped the southern accent, along with the blonde hair, replaced by a cropped brown wig with razor straight bangs. Her light blue eyes had vanished too, now brown with thick black lashes—the result of contact lenses and mascara, I presumed. No tan either. It was hard to tell she was the same person. She'd warned me not to be surprised.

"I have a small crew I work with," she said. "They'll be by tomorrow. Did you tell your husband what I asked you to?"

"Yes, that I'm having trouble with the Mac, and I might want another computer, and maybe we should get a new one for his office too."

"And how did he react to that?"

"Very hesitant, then a definite no—at least for now, he said."

"I expected that."

I could swear her voice had dropped an octave too, and was more matter-of-fact, like the part she was playing—computer repair geek.

"And you told him we're coming the day after tomorrow, not tomorrow, right?"

"Yes."

"Good."

We walked into Trevor's office. "How much time does he spend in here?" she asked.

"Quite a bit. He'll go in after dinner, sometimes as soon as he gets home. It depends on what's going on at work."

"So, he works a lot?"

"Yes."

"Gets home late most weekdays?"

"Yes."

I glanced over at her. She was taping our conversation—so she didn't miss anything—was how she'd put it. I'd given permission, still, it made me nervous. It wouldn't look good if she caught me in a lie later on. I'd been straight with her so far. I'd also shown her Kelly's letter, related my fears about Wolfgang and Trevor, and my serious doubts of any guilt on Josh's part. I'd told her about Sylvia too, and my suspicions. Sue had asked me for videos taken at family gatherings, especially any of Kelly. She'd also asked me lots of questions, some of which I had to admit seemed pure nosiness.

"We'll bug your husband's office, and I'll put microphones and cameras near all the house phones too."

"*Near* the phones? Can't you bug the phones themselves?"

"I could, but I won't. Phone taps are illegal. I could go to jail, get a fine, and lose my license. It's done, but not by me."

"Oh. I thought we'd be able to listen in on his conversations."

Her news was a serious letdown. This was one of the items that had interested me most.

"Sorry, but it won't be necessary. There are other ways of getting the information we need."

"But, even if you don't do it ... can you at least give me a clue as to how it is done?"

"Depends on who you are, law enforcement or an individual." She stopped and eyed me. "*You* could go to jail too, Gwyn. And if your husband stumbles on your home-grown recording device, our cover is blown."

"I wasn't planning to do anything on my own. I was just

curious."

She smiled and raised her brows. "Just curious, huh? I'll tell you this, it's so easy to do it's laughable. It's done all the time, by husbands mostly, checking up on their wives or girlfriends, sometimes both, and sometimes it's the local pervert hoping to get his jollies. In fact, I'll be doing a sweep of your place, just in case your husband thought to listen in on you. Of course, if you are, *just curious*, everything you need to know is on the Internet."

She gazed around Trevor's office, then eyed his computer. "We'll start checking his emails here and at his office, and we'll have him under surveillance twenty-four seven."

"How will you check his emails? You don't know the code to his computer, or the password for his email."

"We'll know it soon enough. Tomorrow he'll have a computer meltdown, supposedly. You'll tell him he might need to reinstall the code. Just say the power went off while we were working, possibly messed things up, and he should check it out. When he does punch in the code, we'll be watching. I'll be installing some special software on his computer as well."

"Where is the camera going to be? Won't he notice it?"

"No. We use what's called a pinhole-lens camera. I'd tell you where it's going to be, but you'd look right at it every time you walked in the room. And keep the maids out of the house for a while. Also, I want to install a microphone in his car. Does he ever let you borrow it?"

"No, I own a Jeep. He'd rather use the Cadillac for business."

"Okay, here's what we'll do. When he gets up tomorrow morning, there'll be what looks like a nasty oil stain under his car on the garage floor. It's not permanent, and easy to remove if you worry about that sort of thing. So, we hope he'll notice, but if he doesn't, you point it out. Then you offer to take his car in for service and let him borrow yours. Chances are he'll be in a rush and will go along with it. Later, if he wants to know what repairs were made on his car and has to talk to someone, you'll have a number he can call. Tell him your regular guy was busy, if you have one. One of our guys will be on the other end to give him the particulars when he calls. Oh, and try to keep him in the house as much as possible after he gets home tonight. We'll be in and out of the garage quick, but it will help if we're not interrupted."

"Okay. I can do that. Of course, my main concern is Wolfgang. I want you to concentrate most of your efforts on him. I think he's the one responsible for my sister Kelly's death. I'm worried for Linda. So far, she's okay. But who knows?"

"Do you want someone watching out for her too?"

"Definitely, but make sure she's not aware of it. She notices everything."

"She won't have a clue. I hope you realize this is going to cost you one very big bundle," she said.

"Whatever it costs, it's worth it to me. I want this guy caught. He doesn't deserve to live."

Chapter 19

I felt like I might be coming down with a cold on the night of Linda's party. The back of my throat was a little sore, and I'd sneezed a couple of times. I was taking a tissue from my purse when Trevor walked into the kitchen.

"Wow, you look fantastic," he said. "Great dress."

"Thank you." I was wearing a cream-colored long sleeved wool dress with a deep V-neck. Though I'd planned on wearing my violet backless beaded dress, I decided against it because of my cold, plus the temperature outside was hovering around fifteen degrees. The wool would be warmer, though not as daring, but with Trevor's gift of diamond earrings and bracelet I could at least pull off a little elegance.

"How do I look?" he asked.

"You look great. You'll be the best looking guy at the party."

"Well, that's a given," he said, grinning back at me. "But thanks for the compliment." Trevor was wearing a custom-made ebony black suit, complete with cream shirt, striped tie, and gold cufflinks.

"Oh," he said, "and thanks again for letting me borrow your car yesterday. Can't figure out how so much oil leaked out from a loose cap. But they checked it out and couldn't find anything else wrong.

No problem today either." He shrugged.

"I'm sure the car is fine."

"Maybe I'll start looking around for something else ... just in case."

"I guess you could, but the Caddie's practically brand new. How many miles did you say it has?"

"Barely any. A few thousand. Yeah, you're right. I'm sure it's fine. Ran good today. Man, first the car, then the computer. I hate it when stuff breaks."

I took a sip of hot tea and watched as Trevor moved about the kitchen, opening cabinet doors, and finally, the refrigerator. He pulled out a block of cheese, drew a knife from the drawer, and began to slice off chunks. "I'm hungry," he said. "I hope she has lots of hors d'oeuvres."

"You're joking, right?"

He chewed, gazing at me. "I hate to walk into a party and right away start stuffing my face. That dress. New, isn't it?"

"Sort of. I haven't had a chance to wear it since I bought it, so I guess it's still new."

"Where's the zipper?"

I pointed over my shoulder. "In the back, but it's covered, of course. Why? Is something wrong? Oh, don't tell me ..."

"Yes, I do see something here." He began to ease the zipper down.

"What?"

He pulled the zipper all the way to the small of my back, then placed his hands beneath my bra clasp and caressed me along the spine. "We have time, don't we?"

"No, honey, we don't," I said, wiggling away from him. "You'll mess up my hair, and my make-up, and you'll probably catch my cold."

"Awww. I don't care about that. I like your germs. We can share them."

"No, Trevor."

"And here I thought you loved me. Come on, Gwyn. You look so good. I won't mess up anything. Promise." He kissed me on the back of the neck, then dropped his head over my shoulder, kissed me again, and looked up at me. "Please?"

"All right. But quick, okay? I don't want to be late for the party."

"Oh, wow," he said, lifting the hem of my dress to my hips. "You're wearing the sexy garter belt I bought you. The one I got you for your birthday. God, you are so incredi-fuckably gorgeous. Thank you, baby. Thank you. Thank you."

We were a half-hour late, but I'd called Linda and made up an excuse, said we couldn't find the car keys. She didn't seem to care, probably into her second martini and feeling happy.

Jazz, the deep resonant notes of a saxophone, bass fiddle, and drum trio, greeted us at the door, opened by a teenaged boy in a tweed sport coat. "Good evening," he said, waving us in. "May I take your coats?" I didn't recognize him, but later learned he was the son of the bartender.

I searched the crowd for Caroline, curious to see if she'd brought her new guy friend, Nate, to Linda's party.

Out of the corner of my eye, I spotted Josh, then glanced quickly back at Trevor, who was picking a piece of lint from his sleeve.

Wolfgang worked his way toward us.

"Dressed to kill," he said, eyeing us both. "Hope you brought something warmer for later. I've got some mean machines parked out back."

"We did," said Trevor. "But Gwyn probably won't be going snowmobiling. She's catching a cold."

"Oh, that's too bad," he said. "You'll miss out on all the fun."

"I still might go," I said. "I haven't decided. Where's Linda? I don't see her."

Wolfgang turned and pointed toward the corner of the room by the Christmas tree. "Over there, last I looked."

But Linda wasn't by the tree, so I tried the kitchen, then spied her walking quickly away from me down the hall. "Linda," I called out.

She stopped and turned around. "Oh, hi, Gwyn."

Something about her didn't look right, as if she were trying to hide tired eyes behind too much makeup. I wondered if she might be getting sick too. "Sorry we're late."

"Well, you misplaced your keys. I'm sure you didn't do it on purpose, right?"

"Well, no."

"So what do you think? How's it look out there? Is everyone having a good time? I haven't had a chance to check."

"It's going great, and the jazz combo is awesome."

"Isn't it?"

"You look nice," I said, noting that she appeared thinner than ever. "Pretty dress. I love that shade of turquoise on you."

"Thanks, you look nice too."

"I'm catching a cold, so don't breathe too deeply around me. Are *you* getting sick?"

"Sick? What makes you think I'm sick? First you compliment me, then you tell me I look sick. Thanks a lot." She shook her head and turned back down the hall.

"Linda, I didn't mean it that way. Linda, please stop."

She did. "No, I am not sick. I'm just tired. Excuse me, Gwyn. I have to use the bathroom."

"Okay. I'll see you out there."

I made my way to the bar set up in a corner of the living room and asked the bartender for a glass of merlot, then meandered to an empty chair and sat down, kicking my high heels off, hoping no one would notice.

I felt a hand lightly touch me on the shoulder. "Hello, gorgeous." Josh stepped around in front of me. "Sore feet?"

I smiled up at him. "Yes, but you weren't supposed to notice," I said, slipping the heels back on.

"Oh, leave them off. Who's going to care? Certainly not me."

I looked behind him, wondering if he'd brought a date. Considering how handsome he looked tonight, I figured the woman would be rushing over to claim him by now. His blond hair fell casually over his forehead, framing eyes that sparkled with devilish mischief.

"I don't know any of these people," he said, kneeling at my feet, his hand cupping my left knee for balance.

"Yes, you do. You know as many as I do. And Caroline will be here soon."

"She's already here. But she has a date."

"Where? I didn't see her."

"She just walked in."

Josh looked me over. "You're more beautiful than ever, Gwyn. You have to promise me a dance later."

"Of course ... if I can."

"Oh, your husband will survive it. Looks like he's preoccupied already."

I turned in the direction Josh was nodding. Trevor was standing at the bar with Bob Morris and Sylvia Breslin. Last year, Bob had attended Linda's party, but unfortunately, this year he'd brought Sylvia. "Sure, Josh, we can have that dance. Why not?"

Josh laughed. "She's a troll compared to you."

"She's a business associate of Trevor's," I said. "In fact, we spent a weekend in Aspen with them recently, as their guests ... well, her guest, actually."

"Is that her guy?"

"Her date, not her guy. It's purely platonic, Trevor says. I like Bob though. He's nice."

"Looks like you need another glass of wine. I'll get it for you. Merlot?"

"Yes, thanks."

He rose and approached the bar, shook Trevor's hand, then made introductions with Sylvia and Bob. Trevor noticed me watching the four of them and waved, then stepped away from the group and walked over.

"Why don't you join the party?" he asked, taking a seat on the arm of my chair. "You took off and left me with Wolfgang. That wasn't very nice. He was giving me the make and model of every snowmobile he's rented for tonight, and I'm thinking I won't even go."

"Sorry."

"You should be."

"I didn't know Sylvia would be here."

"And neither did I," he said, emphasizing each word, "but I have to be polite, don't I? It might look a little ungrateful if I just ignore them."

A moment later, Caroline came around the corner of my chair with Nate. Trevor rose to his feet. "Oh, don't get up," she said, her eyes twinkling as she brought her guest forward.

Nate reached out to shake each of our hands. "Hello, Gwyn, Trevor. Nice to see you again."

Caroline whispered down toward my ear. "Where's Linda? I wanted to say hello, but I haven't seen her."

"I don't know. I talked to her earlier. Must be busy with something." I scanned the roomful of people, but Linda wasn't among them.

"Oh, well, I'll find her eventually." She turned to Nate. "Want something to drink?"

"Sure." He turned to us. "Could we get you anything while we're up there?"

We shook our heads. "Thanks, we're good," said Trevor.

Nate led Caroline away.

I tapped Trevor on the arm, but his gaze had moved in the direction of the hors d'oeuvres table. "She likes him," I said. "I haven't seen her look that happy in a long time."

"That's nice. Let's get some food. I'm starving."

I noticed Josh making his way toward me with the glass of wine he'd promised. "One second," I said.

Trevor spotted Josh also, but grimaced, manufacturing a smile as Josh neared. "Hey, Josh," he said, watching as Josh offered me the wineglass. "So what's been going on with you? How are you these days?"

"Great. And you?"

"Can't complain. Didn't expect to see you here though. What brings you to Glenwood?"

"Oh, visiting the family, enjoying the holidays."

"How are they?"

"Fine."

"That's good. You planning on going out with the guys later, on Wolfgang's snowmobiles?"

"No, I thought he was joking."

"Don't think so."

"I didn't bring a change of clothes," Josh said.

Trevor waved a hand. "I'm sure Wolfgang's got extra stuff you can borrow. You're not going to stay inside with the women, are you?"

"I thought the women were invited too?"

"Yeah, but Gwyn's not going. She has a cold."

"I haven't decided that for sure," I said, "but you're right, probably not."

"Sure, I'll go," Josh said, "if Wolfgang can suit me up. What the hell?"

"Yeah, what the hell," Trevor said, smacking Josh on the back so hard his drink slopped over the side.

Josh narrowed his eyes at Trevor, then excused himself and walked off toward Caroline and Nate.

"Doesn't that guy ever bring a date?" said Trevor. "If he wasn't your ex, I'd swear he was gay."

"I thought you said you weren't going out, that you'd changed your mind."

"Well, I changed it back."

"It's a bad idea and you know it. It's freezing out there and you've had too much to drink. How many is that anyway?"

"Don't worry. I'm fine. I'm hungry and I'm getting some food. You coming?"

"Yeah, I guess."

After the snack, I ditched Trevor and searched for Linda. I'd spied her once, briefly, when she'd stopped to talk to a few guests, but just as quickly she'd disappeared again.

I looked for her in the kitchen, then in the rooms off the hall on the main floor. Finally, I found her in the room Linda referred to as the library, a grouping of chairs and loveseats surrounded by bookcases only partially lined with hardbound books.

"What are you doing in here?" I asked.

"Nothing, trying to find a little space."

"Oh. Just wondered where you were. I can leave if you'd rather be alone."

"It's okay. Go ahead. Sit if you want."

I noticed a weird odor in the room, masked somewhat by the heavy scent of Linda's perfume. "This room smells a little funky, don't you think?"

She sniffed the air. "Yeah, guess it does. Books are probably moldy. Nobody actually reads them. If I opened one up a moth would probably fly out. It feels cold in here too, doesn't it?"

"A little chilly."

"I'll start a fire." Linda rose and turned on the gas jets for the fireplace. "If this damn thing works."

After a few seconds, flames ignited. We sat quietly, staring at the fire.

"Looks real," I said.

"It should. I spent enough on it."

It was then that I noticed a tear slip down her cheek, then another.

"Sweetie, what's wrong?"

"Nothing. It's nothing. Don't—"

"No, tell me, please."

She sat very still, then lifted her head and smiled sadly. "Have I always been such a loser? Did I ever do anything right?"

"Linda. What are you talking about?"

"Nothing. Just that no one really gives a shit about me. Except you. And then ... maybe not you either. But how could I blame you? I'm such a pain in the ass."

"You're not."

"I will bet you that not one other person noticed I'm missing from my own party."

"That's not true. Not true at all. Caroline was looking for you. And a lot of other people asked me where you were."

She shrugged.

"Linda, everyone likes you. You have tons of friends. Everyone goes on and on about how much fun you are, and you give these great parties."

"Yeah, my great parties."

"Did something happen? Something must have happened."

She stared ahead, her eyes glazed over.

"Wolfgang?"

"I don't think I want to talk right now."

"Tell me. What happened? What did he do?"

"Not *now*, Gwyn."

"Okay ... okay. Then we'll just sit here."

She took a deep breath, let it go. "I'm glad I have you, Gwyn. You know that? I don't say it very much, but I am."

"I know." I moved in close and put my arm around her. "I love you, Linda. I do. Please believe that. And everything's going to be okay. From now on. I won't let anything bad happen to you—not to either of us."

This only made her cry harder. She stayed tucked under my arm for several minutes, and then finally shook herself loose.

"I'm better now," she said, sniffing. "I'll just go upstairs and fix myself a little, then I'll be back down."

"All right," I said.

She rose to leave.

The first thing I did was go look for Wolfgang. I found him near the bar, flirting with Sylvia of all people, though she didn't appear to be paying much attention. Instead, she was craning her neck in the direction of Trevor and Bob.

I turned away in disgust and cruised the room trying to find Caroline and Nate. They were seated on one of the couches near the Christmas tree, the lighting lower on that side of the room. Caroline scooted closer to Nate to make room for me. "Enjoying the party?" she asked. "You look tired."

"I am. I have a stupid cold. I hope I don't give it to you."

"I'm not worried. Hey, is that the infamous Sylvia? The brunette?"

"In the flesh."

"Kind of the painted lady, isn't she? Puts that makeup on with a trowel. I haven't seen Trevor talking to her much. In fact, I think he moves around the room just to avoid her."

"Yes, but what does that mean? He knows I'm watching him."

"True. But maybe it means he's telling the truth. Maybe he's not interested in her."

"No, maybe he isn't. But she's not the only woman he knows. And maybe he doesn't want to make it too obvious. Oh, who knows? Who cares?"

"You care." Caroline leaned in close. "So, how's it going with—you know? Anything happening yet?"

I shook my head. "Not a lot yet, but I'll tell you when we're really alone. I'm a little paranoid. I feel like everyone can hear me, no matter how softly I talk."

"From what you told me about—you know—maybe they can." She looked suspiciously at the couple seated across from us. "I did talk to Linda, finally. It took me a while to find her."

"I don't think she's in a people mood tonight," I said. "These parties really wear her out. All the planning involved." I motioned toward Nate, who seemed content to gaze around the room while Caroline and I conversed. "Is Nate having a good time?"

"I think so. But he's all talked out. He was on duty since early this morning. Needs some quiet time, I guess."

"So it's going good?"

"So good it's scary. I hate feeling this way." She leaned in closer still. "He's a great kisser. But that's *all* I know so far. I'm not going to rush into anything with him. And he's not pushing me."

"He seems really nice."

"Yeah, he does. But he hasn't gotten to know me yet. I don't know if I can keep my apartment clean for much longer."

I laughed. "If he takes the time to get to know you like I do, he'll adore you."

"Whatever," she said, but grinned. "I saw you talking to Josh when we walked in. How did Trevor handle that?"

"How would you expect?"

"Hand to hand combat, right?"

"Trevor plans to go out and challenge Josh on a snowmobile. I did, of course, try to talk him out of it."

"The whole idea is hilarious. A bunch of drunk guys out tearing around the property. Wolfgang's idea?"

"Who else? Maybe Nate can put a stop to it."

"Private property. As long as they don't go out on the public roads, he can't do much. And I don't think he'd want to. He'd be the guy on the outs with the host, and he doesn't want to ruin Wolfgang's party. Maybe he can keep an eye on things. I sure hope Wolfgang thought to update his liability insurance though."

The hors d'oeuvres trays were moved out and replaced with a hot buffet. Trevor filled a plate, but I wasn't hungry.

"I'm getting tired, Trevor. Why don't we just go home afterwards? Okay?"

"No, but I'll take you home if you want."

"Earlier tonight you said you didn't even think you'd go."

"I changed my mind."

"Why is this so important now?"

"It isn't. I just don't want to be the only one not out there."

"It's a stupid idea and you're not even sober."

"I'm sober enough. Don't bother to argue. I'm going."

The trio of jazz musicians kicked it up a notch, and a few couples moved onto the area set aside for a dance floor. Though still angry at Trevor, I accepted his invitation to dance when the tempo again slowed.

"No talking," he said.

"But—"

"No, if we don't talk, we won't argue." He pulled me close, his fingers pressing lightly in at my waist, then moving upwards, rippling along my spine. I began to relax, feeling much more forgiving.

He looked down at me. "Better now?"

"Yes." Moments later, I spotted Sylvia watching us, and pulled Trevor closer still. "Can I ask one favor?"

"What?"

"Don't dance with Sylvia if she asks."

"What makes you think she'd do that?"

"That's easy, she hasn't let you out of her sight since we walked in. It's perverted the way she stares."

He glanced at her, then laughed. "She's not watching me. She's talking with Bob. You're imagining things."

"Yeah, sure I am."

As the music died away and Trevor led me off of the floor, Sylvia suddenly appeared in front of us.

"Oh, hi, you two. Glad I ran into you. Gwyn, could I borrow Trevor for a minute? Bob refuses to dance with me anymore. He says his feet hurt."

I started to open my mouth, but before I could answer, Sylvia quickly pulled Trevor onto the dance floor.

He looked back at me, raising his brows as if to ask, *What am I supposed to do?*

I watched as Sylvia attempted to draw Trevor tightly into her arms. It was several seconds before I noticed Josh standing beside me.

"Aggressive lady," he said.

"What?"

"Sylvia Breslin. Over there, the one practically wearing your husband."

"She doesn't bother me."

He chuckled. "Oh really."

I began to walk away.

He caught my arm. "I'm sorry, Gwyn. I am. I shouldn't make fun."

"You're right. I hate her."

"Understandable."

I glanced up at Josh, but he was watching Sylvia and Trevor.

"You know," he said, "she's planning to snowmobile after the party. She told me. Listen, I'll foil her plan, make sure she's not on the back of your husband's snowmobile. I'll take her on mine. Unless Trevor stops me. You'd like to know if he does, wouldn't you?"

"Yes, I would."

"Want to dance?"

"Love to." Though he held me at a comfortable distance, I purposely drew him closer. "Not to be nosy," I asked. "But why didn't you bring a date tonight?"

"What you're really asking is, am I here alone because of you."

"No."

"Gwyn? Truth?"

"Well, no. It's just that I know lots of women who would have loved to be your date. Half the women in this town."

"I'm here alone because I didn't know if I'd actually be able to make the party. I wouldn't want to cancel and break some woman's heart."

"Yes, that's true."

Josh brought his lips close to my ear. "Trevor's watching us. I don't think he likes me right now."

"So? That's his problem."

"We'll teach him."

I began to giggle in spite of myself. "We've known each other a long time, haven't we, Josh?"

"Yes, a very long time. And I've enjoyed every minute of it ... well, almost."

"I am sorry."

"Sorry?"

"About ... before."

"Oh. I knew that. Don't give it another thought."

"You do deserve better," I said. "You deserve the best."

He looked out over the crowd. "Your husband dumped her. At least for now." Josh winked. "The games begin." He motioned toward Wolfgang, who had already changed into his bulky snowmobile suit.

"Isn't he rushing things?" I said. "Linda's party is not exactly over."

"This could be a major hint that he'd like it to be."

The jazz trio ended its number and Wolfgang disappeared from the room. Shortly after, I heard the loud buzz of a snowmobile warming up outside.

"Well, Gwyn, it's been a pleasure," said Josh, "but hubby is coming this way and he's not exactly smiling. Catch you later."

"Bye, Josh."

Trevor marched toward me, his face fiery red. "What was that?"

"What was what?"

"You, dancing with that loser. What? To get back at me? Pretty childish."

"No, and lower your voice. Who's being childish?"

"Oh, to hell with it. I'll be outside. I'll see you when I'm done."

I watched him stalk away. Funny how he'd just assumed I wasn't going.

The jazz group put their instruments back in their cases, and the help staff began to clear the room of stray glasses and plates. Guests either said their good-byes, or headed to designated rooms to change clothing. Coffee was offered to those left behind.

I wandered to the rear of the house and drew the curtains aside. I could see the headlights of a few snowmobiles parked outside or moving slowly toward the acreage beyond. Josh was gone. Trevor was gone. All of the men had left.

I went off to look for Linda and Caroline.

I found Linda standing alone in the kitchen.

"Aren't you going out?" I asked.

"No, not in the mood. Aren't you?"

"I don't know. I have this cold, and I'm tired. But Trevor's going."

"I wish they'd all go home. The neighbors might get testy if this thing gets too noisy, though a few of them said they'd join in. Wolfgang's planning a big bonfire afterwards." She walked to the kitchen table and sat down. "You want something? Coffee?" she asked.

"Not unless it's decaf."

"It isn't."

I sat down with her. "Your party did turn out great."

"I suppose it did, but I probably should have cancelled, considering how much I've had to do lately."

"So when are you leaving for Hawaii?"

"Thursday ... if I go."

"What do you mean? If you go."

"Because Wolfgang's a colossal jerk." The buzzing of the snowmobiles intensified. She glanced toward the window. "I hope he runs himself into a tree, the bastard." She turned back to me. "Don't worry. I'm not serious—not yet anyway. It looks like we'll be in Maui the first week, at the Grand Wailea Resort. After that, I don't know. Wolfgang says he wants to surprise me. I'll send you a postcard."

"I'd rather you call."

"Sure."

"Can't talk you out of it?"

"No."

"Have you seen Caroline anywhere?"

"I think I saw her head outside. That's a nice guy she's with. Does she like him?"

"Yes."

"Well, I hope it works out for her."

After a while, Linda left to go upstairs and I again tried to watch the others from a window. Lights bobbed up and down invisible mounds of snow and through the trees at the back of the property. Up by the house, I caught sight of two snowmobiles idling, waiting for passengers. I couldn't stand it one minute longer. I had to know if Trevor was with Sylvia.

I changed into heavy clothes, picked out a helmet from a pile near the door, then hopped on a snowmobile that didn't appear to be in use. I gunned the engine and charged off.

I knew the property fairly well, enough to know the hazards. Linda and I had walked it several times before she'd made the decision to buy it.

Most of the snowmobiles were still at the back of the property, following the trails that curved through the woods. I sped across the snow, crouched over the snowmobile as it smacked down over several small rises. Gripping the handlebars tighter, I stood, straddling the machine like a steed in full gallop. I cranked open the throttle, giving it gas. Reaching the open field, I raced across it, then braked momentarily to locate the trailhead. I saw it, and punched the throttle open, flying up the curving path. I was gaining on them. I could see their headlights in the near distance through the woods. So concentrated on their lights was I, that I nearly missed the next turn. I slammed on the brakes and slid out so fast the tail end of the snowmobile arced a hundred and eighty degrees. I'd narrowly missed a big sturdy pine. I stopped and caught my breath, thinking that it wasn't necessary to die and make it easier for Sylvia and Trevor to be together.

Before I could start out again, I heard what sounded like a *whump*, then screams and shouts. All activity stopped.

I raced up the trail and saw snowmobiles scattered all over. I jumped off and started running.

People were standing over someone on the ground. Headlights were trained on the body, lying still on its back. Two men crouched near it. As I approached, I could see that the body was a woman's. One of the men crouching over her was Trevor. I ran toward him.

"What happened?" I shouted, but he didn't seem to hear me. "Trevor, what happened? God, is it Caroline?"

I stopped, and someone grabbed my arm. "No, Gwyn. It's not. I'm perfectly fine."

"Oh my God, Care. Then who is it?"

"It's Sylvia."

"Oh.... She's not dead, is she?"

"No. But it looks serious. She hasn't moved since she got thrown off. Nate is taking care of everything, along with Trevor. They called an ambulance."

"Did you see what happened?"

"No. Nate and I were at the back of the line. I couldn't see much of anything."

"It's not my fault," said a male voice behind us. I turned to see Josh standing a little ways back. Several men turned around as well and glared at him. I looked from the men to Josh.

"It's not my fault," he said again, seeming dazed.

"Of course, it isn't," I said, hoping to comfort him.

"Why were they going so damn fast? I couldn't stop. Is she going to be okay?"

"They're taking Sylvia to the hospital," Caroline said.

"What happened, Josh?" I asked, leading him farther away from the men.

"I don't know. They were going so fast. And I don't know how to drive those things. I mean, I've driven them, but ... never at that rate of speed. And every one of those guys has been drinking. It's their fault too. They were going way too fast."

"So, you were riding with Sylvia and she flew off?" I asked.

"No. No. I wasn't with her. I was alone. She was with Trevor."

He seemed to come out of himself, then looked me directly in the eye. "She wouldn't have it any other way, though I tried. I don't know if Trevor was for it or not. Honestly, the woman just jumped on the back. Maybe they'd talked before. I can't say." His shoulders slumped. "I hope I didn't kill her."

"Tell us exactly what you remember," Caroline said.

"Okay, well, I pulled in right behind Trevor and Sylvia. For a while, we drove at a reasonable speed, but then it got faster. The line would speed up, then slow down. Real jerky. I tried to keep a safe distance. It felt safe to me. Then all of a sudden it got really fast, out of control. I kept thinking ... we're going too fast, too damn fast. That's when it happened. I saw a flash of brake lights and then I was on top of them, slammed right into them. I flew off, hit hard. Trevor must have stomped on his brakes. I have no idea why. Maybe someone up ahead did something stupid. Maybe he panicked. But I swear, it wasn't my fault."

"None of this should have happened," I said. "This whole snowmobile thing was a stupid idea. Wolfgang should have known better."

"Have you heard anything about Sylvia?" he asked. "Do you know if she's still unconscious? Maybe I should go over there."

My ears picked up the wail of an approaching ambulance.

"Josh," Caroline said, "you should go too, get checked out at the hospital. You took a heck of a hit too."

"No, I'm okay, just bruised, I think. I'll go later, maybe. I think I'll take off now. Tell Nate he can reach me at my mother's if he needs me. He has the number. I'll see you two later."

"Bye, Josh," we said.

"He's pretty shook up," said Caroline.

"Yes. Thinks it's all his fault."

"Legally, maybe it is. But I sure wouldn't blame him. If I blamed anyone, it would be Wolfgang. You know, just between you and me, I think I saw Sylvia open an eye when she thought no one was looking. But I could be wrong. But maybe she's not as hurt as she seems."

"Trevor's okay, isn't he?"

"He said so."

We watched as the ambulance pulled up and gave one last shriek before stopping. The attendants examined Sylvia, and I saw her lift her head to talk to them. They secured her onto a stretcher, and then carefully loaded her inside the ambulance. I could see Trevor and Bob talking, then Bob hopped in with Sylvia. Trevor looked on as they sped away, then turned until he spotted me. I looked down, pretending not to see him, expecting him to walk over. But when I looked up, he was gone.

"Well," said Caroline, "guess I'll go find Nate. You coming?"

"Sure."

"I heard someone say Wolfgang's still planning to start his bonfire. Guess no one could talk him out of it."

"Linda will be thrilled."

We found Nate and the three of us rode our snowmobiles back to the house. I walked inside, hoping to find Linda, but she wasn't around. I stopped for a drink of water, then headed out again.

Wolfgang's bonfire was blazing, and a small group of people were standing near it. As I drew close, I could see that Trevor was one of them. He saw me too and stepped aside, allowing me access to the fire.

"I thought you weren't going to ride tonight," he said. "How are you feeling?"

"I'm okay. I'll survive. Are you all right?"

"Yeah."

Linda approached the blaze from the other side of the circle, then reached toward the fire, seeking its heat. "What time is it?" I heard her ask.

Wolfgang hefted a log and threw it on the fire, discharging a flurry of sparks. Linda quickly pulled her arms back.

"Late," he said, "but who cares? I'm not getting up early. My self-imposed vacation starts tomorrow. I'll be skiing my butt off this week, and lounging in the tropics the next."

"I'm going back in," Linda said, barely glancing at him.

"Nightie night," he said.

She ignored him and kept walking.

"Did your friend go home?" Trevor asked mildly, but I could detect the undercurrent of anger.

"Yes."

"What an asshole."

I kept my eyes directed at the fire, not rising to the bait.

Later, as guests departed, Wolfgang let the fire die down. Finally, Trevor turned to me. "Let's get out of here."

"Fine with me."

We thanked Wolfgang for a great party, despite the accident, then began walking toward the house. I looked up at Trevor. "I'll just say goodnight to Linda."

"Meet you out by the car."

But I couldn't find her and had to assume she'd gone to bed. That wasn't like Linda, going off to sleep with the house still in disarray.

I steeled myself for the ride home, staring out the windshield, avoiding any possible eye contact with Trevor.

"Fun party," he said.

"Yes, it was ... for a while."

"I hope you see now what kind of a guy he is."

"Can we talk about this some other time? I don't want to fight with you right now."

"Fine." Then he faced me. "No—I need to talk about this now. The guy's an asshole. He ran into me for God's sake. He put a woman in the *goddamn hospital.*"

"Who happened to be riding on the back of *your snowmobile.* Now why was that?"

"Oh, of course—Sylvia. Your favorite subject."

"Well, why was she there? *Why is she always there?*"

Trevor slammed on the brakes at the light. My seatbelt yanked me backward.

"What did you want me to do?" he shouted. "Throw her off?"

"Yes," I shouted back. "Something. You don't do *anything.*"

My chest began to heave, and I turned away, unable to stifle the sobs.

"Okay," he said quietly. "Okay, that's enough."

"Just," I whimpered, my words punctuated with little gasps, "leave

... me ... alone."

I wouldn't look at him the rest of the way home, and grabbed my robe and pillow and made up the bed in the guest room. I averted my gaze each time I passed him in the hall.

He didn't try to talk to me either.

After he'd gone to bed, I got up and walked downstairs to the kitchen. As soon as I sat down, Annabelle jumped into my lap, startling me. "You're supposed to be asleep, Annie-B."

She smiled her doggy smile, then hopped down and trotted back and forth between me and the front door. "Right," I said, "Trevor forgot to walk you, didn't he?" I pulled my robe tighter, shoved my bare feet into boots, and led Annabelle on a leash outside to the driveway.

Chapter 20

The next day, tired and unable to concentrate, I hopped into my Jeep and drove over to the old house. I decided it was a good time to see what kind of progress my newly hired workers were making.

Earlier in the morning, Trevor had knocked on my guest room door and apologized. I was grateful, because I was feeling really low. It was the first time we'd slept in separate beds under the same roof since we'd been together. I hadn't gotten much sleep and felt sick with misery. I didn't ask him if he'd called the hospital, or spoken with Sylvia or Bob, and he didn't bring it up.

Tomorrow, I was meeting Sue at a location as yet to be determined, where she would hand over her first report. I'd tried to push the meeting forward, anxious for any news, but she needed more time to pull everything together, including editing out repetitious ho-hum stretches of videotape.

The old house was a mess when I walked in. Plastic tarpaulins lay everywhere, protecting the furniture and floors from paint splatters. The workers, two industrious men in their twenties, looked down at me from their ladders as I tread carefully between paint buckets and pans.

"Looks good," I said.

They acknowledged me with smiles, and kept on painting. They'd accomplished a lot in the past few days, finishing the upstairs bedrooms and bath, also the living room. Now they were working on the entrance near the stairs. I'd asked them to strip the faded wallpaper in the kitchen, along with the paneling in my dad's little room. They'd accomplished that yesterday, but I hadn't seen it yet. I planned to repaper those two rooms. In fact, my next stop would be in town to pick up samples.

As I entered my dad's room, I stopped in my tracks, startled by the change. The walls beneath the paneling looked awful—yellowed and dirty. Next to my father's desk, a bunch of scribbling covered a section of wall. My dad had made a habit of jotting notes on the wall when he was in a hurry and couldn't find paper. It had driven my mother crazy, hence the installation of dark paneling and a chalk board.

I walked over and ran my hand over his bold inked script—*call Benny in the morning, take order—cancel shipment #5038 to Jake, late on payment—deposit checks by the fifteenth.* And on and on …

I continued reading, knowing this would likely be the last time I'd ever see these long ago messages. Then I stopped. No, that didn't have to happen. I ran out to the Jeep and grabbed my camera, then spent the next few minutes taking close-up shots of the wall. I didn't want to lose these mementos. Now, I could keep them with me always.

I stayed for only a few minutes more, then drove into town and picked up my wallpaper samples. When I returned home, Annabelle greeted me, yapping, at the door.

"Ooo, good dog, such a good, good dog," I cooed as she bounced happily at my feet. "Do you want to see what I've got? Oh, yes you do, yes you do." She wiggled so hard I thought she'd lose her footing.

I pulled a tube of wallpaper from the bag and rolled it across the floor toward the kitchen doorway. She chased after it until it stopped, then crouched on front paws and barked at it, presumably waiting for it to come to life and roll again. I lightly kicked the roll, and she was off.

Bringing the bag into the kitchen, I grabbed scissors and snipped open several rolls and spread them across the floor. "Which one do *you* like, Annabelle?" I pointed down at one and she followed my finger, then stopped near the paper. "Yes, I like that one too."

She leisurely sniffed each roll, then moved to a far one and flopped down, stopping to chew the edge of it. "And that one? Yes, it's very nice, one of my favorites. Do you want to go with me and try these out at the house?"

Annabelle barked yes, once I found her leash.

I grabbed a handful of puppy treats for later on, then attached the leash to her collar.

It was late afternoon when we arrived at the old house. One of the workers was loading equipment into his van, getting ready to leave, I supposed. It appeared the other man was still inside.

I entered by way of the back door off the kitchen. The man was washing his hands in the kitchen sink.

"Hi," I said. "Are you planning to leave right away?"

"No, ma'am, I'll be here for maybe another hour. If that's okay?"

"Oh, sure. Stay as long as you want. I just thought I'd try these out." I pointed at the samples. "See if I like them. I won't be in your way, will I?" I pulled Annabelle's leash close, drawing her away from the freshly painted walls.

"No, ma'am, and don't worry. Everything is dry now. Your dog can't hurt much."

"You be good," I said softly to Annabelle, offering her a treat, "or we're out of here." I hooked her leash handle under a kitchen table leg, and though Annabelle whined and tugged at it at first, she finally flopped down.

I tacked up the first wallpaper sample, vertical stripes of pale green and gold fading into each other, then stood back, trying to envision a whole wall of the pattern. Not thrilled, I tacked up another sample, then two at a time, deliberating. Finally, I picked out a print consisting of tiny violets on a white background, and fastened several lengths of that alone on the wall. It was a good possibility. With a nice white or lavender border, it could be charming. I tacked up several more samples to compare.

It wasn't until the shadows in the kitchen grew long that I realized the house was very quiet. Annabelle was asleep. But hadn't I heard the worker's cell phone ring what felt like only moments before? He'd been talking to someone. Or had he been talking to me?

Quickly, I stepped to the front window. The driveway was empty.

"Come on, Annabelle. We're leaving." I gathered the wallpaper and placed the rolls in the bag. As I was rooting in my purse for keys, Annabelle leapt up—teeth bared, growling.

"What is it? What's the matter?" I held my breath, my heart beginning to jump.

A moment later, I heard footsteps at the back door. A man's profile appeared at the window.

Too late, I realized the door was unlocked.

The knob turned.

Annabelle charged for the door, then squealed, yanked back by the leash.

"Who's there?" I called out, then hoping it might be one of the workers, asked, "Who is it? Did you forget something?"

The door opened a crack. I backed away, reaching for my cell phone.

A man's head jut inside. "Hello," he said, smiling. "It's Gwyn, isn't it?"

"Who are you? You've got no business in here without my permission."

He studied Annabelle, then stepped inside and closed the door. "Relax. I guess you don't recognize me."

"And I guess you didn't hear me." I held up my phone. "I already called the cops." I made a swift move toward Annabelle, but the man instantly stepped between us. Annabelle lunged for his leg, but missed.

"Hey, if your mutt gets loose, I'll have to hurt it. Is that what you want?"

"No. Don't. Calm down, girl. It's okay."

She stopped struggling, but continued to growl.

"Listen," he said. "I'm not here to hurt you. I saw you drive up and I need to talk to someone. I'm tired of running from the cops. I'm Craig Foster."

I stared at him. It *was* Craig. The long blond hair was gone, short now, almost a military-style cut, and brown, but definitely Craig. He wore glasses with large unattractive plastic frames, and his pants hung too short, showing discolored white socks. The disguise was a good one. He appeared geeky, a nerd. Nothing at all like I remembered.

"Give me one minute," he said, "then I'm out of here. I didn't kill your sister. For chrissake I was in love with her."

I pulled my arms tightly across my stomach. "Just because you bust in here and tell me you loved my sister, don't expect me to believe you're innocent. If you're so innocent, why did you run from the police?"

"Because whoever set me up, did one hell of a job. And I'm not stupid enough to do time for anybody."

"Okay. But I still don't have any reason to believe you."

"And I don't expect you will, unless I find what I've been looking for."

"What's that?"

"A box."

Annabelle jumped up, barking.

"Why? What's so special about it?"

"I wish I knew," he said, "but I think whatever it is might clear me. I think she was having an affair, and I think he killed her. She used to write these notes, hide them all over the house. I think she was scared."

"How do you know there was a box?"

"Right before she died, she joked that if anything happened to her, to look for a box she'd stashed in the house. I didn't think she was serious. She could be really weird sometimes. I didn't pay much attention—until she died. The thing is, he might be looking for it too. I saw someone take off out of this place the other night."

"Where have you been all this time?"

"Here and there, but I keep coming back to search, but now I've run out of time. You put a for-sale sign out front."

I hesitated, thinking. "I found a note too."

"*So you see I'm telling the truth.* What did your note say?"

"It said she was having an affair, and that she was afraid, and she mentioned a box."

"*You see. You see.* Did she say where she put it?"

"No."

"Then it's probably gone. I've looked everywhere. I've been through every box in this house, in the basement, in the closets. When things quieted down after she died and I thought it was safe, I used to come by and go through them, but there's nothing. I didn't find anything. Did you move stuff of hers? Throw things out?"

"Yes, some things. You're right. Whatever it is might be gone."

"Then I'm screwed."

"I think you should go to the police and tell them what you've told me. I'd be there to back you up."

"Not a chance. They don't give guys like me the benefit of the doubt.... But there is one place I haven't searched yet." He reached up and removed his glasses. "Did she ever mention the initials, T.D., something T.D., maybe a guy's initials or a code word?"

"No."

"I never could figure that out. But I saw it once in a note. I could have it wrong. It could have been some kind of a symbol. Do you know what she might have meant by it?"

"No idea."

"What happened to the furniture she had upstairs? The bedroom furniture. Why did you get rid of it?"

"I didn't."

"Where is it?"

"Actually, I sort of did get rid of it. I gave it to a friend, and she gave it to charity."

He glared at me. "Right. If you've still got the stuff, you don't have to tell me. After all," he said, his voice rising angrily, "*it's only my whole life at stake here.*" He jabbed a finger in my face. "You know, you could be next, if he thinks you're looking too."

"Why would he think that?"

"Maybe he won't, but I'd sure watch my ass if I were you. And I wouldn't go telling anyone about seeing me here either."

The light on the timer switched on in the living room, and he shrank farther into the darkness. "I have to go."

"No. Wait. I need to ask you about that night. I need to know what happened."

"Thought you said the cops were coming."

"No. I didn't get a chance to call them."

"Didn't think so." Still, he glanced toward the street. "What is it you want to know?"

"That night. Were you with her at all? What did she say? Where was she going? Why was she walking out on the road by herself? Why did she get out of her truck?"

"Hey, you're asking me things I can't begin to know. I did see her earlier that night. She told me she was going 'out.' That was just like her, take off and not care what I thought. She didn't tell me to leave though, so I stayed, figured I'd see her later. I watched some TV. Eventually I went to bed. I heard her come home, *I thought*. I heard her truck pull in, heard the garage door close. I don't know what time that was, but I fell back to sleep. I left in the morning, never saw her, assumed she'd come home and took off again. I didn't think a thing of it. But she was already dead by the time that truck rolled into the garage. Whoever brought it back had a lot of guts too. What if I'd seen them? They knew someone was inside. My motorcycle was parked in the drive. I guess they figured they could set me up that way. But since no one saw me here, I told the cops I was at my place, all night. And guess what? They didn't believe me ... and blamed her murder on me." He turned and opened the back door. "That's about it. See ya."

"Wait. How will I find you if I need ...?"

But the darkness had already gobbled him up.

I released Annabelle, locked the back door and left. As I pulled the Jeep's gearshift into reverse, headlights loomed in my rearview mirror. A car peeled in behind me.

Someone got out, slammed the door, then walked to my window. Trevor. I rolled the window down.

He leaned in. "What in God's name are you doing here alone this late? I've been worried sick, no note, no call, nothing."

"I was just leaving."

"Just leaving? It's pitch black out. Why in the name of ...?" He stopped, then shook his head. "We'll talk about this at home."

He followed me all the way back to the house, then inside, still hovering over me as we walked into the kitchen.

"I'm sorry, okay?" I said before he could start up again. "I didn't do it on purpose. I made a mistake."

"What were you doing there so late? I don't know what made me think you'd be there. I get home, no one's here, the lights are off. So I drive over there, and I find you alone in the house."

"I'm sorry. Don't flip out about it. I stayed longer than I realized. I didn't mean to worry you."

"What were you doing?"

"*Nothing*. I was trying out some wallpaper samples. I planned to leave once the workers did, but I got involved and lost track of the time."

"You said you wouldn't go over there alone anymore."

"I wasn't alone. I just said that. Can we please change the subject?"

"Do you have any idea how I'd feel if something happened to you? Do you think I don't worry that maybe that creep will come back here someday? He could. I don't mean to scare you, Gwyn, but he could."

"I know that."

"Then why do you pull these stunts?"

"I'm not pulling any *stunts*. I stayed too long, that's all. I wasn't thinking."

"No, and neither was your sister, or she might still be alive."

It felt like a fist to the gut.

"It wasn't Kelly's fault."

"No, not entirely, but she wasn't exactly the world's best judge of character or she wouldn't have hung out with that creep."

I eyed him, so very tempted to take this a little further, maybe mention that Craig wasn't the only creep that Kelly hung around. Instead, I tried a different tack. "Did you call the hospital?"

"Yes, I did. They discharged Sylvia this morning."

"No brain damage?"

"That's not funny, Gwyn."

"I didn't mean it to be."

"Well no, it appears she's not ... damaged," he said, a hint of a grin appearing at the corner of his mouth. "She came through it okay. They took x-rays and a CAT-scan and there doesn't seem to be—"

"So glad to hear it."

He frowned. "Your buddy, Josh, he'd better hope she doesn't sue his ass."

"For what? Oh, come on. She wouldn't really, would she?"

He shrugged. "You never know with Sylvia."

"God."

Chapter 21

"Are you ready for this?" Sue asked as she breezed through the door of Caroline's apartment. In one hand, she held her briefcase and in the other what looked to be an ordinary shopping bag.

"I guess," I said, nervously swiping my hands across my jeans. I'd arrived a few minutes earlier and unlocked the apartment. Care had left a key for me under the doormat.

Sue looked around. "Thank Caroline for me. This saved me having to find a place. Mmm, I smell coffee."

"Like a cup?"

"Sure would." She dropped her bags and followed me into the kitchen.

I took an empty mug from the cabinet. "Care brewed the coffee. She left a plate of oatmeal raisin cookies for us too. Help yourself."

"So where's she at?"

"Over at her mom's. Guess she owed her a visit."

"Well, we shouldn't be too long."

Caroline had offered to vacate her place so Sue and I could have complete privacy with no interruptions. Care knew I'd feel more comfortable here. Once Sue left, Caroline would be back to sop up all the details. That is, if I decided to tell her any. Best friends or not,

I might not be ready.

Today, Sue wore an auburn wig with gold highlights, and I wondered if Caroline's sun-kissed hair had influenced her choice. The two shades were almost identical. Sue's complexion appeared a milky white and her eyes a bright green, but I wasn't sure if this was her natural color or just excellent makeup and a new pair of contact lenses. And it was impossible to tell.

I hadn't yet found the nerve to ask which identity was the real Sue. And I wasn't sure she'd tell me even if I did. So far, she hadn't gotten all that chummy. I knew virtually nothing about her personal life.

"Would you like to do this in any particular order?" she asked as we settled onto the couch with our coffee.

"Do this?" I said, finding it difficult to swallow.

She smiled then, sympathetically, I thought. "It's okay, Gwyn. There's room for speculation in some of this. It's not all cut and dried. What I meant was, who would you like to start with first?"

"Oh ... well then, Craig. Have you found out anything about him?"

"Yes, I have, and unfortunately it's both good and bad news. He's been spotted recently. Here—in Glenwood. That information came from a couple of different sources."

"He's here?"

"Yes. So you need to be on the lookout. Also be very careful. Don't try to do anything on your own if you spot him. Call the cops. Agreed?"

"Of course."

"What I can't figure out is why he's back. Why would he chance coming back here? I don't think he's that stupid, certainly not if he's eluded the police this long." She stared at me, as if I might know the answer.

I shrugged. "So, what's the good news?"

"That if he sticks around, we'll nail him."

I wanted to tell Sue about my run-in with Craig, but I couldn't. Sue would be after him, possibly ask me to help set a trap, and if Craig sensed the noose tightening even a little, he'd fly. I'd never find out who killed my sister. Craig was onto something, the initials T.D., the whereabouts of the box. My instincts told me to hold off.

Sue pulled a videotape from the shopping bag.

"And now, your husband."

She leaned over to pop the video in.

"Sue—wait."

"What?"

"Well, I want to see ... and to hear it all, but before I do, I need to know, right now. Is he screwing Sylvia?"

"Unfortunately, that's the part that's not absolutely clear. I can't prove anything yet." She leaned toward me. "I thought it might be better to ease you in, let you see what I saw, so you can judge for yourself. I will say that in most of the cases of marital infidelity I've looked into, I'd be able to give you a definite yes or no by now. But something has happened. He's cut off relations with her, if he was having them to begin with. The lunches and a lot of the meetings have stopped. And it looks like it started right after Sylvia's trip to the hospital, after the snowmobile accident. Right after you hired me."

"God."

"Is it possible he knows you've hired a private detective?"

"No, how would he?"

"Maybe something you said? As clueless as some men are, others are incredibly good at reading women. Have you talked about Sylvia recently? Any fights in that vein?"

"Yes. I've mentioned her several times. And yes, we had a big fight in the car on the way home from Linda's party. After Sylvia's accident."

Sue brought her fingers to her chin and looked thoughtful. "You may have scared him off. Could be he's decided to cool things with her for a while, thinking you might check up on him. Maybe *they* had a fight. Maybe he's even called it off for good. Whatever's the case, if he's still involved with her, eventually he'll slip up. I assume you want me to continue surveillance."

"Yes."

"Are you ready for the tape now?"

I nodded.

The V.C.R. buzzed as she slipped the tape in. "This first shot is inside your husband's office—after hours I might add. Everyone else has gone home."

"What time is it?"

"About seven."

I watched as Trevor walked across the small reception area toward the front door. Sylvia called to him from outside. "Trevor, open the door."

He hesitated, then stepped forward. "I'm working, Sylvia. Seriously, I don't have time for you right now."

She jiggled the knob. "Open it. It's not open yet." Trevor released the lock and she marched in. "Since when do you lock the door on me? I told you I was coming."

"And I told you not to. Sylvia, I need to get back to work. We can talk later. Okay?"

"No, and stop making excuses. It's insulting."

He threw up his arms. "Why do I even talk?"

She flew forward and grasped him in her arms, then laid her head to his chest. "I know you're still mad at me. I'm sick about it. Please, don't be. I can't stand it when you're cold to me like this. It scares me."

He carefully removed her and pushed her back. "Sylvia, *go home.*"

"No. And don't talk to me like that. I can't take this, Trevor, waiting for you all the time, wondering when you'll be able to see me. It's driving me nuts. I need you. You have to leave her."

"Sylvia, you are so used to getting your own way you don't know when to quit. Now, I've got someone waiting for me to call back. Do you understand?"

"I don't—"

"I know. *You don't care.* But that's because you have me and a truckload of others making sure you don't have to care."

"Are you coming by tonight or not?"

He gazed up toward the ceiling. "I'll do what I can. Now let me work."

She lifted her face to his.

Trevor, appearing as if he might actually kiss her, instead brought his lips to her forehead.

"Nice," she spat out, then spun away. "Don't stand me up. I won't forget it this time."

The tape dissolved to white space. Sue reached over and stopped it. She looked at me. "On the positive side, we tracked him and he never showed up at her apartment. She has a place in Glenwood she's renting, though she's not there most of the time. Appears to travel a lot on business. We don't have one shot of your husband showing up there. He didn't call her back that night either. But they have been meeting for lunch, like I said, at least until recently, sometimes alone, sometimes with another man, Robert Morris. We got that information from restaurant employees who know your husband, and notes on his daily calendar. We have snapshots of the most recent lunch with Sylvia, but none of it proves anything."

"He didn't kiss her, not a real kiss."

"No, he didn't. But could be he's in the middle of breaking it off with her. Maybe she's gotten too weird. Doing a *Fatal Attraction*. He can't out and out dump her because he does business with her, plus she might go off the deep end and decide to take revenge, tip you off. Lots of women aren't above doing that—the anonymous caller, note in the mailbox routine."

I closed my eyes. *You have to leave her. You have to leave her.*

"Gwyn?"

"What?"

She shook her head. "Where did you go? Are you okay?"

"I'm ... no, I guess I'm not."

"This stuff is never easy. Do you want to continue?"

"Yes."

She pulled a large manila envelope from the shopping bag. "I have copies of recent emails between the two of them. Most of that is business related. You can look at them privately if you'd prefer. Also, I have his end of phone calls, the office, the cell, audiotapes and transcripts of everything, but I've only included the calls to and from Sylvia. Unfortunately, there's nothing conclusive there either. You'll see what I mean."

"What about Kelly? Is there any chance Trevor was involved with her, that he killed her?"

"I did another background check on your husband, like you asked. It checks out, same as the other one, clean record, no priors. But we also checked the telephone records from his office on the night your sister died, and no calls went out. If he was there, there's no evidence of it. In a few days, we'll have the numbers he called from his cell, but I don't expect to find anything. The cops would have checked that out too. We're also checking to see if anyone spotted him with her, either that night, or on other occasions, maybe at her place, or the local motels. Some motels run a hidden camera of who goes in and out, in case they get robbed. Of course, your husband may have rented a place, wouldn't be too difficult. We're still looking into that."

I looked down, my heart pounding so hard I was sure she'd hear it.

"To tell you the truth," she said, "I'm more worried about your sister."

"Linda? Why?"

"Her husband beats her up."

"Oh God. I knew it."

"We found out he's put her in the hospital at least two other times, other than the time you told me about. Could be he's the one that was involved with your sister Kelly. Appears he doesn't mind sleeping around. That doesn't mean he killed her, of course, but it doesn't mean he didn't. I plan to go deeper into his background—with your permission. Try to tie some things together."

"Yes. Of course."

"Listen, if it looks like he's about to hurt her, we could bring in the cops. Stop it. Right there. Haul his ass to jail. It's up to you. I've got someone listening in every minute."

"Yes, *please* make sure she's protected. If he knows about the surveillance, then he knows. I don't care if Linda hates me either. That *scum*."

"Sure is." She eyed me. I'd started to shiver. I crossed my arms and held them tight to my body in an effort to stop it.

"Maybe we should take a breather," she said. "Finish this later."

"No. Please. Go ahead."

"Okay, about your friend Josh. Though the police never seriously saw him as a suspect, I do find it odd that he left so soon after your sister's death. That always raises a red flag in my book. He left the States for two months. We traced him to Vancouver, British Columbia, where he rented office space with attached living quarters. Did he ever mention to you why he was there?"

"No, I never got a chance to talk to him after we broke up. He wouldn't see me. I've only talked to him recently."

"Well, we're doing some checking in that direction." She stopped, reached for her coffee. "Is there anything you'd like to ask me? Maybe something you'd like to tell me? I know all of this has come at you pretty fast."

"I don't know. No. Not right now."

"Well, probably you'll have questions later."

"Yes."

"There's more to look at on the tapes, but no more declarations from Sylvia toward your husband, just more business talk, and some other stuff that's open to misinterpretation. Don't take much stock in it. I also have the tape from inside Linda's home, of Wolfgang threatening her, and one fight that came close to escalating. I have tapes of the more mundane stuff too, if you're interested. Each is labeled. Also lots of photos, transcripts of emails, audiotapes. You'll be busy for a while. I wouldn't keep any of this at home for obvious reasons, unless you have an incredibly good hiding place. Maybe a safe."

"Trevor has the combination."

"Then I'd rent something, a small storage locker, something like that. I have the names of a few places." She reached into the shopping bag and drew out a notebook. "The information is written down here. Or, if you want, I could locate something for you."

"I'll let you know."

She nodded. "I'll have another report for you fairly soon."

"Good." I rose from the couch. "I think I'll stay here for a while longer, review some of this. Caroline won't mind."

"Sure."

I walked her to the door.

It was two hours before I called Caroline. I'd gone through the videotapes, fast-forwarding through sections of them, then skimming the emails and listening to bits of conversation on the audiotapes. Sue was right. I'd be busy for a while.

"Hey, Care."

"God, I thought you'd never call. My stomach's been doing flip-flops for hours. So?"

"Come pick me up. We'll go for a drive in the mountains, to our usual spot. I'll tell you on the way."

"Be there in five minutes. Oh, wait ... I have to stop for gas."

"Don't bother. We'll take the Jeep."

When she pulled in, I ran downstairs with the shopping bag.

"What's that?" she asked as I approached.

"Everything. You drive."

I handed her the keys and we hopped in.

"So how bad is it?" she asked.

"Pretty bad."

"Is he ... cheating?"

"Looks like it."

"Oh, man." Caroline shook her head sadly, then reached over and touched my hand. "I'm so sorry, Gwyn. I swear. I never would have believed it."

"Sue didn't catch him in the actual act. From the looks of it, he stopped seeing Sylvia recently, maybe for his own reasons, or maybe because he thinks I might check up on him. That's what Sue thinks. It all looks pretty suspicious."

"So what are you going to do?"

"I don't know. I want you to look at the tape. Maybe I'm wrong. I hope I'm wrong."

"As soon as we get back."

"Can I leave this stuff with you?" I pointed to the shopping bag. "I can't take it home, and I want to study it some more."

"Of course. And I promise I won't look at it unless you're there."

"Doesn't matter. You might as well. You might see something I missed."

"What about Craig?" she asked. "Did Sue find out anything about him?"

"Yes. He's been spotted here in Glenwood. She thinks they'll grab him if he sticks around."

Caroline's eyes opened wide. "God, what if Craig was the one in your old house? I'll bet it *was* him. I mean, it makes sense. It would be easy enough for him to figure out the place is empty. All he'd have to do is drive by a few times. Probably thought it'd be a good place to hide out."

"Yes."

"But why is he back? He must want something." She turned quickly to me. "And that's another good reason for you to stay far away from there."

We wound our way up the mountain and parked in the woods alongside the road, our spot, a stretch of dirt road we hiked often. I quickly filled Caroline in on Wolfgang.

"What?" she said. "This gets worse and worse. How could Linda stay with that bastard?" She shook her head, then stared out the windshield. "God, Wolfgang could be the one Kelly was talking about in her letter. Craig might be innocent. Maybe he only ran because he knew no one would believe him. Maybe he came back to look for proof to clear himself."

"It's possible. Hey, Care, do you ever remember Kelly talking about someone with the initials, T.D.?"

"T.D.? No, why?"

"Oh, I read something in one of her journals. It just got me thinking. Maybe there's a connection somehow."

"Did she write anything about Wolfgang?"

"Not that I saw, but some of her journals, the most recent ones, are missing."

"Who took them?"

"I don't know."

Caroline drew a sharp intake of air. "_Wolfgang._ Or Craig. Yeah. Maybe he knew about Kelly's journals. The guy practically lived with her. Maybe he thought he'd find some answers in them. _Maybe he did._" She looked over at me. "Maybe he's filling in the puzzle pieces before he goes to the police."

We drove back to Caroline's apartment and she viewed the video scene between Trevor and Sylvia.

"God, she's such a bitch," was the first thing out of Care's mouth. "How could Trevor even like her?"

"Maybe he likes the sex."

"This tape doesn't really _prove_ anything. It looks bad, but it doesn't prove that Trevor's nailing her."

"It's okay, Care. Don't try to defend him. I know how it looks."

I handed over a few of the emails.

She read one aloud, mimicking Sylvia's syrupy sing-song voice. "I can't wait to see you today, baby. Let's go to our favorite restaurant. I want to be alone with you. I miss you. I can't keep my mind on my work. Meet me at twelve-thirty. Don't be late."

"And this is Trevor's reply," she said. "Don't wait for me. My meeting with Larry could run long. I'll try to make it, but I'll let you know."

Care looked over to me. "This does not sound like a man in the

throes of a love like none he's ever known. He's barely civil to her."
She read a few more emails, then gazed up. "And it looks like all
these are like this. Trevor is short with her, doesn't say anything even
remotely romantic. He's almost rude."

"Yes, it could be over. I agree. But the point is ... *was* he having an
affair with her? Even if Trevor only used Sylvia to cement this condo
project, or slept with her out of sexual curiosity, or just wanted to feel
up her great tits, it doesn't matter. If he fucked her, we're through."

"Yeah."

We flipped through some of the photographs, Trevor and Sylvia
at lunch, she leaning in, whispering something into his ear. Trevor
and Sylvia outside the restaurant, Trevor's hand behind her back,
helping her across the street. It was an intimate gesture, but one that
could also be viewed as polite, depending on what you wanted to see.
I'd seen Trevor do the same type of thing with his mother. *One of the
many photographs that could easily be misinterpreted.* Like Sue said.

I showed Caroline the tape of the fight between Linda and
Wolfgang. It started as a shouting match, then escalated to Wolfgang
making a grab for her, then Linda sprinting to the bedroom where
she locked herself inside and threatened to call the police.

"If you touch me, I'll do it," she screamed. "And if you *ever* fucking
hit me again, I'll kill you. I'll kill you, you fucking *lunatic.* You stay away
from me, you piece of *shit.*" Then Linda started crying, and Wolfgang
stalked out of the house, first hurling a lamp against the wall on his
way. I heard a car engine starting, then a screech of tires as he took
off. The tape skipped forward, showing Linda cautiously exiting the
bedroom, then peeking outside to the drive, then also leaving the
house in her car. The tape skipped forward again, showing Wolfgang's
return hours later, then a call to Linda on his cell, apologizing, begging
her to come back, crying himself, promising not to *ever, ever* hurt her
again, that he was sorry, sorry, so sorry....

Later on, after I left Caroline's, I called Linda. She was working
out with Wolfgang in their private gym. She couldn't have sounded
happier.

Chapter 22

Trevor wasn't home when I returned from Caroline's, and that was good. I had no idea how I was going to hide the way I was feeling right now. According to his message on my cell, he'd be home on time tonight, by six. But I was ready for a last minute excuse. If he did call, I'd act the part of gullible wife, say I understood the delay, then hope Sue would finally get the goods on film and put an end to any remaining doubts.

Annabelle met me at the door, my faithful Annabelle. I stooped to pet her, then brought from the closet the warm wool holiday coat I'd bought for her, red with tiny gold jingle bells attached. She squirmed as I snapped her in, but her tail was wagging, knowing we'd be taking our usual walk around the neighborhood.

Lights were coming on in the houses, and I was able to see Christmas trees shimmering in the windows, and reindeer posed mid-prance in the yards. Usually it made me smile. Now I felt dead.

Annabelle stopped to nose around a bush, preparing to provide extra fertilizer. I'd been going over and over what Craig had told me, what Kelly had written, trying to pull this stubborn rabbit out of the hat. Kelly had left clues for us to find, hidden in a nook here, a cranny there, just in case her worst fears were realized. How I wished she could speak to me now, tell me what I needed to know.

I looked up to the heavens, at the slate gray sky and scudding clouds overhead. I'd been feeling her presence more and more these last few days, drifting at the edge of my thoughts. Perhaps she was trying to lead me to the truth, set my feet in the right direction, if only I would listen.

Oh, Kelly, please help me. I miss you so. Are you somewhere up there, baby? Looking down on me now? What is it you want me to know? I'm listening. I'm here, and I'm listening. You can tell me, whatever it is. No matter what happened back then, don't worry. I love you and I forgive you. I forgave you a long time ago....

I fell asleep on the couch after the walk, Annabelle near me, curled against my stomach. I didn't wake until the headlights of Trevor's Cadillac flashed alongside the house as he pulled up the drive. I wiped the sleep from my eyes and stumbled to the kitchen. The clock read six-fifteen.

I heard Trevor's footsteps cross the tile floor, then he called out my name, coming up behind me as I stood at the counter. Frigid cold wafted off his clothes. He hugged me, and I shivered.

"How's my Gwyn?" he said, kissing me on the back of the head. "I'm home on time. Did you notice? Just like I said I would be."

"Guess I didn't believe you. I don't have anything planned for dinner." I shrugged away from him.

"I'm not hungry, not right now. Maybe we can order a pizza. Or go out."

"Maybe."

He pulled me around to face him, his eyes large and dark like liquid black buttons. It was then that it hit me, like an electric shock. What Kelly had meant by the initials T.D. "Oh," I said, my heart revving so fast I could barely think.

"What?"

"I just remembered ... something. I was supposed to call Caroline. She asked me to call ... about.... I don't know. I'd better go call her."

"Sure." He seemed slightly confused.

I felt him watching as I bypassed the kitchen phone and fled down the hall to my studio.

Oh, please be home, Caroline, please.

"Hey," she said, "what's up?"

"I need a favor. Can you meet me at the old house—right now? I don't want to go there alone and I left some wallpaper samples I need. I'd go by myself, but you said—"

"What's going on? Is something wrong? Is Trevor there?"

"Yes."

"Sure, I can meet you. Nate's here too. We'll both go. But wait a few minutes before you leave. Give us time to check out the house."

"Trevor," I yelled as I ran back down the hall and grabbed my coat. "I'm going over to Care's. She wants to show me something. I won't be long. Do you want me to stop for pizza on the way home?"

He came up behind me as I was about to escape through the side door. "You're leaving? But I just got home. What's the big rush?"

"I don't know. It's Care. She's excited. She wants me to see something she bought. I won't be long. I'll get the pizza."

"Don't bother. We can get it later."

Nate's squad car was parked in the drive when I pulled up. Caroline sat alone in the passenger seat. She waved me over. A few seconds later, Nate, carrying a big flashlight, emerged from around the back of the house. He gave the two of us a nod and we followed him inside.

I walked directly to the kitchen and scooped the bag of samples off the kitchen table.

"So, is that everything?" Caroline asked.

"No, just one more thing." I headed for the basement, flipping on the light at the top of the stairs as I started down.

"Wait," she said. "Wait for us."

I began searching through the cardboard boxes containing Kelly's belongings, tearing the boxes open and pulling stuff out.

"What are you looking for?" Care asked.

"I want to find a teddy bear we used to have. I need it for a painting I'm doing, kind of a Christmas thing."

"A teddy bear? Couldn't you just buy another one?"

"No, this one is special."

Caroline helped me rummage through the boxes, and then Nate.

"How big is it?" Care asked. "Little or medium sized?"

"Kind of medium," I said. "Like this." I pulled it out.

It reminded me of a teddy bear corpse, sealed in plastic as it was. I unzipped the bag and reached inside, relieved to find the old bear dry and unharmed. I stared into its round black button eyes. "We can leave now."

When they'd turned their backs and started for the stairs, I pressed on the bear's stomach, and thought I felt something.

We met at the top and Caroline gave me an odd look, knitting her brows. "Are you not telling me something? You seem awfully nervous."

I shook my head. "Can't talk about it now."

I thanked them both for helping me out, then hurried home. I left the bear outside in the Jeep. I'd finish my examination of it once Trevor wasn't around.

He was standing in the kitchen when I walked in, a frown on his face.

"Were you expecting something?" He took an approximately eight-inch square package wrapped in newspaper off the table. "I found this on the front porch. Someone knocked on the door just before you drove in."

"Who was it?"

"I don't know. They didn't stay."

"Is there a label on it?"

"No—no label. Think we should open it?"

"As long as it isn't some kind of letter bomb." Then a thought struck me and I reached for the package. "Let me see it." He handed it over. It felt slightly heavy. "Maybe we should wait," I said. "Could be a surprise Christmas present or something. Maybe Caroline brought it over."

"Caroline? Why would she do that?"

"I don't know."

"I think we should open it now, find out for sure."

He wasn't going to budge. There was no way to avoid this.

I slowly tore away the paper. Eventually, a black lacquered jewelry box appeared, one I recognized immediately.

"Well, I was right," I said. "It is from Caroline. I saw this in town and looks like she decided to buy it for me. I'll have to call and thank her."

"Why would she drive over and just dump it on the porch?

Especially since you just saw her."

"I don't know. Maybe she wanted to surprise me."

"Yes ... maybe." He eyed me, then turned his back and headed through the foyer toward the living room.

Quickly, I carried the box out of the kitchen and down the hall toward my studio. I entered, holding onto Kelly's old jewelry box tightly, a box I hadn't seen since she died. Hands shaking, I undid the small latch and lifted the lid.

Inside was a note, and below it a cylindrical metal canister used for film. I opened the note.

This is what he was looking for. Watch out! I'll contact you soon. I have something else. Could be proof if I'm right.

I heard Trevor approaching and hid the note and film container behind my back, then realized how suspicious that looked, and chucked them both onto a nearby table. The canister rolled until it found the edge of the table and dropped to the floor.

"So did you call her?" Trevor stood in the doorway.

I stared down at the jewelry box I still held in one hand, aware that my face was reddening despite willing myself to be calm. "No, I'll call and thank her tomorrow."

"Won't she want to know that you got it okay?"

"She won't care."

"I think you should call her. Why wait to thank her? I might want to thank her too."

"All right. If it will make you happy, I'll call." I dialed Caroline's number at home, but she didn't answer, and I was not about to leave a message. If she called back, Trevor might get to the phone before I could. "Not home," I said, hanging up.

"Probably left for work," he said, "or went out with Nate."

"Yes, probably."

He stood there quietly. "Why don't you tell me who really gave you that jewelry box?"

"I did tell you."

"Josh gave it to you, didn't he?"

For a moment, I was struck dumb.

"Why don't you tell me the truth? Are you seeing him again?"

"No, Trevor. I'm not."

"Then where did the box come from?"

"I told you. Caroline."

"Look at you. Your face is red all the way down past your neck. You're not a very good liar, Gwyn." He turned to leave, then an instant later popped back in the doorway. "You met him just now, didn't you? Did he forget to give you a present? You know, if you really want that weird son of a bitch instead of me, don't worry. I won't fight you. I'm sick of it all." He smacked the doorjamb with the butt of his hand, then stalked off.

For a moment, I was tempted to go after him, then remembered the film canister down on the floor. I dropped to my knees, still watching for him to make another appearance, then felt under the table for the container. I grabbed it from behind a table leg, scrambled up, and hid it behind a cup of sketching pencils. I took the note and placed it beneath a magazine.

I waited, listening, but couldn't tell from the relative silence where Trevor might be in the house. Deciding to chance it, I grabbed the can from off the table and ran for the hall bathroom.

But Trevor appeared suddenly from around a corner, blocking the hallway. "Are you really going to try and deny it?"

"Yes—I am. Excuse me, please." I pushed past him to the bathroom and locked the door behind me. Taking a few quick breaths, I screwed off the cap and shook out the contents. It was developed film, two strips of five frames. Not much. Maybe Craig had kept the remainder of it.

I handled the faded negatives as carefully as possible with shaking fingers, trying not to smudge the images. I tilted them up to the light. At first, I couldn't even guess at what I was seeing, and then it became agonizingly clear. Kelly, naked, her body parts flagrantly exposed, was with a man, his genitals also open for viewing. Considering the angle of the shots, they must have taken the photos themselves. But I couldn't see the man clearly, his face was turned away or looking down, the top of his head cut off . Even squinting, I couldn't tell anything for sure. I placed the film back in the container, then flushed the toilet in case Trevor was standing outside the door.

He wasn't.

I hurried to my darkroom and hid the film canister at the rear of a drawer. Leaning back against the counter to steady myself, I closed my eyes. I could still see the images. It could have been Trevor. It could have been, but I wasn't sure. As soon as it was safe, and with sufficient time to do it right, I'd develop the negatives into prints.

I found Trevor sitting in the kitchen, his face in his hands. He straightened as I walked in, glanced toward me, then away. His face seemed swollen, as if he'd been crying.

"I'd appreciate it if you could *at least* be honest with me," he said. "I know you're lying. Caroline did not bring that over."

I didn't bother to reply.

"How long has this been going on? What did he do? Stop over when I was out of town? And it went too far?"

"No."

"Just tell me the truth, Gwyn. You don't have to worry. I won't leave. I know you've been having some serious emotional problems, and I haven't helped. I'm not around like I should be. You going to him ... it's probably my fault. So I've decided to forgive you, because we're *married*, and we made a *commitment* to stay together. I made a *commitment* to you. And I've kept my end, because I love you."

"Is that right?"

His mouth hung open. "What? How many times do I have to say it? How could you believe anything else?"

I turned, walked away, afraid I would blurt everything out.

"Gwyn, don't turn your back on me. We need to talk."

"I don't feel like talking."

I continued to my studio. He didn't follow me. A few minutes later I heard the side door slam and saw Trevor backing his Cadillac down the drive. I watched as he turned into the street and sped away.

It was my chance. I ran to the garage and grabbed Kelly's bear out of the Jeep, carried the bear upstairs. I stopped to find a pair of nail scissors, then entered the room containing Kelly's bedroom furniture. I shut the door and sat on the bed.

I unzipped the plastic bag and eased out the bear. On the way home from the old house, I'd discovered something. The seam along the left side of the bear didn't quite match the right. It appeared to be hand-stitched. I picked up the scissors and snipped away at the threads.

Roosevelt was the bear's official name, but not its original. As a toddler, Kelly had called her favorite toy, teddy, like most children. But the halting words issuing from her baby lips sounded less like teddy, and more like, tee dee. She'd decided to rename the bear after entering kindergarten. During a history lesson, her teacher glowingly explained the origin of the teddy bear, how it was named after President Teddy Roosevelt and his one particularly unsuccessful bear hunt in the wilds of Glenwood. From that day on, Kelly had asked our family to call her teddy bear, Roosevelt. We had, and that's why I didn't remember. Kelly, I suspected, may have found the name change difficult, and eventually reverted back to her original and beloved, T.D.

I carefully opened the seam to expose the bear's stuffing, then slipped my fingers inside and poked around, working my way toward the center of the bear's belly. I hit pay dirt. One by one, I pulled out the items, laying each of them out on the bed. Before me was a U. S. passport, a slip of paper wrapped around a key, a compact roll of cash, and a folded airline ticket.

I picked up the ticket. The designated airline was Alitalia, the destination Milan, Italy. It was a one way ticket, the departure date, October sixth, the day after Kelly died. The name printed on the ticket was Lydia M. Linden. It didn't sound familiar.

I put the ticket down and picked up the passport, and as I did, several items fell from it, a driver's license, a social security card, and a photo of Kelly's smiling face. I studied the photograph for a moment, then examined the driver's license. An identical photo of Kelly appeared there, but instead of Kelly's name, the name listed was again, Lydia M. Linden. The passport held Kelly's likeness also, but again with the wrong name and wrong date of birth, likewise the social security card.

Obviously, Kelly had planned to fly off to Europe with fake identification, but was murdered a day before it could happen.

I picked up the roll of cash, five one hundred dollar bills. I wondered if this token amount could be from the cash Kelly had withdrawn a few days before her death. According to bank records, she'd withdrawn three hundred and fifty thousand dollars, all in cash, the majority in one hundred dollar bills. We'd never figured out what she'd done with it, but now I wondered if possibly she'd forwarded it to another bank account, maybe to her destination in Europe ...

under her new name.

I looked at the key wrapped in paper, unfolded the paper and studied it. Kelly's handwriting was on the paper, but I could make no sense of what she had written. It appeared to be a code of some kind.

4 TL HE 3 TR IS 2 TL ME 1 TR STP.

I fingered the key. I had no idea what lock this key might be meant for either. The only thing that did appear familiar was the actual words interspersed within the code, HE ... IS ... ME, and the numbers in a backwards sequence, 4, 3, 2, 1.

He is me. What was that supposed to mean?

I placed the items in Kelly's drawer. Though the code made no sense to me, I wondered if it would to Craig. But I'd have to wait to find out, until he contacted me again.

Trevor showed up later, carrying a pizza box. He placed it on the kitchen table.

"We have to eat," he said.

"Yes."

We ate in silence until finally Trevor set his slice of pizza down and his stillness drew my attention. "I'm sorry," he said when I looked up. "I'm sorry I lost it. If you say nothing's going—"

"Stop."

He did, and stared at me.

"I don't think it's a good idea for us to talk right now. Okay?"

"Okay."

Later, we watched television, Trevor on one side of the room, me on the other. Occasionally he'd look over at me, but didn't speak. He finally rose from his chair and started up for bed, saying only "goodnight" as he passed by me.

It was one o'clock in the morning before I felt safe enough to enter my studio. I closed the door silently behind me and then stepped into the darkroom. Opening the drawer, I drew out the film container and held it. I stood there, thinking. These were color negatives, and I didn't have the proper chemicals on hand to make color prints. More than that, I rarely worked in color, preferring to work in black and white which allowed me use of a safelight.

I listened for any hint of movement upstairs, then reached over and locked the darkroom door.

Because I was printing color negatives on black and white paper, I would have to use a special paper, Panalure. And as with color, I would have to do the developing without a safelight, without any lights at all, in total darkness. I lifted my hand and stared at it. It was shaking. I sighed deeply, then began.

With the lights still on, I mixed the developer, diluting it with water according to instructions, then poured thirty-two ounces into my graduate, a measuring device. My four trays sat before me on the counter, clean and empty, ready for use. The first tray would contain the developer, the second the stop bath, the third the fixer, and the fourth I would use to wash the prints. I had done it all many times, but only a very few times in total darkness, and never as nervous as I was, with the stakes so high.

I filled each tray, then looked around to check my bearings. I decided to do a preliminary trial run.

Eyes closed, I pretended to position the invisible sheet of eight-by-ten photographic paper in the easel, remembering I would need to set the enlarger's height for proper magnification before actually turning out the light. I then pretended to turn on the timer to expose the paper. Eyes still closed, I carried the nonexistent paper to the first tray and felt for the edge of the counter, located the first pair of tongs.

Normally, a photographer would use bare hands, especially in a situation like this. But I'd developed an allergy to the chemicals. Even a brief exposure brought on severe swelling and itching. Hardly worth it, considering I was fairly adept with tongs.

I secured a corner of the imaginary paper, then pretended to dip it into the developer and to agitate the tray. Timed perfectly, I moved to the next step, the stop bath, repeated the process with a clean set of tongs, then finally, placed the print in the fixer. After the fixer, I opened my eyes. The rest I could accomplish, without harm, with the light on.

There were two strips of negatives, each with five frames. I looked them over and chose a frame with a fairly decent head-shot of the man, then transferred the remaining strip to a clear negative sleeve, for possible use later. I took another deep breath.

Before beginning in earnest, I listened once more for any sound from outside the door, then reassured, positioned the frame in the negative carrier, adjusted the composition of the image and the focus on my enlarger.

I gazed around to get my bearings, then turned out the light. I waited for my eyes to adjust, making sure no light from any source had infiltrated the room. But it was as if I were blind.

I pulled out a sheet of Panalure paper, held it by one corner, then secured the one remaining sheet. Positioning the photographic paper in the easel, I suddenly stopped ... froze. Had I remembered to re-adjust the f-stop to f-8, my normal working aperture? I'd been experimenting with different settings earlier in the week. No, of course I'd remembered. I was worrying for nothing.

Familiar with the position of my enlarger timer, I hit the switch— projecting light through the negative onto the paper for real.

Carefully, I slid the paper from the easel, then locating the tongs, gripped a corner of the paper. I eased the sheet into the developer and began to time the process, continuing to tightly hold onto the edge of the paper, knowing that if I let it go, I wouldn't be able to see to pull it out again.

At that precise moment, I heard a loud *thunk*. But it had come from outside the house, on the roof. Probably a tree branch had fallen as wind picked up outside.

I listened for a moment, hoping the noise hadn't awakened Trevor, then, the timing for the development process complete, lifted the print. I could tell immediately from the weight of it that nothing came out with the tongs. Blindly, I poked around the tray searching for the paper, but couldn't find it.

I tried not to panic. But it was all taking so much time. Trevor could wake up and begin searching for me.

Finally, I located the print and lifted it out. I felt around for the next clean pair of tongs, again secured the print and let it slide into the stop bath. I released my breath, realized I'd been holding it.

I completed that step and the next without a problem. I turned on the light.

To my utter dismay, the print was ruined, the images too dark to tell anything. The enlarger light had been too bright. I looked closely and saw that the enlarger lens aperture was set to f-4, not to f-8. Now I had only one sheet of Panalure paper left.

I rubbed my eyes with the back of my hand, my skull throbbing from the tension, and began again.

This time, I worked more slowly, hoping to compensate for the gaps in my thinking that might cause me to fumble simple, but crucial details. Silently, I talked myself through it, told myself to be careful, to stop and consider ... to make sure ... to get it right.

This time, when I turned on the light, the print lying submerged in the tray revealed everything.

Wolfgang. Wolfgang and Kelly. Not Trevor ... not Trevor.

I let my body sway back against the counter. For a moment, I allowed myself a grim sort of gratitude. It wasn't Trevor. It wasn't him after all. He hadn't had sex with Kelly, and then murdered her. It had to be Wolfgang. Everything pointed to him.

I perched onto my stool, my stomach a big painful knot, my head pounding. I reached for the print and pulled it from the tray. But God. *My poor Linda.* Married to that *sick, sick* monster. I had to get her out of there. I had to get her the hell out of there—fast.

I picked up the phone, then stopped. What would I say to her? You didn't call Linda in the middle of the night without a very good reason. And Wolfgang would certainly ask what was up. I couldn't think of a thing that would get my sister out of that house. I couldn't mention the negatives, not over the phone. Wolfgang might overhear us. And Linda would need something more incriminating than the negatives anyway, no matter how damning they were, to believe her husband was a murderer. Unfortunately, Craig was the only one who could provide the remainder of the proof.

Sue. I could call her, have her remove Linda from the house, forcibly if necessary. But Sue would ask why it was necessary. She'd know Linda was in no immediate danger. Her people were watching and listening in twenty-four seven. And if I did tell Sue about the negatives, her next question would be to ask who gave them to me. She was smart. She might guess that Craig was involved, and then she'd be watching me like a hawk, and Craig would come nowhere near me.

I stepped out of the darkroom. It was late, very late, past three. My eyes kept closing involuntarily. Maybe I should get a few minutes sleep. I'd be able to think clearer if I got a little rest. Just lie down for a couple minutes. Then I'd be able to figure all this out....

Chapter 23

"Gwyn. Gwyn?" Trevor's hand was on my shoulder, shaking me. My eyes snapped open. "What time is it?"

"Seven ... a little past. I wanted to say goodbye before I left for work. What are you doing out here?"

I didn't remember falling asleep on the couch, but I had. "I don't know."

He kissed me on the cheek. "Call me later. Okay?"

I nodded.

"Okay?" he asked again.

"Yes."

He started for the door, looked back, then closed the door behind him.

I leapt up and ran for the phone. Linda didn't answer, so I called back every few minutes until she finally picked up fifteen minutes later.

"What?" she asked exasperatedly.

"Geez, I call to ask you to go to breakfast with me and that's what I get?"

"Breakfast? Since when do you ask me to go to breakfast?"

"I don't know. Today."

"Well, you're lucky I'm even up. Sorry, but I can't. Wolfgang and I are heading out to ski."

"You are? Where?"

"Cloister Ridge. Did you see how much snow dropped last night?"

"No."

"At least twelve inches. Should be spectacular. I'd talk longer, but I need to finish dressing."

"Can I go?"

She was silent for a moment. "Well, I suppose. You really want to?"

"Sure, it sounds like fun."

"One sec. Let me mention it to Wolfgang."

She'd covered the receiver. I could hear only muffled voices.

"No prob," she said. "In fact, Wolfgang can bring the snowmobile now that we have a third. You know, I would have asked you to go in the first place, but this is all very last minute. Do you want us to pick you up?"

"No, I'll meet you. I have a couple of things I want to do first."

"Okay, see you out there."

I left a message for Trevor on his cell, gathered my equipment, then started out. Snow was still falling steadily. As I pulled the Jeep onto the highway, a snowplow, yellow lights blinking, roared past. Even in this weather, I calculated I could make it to the ridge in under a half-hour.

Snow continued to descend in whirling flakes as I turned onto the narrow mountain road that cut off from the main highway. Only four-wheel drive vehicles could make it up this god-awful stretch of road on a bad day, and this was going to be one of those days. Ahead of me, two sets of tire tracks dug into the heavy snow blanket. I assumed the tracks belonged to Wolfgang's Subaru and the flatbed trailer he'd be hauling behind it.

My Jeep bumped up, then slammed down over what must have been a sizable log buried beneath the snow. Only my seatbelt kept my head from hitting the roof. I gripped the steering wheel tighter, slowed to less than ten miles an hour.

It was another three to four miles of rough going through thick pine forest before I spotted the Subaru and trailer parked off to the side of the road. Wolfgang was sitting atop the snowmobile, backing it off the tilted flatbed.

I parked, climbed out, then trudged through the Subaru's tracks toward him. I noticed Linda still inside the car.

"Hey there," Wolfgang called out, smiling at me. "You picked a great day to join us."

I couldn't look at him now without seeing the eight by ten glossy of him sitting on his knees, his erection visible, Kelly's fingers reaching out, stroking.

"Yes, a lot of snow."

Linda opened her car door. "Gwyn, come sit with me."

I slid behind the steering wheel, then glanced uneasily at my sister.

"How did you know?" she asked.

"What?" I said, startled.

"That we were going telemark skiing. You must have read my mind. You never call that early in the morning."

"Yes ... strange." I watched Wolfgang through the rearview mirror. He was gunning the snowmobile, veering around in circles. "You know," I said, "the weather's looking really nasty. That road was in pretty bad shape."

"Funny. Wolfgang said the same thing, only he thought it was good, keep the others away."

I faced her, and was about to speak, when her door flew open. Wolfgang thrust his head inside. "Move your little butts, ladies, or I'll be the only one with first tracks."

"Well, you just do that," said Linda.

He grinned and shut the door, then began to pull skis off the roof rack. I got out and headed toward the Jeep. As I strode over, I could almost feel Wolfgang concentrating his full attention on my ass. I remembered all those times when I was first getting to know him, how he would move in a little too closely, hug me a little too tightly, on all those special occasions when it wouldn't seem inappropriate. The same way he'd no doubt lured Kelly.

I brought my skis and poles out of the back of the Jeep and placed them on the snow. I sat inside and began pulling on my gear: hat and mittens, neck warmer and goggles, hooded waterproof ski jacket and pants with gaiters, to keep snow out of my ski boots. I grabbed my backpack off the rear seat and did a quick check. Inside were mohair skins for climbing, a compact first-aid kit, shovel and telescoping probe, plus a rope and digital avalanche transceiver. To travel in the backcountry with anything less could be suicidal.

I set the transceiver to "transmit."

Linda and Wolfgang stood waiting for me in full gear and backpacks.

"Linda," I said, "check my transceiver."

She nodded, unzipped her jacket, then lifted the device from a strap around her neck. She flipped the switch to "receive."

I walked toward her. "It's working," she said, her transceiver emitting a beeping signal that grew louder as I approached.

"Now you," I said.

I checked out Linda, then she checked out Wolfgang, though he insisted his equipment worked just fine.

I pointed in the direction of the snowmobile, figuring one of us would be riding it down. "No," Linda said, "not yet. I plan to take at least one trek up without mechanical aid, though I'll probably live to regret it."

The three of us cleared the snow from the bottom of our ski boots, then stepped into the cable bindings attached to the skis. We began trekking, poles in hand, Wolfgang in the lead, Linda following, me taking up the rear.

The ridge was fifty yards away on our right. To get to it, we had to first maneuver a narrow path snaking through the fir trees. It was relatively flat terrain here and up ahead on the ridge, but once over the edge, the mountain dropped off at a heart-stopping angle. No matter how many times I'd skied it, the sight of it always stopped me cold.

We finally reached the clearing, the ridge stretching wide, almost devoid of trees, a rocky inhospitable crest beneath deep layers of snow. Wind swept across the smooth white surface, unmarred except for a few rabbit tracks. Years ago, I'd driven up here on an early spring morning and taken shot after shot of this breathtaking panorama. Then, tiny plant shoots pushed their way between the scaly rock crevices. Now, all traces of that had been obliterated, buried beneath this massive canopy of powder.

I glanced at Linda. My plan was to stop her once Wolfgang started down, tell her as much as was necessary, then rush her back to the car and fill her in on the rest.

But my thoughts were interrupted as Wolfgang let out a whoop, then charged over the side, snow flying as he raced down the slope.

I reached a hand toward Linda, but she managed to dodge me.

"Hey. Wait, Linda."

"No way," she cried out, quickly dropping over the edge. I could hear her laughter as she swooped down, carving an identical set of wavy tracks next to Wolfgang's. Now I understood. She'd planned to take me by surprise, beat me down.

I skied off after her. "Linda, wait up."

In my nervous eagerness to catch her, I hooked a ski tip and tumbled forward into the snow. I came to rest covered in powder, and could only watch as Linda continued down and out of sight. Laying my poles in an x-pattern beside me on the snow, I placed my hand where the poles converged, then pushed, floundering to my feet. I positioned my skis again and started down.

By the time I caught up to her, Linda had rejoined Wolfgang.

"Wasn't that fantastic?" she said. She smiled impishly. "Beat you."

"Yes, you certainly did."

Wolfgang looked over at me. "I doubt you'll let that happen again. Nice line by the way. But this time, try not to leave such a huge crater in the snow." He broke out in laughter.

"Let's get started back up," I said.

I removed one of my skis and stuck it tail first into the snow, then took the mohair skins from my backpack. I pulled the adhesive sides apart, careful not to let the skins fall into the snow and pick up debris. Hooking the skin to the tip of my ski via an elastic strap, I smoothed it down over the bottom of the ski. Finished, I did the same with the other ski.

I glanced at them. Wolfgang was ready, and Linda was just finishing up.

I waited for her, then started up the slope, breaking trail. But Wolfgang would have none of that, and came around in front of me. Fine, I thought, maybe he'd wear himself out, make it easier when it was time to run.

We moved steadily up the mountain next to the tree line, heels lifting off the skis, boots attached only at the toe. We climbed straight up, like climbing stairs, mohair skins gripping the snow. I could feel sweat forming in my armpits and at the back of my neck.

Halfway up, I heard Linda groan behind me. "Can we just stop for a minute," she gasped. "I need water." We stopped, and Linda reached around for her bottle in a pouch at the side of her pack. "God, is this cold," she said, gulping the water down.

A spray of wind-driven snow hit me across the face as I also tipped a bottle up to my mouth. "The wind," I said, "it's getting worse."

Neither Linda nor Wolfgang replied.

We again began our ascent.

At the top, Linda threw her pack to the ground and plopped onto it. "Okay, where's that snowmobile? I've had it with this climbing." She glanced up at Wolfgang.

"My wife is wimping out already. What about you?"

I shrugged. "With the weather so bad ... yeah, I think I'll ride up too. Get more runs in that way."

"The both of you ... wimpy women. I'm disappointed."

"Just get the snowmobile," said Linda. "When we want your opinion of us, we'll ask."

He laughed loudly at this, the sound echoing across the ridge. He turned and trekked off into the forest.

I considered telling Linda now, then changed my mind. Wolfgang might notice a weird look on her face when he returned. Or Linda might lash out at him, completely forgetting how vulnerable we'd be alone out here on the ridge. Better to first use the snowmobile as our means of escape. Leave Wolfgang far below. Then tell her.

Wolfgang roared back out of the trees. He stopped, left the snowmobile on idle, then dropped his skis from under his arm onto the snow.

I skied over and nodded at him. "I'll take it down first. Let you guys get a run."

"No," said Linda. "I can take it. I don't mind."

"Next time," I said.

I planned to take the snowmobile much farther below than we'd gone previously. The more time it took for Wolfgang to march back up, the better.

I straddled the machine and started off. "See you guys at the bottom." I guided the snowmobile down, staying close to the trees. When I stopped, I could see neither Wolfgang nor Linda. I waited, watching for them to appear. Then, off on the far right side of the ridge, I spotted loose snow tumbling down, and my heart rate quickened. I searched for any sign of them, then glimpsed a speck, someone skiing down fast toward me.

Linda.

Still far up the mountain, she fell in a burst of snow. Faintly, I heard her calling to me. I turned back up the slope and raced toward her.

"Gwyn," she gasped as I slid to a stop. "We have to ... help him." She pointed in the direction of the slide.

"Where? Show me."

She tossed her skis and hopped on. I hit the accelerator and we leapt from the snow, charging across the slope. "I told him not to go," she shouted over the engine noise. "He wouldn't listen. Oh God. Hurry, Gwyn. You know what's down there."

I certainly did. And only a fool would venture close to that side of the ridge. Below the line of trees, where the snow accumulated in deep endless drifts, lay a set of cliffs that angled down, the first, a steep narrow step called, God's Hands, to catch the unwary before the mountainside plunged straight down toward the valley.

Loose snow slides were a frequent occurrence near the cliffs, but this was untended backcountry and nature made its own rules. The possibility always existed that an entire slab could tear off and break away. A few big avalanches had been reported over the years, along with the occasional casualty. The locals were aware and kept a respectful distance.

I slowed, glancing uneasily uphill before crossing the slide, but the snow appeared to have settled. I could see no sign of Wolfgang, his tracks obliterated. I clicked on my transceiver, crossed the compacted snow and continued moving in the direction indicated, closer to the cliff. I slowed again, checked the digital readout, the numbers dropping steadily.

Wind whipped and whistled high above us in the trees. "Where is he?" Linda cried out, her voice shrill, competing with the wind. "*Wolfgang! Wolfgang!*" I could feel her body quiver against me as she began to sob.

I drove closer to the edge of the cliff, following it down.

Up ahead, I glimpsed a small dark object sticking out of the snow. It looked as if it might be a gloved hand. Linda saw it too. "What's that?"

I approached, holding my breath. But it was the tip of Wolfgang's ski, the remainder hidden beneath the snow.

"It's not him," I said, "only his ski, not according to my transceiver. Unless ..."

"Unless *what?*" Linda squealed in my ear.

"Wolfgang wasn't wearing his transceiver under his jacket like us. Maybe it got ripped off in the slide."

"Oh God. I told him. Should we dig here? Should we?"

"The beacon says he's still up ahead of us. What do you want to do?"

She hesitated. "Keep going ... I guess."

The signal drew us closer to the periphery of the cliff.

"Take it to the edge," Linda said.

I shook my head. "No, we're already too close. It's not safe."

"Take this thing to the edge so I can look down."

"No."

"*Do it, Gwyn.*" She made a grab for the accelerator.

I swiped her hand away. "Are you crazy? Stop it."

"Do it. Or I will."

"No. Listen to me. He's not worth risking our lives. He murdered Kelly."

"What?"

"He killed her. He did it."

"No. No, he didn't. What are you talking about?"

"Linda, I have proof."

I winced as her fingers dug deeply into my flesh. "I don't *care* what kind of stupid proof you think you have. Now you get this thing moving. Do you understand me?"

"He was having sex with her. I found photos."

For an instant, she didn't say a word, and then her voice, low and cold at the back of my neck, murmured, "That doesn't mean he killed her. Now you get this goddamn thing moving or I'll push you off and go find him myself."

"Linda—don't do anything stupid. You'll kill us both."

"Then don't make me."

I continued inching forward, easing the snowmobile nearer the periphery. A slab of snow broke off and slid over the rim, crashing down. "That's it," I said. "We've got to stop. I don't know where the cliff ends."

"Fine, stop here. I'll take a look." She stood, hands on my shoulders, and peered over the precipice. "I don't see anything. Keep going."

A low groaning came from below us in the snowpack, a sound that sent chills streaking up my spine ... nothing human this sound, but a warning of rifts forming layers below. "Sit down, Linda."

I slowly guided the snowmobile along the edge, following the signal.

She called out again. *"Wolfgang. Do you hear me?"*

Suddenly we both looked up, though at first I wasn't certain of what I'd heard.

"Over there." She pointed.

We crept forward, and Linda stood again. "Yes, I can see him."

"Sit," I said, standing myself and venturing a look. He was partly buried on the narrow ledge, mere inches from the vertical face. "We can't go out there. The snow is too loose. It could let go, and we'll all go down with it."

Wolfgang looked up at me. He shouted over the wind. "My foot is caught. It's the ski. My leg is twisted. I can't get to it."

"We'll get you out, honey," Linda shouted back. "I promise." She leaned forward, stared wide-eyed at me. "We have to do something. Quick."

I studied her face, and suddenly remembered what Janet had said on my last visit. *Did it ever occur to you that Linda knew about the affair?*

I pulled off my backpack and reached inside for the rope. "We'll loop this under your arms, then I'll tie the rope to the snowmobile. You can try to dig him out."

At least this way, Linda would have an even chance to survive if the snow did give way. Maybe. And maybe we'd all be pulled over the edge.

I looped the rope around her, then knotted it tightly to the snowmobile. I handed her the telescoping shovel. "Do it fast as you can, but be careful."

I brought the snowmobile around, facing away from the drop, ready to move fast if conditions warranted it. Linda slid onto the snow and crawled to the edge. When she signaled she was ready, I drove forward and brought the rope taut. I backed toward the cliff, easing Linda over the side.

Minutes passed while I listened for more signs of shifting snowpack, watched for more evidence of loose snow.

I could hear Wolfgang and Linda talking below, but not their words. Finally, Linda shouted up, "He's okay. I've got his leg free. Pull us up."

Carefully, I drove forward and the rope tightened, the knot stretching wide, but holding. I dragged the two of them up, then over the rim. I continued pulling them across the slope, out of the area in immediate danger of sliding.

I stared at Wolfgang and he stared back. One broken ski, still attached to his boot, dangled behind him in the snow.

"Are you injured?" I asked.

"No," he said. "I'm okay."

"Then I think we should get out of here. It's not safe."

"I agree. Guess I'm lucky to be here."

"You are. Linda, hop on. I'll take you up first."

"No." She shook her head. "Take Wolfgang. I can wait."

"Do as she says, Linda," Wolfgang said, his eyes focused steadily on mine. "It's okay. Let her come back for me."

She stared at Wolfgang, then at me. "All right." She climbed on and we took off up the mountain, stopping only to retrieve her skis.

Once we reached the top, she faced me. "Don't go back down there. I'll go."

"Why?"

"Because ... I.... Just do it, okay? Take the Jeep and get out of here."

"Not a chance. You're coming with me. We'll send someone else back for him. Preferably the cops. Linda, I know he beats you up."

She flinched. "No. Where'd you get that idea?"

"Don't try to deny it. But he's not going to do it again. Not ever."

She averted her eyes, looked down toward the valley. "You don't understand how it is between us. It's not that simple. And it's not all his fault. You know how antagonistic I can—"

"Stop it. Don't even *try* to blame yourself. You're finished with him."

"Oh," she said, "so easy for you to say. You with your Trevor, your Mr. Perfect, who never does *anything* wrong. Yeah, Wolfgang is a bastard, but he's all I have, and I won't leave him…. I can't. Believe me, I've tried."

"Don't talk nonsense. Do you have the keys to the Subaru?"

"No. He has them. Gwyn, let me go back for him. He won't hurt me. Not now."

"You're not going anywhere near him. The guy's a vicious killer."

"You don't know that. Not for sure."

"Linda, by now he's figured out something's up. He'll start climbing out. Come on. We've got to get out of here."

She stared at me, then nodded.

I sat at the wheel of the Jeep, maneuvering it down the snow-choked mountain road, now almost impassable.

"What are you going to do?" she asked.

"Call the cops. They can deal with him." I dialed my cell phone, but couldn't get a signal.

"But what if they can't get to him? The road's so bad. He'll freeze. And the cliff … it could avalanche. He'll be killed."

"*Would you stop it? Just stop.* The man's a freakin' monster."

For a second, it was as if she'd turned to stone. Then her eyes flashed with fury and her lips thinned. "*He's* a monster. *He's* a monster. Haven't you forgotten something here? What about your poor dear Kelly? What about *her*? You don't think *she* was a monster? Fucking my boyfriend? Knowing how much I loved him? *She* was the monster. *She* was the goddamned monster." Linda stopped, turned her face away. "She wouldn't let me have anything. Not you—not him. Always taking away the people I loved. Take them away and laugh. She *deserved* to die. The *witch*."

When we reached the house, I led Linda inside, where she began to cry quietly. I hurried to my studio, about to call the police on the landline, when it struck me that Annabelle hadn't greeted me at the door. "Annie-B?" I called out.

I hesitated, picked up the phone, then stopped.

Someone was behind me.

I turned slowly around.

Craig stood with his back to the door, a finger to his lips. He pushed the door and it clicked closed.

"Did I scare you?" he asked.

"Well ... yes."

"I didn't want her to know I'm here."

I nodded.

"Did you see the pictures I left you?" he said.

"Yes, and I was just about to call the police ... to pick up Wolfgang."

"Not yet."

"Why not?"

"They'll need more evidence. We have to put the pieces together, yours and mine. Did you figure out what T.D. meant?"

"Yes."

I turned my head as Linda's footsteps approached from down the hall. Craig squeezed back behind the door.

"Linda," I said. "Wait out—"

But the knob turned and she walked in.

Craig, seeing he was caught, stepped out to reveal himself. Linda let out a shriek.

"It's okay," I said. "It's okay. I was expecting him."

"Who *is* he?" She shuffled over to me.

"Craig Foster."

She did a double take. "What's going on? Why the hell is he here?"

"He's innocent," I said. "He has the rest of the proof. I found something too."

"Okay," he said, "enough talk. I can't stick around here. It's not safe. Show me what you have."

"What about what you have?" I said.

"Just get it, okay? I'll explain soon enough."

"It's upstairs."

I retrieved the bear and brought it back down to the studio. I held it out to him. "This belonged to Kelly. The initials, T.D., were short for Teddy. Kelly hid some things inside." I pulled out the passport, license, key, and a note. "This is the part I don't understand." I handed him the note. "It's some kind of weird code. I can't make sense of it."

He studied it, then smiled.

"Yes," he said, "this is exactly what I need. You have no idea. Now, we don't have much time. You have to help me out."

"What?"

"I need you to drop me off. I left my motorcycle where they can't find it. Outside of town. I'll explain everything once we get there."

"Here," I said, "just take the keys to my Jeep. You can call and let me know where you left it."

"You're not listening. I *need* your help to do this. And everyone's looking for me. They might recognize me if I drive."

"Okay ... I'll drive you."

"Her too," he said.

"Why?"

"Why do you think? She'll spill to the cops the minute we leave."

Linda sat in the front of the Jeep with me. Craig crouched low in the back.

"Which way?" I said.

"Out to the highway, then hang a left."

After several direction changes, I realized we were heading toward the old house. As we approached it, Craig leaned over my shoulder. "Park a couple houses down. I don't want this thing sitting in the drive."

"Where's your motorcycle?" I asked.

"Hidden in the garage."

The three of us hopped out.

"Come on," he said, "follow me."

I looked at Linda, and she at me.

"Well, come on," he said, "before someone spots us. Oh, for ..." He grabbed our wrists and began dragging us across the road. "*Hurry up.*"

We scuttled in and out of shrubbery until we'd reached the back of the house. He finally released us to open the side door of the garage. "See?" He pointed inside at his motorcycle. "Right there. Now do you believe me?"

The minute he turned his back, I gave Linda a push. "*Run!*"

"What the hell?" he cried, and tore off after her. She didn't get very far. He caught her and yelled back at me. "Hey, Gwyn."

I stopped running and turned around.

"Think you should get back here." He took Linda by the hair, pulled her head back exposing her throat, then casually flipped open a switchblade. He pointed the knife at me. "I really think you should get over here."

I complied.

"Listen," he said. "I *am* innocent. Okay? So don't make me do things I don't want to do. Geez."

"Then let us go."

"I will, after you help me. Wait 'til you see what I found. I think you'll be surprised. Hey, you got a key to this place? My way in could be a little messy."

"I have a key."

I turned it in the lock and opened the door.

He pushed us inside. "This way," he said.

He led us toward the basement, then flipped on the light at the top of the stairs. His eyes shifted to the left and right. "Ever notice how creepy this place is? Gives me the willies. Tripped and almost broke my neck last time I came down here."

He motioned for us to proceed ahead of him. We started down and the stairs creaked, louder than usual. Something skittered across the floor.

"What was that?" he said, stopping.

I glanced back at him.

"Did you see that?" he said.

"No." I looked aside at Linda.

"Yeah, you saw it. Fuckin' rats. Probably got a nest down here."

"We don't have rats."

"Sure. Like I'm seeing things."

He jabbed me between the shoulder blades, indicating we should continue down.

I shrugged. "Could be Kelly. Maybe she wants to know what you're doing down here with us."

"What the fuck you talking about?"

"You don't know? She still lives here—in the house. You telling me you can't feel it?" I gazed up at the rafters. "That cold sensation running up your backbone? Like you know somebody's watching? You said it yourself. The house gives you the creeps."

"Quit messing with me and shut the fuck up."

He followed us across the basement. I heard the switchblade click into life.

I glanced back at him—at the knife.

"Oh, you worried about *this*?" he said. "It's just insurance. So I don't have to ask you twice. Stand aside."

We were directly in front of my father's tool cabinet. It stood seven feet tall, four feet wide. The doors were open, the tools exposed.

"So, you know about this?" he asked.

"Know about what?" I said.

He tugged hard on the right side of it and it moved. He reached in behind, fooled around with something, then swung the cabinet out. I realized it was on hinges. Behind the cabinet, on the wall, was a door.

"There used to be a padlock on this," he said. "It took some work, but I finally got it sawed off. Could have used that key you found."

He opened the door and turned on a light.

"So what do you think?" he asked. "Take a look."

The room was narrow and long, maybe five feet by twelve, the walls cement block, no windows. The escaping air felt dank and smelled of mold and rotting insect corpses, reminding me of a tomb. To the far left was a floor safe. To the far right, two file cabinets set side by side.

Now I finally understood where the strange noises had come from while my father was still alive. We weren't supposed to know about his secret room.

"Get in there and sit on the floor," Craig said. "Put your hands behind your backs." He shoved us toward the file cabinets.

Linda looked at me, eyes wide with terror.

Craig turned toward the safe, and I nodded over my shoulder at Linda, calling her attention to the screwdriver I'd shoved down the back of my pants. I eased the tool out, sat on it. Craig held up the note I'd given him and examined it. He set the knife atop the safe.

"How did you find this room?" I asked. "In all this time I never knew it was here."

He ignored me and continued to study the note.

"I'm just curious how you were able to figure it out."

"Shut up."

"I'm just wondering, that's all. I mean, in all these years, I—"

"Okay, just to shut you up, I'll tell you. Look, this is a partial basement, but if you understand construction, you'd know that even with a partial basement, at least one wall follows the foundation. I noticed while I was searching around down here that the last basement window up there is a foot away from the wall. Outside, the same window is six feet away. I figured there could be something built between."

He reached behind the safe and drew out a roll of duct tape.

"And you thought you might find more boxes in here," I said. "But then you found the safe."

"Yeah, sure."

"But you needed the combination. And now I've given it to you. Why didn't you get a locksmith to help you open the safe? You must have known someone."

"Enough with the twenty questions." He picked up the knife and came toward us with the tape.

"Craig, don't ... please," I said. "You don't have to do this. I promise I won't cause more trouble. I know you're innocent. Just let me help you."

"Then do what I say."

I watched as he slit the tape with the knife, ready to bind Linda's wrists. He knelt down, his back to me. I slowly reached beneath me for the screwdriver. The moment he set the knife beside him, I sprang up and plunged the screwdriver down—but his arm shot up and flipped it from my hand.

Blood spread down his shoulder. I'd slashed him, but not deeply.

"Shit," he yelled, his hand flying up to the wound. "You crazy bitch. You fucking crazy bitch." He reached over and grabbed me by the throat, crushing my larynx. I fought for air, fought to loosen his grip.

"Promise you won't cause more trouble, huh? You just wanna help me. Think I'll let you join your fucking dead sister. First—watch this one die." He released me and brought the knife to Linda's neck. A line of crimson droplets appeared.

"No," I choked out. "*You need her.* She's ... the *only* one ... who knows—"

"Knows what?"

"The combination ... the real one. That one ... won't work. *Try it. Just try it.*"

He tossed Linda aside and she flopped against the wall. "I just might do that."

He held the note and began dialing in the numbers. His first attempt failed to open the safe. He tried again. His second attempt also failed.

"Okay, gimme the right combination or I'll cut you open and gut you right here."

Linda had passed out, but was beginning to stir.

"*What is it?*" he shrieked.

Suddenly, the lights went out. I backed across the floor to Linda, gathered her to me. I couldn't see well, but I could hear something ... a soft mournful whisper, like wind corkscrewing through a crack. Then the whisper became louder, more insistent, until it formed recognizable words.

"*Don't ... touch ...them.*"

"What?" he said. "What was that? Who said that?"

The wavering voice grew stronger. "*Don't ... touch ... them.*" The hair rose at the back of my neck. I recognized the voice. Kelly's.

"You're dead," he shouted. "You're fucking dead. You stay the hell away from me." His knife cut the air as he swung it to the left and right.

The stairs creaked, and I heard each frightful footfall as Kelly descended.

"I'll kill you," he shouted. "*I'll kill you again!*"

A blinding light appeared on his face. He held up an arm to fend it off, then screamed, reaching back with the knife.

"Police officers. *Don't move.*"

Craig hurled the knife toward his target.

Shots rang out.

Craig squealed out in pain. "God, I'm shot. I'm shot. For chrissake someone help me. Aaarrrggghhh."

The overhead light came on and I saw Nate holding a gun on Craig. Two other police officers hustled down the stairs. Sue came in right behind them. She pointed at Linda, then shouted, "Get someone in here in a hurry. She's losing blood."

"Are *you* okay?" Sue asked, bending over me.

"Yes."

"I'm sorry. We couldn't get here any sooner. Our man on Linda—he got caught out in the blizzard and couldn't reach us. We didn't know you were in trouble right away."

I watched as medical emergency personnel rushed down the stairs to Linda.

"But ... how did you find us? And ... I heard ..."

"I put a GPS tracker on your Jeep, in the off chance your husband might drive it. When we lost track of Linda, we had to assume she might be with you. The Subaru hadn't moved off the ridge. So we kept an eye out. Then you parked on the street, not in the driveway, and that made our ears go up. One of my guys snuck around the back, found the garage open, a motorcycle inside. We figured it was Craig's.... And the voice? That was me. I'm sorry I had to use your sister in that way, but I had to find a way to distract Craig, get him away from you until the police arrived. I'd only listened to Kelly's voice on the videotape a few times, but I gave it a try, and it worked. It was almost as if she were here, protecting you. I do think she was trying to help me out in the end."

Chapter 24

Two days later, Caroline met me over at the old house. I'd hired a safecracker, just in case the combination I had in my possession failed to open the safe. I already knew what would be inside, the money Kelly had withdrawn from her account, the mysterious three hundred and fifty thousand dollars that had disappeared, the cash Craig was after.

Care and I watched as Herman R. Mathis, a smiling rail-thin man dressed in gray work clothes, knelt in front of the safe and delicately worked the dial.

"Nope, wouldn't want to mess around with this one without the combination," he said, "no you sure wouldn't. Anyone knows his business would take one look at her and say—*no way*. Doesn't surprise me your daddy built a special room for her. You try to drill into this lady and you'll be in a world of hurt."

"How come?" I asked.

"Because she's got cyanide glass packs in the door and the rear of her, plus glass sheets. You drill her and she'll bite ya—bite ya bad."

He pulled open the door. "There you go." He stepped aside. "She'll be needing some maintenance. After you're finished here, I could do that for ya."

"Sure," I said. "That would be fine."

"I'll leave you to your business. You just give me a call when you're done here."

"Okay."

We watched as Herman took the stairs, humming as he went.

I looked at Caroline, then reached inside the safe for one of the largest vinyl packets and unzipped it. Inside lay several stacks of hundreds in bank wrappers.

"Whew, that's a lot of loot," said Caroline. "Do you think Craig knew about the cyanide?"

"No idea. Though he must have known other unscrupulous types like himself. They might have told him the safe was rigged. Maybe the cops will drag it out of him."

"Yeah."

Caroline helped me stack the packets. I counted them, then tossed them into two plastic garbage bags I'd brought to haul up to the Jeep. Kelly's stash did appear to be somewhere in the neighborhood of three hundred and fifty thousand, but I'd leave the actual counting to the bank. I planned to give half of the money to Linda, then donate the other half to a charity or some other good cause Kelly would have favored.

"Sure you don't want a couple of these?" I asked, holding out two stacks of hundreds. "Kelly would approve." But I already knew Caroline's answer.

"No, I don't. But thanks." She smiled. "I like to keep things simple. But you knew that. Weird, aren't I?"

"No."

"I'll let you buy me lunch though."

"Sure."

"So how's Linda doing?" she asked.

"Better. She'll have a two-inch scar on her neck, but the plastic surgeon did a nice job. She's getting therapy too, to help her deal with all this, and she kicked Wolfgang out ... although it might only be temporary. She's ambivalent. Hard for her to let go. She told me she knew what kind of man he was from the beginning, and she knew about the affair with Kelly. Though it practically killed her, she kept quiet, figuring Kelly would eventually tire of him and move on. And she did. Linda says what she needs now is time alone to sort things out. She's delayed her trip to Hawaii until she feels up to the flight, but she still plans to go, and she's taking a girlfriend."

"She should dump the bastard. I can't believe he messed around with Kelly of all people. What an ass."

"I know. Of course, he's begging her to take him back, give him another chance, blaming it all on Kelly. Unfortunately, Linda won't have any trouble believing that part."

"So what did Linda say when Wolfgang asked why you guys left him out on the ridge?"

"Oh, that's when she hit him with the, 'I found out you had an affair with my sister,' info. That was enough. She didn't have to add that I thought he'd murdered Kelly too, and that Linda wasn't too sure about him either. She probably knew it wouldn't help if she decided to take him back. God, I hope she doesn't. But I can't convince her. Maybe the therapy will help her see the guy for what he is. She's not going to tell him she hired a private detective. At this point, I'm not saying anything either."

"So ... what about you and Trevor?"

"I haven't confronted him about Sylvia. But I will. I also need some time myself, before I say or do anything. Sue is still keeping an eye out though, in the off chance Trevor slips up."

I heard Annabelle bark, then bark a couple more times for emphasis. I'd left her on a leash in the backyard while Herman was working inside the house. Now she wanted back in. Caroline and I scrambled up the stairs.

I opened the back door and Annabelle jumped up, dancing on hind legs. I scooped her into my arms, releasing her leash. "Well, yes, come in, my little girl. Yes, you can come in now. Did you miss us?" Her tail wagged vigorously.

I glanced back at Caroline. "I wasn't sure if I'd ever see her again. I thought Craig might have killed her. I was terrified to ask." I nuzzled her nose against my cheek. "Craig broke in through the window in Trevor's office. My guess is he reached over while he was up there and pushed open the door wall. In all the excitement, Annabelle ran out. Trevor found her wandering outside when he drove up."

"I can't believe I almost lost you," Caroline said. "You should have told me what was going on."

"I know. And I'm sorry. But I knew you'd tell Nate, and I was buying time until Craig could prove his innocence. I wanted to believe him. He was convincing. After I saw the photos of Wolfgang and Kelly, I was certain. But I started having doubts after Craig broke into the house. He was very agitated. High on something, I think, and angry. When I went upstairs for Kelly's bear, I decided to forge a note resembling Kelly's, but with the wrong combination. I didn't want to give Craig the real one until he'd proved himself. By then, I'd figured out that Kelly's code was a combination to a lock somewhere. Something just clicked in my head, and I went back and flipped through the photographs I'd taken in my dad's office. I saw it, Kelly's code, in the photo taken of the wall near my dad's desk. The only difference between Kelly's code and the combination my father wrote down was that part of Kelly's was in letters, HE IS ME, which corresponded to numbers on a telephone dial, H for four, E for three, etcetera. Dad had scribbled 'combo' beside his. I knew there had to be a safe or a storage locker ... something ... somewhere. I hoped it would provide the identity of Kelly's killer."

We finished loading the plastic garbage bags with money, then hauled them up to the Jeep. My cell phone rang as we readied to leave. It was Sue.

"I have news," she said. "Craig confessed. He spilled everything. They offered him a deal and he took it."

"What? Why? Everything?"

"He had a choice, confess here in Colorado to Kelly's murder and the attempt on you and Linda, or be prosecuted in Texas for the murder of a girl there. Smart of him to take the deal. Things might not go as well for him in Texas. Part of the plea bargain was that the Colorado prosecutor won't seek the death penalty. But Craig will still get a life sentence—without parole."

"I need to know everything, everything he said."

Caroline tapped me on the shoulder, her brows furrowed in question.

"Craig confessed."

"Oh my God."

I turned back to the phone. "Can you meet me? Can you meet me somewhere?"

"Sure. I haven't left town yet."

"Okay. Care is with me. Could ... could we maybe meet at her place?"

Caroline signaled a thumbs up.

"Sure. I'll be right over."

We gathered in Caroline's kitchen, hunched over the table with our coffee. We'd just finished listening to Nate's message on Caroline's answering machine, also relaying the news about Craig. Nate had been present during the videotaped confession this morning at Valley View Hospital. Craig was under police guard, recuperating from the bullet wound he'd received to the shoulder. Though Nate had shot to kill, he'd missed as he swerved to avoid Craig's knife.

"Will I be able to get a copy of the tape?" I asked, anxious to know every word Craig had uttered.

"Not until the judge accepts the plea and Craig is sentenced," Sue said. "It's considered evidence now. Can't have his lawyer coming back and suggesting the evidence might have been tampered with."

"I see."

"But I talked with Nate, so I pretty much know what was said. I'm just not sure how much of this you want to hear. All the details, could be upsetting."

"I realize that," I said, "but I need to know. Eventually, I'll view the tape, so you might as well fill me in."

"Okay then. The story is Craig owed big money to a real lethal loan shark based in Vegas. Besides his amphetamine habit, Craig had a real love affair with the blackjack tables. Cops were aware of this before. Craig was also under suspicion for the murder of a girl in Texas. He hung with her off and on, but so did a lot of other guys. Cops found the girl, Allison, dead on the floor of her apartment after she was reported missing—heroin overdose. They suspected foul play since she didn't appear to be a user, just a little ecstasy now and then according to her friends. She'd also made a couple large bank withdrawals within days of her death, but not a dime turned up when her place was searched. Didn't add up.

"Craig said he heard about Kelly from a guy he knew who lived in Glenwood. Chick inherited a bunch of money after her dad kicked off. These are Craig's words, not mine, so—"

"It's okay," I said, waving her on.

"So Craig decides he needs to meet this girl, since his buddy says she's a real looker, plus she has a drug habit and likes to run with wild guys. Craig sees this as a golden opportunity. He makes his move, and being a reasonably good-looking guy, wins her over. But she's not too forthcoming with the money, and after a while he thinks she's seeing other guys as well, and maybe plans to dump him. Plus Kelly is afraid of him now. Cops ask him, 'Why is she afraid?' Craig can't come up with anything, tries to change his story, says maybe she wasn't afraid. Finally, he admits they had a fight and he threatened her, said he knew she was fooling around with this Wolfgang character, and if she didn't start being more generous he might have to tell her sister about it. Craig admits this wasn't a good idea in retrospect. She turns off to him completely now. So he changes his tactics.

"He tells her about needing money 'cause the loan shark is after his ass, thinks she'll be more sympathetic once she knows he might be killed. He says he wants to take her to Mexico; they'll blow off steam, hide out. He says she agrees to take money out of her bank account, then says he's surprised when he learns how much, three hundred and fifty thousand." Sue shakes her head. "No one in the room believes him now, that Kelly voluntarily withdrew that much money, but Craig's on a roll so they let him continue. He asks her to arrange to make fake IDs for the two of them, so that once they hit Mexico, he'll be safe. She does. On the day they're supposed to leave, she brings home the cash. They have a plan so they don't have to worry about someone finding the money while they're on the road. The bench seat in Kelly's pickup truck has a hidden toolbox beneath. After some maneuvering, the seat lifts up to reveal it. No one's likely to be aware of it since this type of bench seat is no longer manufactured. They stuff the bags of money inside. Everything's cool. But that afternoon they get into a big row, screaming at each other. Kelly says he can go to hell and he's not getting any of her money. Well, that's not gonna happen according to Craig, so he smooths things over, knowing he'll kill her that night somewhere out on the highway. They're driving down old Freedom road, mostly a truck route, Craig at the wheel. He tells Kelly he hears a tire thumping, thinks they might be getting a flat. Says for her to get out and check. It's late and the road's deserted. There's a long guardrail running along the right-hand side, a steep drop beyond. Craig knew about this before they started out. He plans to—stab her—then toss her over the side of the mountain. By now,

Kelly can see the tire isn't flat. Craig climbs out of the truck, heads around the back. Kelly gets wise and takes off running. She has a head start, plus it's dark, and Craig realizes that once she's out of the headlights, he could lose her. So he gets back in the truck and goes after her. He runs up behind her along the guardrail, but Kelly sees what's happening and dodges back across the road. But by this time … it's too …"

Sue looked at me, saw I was shaking, stopped.

"No," I said, "tell me the rest. Tell me."

Caroline reached over to hug me. I broke down then, weeping, snuffling, burying my nose in Care's shoulder.

"It's okay," she said. "It's okay."

"No. I miss her. I miss her *so much*. It's never going to be okay."

"I know. I wish I knew how to—"

"I want her back. I want her back. Oh, God."

Sue got up from the table and began to pace while I fell apart, then she took off toward the bathroom. Caroline held me, giving me tissues while I tried to regain my lost composure.

Finally, Sue returned. She looked to be drained from the telling too, and probably anxious to get back on the road. I'd seen her glance at her watch more than once.

"I'm ready," I said. "Please continue, Sue. I really do need to know everything."

She nodded, then took a seat at the table again. She turned a serious face to me. "You have to remember that all of this came out of Craig's mouth. Chances are he lied at any point that suited him. This is *his* story—only. You can be certain there are some serious holes in it." She stopped to rub her eyes. "Okay. Let's finish this. According to Craig, his intention was to push Kelly's body over the side of the mountain and hope nobody finds her for a while. But as he's about to do it, he sees a semi-tracker trailer barreling down the highway. He can't take the chance someone will spot him and get curious, so he just leaves Kelly under the guardrail in the weeds, then hightails it out of there. Later, he thinks this might be a better plan after all. Maybe the cops will think it was an accidental hit and run, that Kelly was drunk or stoned, walked out there on her own—at least until they find the crumpled truck.

"Craig drives back to the house, hides the truck in the garage, unpacks Kelly's duffel, tries to make everything look normal, like she wasn't going away. He goes out to the garage to unload the cash from under the seat. After all, he can't drive the truck now. He plans to hide the money someplace else. That's when he finds out Kelly tricked him.

"Earlier that day while he was out buying supplies for the trip, he says, gone for maybe an hour, Kelly replaced the money in the bags with fake. At some point, she'd hit on an alternate plan, and cut newspaper into bundles. She took the real money out, stuffed the fake money into the bags. She even replaced the fake ID in Craig's wallet with an inferior product—misspelled, wrong dates, unusable. Chances are she planned to ditch Craig herself somewhere that night, make her airline flight the next day, get out of harm's way.

"Craig said he came back to Glenwood strictly to find the money. He figured it still had to be in the house, and he was determined to find it." She stopped. "And that's about it."

I sat thinking ... all the questions I needed answers to. "What about the note, and the jewelry box?"

"What note do you mean?" she asked.

"Craig said he found a note, one that talked about T.D., and then he found the jewelry box. Oh ... but he knew about the jewelry box before he killed ... her. It had the negatives of Wolfgang and Kelly inside. Probably just a way of offering me something so I'd help him, take him into my confidence."

"Yes."

"And Kelly hid notes all over the house. Easy for Craig to find one if he was looking."

Caroline got up and began making another pot of coffee.

Sue looked at her watch, then at me. "I have to run," she said, "but we should meet again soon—this week. Your latest report is almost complete. I should have everything ready by late tomorrow afternoon or early the following day. Unfortunately—or maybe not so unfortunately—there's not much new to add. I'll call you as soon as I have it all in order."

"Okay."

Sue turned around in her chair and smiled back at Caroline, then stood and held out her hand. "It was very nice getting to know you, Caroline. Hope I get a chance to see you again sometime."

"Likewise. Actually, you know what? I do have a friend who might need your services. He wants to check out this guy before he goes into business with him. Would you be interested?"

"Sure, let me know."

Chapter 25

Sue and I sat inside her van, parked outside the Wild River Grill. It was close to noon. She was back to her original disguise, the western look, cowboy hat and boots, but now with a great looking cowhide jacket.

"Everything's in there, same as before," she said, pointing to the shopping bag sitting between us on the floor. "Do you want me to brief you on what I found, or would you rather—?"

"Go ahead. Please."

"Well, like I said, we still didn't get anything on Trevor, and at this point, I don't think we will. I can only guess that if something was going on between Sylvia and your husband, it's sure not now. You will be interested to know that he has known, or knew of, Sylvia, at least three years prior to these recent real estate dealings. He wasn't involved with her other than on a business level, but it appears she was interested in Trevor from the beginning. One of the reasons she handpicked Bob Morris to work with her, we believe, is his close association and friendship with Trevor. I'd say Trevor was her target all along. We were able to get close to a good friend of Sylvia's—female—and she gave us many of these details. We, also, of course, checked out her information soon after that." Sue smiled. "It never hurts to have a great looking guy on the staff. Women find him very easy to talk to, plus the ladies we question get a free meal and drinks out of it—at the very least. You'll find all this in the report in more detail."

"In the beginning," I said, "Trevor never mentioned Sylvia, only Bob. So when Bob said Sylvia was the one that brought Trevor onto the team, I did wonder if possibly they had been involved before. But you say they weren't."

"No. Not according to my sources."

"God, I'm not sure what to do. I suppose there's no reason to keep watching Trevor if it looks like nothing's going to develop."

"No. Although I could keep a couple people working on it, if you'd like. But to be honest, I think you'd be wasting your money. When Sylvia and Trevor do meet up now—and that's not too often— it's always with Bob Morris along."

"Then, I think we might as well call it off. For now anyway."

It made me happy to hear that Trevor was only dealing with Sylvia through Bob, even though everything else indicated that something had been going on.

"Tell me, Sue, what would you do? Would you stay with a man who cheated on you?"

"Can't say. Sure can't say for you. I'd rather just collect the facts and stay out of the rest of it. But, since you asked, I'll tell you this. A lot of men cheat on their wives. I can attest to that. And not every woman tosses the guy out, the first time, or the second. I think it's a personal decision, and in some ways, a cultural one. A lot of women here in the States are taught that if the guy cheats, he's a bastard, and that's that. And if you don't toss him out, you've got rocks in your head. But I don't think it's that simple. I've seen marriages revived after the guy is discovered, and others dissolve. Depends on the couple, what's right for them. But if a man is cheating—and it's not just men, you know—you have to consider the other issues. Health hazards are a big one.

"It's strange," she said, "but the thing I've found to be the most perplexing, is how many guys are willing to forgive a woman who strays. Yeah, the men, they yell and they have a holy fit, but in the end a lot of them will take her back—if she wants to stay. Maybe the guys are more likely to forgive because they know how easy it is to make a mistake. Or maybe their love is just a little less conditional. I don't know. I just know what I've seen."

I looked at her. "Thanks ... for your honesty."

"No extra charge for my dime store psychology. So, on that note, we still have the issue of your sister and Wolfgang. Now that's a whole different ball of wax. I did some more checking, and though Wolfgang has never been married before, your sister isn't the first well-heeled woman he's wined and dined. With his previous women, he either took off when trouble brewed or was tossed out. He spent a few nights in jail in one instance, on charges of abuse. I also checked out that other item you mentioned. And yes, Wolfgang's parents did die in an avalanche. And he did live with an uncle, but not until he was eight years old. Before that, he passed through a series of foster homes. So, we'll give him that. He had a tough time growing up. But we won't give him a whole lot else."

She stopped to look over her notes. "Oh—and Josh. Of course, we know now that he didn't have anything to do with Kelly, or her murder. The Vancouver thing—looks like Josh just wanted to get away for a while. His father lived in British Columbia when he was a young boy, used to talk about it with Josh, reminisce on how much he enjoyed his life there. Then Josh's father moved to the States and married Josh's mother. All in all, from everything I can see, Josh appears to be a pretty all-round nice guy."

"He is."

"There's more videotape for you to look at, more emails, etcetera, but no new revelations, like I said. You might find some of it interesting though. You have any questions for me?"

"Actually, I do have one—if you don't mind. But it's a little personal."

"Go ahead. Shoot."

"You don't talk much about yourself. Maybe that's a good idea in your type of business, but I am curious about the disguises you use, and how you were able to so accurately imitate my sister's voice."

She shrugged. "Actually, it's just fun for me, using a disguise, a way to make a sometimes dull business more exciting. And it can be helpful if I need to hang out at a location where I might be spotted. At least, I look like a different person each time. I think I always wanted to be an actress, play different roles ... though, of course, on an amateur level. I'm not talented enough for the big time, nor would I want to pursue that whole Hollywood scene. And the voice? Kelly's? I do have a gift for mimicry, been having a good time with that since I was a kid. I have what you might call a very good ear and unusually adaptable vocal cords. Plus, I practice a lot."

"Would you do one for me? A voice?"

"Sure. I can do that. Umm, let me think. Okay, see if you can guess who this is. I'll give you a hint. The actress played this particular character in a popular sexy TV series.... *Without shoes, life would be dull, drab, and boring. I absolutely love my new pair of strappy sandals.* I'm not quoting anything here. It's just something I made up that sounds like something she might say."

"Oh, that was way too easy. Sarah Jessica Parker playing Carrie in *Sex and the City.*"

"You guessed it."

"You're absolutely amazing. And I didn't need your hint at all."

"Thanks. I hadn't tried her out on anyone yet. Wondered how close I was." She glanced at her watch. "Well, Caroline's probably wondering what in the heck's taking us so long."

"Yes, she's probably hungry. Are you ready to eat?"

"Yep. Hope she's got them wings a cookin'," Sue said in a very believable southern twang.

"And some ribs," I said.

"Yes indeedy."

On my way home from lunch, I passed by the bank. The garbage bags with Kelly's money were still locked inside the storage locker down in the basement. Today would be as good a day as any to do the unpleasant job of taking it all to the bank to be formally counted.

I walked downstairs and pulled out one of the bags to begin a preliminary count. First, I cleared a table to stack the money, then unzipped one of the smaller vinyl bags inside and shook the cash out, stacked it, unzipped the next. But as I shook out the fifth bag, a sheet of paper slipped out and drifted to the floor.

I picked it up, my breath catching in my throat.

Hello,
If you find this, it's almost certain that I'm dead. I'm so sorry, Gwyn,

Linda, if you are still there to read this, for of course, I've made you suffer ... again.

If you don't know already, my plans were to jet off to Italy, then once aboard the plane, call the authorities and let them know about Craig, and poor David. Again, if it weren't for me, David might still be alive. He deserves a decent final resting place, and his family needs to know what happened to him. He's buried under the woodpile behind the garage. Craig put him there after he drugged, then stabbed him, the same thing I fear he will do to me. David made the mistake of falling for me, then trying to help me. He told me what Craig did to a girl in Texas, some girl named Allison, that Craig wasn't just threatening me, that he'd actually killed her. And he planned to do the same thing to me. All the Mexico talk was just crap. He wants the money. That's all. Craig knew that David told me. The poor guy was so transparent.

Craig wasted no time, killed him that same night. I knew it would happen, and told David to take the cash I'd given him and get out, but he worried about me, and wouldn't leave. Just after dark, I heard something going on out beyond the house. I'd just come back from the gas station for some cigarettes. I could hear voices out there, so I snuck back to take a look. Craig was hunched over something on the ground. Then I saw David. Then Craig lifted up the bloody knife. It made me so sick. And I was scared. I knew it was already over, nothing I could do. I beat it out of there, didn't want Craig to know that I saw. I didn't come back to the house for hours. When I did, Craig was gone.

I searched around out beyond the house in the field, but couldn't find David. At first, I had this crazy idea that maybe he'd gotten away somehow, after Craig left. Then I looked over to the woodpile. It was messed up, rearranged. I knew that's where David was buried. I thought about calling the cops, but I knew Craig would try to involve me, say I was in on it. After all, I withdrew all that money and made fake IDs for both of us. It would look bad. And I don't want to go to jail.

Craig won't do anything to me until he has the money. I know that for sure. But he's not going to get it. I made duplicate sets of bags, real, and fake, with a little real cash up front in the fake ones, just in case he checks. By the time he figures out I've switched the bags and his ID, I'll be long gone.

Like I said though, if you find this letter, something went wrong. Funny, about Dad's secret room, huh? I found it one day while I was chasing after a mouse that ran behind the tool cabinet. I just pushed, and like in some dark tale of castles on the moor, I discovered his hideaway. Dad left the key on a shelf, deep in a corner, the combination along with it. Nothing was inside the safe though. Probably cleaned everything out before he died ... so like our father. But I used the safe to hide the money from Craig, knew he'd never find it there.

I love you. I know you love me too. No matter what happens, I want you to know I'm heartsick and sorry for all the trouble I've caused. I'm going to change. It's not too late. I hope you never find this letter, that instead I come back and open the safe myself, that by then I've bought a little villa in Italy, with vibrant pansies trailing from the window boxes, where I write my stories and flirt with the sexy Italian men. Then we'll all go visit my place together, and be a family again, only better than before. I pray this happens. If not ... I promise I'll be waiting for you on the other side.

Your loving sister, Kelly

Chapter 26

When I arrived at the old house, the street was lined with police cars. Crime scene tape and barricades surrounded the yard. Neighbors stood at a distance in talkative groups or milled around, trying to catch a glimpse of the newest police action on the block. I parked on an adjacent street and set out to look for Caroline, who was the first person I'd telephoned after I finished Kelly's letter. As I turned the corner and the house came into view, I saw Caroline at the edge of the crowd and yelled for her. She crossed the street and jogged toward me.

"Wow, what next?" she said, getting in step with me as we approached the throng of gawkers.

"Have they found out anything yet about this David guy?" I asked. "I don't remember Kelly ever mentioning him, and I don't think his name ever came up during the police investigation."

"According to Nate, the cops don't know who he is either, but they'll sure get busy trying to identify him. The medical examiner from the coroner's office is here, and he's been taking pictures and stuff for a while, doing whatever it is those guys do. They just pulled the body out of the ground a minute ago. Sheeez. Can't think there'd be much to look at after all this time. I sure don't want to look myself, even if they let me, which I'm sure they won't. Did you get a hold of Linda?"

"Yes, finally. But she's not coming. Can't blame her."

"No, guess not."

"And I found out something else," I said.

"What?"

"Linda didn't throw out Kelly's journals after all. She still has them. She said she took them thinking Kelly might have written something about her affair with Wolfgang. Linda said she was only curious, wanted to find out what had been going on and for how long. But I think she was worried I would eventually look through them and blame Wolfgang for what happened to Kelly."

"Yes, sounds about right."

"Where's Nate?" I asked.

"Up with the rest of them. He wouldn't miss this for the world."

I heard a rising swell of oohs as the crowd parted to allow the men hoisting the body bag access to the waiting coroner's van. They placed the body inside, slammed the doors. With an earsplitting shriek, police cars parted the crowd and slowly escorted the van out of the area.

The remaining cops began dispersing the crowd, which drifted farther back, but refused to leave entirely, instead morphing into smaller, quieter groups.

I was about to say something to Caroline, when a sudden blinding flash stopped me, followed by a series of camera clicks and flashes as other reporters followed suit. A large-eyed woman with wind-tousled hair stuck a microphone under my chin.

"Ms. Sanders, a few questions please. Did you know the victim personally? How did you get word the body was buried on your property? Is it true you received an anonymous tip from a friend of the deceased?"

Caroline stepped in front of me. "Hey, leave her alone. She's not talking now. She doesn't know the guy. Doesn't know him at all."

Now the reporters swarmed over Caroline. "So the deceased is male? Can you give us a name? A name? How old was he? Can you give us any idea how long he's been buried here on the property? Did he know the accused, Craig Foster?"

"We don't know anything," said Caroline. "Now that's enough.

Let us through."

Nate noticed the commotion and hurried to our aid. "Okay, back off, people. You'll get an official statement soon enough. Give the ladies some breathing room." He ushered us forward toward the house. Camera flashes followed until we'd closed the door in their faces.

"Sorry about that," Nate said. "I should have warned you they'd be on you like dogs on a scent. It's amazing how fast they figure out who's who."

"Whew," said Caroline, "don't think I'd like being famous all that much."

He laughed. "Are you two okay?"

"Yes," I said.

"Sure," said Caroline. "You find out anything yet?"

"We have an idea about him, just need to confirm his identity. He wasn't reported missing, a drifter mostly, but we're thinking Gwyn's sister will be correct as to the time of death and the details surrounding it. I'm guessing this guy may have known Craig a while before, then hooked up with him here in Glenwood."

"Will Craig confess to it?" I asked.

"Possibly, if his lawyer thinks he can get something for his client. But don't worry. Whether Foster confesses to this one or not, once he's sentenced, he won't be going anywhere outside some very solid walls."

Chapter 27

I watched as Trevor came in the front door, finished with shoveling the morning's new load of snow from the porch. He stomped his snowy boots in the doorway.

"Trevor?"

"What?" He ambled over to me in socked feet. "Did you say something?"

"I need to talk to you. It's kind of important."

"Sure, hon, what is it?"

"Maybe you should sit down first." I patted a spot next to me on the couch.

"Oh, don't like the sound of that." He knitted his brows in question.

"First of all, let me say that I do love you, very much. I have from the beginning. I know you love me too, but I also know we've been having some problems. A lot of it's my fault. I do take responsibility for that. But not for everything."

"Gwyn—"

"No, let me finish. It's better if I get this out all at once. The time I was away in Denver, the time you left me the roses, I smelled perfume on my pillow that night. It wasn't mine, and I wasn't imagining it. I know you're going to deny it, but I need you to tell me the truth. If you've been having an affair with Sylvia Breslin, I need to know it. I have to assume that she was the one here the weekend I was gone, and that it was her perfume."

"Wait, wait, no," he said, bolting upright. "No, she wasn't here. Sylvia has *never* been in this house. I swear to you."

"Then how do you explain the perfume?"

"I don't know. I don't know. Let me think." He walked back and forth, shaking his head and staring at the floor. Finally, he looked at me. "You're absolutely sure about the perfume?"

"Absolutely."

"God, why can't I remember? I was so tired that night. I fell asleep before you got home, and I was trying so hard to stay awake. I remember … yeah. I put the roses in the vase, and then wrote you the note. It took me a while to get that note right. It turned out kind of funny, but romantic too. You liked it, right?"

"Yes."

"I wanted it to be a nice evening for us. I couldn't wait for you to get home. I'd missed you, Gwyn. I arranged the flowers on the table, knew you'd see them as soon as you walked in, then I … *wait. Wait right there.*" He ran for the stairs.

He returned carrying a small package wrapped in Christmas paper. "Open this."

I did. It was a bottle of spray cologne.

"Is that what you smelled?"

I sprayed it on my hand and sniffed it. I recognized the scent right away. "Yes, I believe it is."

"I bought it for *you*, Gwyn. I remember I sprayed it a couple times while I was wrapping some Christmas presents I'd bought for you. I wanted to make sure the thing worked. And I was sitting on the bed when I did it. It must have landed on the pillows. I fell asleep later and then you came home. You never mentioned it. If you'd said something back then I would have—"

"But what about Sylvia?"

He stiffened then, all seriousness. "She's a business associate, and that's all. I love you, Gwyn. Just you."

Still, he hadn't denied it.

I waited for him to continue, not sure what I wanted to do. Finally, he spoke. "I saw you that day in Aspen. I saw you with Josh, the day you were late for lunch."

"Oh."

"I saw you after I parked the car. I saw you go off with him."

"But you didn't say anything."

"Yes—I did. And you lied to me."

"I ..."

"Gwyn, I thought you were seeing him again. I saw the way you looked at him. Then I realized that's why you wanted to go to Aspen in the first place, to meet up with him. You didn't want me along. I thought you were unhappy with me, with our marriage, that you were planning to leave."

"No."

"I know, but it's what I thought."

I shook my head wearily. "I'm sorry. I'm so sorry I made you think that. I should have told you. But I haven't been right. I've been so mixed up lately, for so long now. It wasn't fair to you."

"About Sylvia. I suppose I used her ... to get your attention. She's an attractive woman. I could see you were jealous. I shouldn't have done that either, but I did. The truth is, you have nothing to worry about where she's concerned. Sylvia is an incredibly huge pain in the ass. It's getting harder and harder for me just to be around her. In fact, I've asked Bob to intercede and keep the meetings with her as limited as possible until this project is finished. She doesn't mean anything to me. She never will."

I leaned in and kissed him. "Well, I'm sorry to say I don't think I'll ever be able to wear this perfume."

He laughed, and I could see the relief wash over his face. I hadn't forced him to answer—not directly.

"Oh. Well I have much better gifts for you," he said. "Unfortunately, you'll have to wait until Christmas."

"Not that far off."

"No."

His brow furrowed, and I could see he still had something on his mind. "I know you were worried Sylvia might sue Josh," he said, "for causing the snowmobile accident. You can tell him from me, it won't happen. It was her fault. Sylvia used the brake. Something I said set her off and she decided to get off right then and there, and just reached up and grabbed it."

"Oh. So that's what happened. Okay. I'll tell him."

"And I'm okay about Josh now. I am."

I nodded.

"There's one more thing you should know," he said. "I have a little secret. It wasn't my idea to keep it, but I did because my dad asked me to. I suppose you've noticed how I avoid saying much about him."

"Yes, I've noticed."

"Well, he asked me not to say anything unless I had to. He's embarrassed. My father is in prison, in Pueblo." He paused, waiting for a reaction from me."

"Go on."

"He put together some dicey insurance scams. Finally, it caught up to him. He's due for a parole hearing soon. He's hoping. Those trips I take to Denver, well, sometimes I'm only going to visit Dad. Mom goes with me too sometimes. Dad still loves her, but she's all but given up on him. He says he's going to change, but even if he does, that no one will hire a jailbird. Maybe he's right. When he gets out I was thinking of giving him a job at the realty, get him sort of a start. He is a smart man, when he's not being stupid. What do you think? Do you think I should?"

"Yes, I don't see anything wrong with giving someone a second chance. After that ... well ... then they—"

"Then they deserve what they get. Is that what you were going to say?"

"Yes, something like that."

Chapter 28

A large slim package arrived late in the afternoon on Christmas Eve. Around the same time, Caroline dropped over to show me the diamond heart pendant Nate had given her the night before.

"So why didn't Nate wait to give it to you tonight?" I asked as I signed for the package.

"Because he has to work, poor guy. Everybody wants Christmas Eve off. And we'll be busy driving to his folks in the morning, then back to visit mine in the afternoon. Isn't it beautiful?" She held the pendant out from her neck for me to view again.

"Yes. He has very nice taste. And it's always a good sign when a man buys you jewelry."

She nodded. "No one else ever bought me jewelry. Best thing I ever got was a sweater. Guess I'll have to marry him. If he asks. Do you think he'll ask? Not now, of course, it's too soon. But do you think ...? Oh, don't even bother to answer that. The guy has turned me into sponge cake. Here, let me help you with that."

We worked together to slide the package inside. "It's heavy," she said. "What do you think it is?"

"I have no idea."

She bent down to read the address. "Says it's to Mr. and Mrs.

Sanders. Looks like it's from some company. There's a letter attached."
She shrugged.

Annabelle ran over to see what was going on, carrying her gnawed
rubber cat toy. She offered it to Caroline to throw. "Wow, thanks,
Annie-B. Could you have made it any wetter?" Care tossed the toy
toward the kitchen. "So aren't you even curious?"

"About what?"

"This," she said, pointing to the package.

"It's probably from one of Trevor's clients. Nothing important."

"Maybe Sylvia sent it," Caroline said, smiling slyly.

That made me jump to look.

"Knew that would get your attention," she said.

"Oh my God. It's from Josh. It's from his company."

"Ooo, better yet."

I ripped the envelope off the cardboard and opened it. I read the
letter silently, while Caroline waited expectantly.

*Merry Christmas, Gwyn and Trevor. By now, my mom and I are likely in
the south of France or northern Italy. I decided this was the year to give her
the trip she's always talked so glowingly about taking ... someday. I imagine I
am toured out, holes in my shoes, with enough pictures to paper a cathedral by
now. My dear mother has been feeling much livelier since her doctor changed
her medication. Anyway, I knew you would enjoy this gift. Hope it arrived in
time for Christmas. Have a great one, and love to you both. Always, Josh.*

I handed the letter to Caroline. When she'd finished reading, she
raised a brow at me. "The man is still carrying a torch. What a waste."
She sighed, then fingered her pendant again. "He heard about Craig,
right? That they got him?"

"Yes, Josh called me as soon as he found out. Amazing how quickly
news spreads around here."

"Sure is."

Annabelle was back, having abandoned the cat toy, begging
Caroline to pick her up. Care stooped, reaching down for her. "You
just can't get enough of your Aunt Caroline, now can you? So ...?
Gwyn?"

"What?" I asked, realizing Care was talking to me now.

"Are you going to open that package or am I going to just stand here and die of curiosity?"

"It's addressed to Trevor too. Maybe I should wait until he gets home."

"Oh, come on, Gwyn. Do you really think for a minute Josh bought whatever that is for Trevor? Open it. I can't stand the suspense. And I have to leave soon to meet Nate before he starts his shift."

"But maybe I should wait."

"Look, whatever it is, you're going to need time to come up with a decent story so Trevor won't sulk when he sees it. He's not going to be too thrilled that Josh is still sending you presents."

"No, he's okay about Josh now."

"Right. Gwyn, open it."

I wedged my fingers into the folds of cardboard, then Caroline joined in to help. The staples popped free. We laid the box on its side and I pulled out some of the packing foam. I could see that the object inside was a framed painting. Carefully, I eased it out. "Oh my God. It's the LaRoche. He sent me his LaRoche."

"Is it expensive?"

"Well, yes, but that's not the point. He loved this. I can't believe he sent it to me."

"To you and Trevor."

I eyed the painting of the small boy and the feisty weed he sought to pull. "You know—I think this is Josh's way of saying goodbye—to us, to what we had."

"Yeah, I'd say so."

"Here, help me, Care." We lifted the painting and walked with it to my studio. "I think I'll leave it right here for now," I said as we placed the painting onto an empty easel next to the now completed portrait of my sister. And silently I added, *So I can remember two of the people I loved most, whom I will miss very much.*